GATHERING
of the
CLANS

A MAGNIFICENT EPIC OF
SEVEN TRAGICALLY ENTANGLED LIVES

NOR THINGS TO COME:
A TRILOGY OF THE AMERICAN WEST: BOOK 2

RICH RITTER
THE NEW VOICE OF THE AMERICAN WEST

PUBLICATION
CONSULTANTS
We Believe In The Power Of Authors

PO Box 221974 Anchorage, Alaska 99522-1974
books@publicationconsultants.com—www.publicationconsultants.com

ISBN 978-1-59433-708-6
eBook ISBN 978-1-59433-709-3
Library of Congress Catalog Card Number: 2017937561

Manufactured in the United States of America.

For I am persuaded, that neither death, nor life, nor angels,
nor principalities, nor powers, nor things present,

Nor Things To Come

... shall be able to separate us from the love of God ...
Romans 8: 38-39

TABLE OF CONTENTS

LIST OF EXCERPTS FROM MUIREALL ANNE RAVENSCROFT'S ONE-VOLUME HISTORY OF THE AMERICAN WEST

A Synopsis of Book 1:
The Perilous Journey Begins

by Muireall Anne Ravenscroft,
award-winning author of *A Concise History of the West*
and other acclaimed works of nonfiction.

When Rich Ritter asked me to write a synopsis of the first book of *Nor Things to Come: A Trilogy of the American West*, I initially thought the task unnecessary. After all, I reasoned, why would any serious reader commence the second book of a trilogy without having read the first? But as I considered what I should write to briefly outline the magnificent story presented in *The Perilous Journey Begins* (a daunting task to be sure), it came to me one evening during a pleasant autumn thunderstorm that readers of the first book would almost certainly appreciate a "refreshing of the memory" before diving into the second. It is with this assumption in mind that I have written this synopsis. However, if you are indeed reading this without any knowledge of the first book, then I strongly advise you to go no further. You have an intellectual obligation to find the first book and read it before commencing this continuation of the story. But it is not my right to tell you what to do. If you insist on proceeding, then I can promise that the following synopsis will offer only the most superficial preparation.

Dunnet Head Lighthouse, the Highlands of Scotland, April 1860. Gordania Sinclair, a young girl of thirteen, is accompanying her father, Duncan Sinclair, as he hunts for dinner. When the two are out of sight from the lighthouse—and the prying eyes of Fyona, Gordania's mother—Duncan allows his tomboyish daughter to shoot his 12-gage side-by-side percussion shotgun. Even though the recoil of the first shot throws her backwards and pummels her shoulder, she insists on taking a second. The two return to the lighthouse before noon, Gordania rushing ahead with a plump red grouse slung over her shoulder. After lunch, Gordania and Rose Anne, her younger sister, leave to catch frogs. Erskine Mackay, the assistant lighthouse keeper, warns Gordania to keep a lookout for Andrew Sutherland's missing Border Collie. While searching for crickets and grasshoppers near a loch, they encounter the snarling dog. Gordania tells her sister to run and then confronts the beast, grabbing it around the neck to allow Rose Anne time to escape. The vicious animal tears ragged chunks of flesh from Gordania's stomach and neck before she kicks it away. Woozy from her wounds and loss of blood, Gordania staggers home wondering if her mother has already plucked the red grouse for dinner.

Shiloh, Tennessee, April 6, 1862. Manfred Herrmann slouches against an ancient hickory tree not far from the western shore of the Tennessee River. As he examines the petals of a fire pink, his reverie is ended when Sergeant-Major Gallagher tells him the Seventh Iowa Infantry Regiment is to form up with the First Brigade for parade and inspection by General W.H.L. Wallace. The parade is interrupted by the shrill of bugles and cascading volleys of musket-fire to the southeast. General W.H.L. Wallace orders the First Brigade to advance toward the approaching cacophony. After tromping through tangled oaks and across icy streams and over muddy swamps, the 7th Iowa reforms in a sunken road just beyond a grove of hickory and oak trees. Ethan Plantagenet, a first lieutenant with the 8th Texas Cavalry, watches from a distance as Confederate infantry executes a frontal assault on the 7th Iowa. A young confederate soldier appears from the smoke. Manfred slams him to the ground and presses the tip of his bayonet against the boy's chest. Manfred allows a moment to appreciate the boy's dirt-smudged face, tangled brown hair, and age—fifteen, maybe sixteen at the most—and while tears stream down the boy's dirty cheeks, Manfred thrusts the bayonet in. Then, as his hands tremble, Manfred watches the young boy choke on his own blood and the light fade from his brown eyes.

Nanjing, China, July 1864. Tseng Longwei—born of peasant farmers in 1819, educated in English by missionaries, swept away by the peasant revolt against the corrupt Manchu Dynasty in 1850, elevated to the rank of colonel in the Taiping Heavenly Army during the bloody march on Shanghai in 1861—walks along the top of the stone walls near the east gate of the besieged city of Nanjing after the untimely death of Hong Xiuquan, spiritual and moral leader of the Taiping rebellion. The Imperial Army breaches the heavy gate with wagons loaded with gunpowder. His eardrum ruptured and his mind dazed, Longwei escapes into the city, where he later kills an Imperial officer and dons the dead man's uniform. Now safely disguised, he strolls jauntily across an open plaza swarming with Imperial Army troops. He sees three Taiping women bound together at the neck in a heavy wood slab secured with iron clasps. The middle woman is naked and shivers in the cold. Longwei dresses the naked woman with garments taken from a corpse. She thanks him, but he does not believe she will survive the night. He reaches one of the western gates just before sunrise and uses his rank and bravado to bully his way past the guards. He follows a path to the Yangtze River, where he finds a small but well-maintained junk. After convincing the fisherman that he is not a member of the Imperial Army, they sail downriver toward Shanghai.

Fort Sedgwick, Colorado Territory, June 1867. Joshua Hotah, born of a Sioux mother and English father, pats the neck of his faithful appaloosa as he waits outside for the new captain to finish his conversation with the war general. Inside, Captain Ethan Plantagenet argues against the assignment of a Sioux half-breed to his company for what should be a straightforward mission. General William Tecumseh Sherman exclaims that Joshua is a superb Indian scout and denies Ethan's request. General Sherman gives Ethan a written message and a cigar: the message to be delivered to General Custer's encampment near the forks of the Republican River, and the cigar to be smoked at a later time. After an awkward meeting with Joshua, Ethan and his company of 20 men depart Fort Sedgwick. Two days later they find the abandoned encampment of the Seventh Cavalry. After reading the ground Joshua recommends riding north, but Ethan decides to follow the wagon tracks south. The next day, just before noon, the patrol is attacked by over 100 Lakota and Cheyenne warriors, and after a running battle is forced to take refuge in a rocky gulley near

Beaver Creek. During the terrifyingly black and windy night, all are killed (many mutilated) except Joshua and Ethan. The next morning, Running Bear (Joshua's half-brother) approaches the gulley and tells Joshua he may leave. Joshua refuses to leave without Ethan, and after a testy discussion Running Bear agrees, but only after insisting that the appaloosa must stay. Joshua and Ethan hike south, are eventually joined by the appaloosa, and smoke General Sherman's cigar together. They arrive at Fort Wallace safely. After deciding to begin the search for his lost parents, Joshua shakes hands with Ethan as a friend.

Sitka, Alaska, October 18, 1867. Roshan Kuznetsov, unwashed and stinking of skinned otter, returns to New Archangel after three months of trapping to be told by members of the U.S. Army Band (a tubaist and trombonist) that all of Alaska now belongs to the United States of America. The tubaist asks Roshan to step away because his stench is truly suffocating. Roshan marches angrily to the headquarters of the Russian-American Company to confront Prince Dmitri Petrovich Maksutov, apparently the last governor of Alaska, to protest. Maksutov explains that the sale of Alaska is final and that he can do nothing about it. He offers to arrange transport for Roshan on the USS Ossipee, which sails for San Francisco in the morning. Roshan reluctantly agrees, and the next day is picked up by a small boat manned by a boatswain and six oarsmen. After sucking in an enormous breath of Roshan's stink, the boatswain orders the oarsmen to row as if their lives depended on it. Roshan is quickly escorted aboard and then below decks to find quarters with the U.S. Army Band. The tubaist and trombonist are playing cards when they smell the same stink they smelled at the flag raising. Roshan rushes to their sides and embraces them and explains that he will travel with them on the big ship all the way to California. The trombonist holds his nose, then exclaims to the tubaist, "Oh lucky day."

Budapest, Hungary, May 1869. Csongor Toth strolls along the Széchenyi Chain Bridge above the sun-sparkled Danube River on his way to the Royal Hungarian University School of Law. As he studies the structure of the bridge, he reminisces that he once considered engineering as a profession—but after accepting that his supple mind craved the messy uncertainty of debate and philosophy, he chose the law instead. He joins Kelemen, his roommate, for a drink at a clean little restaurant along the Belgrade Embankment. Kelemen, who is drinking heavily because he is in much pain, shows Csongor his splinted little finger and explains that it was broken by the corrupt policeman Mészáros because of Kelemen's refusal to pay for protection. Csongor agrees to help, but only after receiving compensation equal to the amount demanded by officer Mészáros. Kelemen is furious but acquiesces because he does not want any more broken fingers. Csongor meets Mészáros the next evening at midnight. Mészáros agrees to a large sum to spare Kelemen from his protection, and while he is counting the money Csongor garrotes him with a piano wire. Kelemen awakens the next morning to find Csongor sitting on the settee with his suitcase packed. Csongor hands Kelemen a sealed envelope and tells him to present it to the police should they ever arrive to arrest him because of his involvement with Mészáros. As he prepares to leave, Csongor says that he may never return and instructs Kelemen to burn the letter and scatter the ashes after three years.

Salt Lake City, Utah Territory, May 1871. Priscilla Kimball—brown pigtails bouncing in the sun, white dress swirling across graceful legs, slender arms swinging in tempo, and three months beyond her fourteenth birthday—skips urgently along East Temple Street. Distracted by the whinny of a horse, she blunders into the strong arms of James, her older brother by five years, who reminds her that she was supposed to meet father and mother at the general store an hour ago. After cleverly declining his offer to accompany her to the appointment, she rushes to the Kimball and Smith Emporium & General Store where she finds her parents waiting with respected Salt Lake City banker Thaddeus Haglund. Priscilla's parents explain that Mr. Haglund has graciously agreed to take her as his second wife. Priscilla demurs, but her mother says the decision is already made. One month later, during the wedding reception, Thaddeus leads Priscilla to a nearby corral and barn to see the wedding gift he has purchased for her: a chestnut-colored Arabian horse. Thrilled, she names the magnificent animal Ezekiel and asks if she can sit on it. Thaddeus agrees reluctantly, and the blacksmith saddles and bridles Ezekiel. Thaddeus returns to the wedding reception upon Priscilla's promise that she will join him shortly. Priscilla waits five minutes, then opens the gate and rides out of the corral. When she reaches the boundary of Salt Lake City, she kicks Ezekiel into a full gallop and heads north into an approaching thunderstorm.

East China Sea, October 1867. The Pacific Mail Steamship Company steamer "China" plows easterly through the stormy waves of the East China Sea. A beleaguered first mate (and former harpooner from Nantucket) named Obadiah Hancock is sent by the captain to fetch a lone man clinging to the port side railing. The man tells Obadiah that he is desperately seasick and would rather jump over the side than go below for another foul breath. Obadiah convinces the man to go below to his cabin, where he will give him molasses and ginger to settle his stomach. Once in the cabin, and with the medicinal concoction improving the man's outlook, he introduces himself as Tseng Longwei from Shanghai. Pressed for more information by Obadiah, Longwei explains that he worked for three years pulling British, French, Germans, Danish, and even Americans in his rickshaw. He then tells the story of taking a wealthy Imperial official to the Blue Lotus opium den, but Obadiah is disappointed to learn that Longwei cannot describe the den because he did not go inside. When asked why he is on the ship, Longwei says that he tore a paper off the wall of the Blue Lotus announcing work with the Central Pacific Railroad in America. Obadiah asks if that's akin to stealing; Longwei says it is not because no one going to the opium den is interested in working on the railroad. After disembarking the steamer in San Francisco, Longwei finds a flatbed wagon with representatives of the Central Pacific Railroad waiting to collect men from China. After boarding the wagon, Longwei regrets having stolen the poster from the wall of the Blue Lotus.

Seattle, Washington Territory, May 1868. The enormous blade of the Yesler Sawmill completing its run down the length of a thousand-year-old log, Roshan Kuznetsov and fellow sawyer Erland Bech catch the bark-crusted slab and carry it outside to a large pile of slabs. As they work, Erland asks Roshan to explain why he ended up in Seattle, instead of San Francisco looking for gold. When they break for lunch, Roshan tells his story. When the USS Ossipee docked in Seattle, Roshan asked the tuba and the trombone, "Is this the place San Francisco in the California where I go to find the gold?" The tuba told him, "Yes, Roshan, this is San Francisco, and the place where to go to get on the land and find the gold you are looking." And then the trombone talks again and speaks, "Yes, this is the San Francisco where you go if you must lift your bags and go." Erland declares that the musical instruments lied to Roshan, but he does not think so because they were kind enough to teach him to play poker until all of his money was gone. Erland says that it is sad that Roshan is stuck in Seattle and will never make it to San Francisco to follow his dream of prospecting for gold. Henry Yesler, owner of the sawmill, arrives and asks Roshan and Erland if they are available to accompany a shipment of vertical grain lumber set to sail the next day. The two are dubious and ask where the shipment is heading. Henry Yesler exclaims, "Some big expensive hotel under construction in San Francisco. Interested?"

Liverpool, England, July 1869. A high-necked cotton dress concealing the scars on her neck, Gordania Sinclair enjoys dinner with a dapper gentleman on board the Steamship SS Tarifa. The dapper gentleman, fascinated with Gordania's rustic beauty and emerald eyes, inquires of her travels from Northern Scotland to Liverpool. Gordania describes her entire trip, including running down the platform in a cotton dress before jumping aboard a moving train in Glasgow because she had misjudged the time. She concludes the travelogue by thanking the dapper gentleman for rescuing her from the three brutes who tried to rob her (she had hidden money in her bloomers) in Liverpool. She says that when he arrived and produced a rapier from a walking stick and stabbed the man holding her down through the shoulder ... well, she had never seen a sword disguised as a cane before. The dapper gentleman asks if she has recovered from the ordeal, now that they are safely on their way to America. Gordania says that she has, and asks the dapper gentleman to spell his name so that she can record it accurately in her diary. The dapper gentleman is delighted, and spells his name C ... S ... O ... N ... G ... O ... R ... T ... O ... T ... H. He clarifies that the "C" is silent. After more dinners together and walks on the deck, the Tarifa arrives safely in Boston in late July of 1869. After parting with nary a handshake, Gordania is abandoned on the rain-glistened dock ready to step off into her new life.

Clayton County, Iowa, June 1870. Now in the final week of his final year at the Wartburg Theological Seminary, Manfred Herrmann appears to be dozing during a lecture by Professor Strathmore on the philosophies of Johann Konrad Wilhelm Loehe. Unexpectedly, the grotesque memory of the young boy Manfred killed at Shiloh bubbles into his consciousness. *As a pool of voracious maggots swarm the horrific scene, Manfred drives the bayonet in again; waves of intoxicating ecstasy convulse through his body.*

The pale boy looks up at Manfred and asks the same question he has asked a thousand times: "Manfred Herrmann, why have you killed me again? I am already dead." Professor Strathmore confronts Manfred and accuses him of sleeping in class. Manfred proves that he was not sleeping by reciting the lesson flawlessly, including information that was not yet presented. Professor Strathmore orders Manfred to meet him in his office after class. When the two meet, Professor Strathmore tells Manfred that it is not a requirement for him to always be in a state of suffering. Manfred responds that he does not see life as an experience to be enjoyed, but rather as an opportunity to atone for his sins. Professor Strathmore declares that everyone sins, and runs through the Ten Commandments to prove his point. When he skips the fifth commandment, Manfred confesses that he murdered fourteen men with only his bayonet at Shiloh, and that he enjoyed the slaughter. Professor Strathmore decides to send Manfred to Silver City, Idaho Territory to establish a Lutheran mission church. Manfred agrees reluctantly because he believes other students are more qualified. Professor Strathmore explains that he will arrange for Manfred to stop in Chicago on the way to spend a few days in a civilized city before heading west, then says, "I shall pray for a memorable trip."

Boston, Massachusetts, July 1870. The arrival of a new client now imminent, Csongor Toth waits in his small law office on the top floor of the Revere Bank building. Although not organized in his usual manner, he has prepared sufficiently to carry on any conversation with verve and confidence. Meredith Brewster arrives at precisely three o'clock and immediately informs Csongor that he is not fond of lawyers but finds them a necessary evil at times. Csongor informs Mr. Brewster that his opinion of lawyers does not concern him in the slightest. Mr. Brewster asks for Csongor's credentials. Csongor explains that he was educated at the Royal Hungarian University School of Law in Budapest, that he speaks three languages fluently (and has modest proficiency in French), that he is independently wealthy and has no need for this occupation other than to provide a dash of light entertainment, and that he is absolutely ruthless when it comes to protecting the interests of his clients. Satisfied, Mr. Brewster explains that his current will, which leaves everything to his wife Eva, must be changed because she has become unstable during the last few years. He now wants his son Jonathan, who he admits is a "vindictive little cuss," to inherit everything. Csongor agrees to meet Meredith at his home in Brookline so that he may attest to the fact that Eva is unfit to manage the estate. During the meeting, Meredith introduces Csongor to the new governess, Gordania Sinclair, and explains that she is in charge of his two daughters, Bethany and Bathsheba. Csongor acts as if they have never met, and gives her his business card. Later, Gordania walks upstairs to invite Eva to lunch with the girls. She raises her hand to knock on the bedroom door, but hesitates when she hears sobbing.

Fort Laramie, Wyoming Territory, Late March 1871. After four years of wandering, Joshua Hotah and the feisty appaloosa ride west on the Oregon Trail. A rifle shot echoes to the north. They head in the direction of the shot, and after plunging over a grassy hillock see a magnificent herd of buffalo extending far to the east and west. They continue riding until they stop just behind a lone buffalo hunter. The appaloosa neighs stridently and spooks the nearest cluster of buffalo, causing the herd to stampede away. Disgusted because he only bagged three animals before the herd panicked, he asks if Joshua is some sort of half-breed Indian scout, or something. Joshua introduces himself and explains that his mother was Sioux and his father English, and that he was an Indian scout for two years. The buffalo hunter introduces himself as John Runyan and explains that he has big plans to move to California and find a nice place on the ocean. They agree to travel together to Fort Laramie so that Joshua can buy ammunition for his Henry rifle. After buying the ammunition at Sutler's Store, and also selling a buffalo tongue and three hides, they proceed to the nearby Three-Mile Hog Ranch because John Runyan thinks Joshua has the look of someone in desperate need of a whore. John Runyan introduces Joshua to Martha Canary (also known as Calamity Jane). When Joshua tells Martha that he is looking for his parents, a buffalo hunter from England with a Sioux wife, Martha exclaims that she met them less than two years ago, and that they were heading for Oregon City. Joshua rushes out of the saloon into the pellucid moonlight of a clearing sky and rides toward Oregon City.

The Oregon Trail, Idaho Territory, June 1871. After living more than five years in a dirt-floored shack on a 160-acre homestead of isolated, rocky, windswept, arid, miserable prairie land in eastern Kansas, Ferd Tucker and his wife Joniah and their children Seth and Clarinda are heading west in a lone prairie schooner pulled by four oxen. Ferd and Joniah are arguing about getting separated from the other wagons after fixing a broken wheel. Seth is teasing Clarinda by telling her that he can see prairie dogs riding wild horses and a whole bunch of buffalo and hawks through a magic hole in the side of the canvas cover. Ferd halts the wagon after spotting a small white dot where the meandering trail joins the horizon. Ferd and Joniah speculate that the dot is either Indians or a scout coming back to look for them, but it turns out to be a little girl wearing a wedding dress and riding a large horse. The dress is torn to shreds, her hair is tangled into matted balls of filth, her lips are cracked and swollen from the wind, and her legs are thorn-slashed. The girl concocts a lie that three men have been following her for days, and that she is trying to ride to the safety of Fort Boise. She also claims that she is Mary Smith from Brigham City. Joniah takes pity on the girl and invites her to travel with them to the Glenn's Ferry crossing. Although Ferd objects because it will be dark soon, Joniah begins looking for food and a clean dress.

Promontory Mountain, Utah Territory, April 28, 1869. Burly Sam Logan gazes upon the railroad tracks and adjacent telegraph poles completed yesterday and the hundreds of Chinese laborers swarming along both sides of the railhead as the approaching engine pulling 16 flatcars brakes at the staging area. At precisely seven o'clock he orders the six Chinamen under his supervision (including Tseng Longwei) to load a handcar with 16 rails, kegs of bolts and spikes, and bundles of fish plates. Horses pull the handcar 200 feet ahead to the railhead, where the men unload the materials for installation by Irish rail handlers and track gangs. Sam Logan and his men return for more materials, removing the handcar from the tracks to allow another handcar—with one Irishman, six Chinamen, and the same materials—to pass. This pattern is repeated throughout the day until the nearly 4,000 men (and hundreds of horses) working for the Central Pacific Railroad extend the track 10 miles and 56 feet by seven in the evening, a record-setting achievement. Late that night, Tseng Longwei drinks tea near the warmth of a campfire (one of hundreds on both sides of the railhead) as the eleven exhausted men scattered around him sleep. A man on horseback appears out of the darkness, and Longwei invites him to sit by the fire and share some tea. The man tells Longwei that he is Roshan Kuznetsov, and says he is on his way to Silver City to find great wealth. The two agree to become business partners and travel to Silver City together, but not until the railroad is finished. Early in the morning of May 10th, dignitaries hammer spikes of gold and silver into the final track. Unfortunately, Longwei does not witness the historic event because he is shoved back by the crowd of onlookers. With much sadness in his voice, he tells Roshan it is truly time to go.

Brookline, Massachusetts, May 1870. Not willing to spend any of her meager savings for a railway ticket, Gordania Sinclair hikes over five miles from Boston to Brookline to apply for a position as governess. She is greeted at the door of the Brewster residence by Emma Johnson, the cook and housekeeper, who escorts Gordania to the ornately-appointed parlor. Eva Corrine Brewster arrives a few minutes later to conduct the interview, and after learning that Gordania is literate, has knowledge of English grammar and spelling, and has previously taught children to read and write in Scotland, hires her on the spot. Eva concludes the interview by admitting that she has suffered bouts of melancholy since the birth of Bethany, her oldest daughter. Several months later, Gordania unexpectedly meets Csongor Toth in the same parlor conducting a business meeting with Meredith Brewster. After this troubling encounter, she ascends the stairs to invite Eva to lunch, but finds Eva sobbing in the bedroom. Late that night, as a storm rages and lightning flashes illuminate the foyer, Meredith returns from Boston. His blood seething with alcohol, he tears Gordania's dress and attempts to rape her. She unintentionally kills him by striking him on the head with a bronze songbird. Emma arrives and tells Gordania to run from the house as fast as she can. Gordania walks through the storm to Boston and is waiting on the steps of the Revere Bank building when Csongor Toth arrives for work. After listening to her story, he decides that Gordania must leave immediately. He arranges to have her hair cut short and died black, buys her new clothes, gives her over three-thousand dollars, arms her with a derringer pistol, changes her name to Alexandra Smythe (from Liverpool), and puts her on a train to Ogden, Utah, where she is to arrange travel to Silver City via stagecoach. When Gordania turns to wave goodbye from the car platform, Csongor has already disappeared into the crowd.

Chicago, Illinois, July 1870. Because his train does not leave for several hours, Manfred Herrmann sits on his suitcase and observes the countless people occupying the dusty promenade by Lake Michigan. After a wagon passes, a pretty woman with black hair cut very short and dressed in black is revealed and stares directly at him. He admits that he wouldn't mind meeting her and thinks of waving, but the woman walks away before he can decide. Later, as his train moves out of the station, he sees the same woman running along the platform skillfully dodging left and right around people and obstacles. She appears again in his car after the train bursts out of the great arched opening at the end of the depot. The conductor seats the running woman across the aisle and one row back from Manfred; he feels a rush of warmth when she speaks to the conductor and the lilting cadence and pleasant brogue of Dunnet Head washes over him. An hour passes, and while pacing the aisle to stretch his legs, Manfred notices that the running woman's jacket has fallen to the floor—revealing a small pistol in her hand. When Manfred attempts to cover her, she flinches awake and chides him sternly because she might have shot him. She then tells him to never talk to her again. As the train arrives in Ogden, the running woman apologizes to Manfred for her beastly behavior, introduces herself as Alexandra Smyth from Liverpool, and disembarks. Manfred stays on the train until Kelton, and boards the stagecoach to Boise the next morning. His travelling companions, Arthur and Sarah Pence of Pennsylvania, tell him that they are searching for their lost son. Three desperadoes try to rob the stage less than a mile from Black's Creek, but Major Ethan Plantagenet and his escort of a dozen buffalo soldiers thwart the attempt. Major Plantagenet invites Manfred, Arthur, and Sarah to dinner the next evening at Fort Boise. It is during this meal that Manfred and Ethan discover that they fought at Shiloh on opposite sides. After a long pause, Ethan states that they have been made brothers by their shared experience on the battlefield and asks if he may offer his hand in friendship. After another unpleasant pause, Manfred stands and declares, "I would like nothing better."

Fort Boise, Idaho Territory, August 1870. An overhead line guides Gus Glenn's wood-hulled ferry across the Snake River. After admiring his shadow on the surface of the smoothly-flowing water, Roshan Kuznetsov commences a discussion with Tseng Longwei, who is holding the reins of Roshan's horse. Roshan tells Longwei that it has taken more than a year to travel this far because Longwei had insisted on fulfilling his commitment to the Central Pacific Railroad. Longwei counters that it has taken so long because Roshan did not know which way to turn when they departed Promontory Mountain in Utah. Nonetheless, they both agree that the adventures they have endured—many months in Laramie City learning the trade of the blacksmith, many more months in North Platte learning to cut and sew canvas for prairie schooners, an unfortunate event in Ogden involving a general store and flying spittoons, and many other unfortunate events—have strengthened their business partnership. They eventually make their way to Fort Boise, where Longwei discovers that the Irish not only worked on the railroads of America but also provided the primary source of recruitment for the U.S. Army. Roshan meets with the commanding officer while Longwei waits outside. Roshan introduces himself to Major Ethan Plantagenet by asking if there are any spittoons in the room and if he knows the way to Silver City. Ethan escorts Roshan outside to the front porch, shakes Longwei's hand, and provides directions to Silver City; he tells them they can't miss it. Longwei replies, "You would be surprised, Major Plantagenet, at what things Roshan and I are capable of missing."

Boston, Massachusetts, September 1870. After the death of his father, Jonathan Brewster meets with Csongor Toth to ask him if he will accept the assignment of tracking down the temptress Gordania Sinclair and bringing her back to Boston to be convicted of murder and hanged by the neck until dead. After an inexplicable period of reverie, Csongor agrees, but then warns Jonathan that it could prove difficult and expensive to find her, and once found even more difficult and expensive to bring her back to Boston. Undaunted, Jonathan clarifies that if it is impractical to return Gordania to Boston, Csongor is to arrange for her demise wherever she is found. Sometime later, Csongor meets with a bounty hunter named Dougal Connelly at *The Atwood & Bacon Oyster House.* Dougal reports that he spoke with a train conductor who saw a pretty woman of about the right age and height reboarding the train to Chicago—in Albany, two days after the murder. Jonathan Brewster had told him that Gordania always wore a white dress, had long brown hair, and could run like a man. The conductor said the woman in Albany wore black and had short black hair, and that she ran like a man to catch the train as it pulled out of the station. Dougal believes it was Gordania Sinclair in disguise. Dougal had also discovered that this woman in black had a ticket to Ogden in the Utah Territory. Csongor arranges for Dougal to leave for Ogden the next day. After arriving in Piedmont Station, just before the summit at the line between Wyoming and Utah, Dougal opens a letter as instructed by Csongor. The letter directs him to walk outside to the platform because Csongor has heard that the view is unforgettable. After stepping into the cool moonlight, Dougal is confronted by the conductor, who stabs him beneath the ribs with a stiletto and shoves him off the platform into the deep ravine below. The conductor then removes all evidence of Dougal's presence on the train. Csongor Toth steps off the train in Ogden dressed exactly like Jonathan Brewster. He proceeds to the depot and sends a telegram to Jonathan stating that Miss Sinclair has fled to Brazil, and that he requires $5,000 to pursue her. He signs the telegram "Dougal Connelly." Csongor decides to explore the potential business opportunities in Silver City, but not before he has received the money transfer from Jonathan Brewster.

Boise City, Idaho Territory, August 1871. After an unpleasant dream, Priscilla Kimball jerks to a sitting position in the back of the prairie schooner. Her sweat-soaked dress clings to her shivering legs. She closes her eyes and reviews the fading images of the dream and recalls that the dream had emerged several times before—beginning after the day she rode away from the wedding reception on her new horse, Ezekiel. In the dream a diaphanous phantom holds her down on a bed in the middle of the prairie and pries her legs apart with gossamer talons as an applauding crowd looks on and Thaddeus Haglund prepares to consummate the marriage. Fortunately, she always wakes up just in time. The prairie schooner arrives in Boise City, and Ferd, Joniah, Clarinda, and Seth head over to the general store after Priscilla decides to stay with the wagon. When standing in the middle of the street to inspect the surroundings, three men on horses trot from a side street and head directly at her. She shades her eyes with her hand and squints. The riders are her father, her older brother James, and Thaddeus Haglund. She hides by diving to the ground and rolling under the prairie schooner and then crawling along the top of the wood tongue between the four oxen. As the men ride by, the oxen shift and squeeze her tight against the tongue. When the family returns, Ferd uses a hickory ax handle to pry the oxen apart. When he mentions that they might go to Silver City instead of Oregon (because of a tip from the owner of the general store), Priscilla surprises everyone by announcing that she wants to go to Silver City too, instead of Fort Boise. Ferd reluctantly agrees to take her along, but only if she helps with chores and doesn't make too much noise.

Oregon City, Oregon, September 1871. Joshua Hotah and his beloved appaloosa survey Oregon City from a hillside vantage at the end of the Oregon Trail. After descending the hill and riding past an abandoned hovel, Joshua encounters a little girl with a basket and a little boy with a fishing pole. When the little girl asks Joshua if he is an Indian, he explains that his mother was Sioux and his father an Englishman who hunted buffalo. The little girl takes two apples from her basket and gives them to Joshua and the appaloosa. The little girl asks Joshua if his parents live in Oregon City; he replies that a woman at Fort Laramie told him they might have come here. The little girl tells Joshua that he should speak to her father, because he owns the newspaper and knows just about everything there is to know about Oregon City. Joshua finds Grady Hathcock at the *Oregon City Enterprise*. When Joshua explains who he is looking for, Grady remembers that he took a photograph of a buffalo hunter and his squaw about a year ago. He finds the crinkled page of newsprint with the photograph in a wood file cabinet, gives it to Joshua, and says he remembers that the buffalo hunter was an Englishman, the squaw was Sioux, and that they were heading to Silver City in the Idaho Territory. Joshua thanks Grady and rides out of town. He meets the little girl and boy again. He gives a beaded-leather bracelet, which belonged to his mother, to the little girl, and his wide-brimmed-black-felt Indian scout hat decorated with three feathers, which he no longer needs, to the little boy—to repay them for the apples. He rides east on the Oregon Trail. He decides to show the photo of his parents to the appaloosa after finding a good place to camp for the night.

CHAPTER ONE

Silver City, Idaho Territory
September 1871

P riscilla Kimball, the puckered hem of her white cotton dress swirled by a Friday morning breeze flowing through the Jordan Creek valley, skipped to the centerline juncture of Washington Street and Avalanche Avenue. She formed her little hands into a fleshy telescope and viewed the fresh clouds drifting lazily above the summit of War Eagle Mountain to the southeast.* She squeezed her fingers to reduce the size of the aperture and focused on a specific cloud. She rotated her fists in opposite directions and scrunched her eye against the rear thumb until the image of the cloud sharpened. *Just as I thought: a whooping Indian shooting arrows at a buffalo and riding a galloping wild horse.* Priscilla pirouetted on her heels just before a freight wagon—pulled by eight snorting mules and overloaded with coiled ropes and weathered barrels and crates of explosives—rumbled up behind her. The impatient driver, a young man aged well beyond his twenty-seven years by chronic economic failure, shouted, "Get out of the way ya dang fool!" He cracked an angry bullwhip above the ears of the lead mules in a counterfeit attempt to run her over. Shiny-brown pigtails bouncing pleasantly, the puckered hem rising momentarily above her adorable knees, Priscilla skipped out of the way, spun around, and flipped a girlish wave. The young man glowered and hawked a gob of phlegmy spit mixed with chewing tobacco. The gob fell short of

---

* The summit of War Eagle Mountain rises 8,041 feet above sea level and approximately 2,000 feet above the town of Silver City.

Priscilla's toes. She advanced two paces and examined the brownish pool of spit and tobacco. She watched the gob until the slimy thing stopped jiggling then waved again at the back of the young man's head. The mules and freight wagon turned right near a cluster of wood buildings beyond Avalanche Avenue and headed north out of town.

After observing this peculiar extravaganza from beneath a low roof awning, a slender woman wearing brown leather boots, puffy gray dress, and flowing white apron—one of the local "Cousin Jennies"* on her way to buy shortening and flour at the general store—decided it was her moral duty to admonish Priscilla. "Do not stand in the middle of the road staring up at the sky, child, or another wagon will surely run you down if you do." The woman shook a soot-smudged finger at Priscilla to emphasize the reprimand before scurrying away to complete her errand.

Priscilla watched the Cousin Jenny until she vanished into a group of men standing in front of one of the local saloons. She checked up and down Washington Street to verify the absence of wagons and mules before skipping back to the middle of the intersection. She closed her eyes, cupped a little hand behind each ear, and slowly revolved in a clockwise direction. Florida Mountain rose up steeply west of the rocky edge of the town, and, somewhere near the summit,† she heard the familiar chirps of a golden eagle (a ground squirrel clutched in its talons) returning to a nest tucked into the vertical face of a rocky cliff. She turned until her ears faced north, and heard the dull rumble of an approaching thunderstorm somewhere near the Snake River. She continued around until her ears faced east down Avalanche Street, and she listened to the clattering wheels of a Wells Fargo stagecoach move southerly along Jordan Street after crossing the bridge over Jordan Creek. Priscilla turned again until she faced southeast toward the distant slopes of War Eagle, and a muffled explosion deep within one of the hard rock mines shook the mountain and vibrated the air on her cheeks. She rotated until she faced south down the length of Washington Street, and she heard the agitated voices of three or four angry men shouting at each other in front of the War Eagle Hotel at the far end of the street. She twirled to the southwest, and

---

* A "Cousin Jenny" is the wife of a Cornish miner.

† The summit of Florida Mountain rises 7,667 feet above sea level and approximately 1,400 feet above the town of Silver City.

beyond a neatly-aligned row of wood storefront buildings the metrical clanging of a blacksmith's hammer against an iron anvil reverberated musically against the hands curved behind her ears. She returned to her original compass point facing due west, and the agitated voice of the same Cousin Jenny—returning from the completed errand to buy shortening and flour—interrupted her blissful reverie a second time.

The Cousin Jenny raised her eyes in disgust. "I do swear, little miss... you are not much of a one to listen to good advice when it is given to you. I see you are still standing in the middle of the street looking to get run down by any mules who might happen by, just as I left you not more than ten minutes ago."

Priscilla slapped her arms down against the sides of her white cotton dress and opened the right eye first and then the left. "I did take your advice, ma'am, because this time I looked both directions before walking into the street."

This clever response did not amuse the Cousin Jenny, and she clicked her tongue three times. "Suit yourself, little miss, but I shall not weep a single tear if one of the freighters runs over the top of you." The Cousin Jenny shifted a basket from her left hand to the right. "And have you not got something better to do with yourself than stand in the middle of the street, looking up at the sky and tempting death?"

Priscilla clasped her hands behind her back and strolled youthfully toward the Cousin Jenny. "Why, I do, ma'am. I'm just taking a little while to do it."

"And what is it you should be doing instead of standing in the street trying to get run over by mules?"

Priscilla stopped directly in front of the Cousin Jenny and crossed one ankle over the other. "I should be looking for a job, ma'am. The wagon family I was living with can no longer afford to keep me. They barely have enough food to feed themselves. The father and mother said the time has come for me to fend for myself."

The Cousin Jenny studied Priscilla's pretty face, slender waist, and crossed feet. "How old are you, darling?"

Priscilla focused on the worry-worn face of the Cousin Jenny, now transformed with sympathy. "I was born in 1857. I'm almost 15."

The Cousin Jenny raised a hand and pressed it against her heart. "Goodness, child. A young girl of 14 should not be wandering the streets of a place like Silver City looking for a job. Do you not know someone who can take care of you?"

A hermit thrush landed momentarily on the rusty eave above the Cousin Jenny before singing pleasantly, flitting deftly into the morning air, and flying toward the willows growing along the muddy banks of Jordan Creek. Priscilla watched the thrush dart away before answering, "No one, ma'am. The wagon family took care of me as long as they could, but they're really poor and don't have much food anymore to feed everyone. I've been staying down at a women's boarding house across from the Masonic Hall for a couple of weeks, but they said I have to start paying or I can't stay there either. That's why I'm trying to find a job."

The Cousin Jenny held out her soot-smudged hand. "My name is Tressa. And who might you be, little miss?"

Priscilla raised her hand until it touched the tips of Tressa's fingers. "My name's Priscilla Kimball."

Tressa reached a little more and clasped her fingers around Priscilla's delicate hand. "Well, Miss Priscilla Kimball, would you like to stay with my family until you find the work you are looking for?"

Tressa's strong grip surprised Priscilla, and she pulled her hand away. "I might consider it, ma'am, but I'd like to try to find work first. I can probably stay at the boarding house a few more days before they kick me out. But I appreciate the offer."

Tressa pressed her hands together beneath the basket handle. "If you change your mind, Priscilla, my family lives in a small cabin up on the hillside north of town. If you want to find it, just ask someone where Tressa lives and they'll surely point you in the right direction."

Priscilla clasped her hands together and fell one step back. "I'll keep that in mind, ma'am, but I should be on my way now…so I can commence looking for work so I can pay for the boarding house so I won't get kicked out."

Tressa smiled. "Take care of yourself, Priscilla, and don't forget my offer."

Priscilla answered as she turned to walk away, "I will, ma'am, and I won't." She skipped across Washington Street in the direction of the corner saloon.

San Luis Obispo, California
Summer 1907

Saturday afternoon, and John Ravenscroft sipped the last of his tea before setting the delicate porcelain cup decorated with a feminine floral pattern on the matching saucer also decorated with a feminine floral pattern. He lifted the top half of the manuscript above the bookmark he had inserted late last night. He watched Muireall complete several stitches on her current needlepoint project. He tapped his fingers on the kitchen table. "I was about to start reading this section on Silver City and the Owyhees, but a thought prevented me."

Muireall adjusted her reading glasses and drove three stitches into the white fabric. "And what was the thought, the one which prevented you?"

John nudged the delicate porcelain tea cup with his thumb until it rattled against the saucer. "I was thinking of drinking tea from a cup with a handle large enough to shove more than one finger through it. And something without flowers on it. Maybe just a plain brown cup, something which can hold a proper amount of tea so I can gulp it down if I choose to."

Muireall finished two more stitches and tied a French knot. "Suit yourself. There's a brown mug matching your description in the upper cabinet next to the sink. You can fetch it now if you wish and start gulping tea this very afternoon."

John's brows popped. "You have a brown mug with a big handle? How come you never told me about it?"

Muireall did not look up from the white fabric. "I never knew you cared at all about cups, or I would have mentioned it before."

John pushed himself away from the table, stood abruptly, and walked quickly over to the upper cabinet next to the sink. Before opening the cabinet door, he peeked through the window above the sink and noted the darkening skies to the north. After rummaging through a cluster of different cups, he found one matching his earlier description. He nestled the heavy cup lovingly in his hands as he slowly returned to the table, carefully settled down on the hard wood chair, and poured the cup full from the delicate porcelain tea pot. He shoved three fingers through the handle, pressed his thumb down on top of the handle, slurped a big gulp of hot tea, grinned, and exclaimed, "My cup runneth over."

Muireall lowered her needlepoint. "I didn't realize it was this easy to make you happy."

John slurped another big gulp. "Neither did I. Now, if we could only do something about this dinky little tea pot. It barely holds enough tea to fill my new cup." He finished the tea with a final exuberant gulp, and, satisfied with the fortuitous discovery of the brown mug, commenced reading what Muireall had written of Silver City.

Excerpt from
A Concise History of the West
by Muireall Anne Ravenscroft
Silver City: Jewel of the Owyhees

The story of mining in the American West effectively commenced more than ten years before the beginning of the Civil War, when James Marshall discovered gold in the tailrace* of John Sutter's Mill near Sacramento, California on January 24, 1848. Prior to this momentous find, only primitive mining facilities had operated in the southeastern states, principally in Georgia. But when news of this audacious new discovery spread east to the United States and down to South America and across the Atlantic Ocean to Europe and over the crashing waves of the Pacific Ocean to Australia and Asia, tens of thousands of people (over 95% of them young men) flooded into California in search of unfathomable wealth, which for nearly all became more illusion than reality. The next significant mining event in the American West, the discovery of the vast silver deposits of the Comstock Lode beneath present-day Virginia City, occurred in Nevada in 1858 (western Utah Territory at the time) on the eastern slopes of Mount Davidson in the Virginia Range. The Comstock Lode fuelled the rapid growth of

* A tailrace is the channel below the mill's waterwheel through which the spent water flows.

the boom towns of Virginia City, Carson City, and Silver City (Nevada), and also provided needed wealth to sustain the continued expansion and development of San Francisco well into the 1860s. Motivated by Sutter's Mill and the Comstock Lode, as well as other lesser discoveries, intrepid prospectors spread out across the American West and soon found promising deposits of gold, silver, and other precious minerals in Colorado, Utah, Arizona, New Mexico, Idaho, Montana, and South Dakota. Other famous boom towns erupted overnight from the mineral-rich earth including Deadwood, South Dakota in 1875 and Tombstone, Arizona in 1877: the former made notorious by the murder of Wild Bill Hickok in 1876 and the latter by the "Gunfight at the OK Corral" in 1881. But with this last citation I have progressed many years beyond the founding of Silver City, Idaho -- the primary focus of this article -- and must retreat more than three decades to the Blue Bucket Legend.

Late in the summer of 1845, a wagon train travelling the Oregon Trail stopped for the night somewhere in southern Idaho close to a nameless stream because it offered sufficient water for pioneers and animals alike. The wagon train had followed the so-called "Dry Trail" along the southern banks of the Snake River. Compared to the northern route, this trail was longer, had less grazing potential for the animals, and (as the name suggests) offered fewer opportunities to find potable water. However, the route also eliminated two hazardous crossings of the Snake River, and for this reason alone was preferred by many of the early wagon trains. While the adults turned the animals out to graze and prepared the encampment for nightfall, the children set out with buckets to find good drinking water. When they returned to camp, they had filled a blue bucket to the brim: not with drinking water but with "shiny pebbles" found in the gravel bed of the nearby creek. One of the men tossed a handful of the pebbles into an open toolbox in the back of his wagon and sent the children back to fill the blue bucket with drinking water. The wagon train broke camp early the next morning and continued the drive west -- the urgency of crossing the Blue Mountains before the icy onslaught of cruel winter prevailing over any thought of the shiny pebbles in the tool box and the blue bucket now swinging happily on the back of the wagon. Many years after the pioneers had arrived in Oregon, an individual experienced in prospecting recognized the shiny pebbles as gold, but by that time no one could remember the location of the stream where the children had made their discovery. The Blue Bucket Legend was instantly born, and as prospectors searched from Canyon Creek in Oregon to the mouth of Catherine Creek in southern Idaho, the exact location where the children had filled the blue bucket with shiny pebbles proved as elusive as King Arthur's mythical Holy Grail.

In 1862, Captain Tom Turner led 50 men from the Willamette Valley in an extensive search for the source of the Blue Bucket Legend along the Snake River to a point above Catherine Creek in an area that would later be named Owyhee County.* The men stopped here to rest, and after a long fruitless ride determined to take a vote on whether or not to continue farther along the Snake River. Eight of the Oregonians voted no, and after turning back ran into another group led by a man named Grimes. The Grimes party had been attempting to overtake Captain Turner, but upon hearing the disillusionment of

---

* The newly-formed Idaho Territorial Legislature established Owyhee County on December 31, 1863 and defined it as follows: "That all that part of said territory lying south of Snake River and west of the summit of the Rocky Mountains shall be and the same is hereby organized into a county to be called Owyhee." The county was reduced to its present size in 1879.

the eight Oregonians decided to explore a different direction. Grimes and his men, and the eight Oregonians, crossed the Snake River near the mouth of the Boise River. After following the stream east they discovered gold in the Boise Basin. Within a few months news of the discovery lured thousands of prospectors into the area.

In May of 1863, other promising discoveries in the Boise Basin (as well as the continued promise of the Blue Bucket Legend) prompted a group of 29 men to set out from Placerville, a town near Boise named after the technique of placer mining. Led by a man named Michael Jordan, the group crossed the raging spring waters of the Snake River near the mouth of the Boise and rode southwesterly along the southern banks of the river until they made camp at a large stream they named Reynolds Creek. The group began prospecting along the creek the next day, but did not find anything of interest. At some point (the available history is unclear on this), two men named Wade and Miner separated from the group, and, moving westerly over a high ridge line and down into a valley, discovered a substantial stream flowing northerly.* The next day, May 18th, the other men of the expedition followed the same route and joined Wade and Miner late in the afternoon on the banks of what would later be named Jordan Creek. Before the men had begun unpacking some of the nearly 60 heavily-laden horses and mules that accompanied the group, a man named Dr. Rudd immediately grabbed his shovel, scooped a load of gravel from the creek, panned it out, and discovered gold. Within ten minutes every man in the group, except one individual who evidently had a well-deserved reputation for sloth, began digging and panning. The men prospected up the creek for another twelve days, where at a place dubbed "Happy Camp" the group established

---

* Jordan Creek eventually flows to the west until it joins the Owyhee River in southeastern Oregon.

and adopted the laws of the mining district, located the claims, named the creek after Michael Jordan, and named the mining district after W. T. Carson (one of the other members of the party): a process faithful to the traditions of earlier prospectors in Nevada, California, and Oregon.

Reports of this discovery inspired a stampede into the Owyhee Mountains, with some historians estimating that over 2,500 gold seekers abandoned the claims of the Boise Basin for the new location. Unfortunately, the vast majority of these men would encounter abject disappointment because the original 29 men of the Jordan party had established claims to nearly every tract of promising ground. In the end, less than ten percent of these early stampeders remained to work the gravels of Jordan Creek and the rich veins of War Eagle Mountain; the rest dispersed to other areas or returned to their original claims in the Boise Basin. Subsequent to these events, in the summer of 1863, the first town of Owyhee County (and the first county seat) sprang from the banks of Jordan Creek at the mouth of a canyon nestled between the rugged mountains. At first called Booneville, the name of the town was later changed to Dewey. A second town with more space and better water was soon established on Jordan Creek approximately two miles to the southeast, and was given the name of Ruby. During the winter of 1863 approximately 250 men inhabited each of these towns, and another 500 worked in the Carson Mining District outside of the towns. By the end of 1864 the population of Ruby had increased to over 800. But in the same year, prompted by the discovery of gold on nearby War Eagle Mountain, a rival town named Silver City began forming on the banks of Jordan Creek about a mile to the south. Using Ox teams and other devices, men began moving the buildings of Ruby to the new town over a recently-completed toll road, and by 1866 the once proud town of Ruby was substantially reduced and the county seat relocated to the fledgling boom town of Silver City. During this same year, the first....

Standing with her ankles crossed in front of the two-story saloon on the corner of Washington and Avalanche, Priscilla Kimball mouthed the words as she read the crude letters scrawled across a tattered sheet of paper with three corners nailed to the vertical wood siding several feet to the left of the entry doors. A warm gust flipped the free corner up, partially blocking the message; Priscilla pressed it down with a thumb to finish the last two lines.

> HELP WANTED ONE
> OR MAY BE TOO
> WOMAN NEEDED ASK
> THE BARTENDER HE
> WILL TELL YOU
> WHAT FORE

She read the message a second time and thought: *I guess I'm a woman now... since I'm married... although nobody around here knows it... but I could always tell them... if it helped me to get the job.* She uncrossed her ankles and stepped over to the nearest of the doors and peeked through one of nine wood-mullion-framed rectangles of glass in the upper half. She cupped her hands around her face to block the light and pressed her pixie nose against the glass only seconds before an enormous man stomped up inside the saloon and twisted the brass knob. She jumped back when the door swung open, but caught a heel on the head of a rusty iron spike that had worked loose because of all the patrons tromping in and out of the saloon. Priscilla fell hard on her little rump and her dainty legs shot up into the air when she rolled backwards and then her legs whipped forward and her calves and heels slapped the weather-cracked wood boards when she rolled forward again and sat up. She rubbed her forehead and an expression of bewilderment glazed her face.

The enormous man, probably a laborer from one of the hard rock mines on War Eagle, stopped a few inches from Priscilla's feet and loomed over her. The man adjusted his suspenders to pull his pants up a little higher and then loomed a bit more. "Gonna get your pretty little white dress all dirty sitting on the ground in front of the saloon. All manner of filth on those boards."

Priscilla pushed the dress down over her knees. "I'm just resting a bit before I go into the store."

The enormous man chuckled and wiped a shirt sleeve across his moustache. "That there's no store little girl. That there's a saloon for drinking and gambling and whoring. If you be wanting my opinion, I don't think the likes of you should be going inside such a place."

"I saw a sign saying they're looking for a woman, and since I'm a woman who needs to find work I thought I might apply for the job." Priscilla pulled her knees up against her chest.

The enormous man rose up and laughed, and when he had finished laughing he snapped his suspenders. "Some in this town might find a little girl like you just the ticket, but I think it best if you run along and find work elsewhere. Head over to the general store and ask if they're hiring." Then he laughed a final time and adjusted his suspenders again before bounding around Priscilla and striding across Washington Street.

When the enormous man with suspenders had passed, Priscilla jumped up, brushed some dirt off her butt and legs, and yelled at him, "I already tried the general store and everywhere else in this town. I haven't found any work yet."

The enormous man climbed up to the boardwalk and swung around. He waited until a buggy pulled by a prancing mare rode by before yelling back at Priscilla, "Then I reckon you should leave town and find someplace else to live where there's not as much drinking and shooting and gambling and swindling and whoring and anything else you can think of." The enormous man adjusted his suspenders and wandered south along Washington Street.

Priscilla waved at the large man, skipped to the double doors, patted her butt one last time, opened the door to the right, and strolled into the dusky ambiance of the saloon. She waited for her pupils to dilate before assessing the place. Round tables to the left with a few men and women playing cards and two brass flower vases without any flowers in them sitting on the floor next to them. A long, high table to the right with men standing and drinking from strange glasses and women wearing gaudy dresses standing next to it. Brass lanterns hanging from the ceiling, but not lighting the place up much. Priscilla studied the faces of several of the men. *Now, which one do you suppose is the bartender who I'm supposed to talk to? Maybe the fellow with the scar across his cheek? No, he looks too mean. Maybe the gentleman with the flamboyant vest playing cards? No, couldn't be him, because I don't imagine the bartender would be playing games at this time of day. Better ask someone.* Priscilla's gaze swept across the room then froze on a slender woman standing by the long table and wearing a colorful dress and a fuzzy headpiece with a flower in it. *She looks like she would know who the bartender is. I'll ask her right away.* Priscilla almost skipped, but quickly reminded herself of the need to walk like a real woman if she expected to have any chance of getting work. When Priscilla arrived at the bar, the slender woman emptied the amber contents of a small glass into her mouth, slapped the arm of the man standing next to her, and laughed.

Priscilla tried to lower the pitch of her voice to sound older. "Excuse me, ma'am." The slender woman ignored her. Priscilla raised the volume of her voice, but this diminished her ability to lower the pitch at the same time. "Excuse me, ma'am, but I'm looking for the bartender. Do you know where I might find him?" The slender woman laughed again and slapped the top of the long table. Priscilla increased the volume of her voice until the pitch reached a level her mother would have found annoying. "Excuse me miss, but I'm looking for the bartender."

The slender woman slowly turned to identify the source of the annoying voice. She spoke with soothing tones in the lower pitch range Priscilla had hoped for. "What do we have here? A young girl in a saloon in Silver City? What is this world coming to?"

Priscilla wrinkled her forehead. "I'm not a young girl, ma'am. I'm nearly 15. That makes me at least a young woman."

The slender woman touched one of Priscilla's pigtails. "Yes, I can see it now. I do apologize for my mistake. Must have been the poor light."

Priscilla relaxed her forehead. "It's alright, ma'am. A fellow I just ran into outside the store made the same mistake, but I set him straight right away."

The slender woman smiled broadly and rested her elbows on the rolled edge of the bar. "I bet you did." She adjusted the position of her elbows.

"You may call me Nadia." She settled into a more comfortable pose. "And what should I call you, my young lady with pigtails?"

Priscilla clasped her hands behind her back and rocked on the heels of her shoes. "You can call me Priscilla Kimball." She rocked some more, then observed, "And if you don't mind me saying so, ma'am, I think you're beautiful."

Nadia heard this assertion constantly in her line of work, but hearing an authentic opinion from a young "woman" touched her heart. "Why... thank you for the kind words Miss Priscilla Kimball. I do appreciate it. I really do."

At last Priscilla smiled. "You're welcome, ma'am."

"Please call me Nadia. "Ma'am is so formal."

"You're welcome, Nadia."

The man standing next to Nadia clanked his glass down on the bar and grunted. "Nadia, explain to me what is going on here? I'm paying good money for this conversation, except I'm not getting any of it."

Nadia slapped the man's arm. "Shut up Benjamin. Just because you paid doesn't mean you own every second of my time. I'm allowed a break once in a while, especially when I'm with you." The man grunted even more and waved at the bartender for another whisky. Nadia continued her conversation with Priscilla. "Tell me, Miss Priscilla, what brought you into this saloon? Certainly you are not here to drink or play cards."

Priscilla set her hand on the edge of the bar and pushed up on her toes. "No Miss Nadia. I'm here looking for work. I saw the sign outside the store and I'm looking for the bartender so I can ask him for a job."

Nadia's shoulder muscles tightened and she sucked her tongue. "I don't think you understand, Miss Priscilla. You're not the kind of woman they're looking for. You should head out of here right now and look somewhere else for work."

Priscilla's lip quivered. "But Miss Nadia, I have to find work, and I've tried everywhere—even the general store and the livery stables—and if I don't find something soon they're going to kick me out of the boarding house because the wagon family can't afford to feed me anymore because they don't have enough food for their own family and then I won't have anywhere to go and I saw the sign on the front of the store and since I'm a woman now I've just got to talk to the bartender because I don't know where else to go."

A stocky woman dressed in black from her high-necked collar down to her shiny leather toes slithered up to the bar and scolded Nadia. "Nadia, you're here to work, not to while away the time talking to little girls who shouldn't even be in this saloon in the first place when we've got paying customers waiting for you to spend time with them. Now tell this little darling to move along and get back to work."

Priscilla intervened before Nadia could explain. "I'm here about the sign looking for women, Ma'am. Do you know where I can find the bartender?"

The stocky woman examined Priscilla from the top of her shiny brown pigtails to the puckered hem of her white cotton dress and then back again to Priscilla's youthful face. "There'd be some in this town who'd pay good money for a young one like you, but there's others who'd try to run me out of Silver City for offering the opportunity. I don't think you need to waste the bartender's time about the sign out front. You just run along now, little darling. It's time for Nadia to get back to work."

A tear rolled down Priscilla's cheek. "But ma'am, I have to find work. If I don't find something soon they're going to kick me out of the boarding house because the wagon family can't afford to feed me anymore because—"

Nadia interrupted, "Come now, Margaret. Of course we wouldn't hire her for that. But what about giving her a cleaning job? Francis hates cleaning the rooms and would rather spend as much time as possible on her back. Why not give the cleaning job to little Priscilla?"

Margaret moaned softly. "She looks too young to me, and I don't really see how's she's going to manage the—"

Priscilla implored, "I can clean rooms for you! My mother taught me how to clean house and iron and wash and everything. I'm real good at it."

This announcement interested Margaret. "You really know how to wash and iron?"

Priscilla pushed up on her toes. "Sure do."

"Can you make a bed?"

Priscilla dropped back on her heels and rocked. "Sure can."

Margaret stroked the sagging flesh beneath her chin. "Alright then, you're the new cleaning girl...I mean woman. I'll pay you wages every week, but don't expect a lot because I'm subtracting the cost of your room and board."

Priscilla clapped her hands and pushed up on her toes at the same time. "Thank you, Miss Margaret. I'll do whatever you want, and I'll do a really good job because—"

Margaret jabbed a chubby finger at Priscilla. "But if you break anything..." then she scowled at Nadia, "...I'm taking the cost of it out of Nadia's wages. Understand?"

Nadia breathed deeply. She leaned forward until her nose nearly touched Margaret's and sneered, "Fine, Margaret. Just fine."

The man standing next to Nadia, his patience finally waning, waited for Nadia's sneer to diminish, then asked, "Are you done yet? I think I deserve a big discount for having to listen to the three of you argue while I'm paying for Nadia at the same time."

Margaret pushed Nadia aside and rested her hand firmly on the man's shoulder. "Step into the back room, Benjamin, and *I'll* give you a big discount right now."

CHAPTER TWO

Silver City, Idaho Territory
September 1871

Manfred Herrmann waited for Father Nero Aguilar beneath the imposing portico of the War Eagle Hotel (near the southern end of Silver City). He pressed a shoulder against one of the square heavy-timber columns and looked northwesterly along Washington Street. Although the surging bedlam of freighters and mules and pedestrians and wagons and horses and stagecoaches and oxen and buggies and the occasional cow made it nearly impossible to identify an approaching priest, he did glimpse something quite odd during a momentary opening in the chaotic traffic: a small girl in a white dress standing in the middle of the street near Avalanche Avenue. An advancing pair of sweat-lathered horses pulling a small wagon rushed across his view of the girl just after a heavily-loaded freight wagon rumbled north and drove straight at her. When the sweat-lathered horses and wagon cleared his line of sight, the little girl had vanished in the swirl of dust trailing the freighter. Manfred cringed and rushed into the street, but still could not see anything of the little girl. He began jumping up and down to see if the freighter had run over her, but every time he leaped a new obstruction emerged to block his line of sight. First another wagon pulled out in front of him. Then a gang of tromping miners carrying pickaxes and shovels staggered across his path from the opposite direction. When he jumped a third time, a prairie schooner swerved in front of him. Manfred began to run, and, keeping his eye on the spot where the freighter had almost certainly crushed the little girl to death, nearly plowed into a threesome of chattering women. He hastily bowed and apologized to the ladies after the near collision and started to run again, but when his eyes refocused the little girl reappeared in the middle of the street, this time oddly turning in slow circles. Manfred halted, set his feet apart for balance, shoved his fists against his hips, and watched the pirouetting girl through new breaks in the frenzied street traffic. Without thinking, he announced in a soft voice, "Well I'll be a horse's a—"

"Manfred! Quit jumping around in the middle of the street before something runs you down." Father Nero Aguilar, the hem of his black cassock* smeared with dust, yelled at Manfred through cupped hands from beneath a drooping canopy north of the War Eagle Hotel.

Confident the little girl could take care of herself without his intervention, Manfred turned to address the priest. "I've been waiting for you in front of the War Eagle Hotel, but something in the street caught my attention."

Father Nero beckoned Manfred to his side. "I see. But please get out of the street and walk with me to the hotel where we can retire to the relative safety of the dining room. There is no reason for you to continue risking your life, or to give anyone else in Silver City the impression you may have lost your mind."

Manfred glanced right, then nearly banged into a galloping horse. He let the horse pass before advancing to the canopy where Father Nero waited. The two men shook hands. "Thank you, Father Nero, for finding the time to meet with me today. I know you are a busy man."

Father Nero nodded, and began walking toward the War Eagle Hotel. "Yes, especially in a place like Silver City. There is more than enough trouble here to keep a lonely priest occupied."

Manfred stepped to Father Nero's side. "You speak the truth."

Father Nero quickened his pace. "This is why I am thinking the two of us might find a way to work together. There is more than enough sin to go around. Another man of the cloth, even one who is not a Catholic, may be a useful addition to this town."

---

* A cassock is a long garment with a close-fitting waist and sleeves worn by Catholic priests and other clergy.

Manfred increased his gait to match Father Nero's pace. "Indeed."

When they arrived at the main entry to the War Eagle Hotel, Father Nero opened one of the glass-filled doors and motioned Manfred in. The two clergymen walked from the clear sunlight of Washington Street into the formless shadows of the hotel office and lobby. They maneuvered around a grouping of three fabric-covered chairs and a small table toward a framed opening that led to the dining room at the back of the hotel. A young clerk, sitting on a stool behind the high counter in front of the hotel office and reading the local newspaper, nodded when he recognized Father Nero. The echoes of breaking glass and swearing reverberated from the saloon fronting Washington Street to the north of the lobby, and then a chair shattered against something hard and a wayward spittoon rattled along the hardwood floor before gyrating to a standstill. An upright piano started playing a cheerful tune. A woman laughed.

A Chinaman dressed in a white apron splattered with tomato soup greeted Father Nero and Manfred Herrmann when they entered the dining room. "Have you cared to join for lunch today? We have many good specials on the menus you can see for yourself today. Or you can ask to me, and I will tell you many good specials today."

Father Nero replied, "Yes, we are here for lunch. Do you have a table by a window? My friend and I would like to watch the activity on Jordan Avenue while we dine."

The Chinaman grinned and bowed. "Oh yes, we have many special tables on the street through the window. I take you there today." He popped up and led the way to a rectangular table covered with a white table cloth (and decorated with a glass kerosene lamp) near a sun-streaked window. "I bring you menus and you can eat the many specials we have today."

The two men pulled wooden chairs out and sat facing each other. Father Nero asked the waiter, "Do you have fresh coffee? I feel like a cup of fresh coffee. Manfred?"

"Yes, I'll have a cup of fresh coffee too, and a glass of water, please."

The Chinaman slapped his apron with both hands and grinned. "Oh yes, we have the fresh coffee and the fresh water today for you to have together. I fetch them for you soon, and bring the menus today." The Chinaman scurried away to fetch the coffee and water and menus.

Father Nero tapped the table with his knuckles. "I like this place. Although some in this town may prefer the Idaho Hotel because of its more sedate environment, I believe the War Eagle serves the best food in town."

Manfred looked through the window across a wide opening between two buildings at the back of the hotel and watched a line of oxen plod north down the middle of Jordan Avenue. "I've never eaten here before, but I'll take your word for it."

"Have you eaten at the Idaho Hotel?"

"No, haven't eaten there either."

The Chinaman arrived with two cups of coffee. "I bring you the fresh coffee today. I will return later today with the water and the fresh menus." And he scurried away.

Father Nero poured three spoons of sugar into his fresh cup of coffee, speaking while he stirred. "So, my fellow man of the cloth … what brings us together today—something trivial or something important? Would you like some sugar?"

Manfred sipped the fresh coffee. "No thanks. I prefer to drink it without sugar. I believe it is something important. I would never waste your time to discuss something trivial."

Father Nero finished stirring and set the spoon on the table. "I have noticed that you are a very serious person. But do not be afraid to share a meal with me to discuss something trivial. I am always available to anyone, even Lutherans who have drifted away from the true Catholic Church."

Manfred smiled faintly, but not enough for Father Nero to notice. "Then I should make something clear before we speak more, Father Nero. As far as I'm concerned, the Reformation is water under the bridge."

The waiter returned with two glasses of fresh water and one menu. "I thought the both of you would love fresh water today and you can see the special menus at the same time. I come again today to hear the food you wish, and bring more coffee today if you wish it."

Father Nero answered, "Yes, more coffee would be appreciated," then spoke to Manfred. "I agree completely. As you say, water under the bridge. Although I fear the Pope is to this day not terribly fond of Martin Luther, especially his marriage to a nun. I imagine it caused quite a stir in Rome at the time."

Manfred lifted the glass of water but did not drink. "I see that you have not entirely ignored the history of the Lutheran Church."

"Quite the contrary. I find it absolutely fascinating, if a bit misguided at times."

Manfred drank, set the glass on the white table cloth without removing his hand, and slid forward in his chair. "When you say 'misguided,' are you referring to Martin Luther's Ninety-Five Theses to protest the sale of indulgences and other unfortunate abuses by the Catholic Church, or do you mean the translation of the New Testament into German to allow the common man to read it without translation by a priest? If I remember correctly, the Catholic Church sold indulgences for the absolution of sin to raise money for the renovation of Saint Peter's Basilica in Rome. The Ninety-Five Theses must have caused great consternation for the Pope's fundraising committee."

"And I see you also have not ignored the history of the Catholic Church, at least the parts which do not shed the best light on it."

"Quite the contrary. I have studied the history of the Catholic Church extensively, and find it equally fascinating; and, as you say, a bit misguided at times."

The Chinese waiter appeared. "I have come today to hear your food. Have you seen the menus and the many special?"

Father Nero picked up the menu but then set it down without looking. "Even though the hour approaches noon, I feel like breakfast. Can I have scrambled eggs and bacon?"

The waiter grinned. "Oh yes. We can do breakfast anytime today, even in the dark." He bowed to Manfred and grinned. "And your food today?"

Manfred slid back in his chair. "I'll have the same. Scrambled eggs and bacon sounds pretty good right now. And some more coffee, please."

The waiter picked up the menu and clutched it against his breast. "I return today with scrambled eggs and bacon and coffee. You will see." He scurried away, pausing to talk to another guest a few tables down before rushing to the kitchen.

Father Nero, his brows scrunched in amusement, resumed the conversation. "Then I suppose there is no reason to discuss the Spanish Inquisition before we eat?"

Manfred's countenance relaxed. "Certainly not. And I would also recommend avoiding the Thirty-Years War, which I have always found disagreeable."

"To be sure. I believe we are both implicated in that unfortunate episode. But, for better or worse, I cannot shake my interest in Martin Luther's marriage. Do you have any plans to take advantage of this trivial distinction between Catholic and Lutheran clergy?"

A wagon wheel squealed on Jordan, and Manfred turned to look. The recollection of the mysterious woman dressed in black running along the train platform in Chicago flashed into his mind and obscured his vision of the freight wagon. *Alexandra Smythe.* He watched the woman skillfully maneuver around people and suitcases and carts and iron columns as she ran swiftly along the platform. He smiled when she used her canvas bag to provide balance when she bounded around each new obstacle. *Alexandra Smythe.* Then his mind skipped ahead, and he glimpsed the derringer in her hand and heard the mysterious woman tell him to never speak to her again. *Alexandra Smythe.* He remembered her final words with uncanny clarity, and the remembrance provoked a small shiver to tumble across his shoulders: *"I cannot speak more. I only wished to apologize for my beastly behavior. Goodbye, Mister Herrmann."* He focused on the lovely way her mouth formed each word, and then allowed himself the troubling pleasure of repeating the scene. *Alexandra Smythe. Alexandra—*

"Manfred, do you find me so thoroughly boring that you have fallen asleep?"

Manfred shivered again and snapped his attention back to Father Nero. "I apologize, but I was thinking of another time. I did not mean to appear bored. I don't find you boring at all. Quite the contrary."

"Good. There is nothing worse than a boring priest. Nothing worse."

"Yes, I have thought of marriage."

"How delightful. And do you have a particular woman in mind, or are you just thinking of marriage as a general concept to be accomplished sometime in the future?"

Manfred looked through the window again, but the freight wagon with the squealing wheel had moved out of view. "No, I don't have anyone in mind."

The Chinese waiter suddenly rushed to the table with two plates of scrambled eggs and bacon balanced in one hand and a pot of steaming coffee clenched in the other. He deftly refilled the coffee cups without spilling a drop while gliding the plates onto the table at the same time. "The cook added cheese and onion to the scrambled eggs today. My hope you like it."

Father Nero grabbed his fork and poked at the scrambled eggs. "This is why I eat here so often, my good waiter, because the cook always adds interesting ingredients to the scrambled eggs." He speared a chunk of eggs mixed with cheese and onion, shoveled it into his mouth, chewed a few times, swallowed, and exhaled. "Delightful my good waiter. Absolutely delightful."

The waiter grinned and bowed. "I tell cook you good with the egg today." He scurried away, stopping again to talk to the same guest a few tables down.

Father Nero set his fork down, found the spoon, and began shoveling large mounds of sugar into the refilled coffee cup. "Such a pity. I imagine there are many fine women in the world who would be glad to wed a man of your temperament. I'm sure the Lord will present her to you when the time is right, although the chances may be a little slim in Silver City."

Although he did not believe a word, Manfred suggested, "Yes, I'm sure the Lord is searching for a good wife for me at this very moment." The unsettling memory of the young boy at Shiloh flitted beneath Manfred's consciousness, but he refused to look at it.

Father Nero chewed down a thick strip of greasy bacon and swallowed another mouthful of scrambled eggs. "First you find me boring and fall asleep. Now you are making fun of me."

Manfred chuckled. "Once you get to know me better, I think you'll understand that I'm far too serious to ever make fun of anyone. It is one of my numerous, if less serious, faults."

Father Nero popped the last piece of bacon into his mouth and ran a fork over the plate to capture the last of the scrambled eggs. "We all have faults. Maybe the Lord will find you a wife with a cheerful disposition to offset your serious nature."

"I'm sure the Lord would find that amusing."

"I think the Lord finds many things amusing. Otherwise, how could he stand to be around us all the time? But let us discuss what I believe is the primary purpose of this meeting: your request to use *Our Lady of Tears* Catholic Church to hold Lutheran services."

"Yes."

"As promised, I earnestly discussed this idea with the Bishop during my recent trip to Boise. I told him it would be a good thing for the specific setting of Silver City, but sadly, he has denied your request. I am sorry, but any collaboration must stop short of a Lutheran service in the church. I did my best."

Manfred sipped his coffee. "No need to apologize. I believe you. I did not really expect a positive response, but thought it worth asking the question anyway."

Father Nero set his fork down. "Now that I understand how serious you are, I believe you when you say you expected this answer from the Bishop. When you find the right woman, maybe she will help you to be more optimistic."

Manfred stood without smiling. "Well then, we should pay our bill and be on our way."

"Do not worry about the bill, Manfred. You can pay for our next meeting. But I do have another idea for you to consider."

Manfred sat again and rested his forearms on the table. "Another idea?"

"Yes. Although not ideal, the saloon on the corner of Washington and Avalanche has a large room at the back with a few windows looking into the street. With a little cleaning and rearranging, it might prove adequate for Sunday services. I suggest you make an inquiry to the owner, an incorrigibly surly woman named Margaret."

"A saloon for church services?"

"No, the back room of a saloon. I see a distinction, even if you do not. You should find the place relatively quiet on Sunday mornings, especially if you hold services before noon."

"A saloon?"

"The back room."

"Alright then, the back room. But of a saloon?"

Father Nero could not hold back a chuckle. "Should the need arise, you are always welcome to buy indulgences at *Our Lady of Tears*."

Manfred Herrmann sat awkwardly across the beverage-stained table from the owner of the saloon on the corner of Washington and Avalanche. The woman, dressed completely in black from her pudgy neck down to her toes, appeared to have temporarily lost the ability to speak. Manfred prompted her. "Margaret?"

Margaret sighed. "What a day I've had. First a little girl with pigtails and a white dress asks for a job as a whore, and now a preacher man wearing a suit and tie wants to use my saloon for a church. What a day. What a day ...."

Manfred protested, "The back room, not the saloon itself."

Margaret perceived the seriousness of Manfred's manner. "I can tell by the look of you that this is not some sort of stupid joke, otherwise I'd have you thrown out into the street with a snap of my fingers."

"No, ma'am, this is not a joke, stupid or otherwise. Father Nero was the one who suggested the idea of asking you about using the back room for church services. We just had lunch together."

"Father Nero. I should have guessed. This is not the first time he's caused trouble for me. But the real question is, how much are you willing to pay me to use the back room?"

"Why, I'm willing to pay you nothing, Margaret. I don't have any money for such things. I was hoping to use it for free. It's only once a week, on Sunday mornings. It shouldn't cause you any trouble."

The sagging skin beneath Margaret's chin tightened. "You were expecting to use it for free? I suppose this was Father Nero's idea too. He's probably trying to run my saloon out of business by bankrupting me."

"We didn't discuss the rent. It was my idea."

Margaret's foot tapped the floor a few times. "Actually, having a church service in the back room from time to time might give the place a little respectability. It might even get Father Nero out of my hair for a while."

"Almost certainly."

"I think I'll do it. But first, I got some rules."

"Rules?"

"Yes. You have to do your own cleaning. And you have to keep the noise down in case someone's sleeping off a hangover from Saturday night. No fire and brimstone either, because it might upset the paying customers. And—"

Manfred frowned. "And?"

"And I don't want any sermons about the sins of gambling or drinking or whoring."

Manfred allowed himself a little sarcasm. "You've made quite a list. Are you sure you haven't forgotten anything?"

Margaret cackled. "Oh yeah. Thanks for reminding me. And no sermons about swearing either. If you want to talk about lying... fine, but don't make it sound like any of my customers have been doing it."

"I see. How about the sin of coveting your neighbor's ass? Can I talk about that?"

Margaret slammed her hand on the table. "That's a good one, preacher. I was beginning to think you didn't have any sense of humor at all. Yeah, go ahead and talk about asses. We've got plenty to choose from in Silver City. Just don't tell anyone you got the idea from me."

Manfred stood and stretched out his hand. "Then I believe we have an understanding."

Margaret stood and shook Manfred's hand vigorously. "We certainly do, preacher man. See you Sunday. You may want to get here early to clean up a little and fix any broken chairs."

Manfred pulled his hand from Margaret's overly firm grip. "Indeed."

CHAPTER THREE

Silver City, Idaho Territory
October 1871

C onrad Airingsail—wide-brimmed hat scrunched down on top of
ears and spectacles to block the afternoon sun...unraveled hem
of a gray bandana stretched beneath a small dirt-smudged nose to keep
some measure of dust out...cowboy spurs with the rowels* filed down
strapped to boots splattered with dried mud from a morning of fence-
mending...long flannel sleeves buttoned down tight and tucked snugly
into leather work gloves...leather chaps knee-puckered from too much
crawling around on the rocky ground and polished smooth from too
much saddle rubbing—tugged on the reins leading to the bridle of
Abigail, his favorite mule, to cajole both animal and antique buckboard†
to a stop on the east side of Washington Street midway between Second
and Dead Man's Alley directly in front of the general store where he preferred to do business. Conrad Airingsail tied the reins off to the handle
of the wheel break and hopped down. The spurs jingled when his boots
hit the ground. When he walked to the rear of the wagon to fetch a sack
of fresh vegetables, the 12-gauge-sawed-off-pistol-grip-double-barreled
shotgun secured to his back in a quick-release harness he had fabricated

---

* The rowel is the star-shaped disk with radiating points attached to the end of
the spur shank. A working rancher or cowboy usually filed down the sharp
points of new spurs to avoid hurting the horse.

† A buckboard is a four-wheeled open carriage with the seat attached to a flexible
board running between the front and rear axles.

himself swung into view. Another weapon, a small-caliber five-cylinder revolver carried in a shoulder holster, remained concealed beneath the left flap of his sweat-stained vest. A throwing knife, sheathed at a good slant for instant retrieval, adorned an otherwise undecorated belt between a sweat-tarnished buckle and a neat row of eight 12-gage shotgun shells. And something more: Conrad Airingsail smelled of fresh manure.

Conrad Airingsail walked slowly around the rear wheel of the buckboard, each step spur-jingling, and seized the canvas sack. He opened the sack to confirm that none of the contents had rolled out during the five-mile ride to town, and then counted each item: four potatoes, six carrots, and a large onion. He pinched the sack closed with a gloved hand and dangled it at his side before spur-jingling toward the board walk in front of the general store. He paused to read the neatly-painted wood sign cantilevered off the angled metal roof of the canopy and extending the entire width of the store: *The Sommercamp Emporium & General Store - Est. 1867.* When he had finished reading the sign, he stepped up to the wood-planked walkway below the canopy and spur-jingled to the entry. Someone had propped the door open with a small cask of iron nails, and he walked straight in. He waited just inside the general store to allow his pupils to dilate, but he did not pull the gray bandana down or remove the wide-brimmed hat. When his eyes had adjusted to the light, he searched the store until he spotted Mr. William F. Sommercamp standing near the back, next to a long glass-fronted counter littered with cans of different sizes and colors. He maneuvered around a display of hammers and saws and approached Mr. Sommercamp, each step spur-jingling ominously on the hardwood floor. When he arrived directly in front of Mr. Sommercamp, he stood rigidly with the sack of vegetables still dangling at his side and did not move or speak.

When he heard the sound of spurs cease, William F. Sommercamp wrote a final note on a sheet of paper, set a can of beets down on the counter, and looked up. He studied the strange man standing in front of him before speaking. "Mr. Airingsail. I haven't seen you for at least two months. Maybe three. And what brings you to my general store today?"

Conrad Airingsail reached into a vest pocket in front of the concealed pistol, pulled out a neatly-folded piece of paper, shook it open with one hand, and presented the note to William Sommercamp without saying a word.

William Sommercamp bent the paper to flatten out the creases and mumbled while he read the neatly-penciled list of items: *1 sack of flour, 2 pounds bacon, 1 pound lard, 2 pounds coffee, 1 pound sugar, 1 gallon coal oil,* *2 pounds beans, 1 new shovel, and a few eggs if you have them. I brought some fresh vegetables for your family.* He lowered the note. "Yes, Mr. Airingsail, it just so happens that I received a shipment of eggs yesterday afternoon." He read the last sentence of the note again. "And the children always appreciate it when you provide fresh vegetables for the Sunday dinner. My wife appreciates it too."

Conrad Airingsail lifted the canvas sack of vegetables up and handed it to William Sommercamp, but did not speak or look up from the sack.

"Thank you, Mr. Airingsail. I'll put this in the back of the store where it'll be safe from thieves, then we'll find all the items on this list and you can be on your way." William Sommercamp returned with a sack of flour and a can of coal oil. "How many eggs did you want?"

Conrad Airingsail held up both hands.

"Six? You sure you don't need more? I've got plenty."

Conrad added a finger.

"Seven? Okay then, seven it is."

Two women entered the general store together, but when they spotted Conrad Airingsail they whispered to each other and skittered out of the store. Conrad did not appear to notice them.

"Don't mind them, Mr. Airingsail. They probably forgot about something else they had to do. How much flour do you want?"

Conrad Airingsail pointed at one of the 98-pound sacks of flour piled up next to a table of shirts and pants.

"You want a full sack? Well, I guess I won't be seeing you for at least another two months then, or longer, so that makes some sense." William Sommercamp attempted a small joke: "You must like to eat a lot of flapjacks for breakfast. Can I interest you in a bottle of maple syrup? Just got a case in from Boise this week."

Conrad Airingsail said nothing, and William Sommercamp could not tell if this strange customer had smiled because of the gray bandana stretched across his mouth and the wide-brimmed hat scrunched

---

* Coal oil is an early form of kerosene.

down on top of his ears. Conrad Airingsail pivoted on his boot heels and spur-jingled over to the sack of flour, lifted it to his shoulder without making a sound, and trudged out of the front door of the store to load the flour on the buckboard. When he entered the store again, he waited again for his pupils to dilate.

A little embarrassed by the failure of his joke to provoke any response whatsoever, at least none he could see or hear, William Sommercamp had busied himself with packing a splintered wood crate with the food items from the list while Conrad Airingsail lugged the sack of flour out to the buckboard. This time he watched Conrad enter the store. Conrad Airingsail spur-jingled across the wood floor again, stopped in front of William Sommercamp, pulled a second piece of paper from his vest, shook it open with one hand, and presented it.

William Sommercamp bent the second note to flatten out the creases and mumbled again while he read the neatly-penciled sentence: *How much do I owe you, Mr. Sommercamp?* "Well, let's see what we've got here." William Sommercamp picked up the first paper note and began writing down prices. He recited each item and price clearly so Conrad Airingsail could hear his calculations. "One sack of flour, thirty-two dollars... I'll sell it to you for thirty since you carried it out yourself. Two pounds of bacon at seventy-five cents a pound will be a dollar and a half. One pound of lard is seventy-five cents. Two pounds of coffee at seventy-five cents a pound is the same as the bacon. One pound of sugar is sixty cents. One gallon of coal oil, that'll be eight dollars even. Two pounds of beans at thirty-five cents a pound is seventy cents. The eggs are three dollars a dozen, six is a buck-fifty, and I'll throw in the seventh for free and call it even. And the shovels are four dollars each. You can go over to the tool bin and pick one out that suits you. So your grand total comes to..." William Sommercamp scratched a crooked line under the column of numbers and began adding and carrying. "...a total of... forty-eight dollars and fifty-five cents. Why don't we make it an even forty-five dollars since you're a regular customer, Mr. Airingsail."

Conrad Airingsail pulled the glove off his right hand and fished through his right pants pocket and pulled out two ten dollar bills. Then he pulled the glove from his left hand and fished through his left pants pocket and retrieved four fives. Then he dug four one-dollar bills and four quarters out of an inside vest pocket. He unfolded the bills as best he could and handed the wad of money and change to William Sommercamp, then grabbed the second piece of paper from the counter, scribbled a note on it, and held it up.

William Sommercamp leaned forward and squinted to read the note: *Thank you.* "Why, you're welcome Mr. Airingsail. It's always a pleasure doing business with a customer who always pays his bills right away."

Conrad Airingsail nodded without saying a word, pulled the leather gloves on, lifted the splintered wood crate off the counter with both hands without making a sound, and spur-jingled out of *The Sommercamp Emporium & General Store*. William Sommercamp followed closely behind with the shovel and coal oil.

Manfred Herrmann sat on a creaking wood chair and hunched over a wood table (with two of the legs cut shorter than the others) next to the only window in a small shack a few hundred yards from the southern fringe of Silver City. He picked up a metal cup by the sides (the former owner must have broken the handle off) and poured off two gulps of strong coffee. He set the cup down, shoved it near the edge of the table, picked up the last shred of paper he owned, and with a graphite wood pencil wrote the same message he had written on the previous fifty-seven shreds of paper. He held the finished product up to the light glowing through the small window and proofread the smudgy text. He found a small but significant spelling error. He flipped the pencil around, neatly erased* the offending word, and penciled in the correct spelling. He reminded himself to buy a good dictionary and a better pencil when his financial situation improved. He proofread the message a second time, and finding no further errors pressed the shred on top of the pile of other shreds. He set the pencil down. He watched it move and gradually gain speed before rolling off the table. The pencil rattled pleasantly when it hit the floor, then continued rolling across the uneven planks to the other

---

* Hyman Lipman received the first patent for attaching an eraser to the end of a wood pencil in March 1858.

side of the shack, clicked against the wall, rolled back about a foot, and dropped through a wide crack between two uneven floor boards. He watched his last pencil vanish through the floor, and decided to attempt recovery of the errant pencil later.

The task of preparing the notices complete, he pulled on his wool suit jacket, stuffed the packet of shreds into an inside pocket until it bulged, threw open the front door with a prolonged squeal of the hinges, and stepped out to the narrow covered porch (which thus far had prevented the northern wall of the shack from collapsing). He stretched his arms out horizontally and breathed in a full breath of the late morning breeze. *Quite a bit cooler than yesterday.* He stepped forward until he could see the top of Florida Mountain. *The skies have the look of autumn. A spread of blue to the north, but gray clouds to the west. I fear summer has finally come to an end.* He closed his eyes and listened to the pleasant water sounds of nearby Jordan Creek. A thrush chirped, and then something rubbed against his leg. Manfred opened his eyes and looked down.

"You again. I thought I told you yesterday to stay away. There's nary enough food for me, let alone a second hungry mouth to feed." Manfred waved his arms. "Off with you, and don't come back again."

In a display of utter disobedience, the cat rubbed Manfred's leg again, meowed expectantly, and purred.

Manfred kneeled down to inspect the cat more closely but did not touch the animal. Black fur, white paws and chest with a flash of gold around the shoulders, crystal blue lizard eyes a bit crossed, a little mangy around the tail, a small chunk missing from the left ear. "Look...like I told you yesterday, I don't have any food for you, and as the Lord surely knows, I harbor no love for cats, especially in my present circumstances. If He had sent me a dog, I might have considered it."

The cat purred even louder and rubbed against Manfred's knee.

When he stood, Manfred nearly tripped on the cat. "Get away from here. I'm off to run some errands in town, and I expect you to be gone when I return. Understand?"

The cat rolled up into a ball and began licking its tail and purring at the same time.

Manfred strolled away. *Disgusting little varmint.* He hiked along the narrow dirt road that loosely followed the western banks of Jordan Creek, taking special care to steer around the numerous rocky outcroppings. He soon arrived near the southern limits of Silver City. He hastened his pace and walked briskly past the nondescript wood buildings scattered along the southern end of Jordan Avenue—an area the locals called "Chinatown." *No reason to waste my time trying to hand out notices for a new Lutheran Church to the Chinese. They've got their own religion to deal with.* He walked by a Chinese laundry, then a Chinese restaurant, and noticed three men loitering in front of the wagon shop across the street. He marched right up to the men. When he approached within twenty feet, he overheard one of the men speaking about the local courtesans.

The man, a stumpy fellow named Will with a scruffy beard and sleeves rolled up tight above the elbows and knee-high leather boots smeared with sluice mud, pointed his finger in the face of the man standing in the middle of the trio. "You got it wrong, Josh. I got nearly twice as much time with Emily for only a dollar more, and she bought me a whisky for free to boot. There's no way you can beat the deal she offers. And if you think of—"

Manfred Herrmann interrupted. "Excuse me my fine gentlemen. May I have a word?"

Will glimpsed Manfred's shoes, then continued his conversation with Josh. "As I was saying before, if you think of—"

Manfred tapped Will on the shoulder. "If you don't mind, I would like to have a word with you and your associates. I promise it will only take a brief moment of your time."

This time all three men perused Manfred in unison, but only Will said anything. "My associates?" He smirked. "Where did you come from with such highfalutin phraseology? Haven't heard such uppity words since I left San Francisco. You some sort of lawyer?"

Manfred bowed his head slightly. "No, I'm not a lawyer. I'm a Lutheran Pastor, and I want to tell you about church services in the back room of Margaret's Saloon every Sunday morning at eleven. I have a notice with the details." Manfred reached into his jacket pocket, pulled out one the shreds, and attempted to give it to Will.

Will thrust his hands into his pants pockets. "No need to waste one of your pieces of paper on any of us. We got too many things going on Sunday mornings to spend any time at church. Although I have to say, it's mighty convenient to hold the church service in the same building as the whorehouse. Sounds like Lutherans are not so particular as the Catholics." A few seconds passed, and then all three men broke into wild laughter. Josh laughed so hard he inhaled a gob of spit and nearly choked to death. Will blew a string of snot out of his nose. And the third man developed a fearful case of hiccups.

Manfred could see that the conversation had more or less ended. He bowed his head again and said, "Thank you for your time, gentlemen. Maybe we shall speak again in the future." As he withdrew the laughter increased and the string of snot lengthened.

Manfred continued north along Jordan Avenue. He spotted another trio of miners standing in front of the livery stables, but did not have the courage to risk a similar incident. A little farther on he encountered two women leaving a female boarding house (one of several in Silver City), and determined to try again. He angled to the right until he intersected the path of the two women, and this time pulled one of the notices out of his pocket before speaking. "Excuse me ladies. May I have a brief word with you?" The slender woman to the left, the one wearing a white apron smudged with coal dust, whispered something in her friend's ear and then both ladies quickly reversed direction and scurried away before Manfred could speak.

Manfred persevered in his mission to announce church services to the sinners of Silver City all the way to the northern end of Jordan Avenue, but after approaching more than a hundred residents he had convinced not a single person to accept one of the hand-written notices. He turned left at Avalanche, crossed Washington Street to the front of an impressive granite building constructed in 1868 and housing a drug store and a general mercantile, and was again rebuffed—this time by one of the local bankers. Manfred slumped on a stone step and gazed down at the wretched handwritten notice now wrinkled beyond readability in his hand. He spoke to himself out loud: "Lord, give me strength." He stood, crumpled the notice and tossed it into the street, pulled a fresh notice from his jacket pocket, and proceeded south along Washington Street. He was rejected seventeen more times until—late in the afternoon when the last remnants of the afternoon sun cast long, dark shadows over the street— he arrived at the front of The Sommercamp Emporium & General Store.

Manfred decided to remove a pebble from his shoe, and as he balanced himself against a wood post and shook the shoe a peculiar little man wearing a wide-brimmed hat jammed down over his ears and spectacles and jingling spurs and a short-barreled shotgun slung menacingly across his back burst from the store carrying a dilapidated wood crate followed by William Sommercamp carrying a shovel and a tin of coal oil.

Manfred walked over to the buckboard holding the shoe in his left hand and the notice in his right. "Gentlemen, do you have a moment to speak about something of the utmost importance?"

The spurs suddenly went silent. Conrad Airingsail set the wood crate on the back of the buckboard and reached into his vest until the fingers of his gloved hand touched the handle of the revolver.

William Sommercamp, still holding the shovel and coal oil, asked, "What happened to your shoe, Manfred? You could stub your toe walking around in your stocking feet like that."

Manfred lifted the wayward shoe and then hopped around comically as he pulled it on his foot and talked at the same time. "I'd like to invite the both … of you to … the back room of … Margret's place … this Sunday morning…" The shoe finally on, he stopped hopping. "…at eleven o'clock for church services. I have a written notice here so you won't forget." Manfred held the shred out.

William Sommercamp inquired, "Isn't that a saloon?"

Manfred objected. "No, it's the backroom of a saloon. I would argue a subtle but important distinction between the two."

William Sommercamp slid the shovel and tin of coal oil onto the buckboard. "Much obliged, Manfred, but my family attends *Our Lady of Tears* on Sunday mornings. And Conrad here … well, he only manages to get into town about every two or three months. I don't think he'd be much interested either."

Conrad Airingsail spun around. He quickly pulled his hand away from the vest and reached out and snatched the notice from Manfred's extended hand. He held the shred of paper close to his face and squinted through the dusty spectacles. When he had finished reading, he blinked twice, shoved the notice into a vest pocket, mounted the seat of the buckboard, snapped the reins to tell Abigail it was time to leave, and clattered away.

Manfred stared at his empty hand. "That's the first notice I've handed out all day. Why didn't he say anything? He just took it and rode off."

Equally amazed, William Sommercamp watched the wagon turn left on Second Street. "Conrad Airingsail is a mute, Mr. Herrmann. No one's ever heard him say even a single word. Matter of fact, most people are afraid of him."

"Afraid of him? Why?"

William Sommercamp hooked his thumbs around the arm holes of his vest. "Afraid he's going to pull that shotgun off his back and shoot someone, I guess. He's an odd one, Mr. Herrmann. Keeps to himself. Never says a word. Never drinks or plays cards. Always smells like he's slept in a pile of fresh manure. Wears those big spurs that jingle like a brass band. But I must say he is a good customer who pays his bills right away. I've got no complaints about him."

Manfred reflected, "Yes, but odd or not, he is still a child of God."

William Sommercamp unhooked his thumbs. "I suppose you could make such an argument, not that anyone in town would believe you. Give me some of those notices. I'll nail one up in the store and set the rest out so people can take them. Maybe one of my customers will see fit to attend your church service."

Manfred pulled a packet of notices from his jacket pocket and handed it to William Sommercamp. "Thank you. I need all the help I can get."

Manfred strolled south along Washington Street without bothering to hand out any more notices. He briefly reconsidered the idea of heading over to Jordan Avenue and trying to hand out shreds in Chinatown, but the fading light and rapidly plunging temperature convinced him to head straight back to the shack. When he reached the last building on his route, flashes of lightning illuminated the mountains and thunder shuddered down the valley. The rain began seconds later, and within a minute sheets of muddy water roiled across Manfred's path and slowed his pace. Twice he tripped and fell on unseen rocks made invisible by the rain. When he finally arrived at his shack—soaked, bruised, muddied, discouraged— the cat lay curled up beneath the protection of the porch roof, waiting for him. But his long day of unpleasant ordeals had not ended yet, for awaiting him at the threshold of the doorway was a dead shrew.

CHAPTER FOUR

Silver City, Idaho Territory
October 1871

Roshan Kuznetsov, the splintered hickory shaft of a rusty shovel stabbing into his fingers with each stroke, loaded another heavy scoop of dirt into the hopper of a recently-procured gold rocker. He tossed the shovel down and examined a torn blister below his right thumb, then used his other thumb to push the flap of skin down against the reddened wound. He peeled off his sweat-soaked hat with a flamboyant sweeping motion and shook the sweat out while observing a wispy curl of cloud floating above New York Summit. He squashed the hat back on his head and bent over to pick up an oversized ladle, then tromped down to the gravelly banks of Jordan Creek. He spoke sarcastically to his business partner, Tseng Longwei, as he jabbed the metal ladle into the gently flowing waters of the creek. "This rocker of gold, which I have now had the pleasure to work for the many of three days in the past, is a very good piece of the shit, if you ask me to tell you what I have thinking about it. We have not found the speck of gold with this not the good rocker of gold. I have the thought we should use it to build of the fire tonight, if you agree with my think, and you should say to it."

Tseng Longwei, his knees submerged below the waterline of the creek and his hands gently swirling a load of sand and water in a rusty gold pan, suggested, "Maybe you are doing it the wrong way, my blasphemous friend who throws bad words around without a second thought. Are you sure the fellow who sold you the gold rocker gave you good instructions on its use? I agree it is not working, but maybe the fault for this is our own."

Roshan issued a rattling harrumph to display his irritation. Without removing his hat, he splashed the first ladle of water over his upturned face. He opened his mouth and allowed some of the water to pour across his tongue. When he had finished, he spit a narrow stream of water into the creek. "I am of the surest this man gave me goodly instructions for this rocker of gold. It is of the simple, my long-haired partner of the business. There is nothing to do for it but scoop the dirt over the top, pour water into the rocker of gold, shake the rocker of gold with the stick with a good hand of strong, and the gold will come out of the dirt like a thing of magic to see you won't believe. This is of the simple."

Longwei pulled the pan close to his face and searched for flecks of gold. "It does sound simple enough, but after three long days of hard work you only have blisters and a sore back to show for it. Maybe we should return to Silver City, find this man who sold the gold rocker to you, and ask him to give the instructions again."

Roshan refilled the ladle and cradled it in his free hand. The cool metal temporarily soothed the aching blisters. "Listen to my lips of again. I do not think you are of the understanding of a thing. I do not know if this man lives in the City of Ruby or the City of Silver, or maybe in the city I have not told about. But I cannot tell to you the liar: I listened to the instructions of this man with much of my ears to use the rocker of gold. Have not the fear of my ears, to be of the sure."

Longwei cleaned out the gold pan and scooped another sample of sand and gravel and creek water. "This may be true, but we still have not found even the smallest morsel of gold. But the gold rocker is not the only problem. I have not found the smallest morsel of gold with the gold pan either. We have both found nothing to brag to the other about."

Roshan prepared to trudge up the hill with the ladle. "You speak of the truth, but I do not know of other ideas I can tell to you about."

Longwei stood and stretched the sore muscles and ligaments of his lumbar. "I say we should work for three more days with the gold pan and the gold rocker. If we still do not find any gold, we should track down this man who sold the gold rocker and ask him to tell the instructions of its use to both of us at the same time."

Roshan objected. "I do not know of the way to find the rocker of gold man."

Longwei countered. "We will ask around. Someone in Silver City or Ruby must know who he is. Can you tell me of this man's appearance?"

Roshan harrumphed a second time. "You ask of the silly. It is of the simplest. The gold rocker man wears the boots of leather, the big hat, and the shirt of stripes."

"Is this all you can remember?"

"No, there is more to say. A beard of the black...no, the brown...yes, it is not it...of the black. Of this there is not the question to be sure."

"You have described more than half the men in Silver City. Is there not a special thing we can use to find this man? How tall was he?"

"It is of the simplest too. He was of the same tall."

"The same tall as what?"

"Why do you ask much of the silly questions? He was of the same tall as men in the City of Silver who wear of the beards and the boots and the big hat and the shirt of stripes. It could not be of the more simplest."

Longwei picked up his gold pan and held it across his chest. "I fear, my beloved business partner who always tells the truth, that we are almost certainly doomed."

Roshan laughed broadly, spilling some of the ladle's water down one leg. "But there is not to worry about a thing. I told you of before, Roshan listened with much of his ears to the instructions of the cradle of gold and there is surely not to worry about a thing to think of it. You may have not of the fear. But I do have the same idea of three days."

Longwei flipped the gold pan over and dropped it in front of his crotch. "Three days?"

"Yes, three days. If we do not find of the gold speck in the three days, we look for the man who wears the boots and the beard and the big hat and hear the instructions with most of our ears. I have not the problem with the three days."

Longwei sighed. "We will never find this man. At the end of the three days, we should just burn the gold rocker like you advised in the first place."

Roshan grinned and spilled the remaining water from the ladle over his crotch. "You are a good one, Longwei. It is my wish to burn the rocker of gold today, but I will wait of the three days to give the speck of gold the chance to find us."

Longwei answered, "Then we are in agreement. Three more days and we reconsider the fate of the gold rocker."

Roshan nodded, stumbled down to the creek to refill his ladle, and tromped back up the hill to the gold rocker that could not find even the speck of gold to pour water over the huge pile of dirt he had shoveled on top of the hapless device. Thankful for the three additional days, Longwei diligently worked the sands and gravels of the creek with his rusty gold pan.

Excerpt from
A Concise History of the West
by Muireall Anne Ravenscroft
From Las Medulas to Silver City: The Techniques
and Implements of Mining

After the conquest of northern Hispania* in 25 B.C. by the legions of Julius Caesar Augustus (historians often consider him the first Emperor of the Roman Empire), engineers promptly began development of the vast gold fields of the region using a hydraulic mining technique called "hushing." One of the most important -- and profitable -- sites was located in Las Medulas (near present day Ponferrada in northwest Spain), where the Romans eventually constructed seven thirty-mile-long aqueducts to provide the vast quantities of water necessary to work the rich alluvial deposits of the area. Although used as a viable mining technique as recently as 1842 in the lead mines of northern England, hushing is primarily an ancient method whereby a flood or torrent of water is delivered to a specific point to strip away overlying soils and expose the hidden mineral veins. There is convincing archeological evidence that the Romans used immense waves of water to undermine and then collapse entire hillsides in their efforts to release ore-bearing material. The Romans also

---

* "Hispania" was the Roman name for the Iberian Peninsula: present day Spain and Portugal.

employed hushing as both a prospecting technique and to exploit the discovered veins. Because of its effectiveness, hushing remained the primary mining technique from early in the 1st Century B.C. to the very end of the western empire (476 A.D.). Thus it can be said that placer mining, a technique still in use today, dates back to the most ancient of times.

An aside is necessary to define several of the technical terms used in the previous paragraph and throughout the remainder of this article, as well as other sections of this history. "Placer mining" is the mining of alluvial deposits for minerals. "Alluvium," from which the phrase "alluvial deposit" is derived, is sediments of soil deposited and shaped by flowing water, such as in a riverbed or delta. "Hydraulic mining" is a specific type of mining that uses water, typically under pressure, to dislodge minerals from sediments or to simply move the sediments away to expose underlying minerals. The Roman technique of hushing was therefore an ancient example of hydraulic placer mining. A "sluice" or "sluice box" is an artificial channel for conducting water, usually built with a gate or valve to regulate the flow of the water, and "sluicing" is to wash or flood with water. "Hard rock mining" refers to any of several underground mining techniques used to excavate hard minerals, and includes (but is not limited to) the familiar construction of tunnels and shafts in mountains. A "mineral" is a naturally-occurring, homogeneous inorganic solid substance having a definite chemical composition and crystalline structure, color, and hardness. Examples of minerals include arsenic, copper, diamond, gold, lead, mercury, pyrite (also known as "fools gold"), quartz, and silver. "Ore" is a specific mineral or aggregate of minerals from which a valuable constituent, especially a metal, can be profitably mined or extracted. A "metal" is any of a category of electropositive elements that usually have a shiny surface, are generally good conductors of heat and electricity, and can be melted or fused, hammered into thin sheets, or drawn into wires. From the previous list only copper, gold, lead, and silver qualify as metals under this definition.

But before we explore some of the more complex and sophisticated mining techniques and implements of the American West, let us begin with the simplest. Gold panning is a type of placer mining that extracts gold from an alluvial deposit using a heavy-gage pan with rolled edges typically measuring 10 to 17 inches in diameter and several inches deep. The technique relies on the physics of specific gravity.* The prospector (or miner) scoops sediment from an alluvial deposit into the pan, adds a portion of water, then swirls and agitates the pan to cause the materials with a high specific gravity to sink to the bottom and those with a low specific gravity to spill over the edges. The materials remaining in the pan after this process is completed are then examined, and any metal dust carefully gleaned. Although this technique occasionally discovers significant amounts of gold dust, or even gold nuggets, these latter results are exceptional. Gold panning is therefore primarily a gold prospecting technique used to discover the larger veins that are the origin of most placer deposits.

Next we consider the gold rocker (sometimes called a rocker box), a modest but nonetheless significant

---

* Specific gravity is the ratio of the mass of a solid or liquid to the mass of an equal volume of distilled water. The specific gravity of gold is 19.3, which by definition means gold is 19.3 times heavier than distilled water. By comparison, the specific gravity of lead is only 11.3, and the specific gravity of wet sand is a paltry 1.9. Gold is therefore 10 times heavier than wet sand.

improvement to the gold pan. Relying on the same physics of specific gravity, but incorporating the additional advantages of a sluice box, the gold rocker was used extensively from California to Idaho to the Klondike, and still enjoys widespread popularity throughout the American West as I write this history in the year 1907. A relatively straightforward device that an enterprising miner could build with rough-sawn lumber, a handful of nails, a few remnants of canvas fabric, and modest carpentry skills, the gold rocker generally consisted of the following components: 1) an open-topped sloping box three-to-four feet in length and one-to-two feet in width (with horizontal riffles on the bottom) mounted on semicircular pieces of wood to allow use of a vertical handle attached to the high end to impart a side-to-side rocking motion (hence the name "rocker"); 2) a removable hopper (located at the high end of the sloping box, this is where the soil was introduced) with a perforated metal grizzly at the bottom to filter out larger rocks and debris; and 3) two opposing, slanting, removable baffles or aprons typically constructed of canvas stretched over wood frames and located just below the hopper but not touching the grizzly. To use the gold rocker effectively, a man shoveled a small amount of alluvium into the hopper, and then poured water from a dipper into the hopper while simultaneously using the vertical handle to impart a constant rocking motion. The agitation of the rocker and the sluicing of the water quickly disintegrated the alluvium and separated the heavier gold particles which, theoretically, deposited on the canvas baffles while the remaining lighter material washed down the box and poured out of the lower end. The riffles mounted on the bottom of the sloping box were intended to catch any gold particles that might have escaped the grasp of the canvas baffles. From time to time -- depending on the quality of the alluvial deposits but typically up to four times a day -- the hopper was inspected for gold nuggets, the canvas baffles were slid out and washed in a bucket of clean water to recover any gold, and a spoon was scraped along the back of the riffles at the bottom of the sluice box to collect any gold particles deposited there. Although the gold rocker could be operated near an alluvial deposit some distance from a stream or creek -- depending on the constitution of the operator -- a convenient supply of water was still required for efficiency. The Chinese, because of the excessive thoroughness of their technique and the persistence of their efforts, may have achieved more success operating the gold rocker than any other class of miners. This, however, is a subjective conclusion based on circumlocutory evidence, and is only offered as a personal insight.

Similar in concept to the gold rocker, but frequently larger in scale and also requiring a steady flow of water to operate properly, the sluice box is constructed with barriers on both sides and the bottom, and incorporates the same riffles as the gold rocker to capture gold particles as water washes the alluvium along the box. In the American West, sluice boxes were constructed as short as a few feet or longer than 10 feet. During my early research, I discovered an interesting photograph taken in California, probably in the late 1880s (but this date is not confirmed), showing three miners with shovels working two parallel sluice boxes, each (from an approximation of the men's height and allowing for the distortion of perspective) appearing to extend more than 80 feet in length. It is also clear from the photograph, when one considers....

John Ravenscroft felt the soles of his shoes vibrate on the floor of the dining car and listened to both tea cups rattle on porcelain saucers when the train wheels clattered through a track switch a few miles north of Santa

Barbara. The rattling cup reminded him that he had not finished his tea. He set the page of manuscript down and lifted the cup to his lips and swallowed the last of the honey-sweetened beverage in one smoothly-connected motion. When he set the cup down, a dark-haired waiter sheathed in immaculate white and sporting a glorious moustache appeared (from where John did not know) and quickly refilled it. The mid-afternoon sun, floating southwesterly above the serenely-sky-dappled Pacific Ocean, glinted across the tea pot when the waiter tilted it down to pour. Muireall appeared just as mysteriously as had the waiter, and he deftly swung the pot across the table and filled her tea cup before she had finished sliding into the upholstered dining chair.

John dribbled a spoonful of honey into the refilled cup and stirred from the wrist. "I must remember to leave a little tea when I'm finished. The waiter with the enormous moustache is too efficient: he refills my cup the moment I set it down. Once he even started filling it before I set it down. Frankly, I'm even afraid to make eye-contact with the fellow lest he race to my side and knock me over." John lifted the cup and sipped.

Muireall, dressed in a long-sleeved cotton blouse and ankle-length black dress, offered a measure of sympathy. "Travelling on the new Sea Shore Express* is such a bore. Nothing to do but relax and enjoy the gorgeous view. We shall travel by car the next time you decide to visit your sister in Anaheim. You do enjoy driving, and there are no bothersome waiters lurking in the back seat to constantly refill your tea cup."

John set the cup down and tugged his collar. "I see your point, although I am nearly certain you had no intention of making one. I shall stop complaining about the waiter and his ubiquitous tea pot. And I do agree with this note to the editor."

Muireall slid her elbows over the linen table cloth and entwined her fingers beneath her chin. "Which note to the editor are you speaking of? There are hundreds."

---

* The Southern Pacific Railroad inaugurated the *Sea Shore Express* between San Francisco and Los Angeles (with a stop in San Luis Obispo, of course) on December 6, 1906. They also offered the all-parlor *Shore Line Limited* in 1906, which could complete the trip from San Francisco to Los Angeles in an amazing 13-1/2 hours.

John held up the page of manuscript and pointed. "This one, about making this nearly incomprehensible list of mining definitions a sidebar."

Muireall frowned. "Incomprehensible?"

John smirked. "I said nearly incomprehensible. I don't think you should tell the editor to consider it. I think you should simply tell him to do it. Then the average reader, which includes most of us, won't have to bother with it."

Muireall settled back in her chair and contemplated the sparkling ocean through the window. "You don't think the average reader will want to read this?"

John sipped his freshly-poured tea. "I should say not, especially stuff like '... naturally-occurring, homogeneous inorganic solid substance having a definite chemical composition and crystalline structure....' Do you really think anyone will care about crystalline structure? And if someone accidently reads it, do you really think they will know what you are talking about?"

"I care."

"I know you do. But you must think of the reader first."

"I always think of the reader first. It is my most sacred principle of writing."

John lowered the cup. The waiter swooshed by the table, but seeing that the cup was not empty continued on. "I know you do, but I think you forgot about your most sacred principle this one time. I'm not saying you should delete the paragraph. It's certainly impressive, and there are likely a few dozen readers in the country who might find it interesting, especially if they have a college degree in geology. Just make it a sidebar. That's all I saying."

"But it took a lot of research to figure this out. And a lot of time, too. I'm loath to give it up so easily."

"I didn't say to give it up. Just make it a sidebar."

The first buildings on the northern boundary of Santa Barbara scattered angular shadows across the table. The waiter raced by with his teapot to fill an empty cup two tables away. "Okay. I'll ask the editor to make it a sidebar. Anything else you care to say"

John smiled. "I really like your hair today."

Muireall hesitated, but then smiled too. "Oh shut up, you cad."

Roshan Kuznetsov warmed his blistered hands near the flaming relic of the unfortunate gold rocker. At the same time, he nudged a cast iron pot of simmering beans into the hot coals now glowing below the collapsing mining implement. Roshan spoke to his business partner—who sat quietly on a smooth rock a few yards away polishing the rusty gold pan—without looking up. "It is much to say, my goodness friend of business, of we have now the value from gold rocker. It worried me to the end it would come of no good to the both of us. But now I warm my thumbs in the heating of the good for the nothing gold—"

Longwei interrupted, "I think you should stop calling the gold rocker names. I still do not believe we used it correctly. But I must say, I did agree to the three—"

Roshan interrupted, "In this you must not say of it you have the agreement because of the three days we spoke of three days ago. And if I must tell of you—"

Longwei interrupted, "You do not need to waste your breath reminding me of the three days. Yes, I agreed to the three days. But in truth, I thought the gold rocker might find some gold in that time. I did not believe you would not find even the smallest speck of—"

Roshan interrupted, "I do not think it is of the wise to waste our breathing speaking more of the rocker of gold. I used it of the best, and it is not to my fault the rocker of gold did not find even the speck of—" Roshan stopped before completing his sentence when a burro snorted down the hill near Jordan Creek. The beans sizzled and a steam geyser hissed from the cast iron pot.

Longwei whispered, "Did you hear the noise? Can you see who is coming?"

Roshan used a charred stick to pry the iron kettle of beans away from the hot coals. "I do not see of the thing. Should I roll down the hill to take of the look?"

Longwei stood, holding the gold pan across this chest. "No, wait. It may be someone who we do not want to meet. Someone who is dangerous. Someone with many guns."

Roshan stood, still holding the now smoldering stick. "Of this I do not think there is a worry. It is of my most opinion to say almost everyone in Silver City is of the dangerous, and if you think of it in the—"

Longwei dropped the gold pan to his side. "You cannot say such a thing. You cannot say the children of Silver City are dangerous. You cannot say the women of Silver City are dangerous. You cannot say the—"

Roshan pointed the smoldering stick at Longwei. "Of the last you say I must speak the opposite. I have seen of the many women in Silver City of the dangerous. Of this you cannot say of the opposite because—"

Longwei shook the gold pan at Roshan. "Alright, my easily terrified friend. I am willing to admit at least a few of the women in Silver City might be dangerous, but only when there are more—"

Longwei stopped before completing his argument when the burro snorted a few steps beyond the fire. Both Roshan and Longwei turned. A grizzled old man wearing tattered red suspenders and a filthy sweat-smudged hat with the front of the brim folded up introduced himself. "Howdy, men. Mind if I join you for dinner? Them beans smelled mighty good when I was riding up this hill, and I didn't have much in the way of any dinner plans tonight."

Roshan dropped the smoldering stick into the fire. "If we have the much of anything, it is of the beans. It would do me the best to send many beans to you."

The grizzled man swung his leg over the burro's hump and landed on the ground stiffly. His knees cracked when he straightened up. "Why, I'm much obliged." He patted the burro on the head then bent down to warm his hands. "Got any whisky? I'm a might thirsty too."

Longwei wedged the gold pan against a roll of canvas. "We have no whisky, but we have plenty of water from Jordan Creek. May I ask what is your name before we share our beans?"

The grizzled man studied the fire. "I see you been doing some mining with a gold rocker. Didn't know there was any placer mining left to be done in this valley." He sniffed at the air and wiped a sleeve across his nose. "Name's Gustus De Angeles, and I've been working these parts since way back in 1863, long before I suspect you fellows even arrived with this here gold rocker, the one cooking your beans. Sure smells good. Too bad about the whisky."

Longwei brought his feet together and bowed. "My name is Tseng Longwei, from Nanjing, and this is my business partner, Roshan Kuznetsov, from Sitka. You are correct. We only arrived a few weeks ago, and as for the gold rocker, it is—"

Roshan interrupted, "I tell you what it is. It is piece of the shit who cannot find even of the speck of gold for the many of six days. And I tell you this, Mister Angeles, if I of luck find the man who sold this—"

Gustus De Angeles interrupted, "Call me Gustus. The rest of the name you can leave off. I don't much care for it anyway. Say, I just had an idea standing here talking to you fellows."

Roshan shoved his hands into his pockets. "An idea?"

Gustus hooked his thumbs behind the tattered red suspenders. "Sure did. Seeing how you two haven't had much luck with your gold rocker, and seeing how you're kind enough to share your beans with me when we only ran into each other a few minutes ago, and setting aside the fact that you don't have any whisky to offer a fellow so he can wet his whistle, how'd the two of you like to come and help me work my claim?"

Longwei spoke with uncharacteristic excitement. "You have a claim? What kind of claim? And why do you need our help. There are plenty of men in Silver City you could hire."

Gustus snapped the suspenders and laughed. "There's where you got it all wrong. There ain't a single one of them who'd work for me. They're all working at one of the big mines on War Eagle Mountain."

Roshan introduced a dose of suspicion to the conversation. "And must I ask, if you do not take the time to tell me where of it, why we should do of the same as not any the other men?"

Gustus asked Longwei, "What in the world did he just say?"

Longwei explained, "Roshan asked why we should work for you when no one else in Silver City will."

Gustus frowned. "Didn't sound much like what he said, but I'll take your word for it. The men all want to work for one of the big mines that's already struck it rich: the Oro Fino, Poorman, Ida Elmore, Golden Chariot, and the others. Oh, I neglected to mention the Morning Star. It's right popular too. I got a hard rock mine myself on War Eagle Mountain near Mahogany Gulch. Been working it since I staked the claim in 1863. Haven't found anything to brag about yet, but I got a feeling about it. I just need a couple of strong fellows like you to help me out. I know there's a big vein that's been waiting to get found all these years. I just know it."

Longwei answered inscrutably, "I see."

Gustus sweetened the offer. "I'll pay you each five dollars a day."

Roshan asked, "You have money to give to Roshan and Longwei after finding of the nothing these many years from now when we stand hearing our ears speak of it?"

Gustus snapped the red suspenders and cackled. "I still got money left over from my big strike in California. It's almost gone, but there's enough left to pay the two of you for another year. And I've got enough left over from my strike in Nevada to buy supplies for even longer if need be. But the thing that worries me the most right now, is I just understood what you said."

The beans sizzled.

CHAPTER FIVE

Silver City, Idaho Territory
October 1871

C songor Toth, the brilliantly-white collar of his freshly-laundered dress shirt lending a sculptural quality to his head, admired the sign that would announce his new business with understated grandeur. The young man holding the sign above Csongor's desk, a mere errand boy for the master carpenter who had carved and painted the sign, grew weary and lowered the heavy placard to the desk. Csongor immediately encouraged the boy with politely-assertive words. "Come, come my boy. Hold the sign up so I can see it properly in the light. I am not finished examining it." The boy lifted the sign again, and this time wedged both elbows on top of his belt to provide additional leverage. Csongor's blue eyes scanned across the letters of the sign:

CSONGOR TOTH, ESQUIRE
MINING CLAIMS LAW
(PAYMENT IN GOLD PREFERRED)

After what seemed to the boy an eternity, Csongor linked his fingers below his chin and rendered his judgment. "This sign will do quite nicely my lad. I am especially fond of the subtle swell and curve of the parentheses. Please tell your master to have the sign installed by the end of the day tomorrow." The boy hesitated, forcing Csongor to speak more than he preferred. "That will be all, young man. You may leave the premises now." The boy—now a little frightened of Csongor, although he did not know why—swung the sign under his left arm and backed away clumsily until his groping hand found the door knob of the entry door. His hand still grasping the knob, he turned and opened the door at the same time, and taking care not to bang the sign on the door frame, he lifted his foot and minced across the threshold.

Csongor shot up from his chair and lunged over the desk. "Wait!" The boy froze mid-stride. "Come back here. I neglected to inspect the other side." The boy turned and closed the door at the same time, again taking special care not to bang the sign against the door frame. He returned to the front of Csongor's desk, flipped the heavy sign around, and again wedged both elbows into his belt when he held the sign up.

CSONGOR TOTH, ESQUIRE
MINING CLAIMS LAW
(PAYMENT IN GOLD PREFFERED)

Csongor lowered himself slowly into the chair, touched the tips of his fingers and thumbs together, and raised his hands until the index fingers rested beneath his nose and the thumbs supported his chin. "Such a pity. All that work. Such a pity."

The boy, who had remained silent until now, found the courage to speak. "Is the sign the wrong color, or something?"

Csongor lowered his hands. "No, my fine lad, the color of the sign is exactly as ordered."

Emboldened, the boy asked, "Is the sign too small?"

Csongor answered without expressing any particular emotion. "No, no, my illiterate young man. The sign is exactly the right size."

The boy tried the last thing he could think of. "Then is some of the letters crooked?"

Csongor stood again. "Straight as an arrow, my boy. Straight as an arrow." Csongor crossed his arms and squinted. "My good lad, tell your master the sign is acceptable. And tell him I would like it installed by the end of the day tomorrow."

The boy grinned. "Then you like the sign?"

"Yes, yes, yes. Tell your master I am overjoyed with the quality of the sign. Not only will it announce my new law firm with appropriate verve, but it will also allow me to judge the literacy and powers of observation of potential clients without having to ask directly. Tell your master the sign is perfect in every regard. And now you must run along, my lad. I have an appointment in 17 minutes and must prepare a few notes."

The boy swung the heavy sign around to his side, pivoted on his heels, and shuffled through the office door. An artificial breeze fluttered several papers on Csongor's desk after the door slammed.

Three of the more celebrated miscreants of Silver City stood in a ragged line directly in front of Csongor Toth's recently-restored and exquisite-ly-polished office desk. Csongor studied each man's facial expressions, posture, and clothing—a process which consumed a full minute—before speaking. One of the men, the one on the left, fidgeted the entire time. "Gentlemen. Before we begin the business of this meeting, please tell me a little about yourselves. Let us begin with you." Csongor waved his hand loosely at the fidgeting man on the left.

The fidgeting man jammed his thumb against his chest. "Me?"

Csongor answered flatly, "Yes, you."

"What do you want to know? There ain't much to tell."

Csongor's lips tightened. "Then begin with something easy. For example, what is your name, and what did you do before you arrived in Silver City?"

The man fidgeted. "Well, not much of anything to talk about. Name's Seth. Mostly got into trouble with the law. Don't like lawmen much. As a matter of fact, can't think of a single one of 'em I like."

Csongor stroked the thinly-manicured line of his moustache. "And what is your surname?"

Seth scrunched his right brow and lifted the right side of his upper lip. "My what?"

"Your family name."

"Don't know what that means neither."

"Your last name. What is your last name?"

Seth relaxed his brow and lip. "Don't got one. I'm just Seth."

"I suppose this does simplify things." Csongor shifted in his chair and swung his gaze to the stumpy man in the middle. "And you, good sir. What is your name and what did you do before coming to Silver City? I trust that you, unlike our friend Seth, have a last name?"

The middle man, his hands concealed inside the pockets of his grease-stained canvas pantaloons, stood motionless. "Name's Jackson, Bill Jackson. But you can call me Jackson, like everyone else."

"I see." Csongor opened the cover of a leather bound notebook and scribbled a short note with a pen. "And why do you use your surname as your first name?"

Jackson scowled again. "My what?"

Csongor sighed. "Oh for heaven's sake. Your last name. Why do you use your last name?"

"Oh. Don't know. Just like it better. Never liked Bill. I like Jackson." And then he leaned forward menacingly. "You got a problem with my name?"

Csongor did not react to the subtle threat, and replied with icy calm. "Not at all, my good fellow. Not at all. Then Jackson it is. And your experience before Silver City?"

Jackson stiffened. "The usual. Robbed a few stagecoaches. Robbed a few trains. Robbed a few banks. Robbed a hospital once, but wasn't as much fun as robbing a train or a stagecoach, 'cause it wasn't moving."

Csongor nodded. "Robbed a hospital? Excellent. A man of limited scruples. Exactly what I'm looking for."

"What's that?"

"What's what?"

"Screw pals. You talking about a bunch of friendly whores?"

"Nothing of the sort, my dear Jackson. A scruple is an uneasy sense of conscience which hinders action. Scruples is the plural thereof."

Jackson scowled. "What you just said don't make no sense."

Csongor tapped the pen on the notebook. "It does not matter. And you ... " he said, pointing the inky tip of the pen at the third and final man, " ... what is your story?"

"Story? You mean, like a bedtime story?"

Annoyed, Csongor resumed tapping the pen. "Of course not. What is your name and what did you do before arriving in Silver City?" Csongor stopped tapping the pen and began rolling it back and forth on the desk.

The third man slouched into a more carefree posture. "Ain't much to tell either. Name's Miguel Cervantes. Worked in hard rock mines in Nevada before coming here. Worked in the Poorman Mine up on War Eagle Mountain after I got here. Worked with dynamite until the boss caught me stealing a few loose sticks from the storeroom. Had to break the lock to get in. I like blowing stuff up. Didn't think anyone would get upset about a few sticks."

Csongor allowed himself a marginal grin—an extraordinary event. "So you are a man of letters and an explosives expert? Charming. These qualities are potentially useful to my future business plans."

Miguel sniffed. "A man of letters? Never wrote a letter in my life. Don't know how to write. Never read one neither. Don't know how to read. Just like blowing stuff up. Like it more than anything else there is to do."

Csongor stood and motioned to the three men to sit with a sweeping gesture. "Gentlemen, please take a chair to allow us the opportunity to discuss my business proposition in relative comfort. Would anyone care for a cup of coffee? My assistant brewed up a fresh pot not more than an hour ago."

Seth, Jackson, and Miguel each pulled up one of the curved-back wooden chairs scattered around the front of Csongor's law office and arranged them in a messy semicircle in front of the desk. After sitting down, Jackson snorted, "You got any whisky? I don't drink coffee until after dinner, but whisky's good anytime of the day, especially with flapjacks and bacon first thing in the morning."

Csongor cringed. "Whisky, with flapjacks and bacon in the morning? I doubt my delicate constitution would tolerate such a gastronomic onslaught. But yes, I do have a bottle of whisky." Csongor opened a side drawer in his desk, pulled out an unopened bottle of Old Pulteney,* and set it on the desk next to an ink well without removing his hand. Jackson reached across the desk to seize the bottle, but Csongor pulled it back.

---

* The Pulteney Distillery was established near Wick in the far north of Scotland in 1826.

"Now, now, Mr. Jackson, or should I say just Jackson. Let us wait until we have consummated our business meeting before imbibing of this superior single-malt beverage from the land of Scotland."

Jackson lowered his hand to the desk and slowly rolled the fingers into a fist. "Thought you said it was whisky?"

Csongor released the bottle. "It is, my unsophisticated future business associate. It is whisky distilled in the Highlands of Scotland, likely a bit different from the rotgut you normally drink. I had a case shipped in a few months ago. But alas, I prefer the sweetness and bite of pálinka,* and have only finished one bottle. I have not, until now, had the inclination to commence another."

Annoyed, Jackson slammed his fist on the table. "Enough fancy words. What are we doing here, anyway? I got plenty of things to get done besides sitting in a room listening to a bunch of fancy words which half the time don't make no sense."

Csongor did not react to the aggressive display. "Ah…a man of action who wishes to get to the point. And apparently a leader of men as well. Then, Jackson, we shall segue into the purpose of this gathering without delay."

Jackson groaned. "More of them fancy words. Let's just drink the whisky and get out of here." He shifted left and then right as he spoke to the other two men. "Seth, Miguel, what do you say? You see any reason to stick around and listen to a bunch of fancy words when they don't make a lick of sense?"

Csongor reached into the side drawer, pulled out two more bottles of Old Pulteney, and set them on the desk in a neat row aligned with the ink well. "There's a bottle for each of you, if you can maintain sufficient patience and attentiveness to listen to my business proposition from beginning to end. Does anyone care to hear me out?" Not one of the men said a word, but all three heads nodded. "Good. Then let us begin our discussion with a simple question. Has any one of you ever killed a man?"

Surprisingly, Miguel spoke before Jackson. "Don't know. Might of killed a few when I blowed something up. Probably did, but can't say for sure."

---

* Hungarian fruit brandy, similar to cognac.

Csongor rested his elbows on the leather armrests and settled back in the chair into a pose of mock contentment. "And how did it make you feel?"

Miguel crinkled the bridge of his nose. "How'd it make me feel? Didn't feel nothing. Not my fault if someone didn't get out of the way."

"Excellent response. Just as I had hoped. And you, Jackson?"

Jackson snarled. "And me, what?"

"Did you ever kill a man?"

"I killed plenty. In the war."

"Interesting. Not that it matters to me, but may I ask which side you were on?"

"Wasn't on any side. I was on my own side."

"Another excellent response." Csongor lifted his chin. "And finally, we come to just Seth. What do you have to share?"

Seth fidgeted, and then his cheek twitched. "Don't much like to talk about it."

Csongor prompted, "Oh come, come, my dear man. We are all sharing here. Certainly you will not deny us the pleasure of listening to your daring exploits."

Seth fidgeted. "Only killed two, but they had it coming."

Csongor bent forward. "Who had it coming?"

Seth fidgeted. "My father and mother. But I didn't shoot them or anything. Just blocked the door and burned down the cabin."

Csongor did not exhibit a sliver of emotion. "Yes. Shooting is such a messy business. As a matter of fact, I would have to say—"

Jackson snarled, "Wait a minute. You gotta share too. Ain't fair unless you tell us if you killed anyone. I'm not talking any more 'til you do."

Csongor pondered the request before answering, "Certainly, Jackson. Yes, I've killed quite a few, although the exact count eludes me at this particular moment."

Jackson persisted. "What's 'quite a few' supposed to mean?"

A delicate smile appeared on Csongor's face as he reflected. "It means I can't be bothered with such statistics. But if you insist, I would estimate more than seven but less than twelve. Are you satisfied now?"

Seth sat up in his chair. "That's quite a few. Seems odd you can't remember exactly how many."

Csongor mused, "I suppose I could offer an exact count if I cared to think about it, but unfortunately the delicious exhilaration of killing has blended the individual deaths into a composite rapture that has blurred specific details."

Seth complained, "I don't have any idea what you just said."

The intensity of Jackson's previous snarl amplified, and he slapped his hand on the polished desk, causing the three bottles of Old Pulteney to tremble. "If you ask me, this is a waste of my time. What is it we're supposed to be doing here, anyway? I got things to do better than sitting here talking to someone who speaks in stupid riddles."

Csongor stood, repositioned himself behind the chair, and rested his hands on the back. "Just so. Then on to the primary agenda. The reason I have invited each of you here today is to discuss the possibility of a subsidiary business enterprise. As you can plainly see, I have opened an office to provide legal services for individuals interested in mining claims. However, it is my intention to expand into more lucrative projects. But to do this, I will need the assistance of men like you, men who bring certain, shall we say, talents to the table."

Skeptical, Jackson asked, "What kind of projects?"

Csongor massaged the back of the chair as if it represented a woman's unclothed shoulders. "I have not worked out specific details yet, but these projects will involve activities that I am confident each of you is familiar with: blackmail, larceny, extortion, bribery, possibly even 'blowing stuff up,' as you so charmingly put it. If things go well, we may expand the business into other endeavors of a similar nature."

Jackson smirked. "All fine and dandy, but what do I get out of it? All I see is a bottle you claim is whisky. That ain't nearly enough to keep me interested."

Csongor strolled to a window offering a view into the adjacent alley, and clasped his hands behind his back. "I originally thought a commission would prove appropriate compensation, but I've changed my mind and have decided to pay each of you a salary." He turned and faced the three men. "What do you think of ten dollars a day?"

Seth eyed the three bottles next to the ink well and fidgeted. "Ten dollars a day? I don't make that much in a week."

Miguel smacked his lips. "You mean, you're gonna pay me to blow stuff up?"

Jackson negotiated on behalf of all three men. "Your offer's almost good enough, but not quite. Make it twelve-fifty a day and we got us a deal."

Csongor used his toe to smooth a wrinkle from a Persian throw rug while he pondered the counteroffer. "You drive a hard bargain, Jackson, but after thoughtful consideration I will accept your proposal. And to sweeten the pot further…" Csongor pulled a brown leather wallet from his vest, "…here is an advance of fifty-dollars apiece. I expect you each to buy some decent clothes, shave, and take a bath at your earliest convenience. Report back to this office Friday morning at ten, and we will commence the first program of our fledgling business enterprise."

Seth fidgeted and pointed at the three bottles next to the ink well. "What about the whisky you promised?"

Csongor glanced at the bottles lined up on his desk. "Of course. I nearly forgot. Collect your Old Pulteney before you leave. And when you drink of this superbly smooth nectar, please allow sufficient time to savor both the exquisite aroma and flavor when you imbibe. And gentlemen, promise me one more thing…."

Jackson snarled a final time. "What do you want now? Ain't we talked enough for one day?"

"Promise me you'll drink the Old Pulteney from a clean glass."

CHAPTER SIX

Silver City, Idaho Territory
November 1, 1871

Tseng Longwei considered his options.

Option Number One: Stay in the wagon and continue to endure the rump-thumping, teeth-cracking, back-slamming abuse of this so-called "road" to Silver City;

Option Number Two: Ask Roshan to stop the mules, get off the wagon, and walk back to Gustus De Angeles's ramshackle camp of tattered canvas tents, rusting equipment boneyards, and a half-finished cabin near Mahogany Gulch on the southeast face of War Eagle Mountain—a problematic option to be sure because the wagon had now reached a point northeast of Webfoot Gulch, more or less halfway to Silver City;

Option Number Three: Ask Roshan to stop the mules, get off the wagon, and walk the rest of the way to town—also problematic because the wagon had now reached a point northeast of Webfoot Gulch, more or less halfway to Silver City; and,

Option Number Four: Ask Roshan to stop the mules, get off the wagon, find a comfortable rock or stump, sit on the rock or stump, wait for Roshan to drive the wagon to town and return with supplies, get back on the wagon, then endure the rump-thumping, teeth-cracking, back-slamming abuse of the so-called "road" back to Gustus De Angeles's ramshackle camp of tattered canvas tents, rusting equipment boneyards, and a half-finished cabin near Mahogany Gulch on the southeast face of War Eagle Mountain.

Tseng Longwei braced hand and knee against the weathered side of the wagon seat when the right front wheel shuddered convulsively over the scarred top of another rock protruding from the narrow roadbed, and contemplated the possibility of better options. After the wagon had encountered three more rocks, seven wind-hardened wheel ruts, and two splintered tree stumps, his nimble mind produced a fifth option:

Option Number Five: Stay in the wagon and appreciate the mystical gift of life and the serenity of a land not torn asunder by the ravages of brutal civil war.

Longwei's remembrance was not of the American Civil War (of which he had no knowledge), but of the Taiping Rebellion in China, and as his mind refocused on the gossamer clouds floating serenely across blue-gray skies and the natural tranquility of the Jordan Valley, the unrelenting cruelty of the rollicking wagon slowly faded away. When he had nearly achieved a complete peace....

Roshan snapped the reins leading to the four mules and shouted into Longwei's ear, "I do not know this of you, but the road full of rocks below the wheels is kicking this ass out of my crap. I have much thought of walking to the City of Silver and leaving the wagon and mules in a spot you do not know. I hope you feel not of the same, because one of you must ride the wagon for the mules to find the supplies Gustus sent for us."

The calming thoughts of peace and tranquility vanished, and the unpleasant thoughts of rump thumping and back slamming reappeared. Longwei's teeth chattered when the wagon skidded along another rut. "Thank you for reminding me of the road. I had nearly forgotten about it, but now I believe it is even worse than before."

Roshan pondered the jittering clouds and laughed. Then he pulled the reins hard to the left and the wagon nearly pitched down the mountainside before the lead mules finally disobeyed and guided the wagon away from the meandering edge of the road. "You have it of the wrong this time. This road is always worse if I believe before, and I am in the thought to say the road will be worse than before when we make the back. Of this you can be of the sure."

Longwei fell against Roshan when the mules yanked the wagon to the right. "I fear your observation is wiser than it sounds."

Roshan laughed again. "There I must say again, the observation of Roshan is always wiser than it sounds. This is of the way with me. Of this you are sure to be."

The wagon rolled northerly above Slaughterhouse Gulch—a point about 4,000 feet east of Silver City and 700 feet higher in elevation—and followed Golden Creek in a sweeping westerly arc. At the terminus of the arc, the wagon angled due west and plunged downward toward Jordan Creek along a steep grade that was the first part of the roadway covered with ice in the fall, the last part of the roadway to thaw in the spring, and prone to catastrophic washouts during heavy rains. Fortunately, Roshan and Longwei would not learn of these afflictions on this particular day, or their misery would have increased beyond what they could have endured.

Roshan shook the reins when the mules and wagon began the descent, and shouted to Longwei, "It is all down to the hill from here we go to be sure," and then he snapped the reins violently against the backs of the mules and barked an obscure command in Russian. Startled by the whipping leather— and confused by the Russian—the four mules charged into a gallop.

Alarmed by the wild acceleration, Longwei shouted back at Roshan. "Maybe you should slow us down. What if we hit a rock?"

At the moment of Longwei's warning, a ponderous boulder erupted from the middle of the roadway and raced down the center of the two pairs of galloping mules and slammed against the underside of the wagon tongue right on a spot with an unfortunate bit of dry rot and explosively shattered the wagon tongue into two disconnected pieces. Not satisfied with simply separating the wagon from the mules, the boulder also smashed the underside of the front axle, instantly launching Longwei and Roshan into the back of the racing wagon. Stunned, but still alive, Longwei pulled himself above the sideboard in time to see the mules move to the right and then slowly drift back as the wagon overtook them. He watched with growing curiosity when the mules maneuvered in behind the wagon. Longwei shifted his view forward and dreamily watched the approaching New York and Owyhee Stamp mill at the bottom of the hill. Roshan bounced around helplessly until his legs swung above the sideboard and his knees hooked over the top. Although he tried, Roshan could not free himself from his awkward predicament.

Two men—one smoking a stubby briar pipe with a curved stem and one whittling the splintered remnant of a hickory axe handle with a dull jackknife—waited outside the New York and Owyhee Mill for a load of ore from one of the hard rock mines on War Eagle Mountain. The smoking man passed the time by gazing introspectively at the rugged slopes of Florida Mountain, but after he sucked in a fresh breath of smoldering tobacco the dissonant sounds of a clattering wagon distracted him. He lowered his eyes in time to see the wagon—with the torso of a man waving his arms near the front and the same man's legs sticking out above the sideboard near the back—careen into his view. The wagon raced by and bounced across the road connecting Ruby City to the north and Silver City to the south and then plunged chaotically down a shallow ravine into Jordan Creek. A handful of seconds later, a team of four seething mules stampeded by and followed the wagon into the creek. Intensely focused on his work, the whittling man missed the entire spectacle.

The smoking man pulled a match out of a vest pocket, snapped it against the vertical wood siding of the mill building until a flame ignited, and prepared to rekindle the tobacco. He paused to say a few words to the man with the dull jackknife. "Now there's something you don't see every day."

The whittling man grumbled. "I need to sharpen this blade before I cut one of my fingers clean off. What don't you see every day?"

The smoking man held the match close to the pipe and sucked the flame into the briar bowl. "It's sort of hard to describe."

Longwei waited in the street fronting the livery next to the restored wagon and mule harnesses while Roshan paid the proprietor for the repairs. One of the mules twisted his head and nipped at the sleeve of Longwei's black tunic. Longwei pulled his arm away and chastised the surly animal. "It is not my fault the so-called road is full of large rocks sticking out of the ground. And it is also not my fault Roshan told you and your three friends to run down the hill as fast as possible. If you want my humble opinion, you should have ignored him, just like you did when he tried to drive us off the road." The mule ignored Longwei.

Roshan burst from a large swinging door at the front of the livery whistling a Russian folk tune Longwei had never heard before. When Roshan arrived at the side of the mules, he stopped whistling and slapped Longwei on the shoulder. "It cost all the first week of pay for the both of us for the wagon and night in hotel in the room with single bed and much noise of screwing in the other room but now we have a new wagon to give Gustus for his trouble after we find supplies he sent for us in the first place. It is not of never bad as you think, my partner of business to be sure."

Longwei kept an eye on the mule who had tried to bite his arm. "Yes, yes…it is not too bad. Especially when you consider the ride down the hill could have killed both of us. It is truly a miracle to have survived."

Roshan stroked his chin. "This is of the true. Then Gustus De Angeles—you see now I say his name without mistake because I have practice when you are not to hear—would must to wait more days for the supplies if he cared to think of it."

"And we are lucky the mules are not dead too, after the way they followed the wagon down into the creek and up the other side. I expected to find at least five broken legs, but none were harmed."

"This is too of the true, Longwei, because we do not have money to buy even of one mule leg after I give it to the man in the barn for the wagon and harness and the man in the hotel for the room of plenty screwing noise."

Longwei slid his hands into the wide sleeves of the tunic. "Then let us not tempt our luck further this day, and quickly ride the wagon to the general store to buy supplies before more harm befalls us. It is only just past noon and the sky is mostly clear. If we hurry we can buy the supplies and make it back to Mahogany Gulch before dark. I do not want to spend one more night in the—how did you say it?—room of plenty screwing noise."

Roshan nodded his agreement, and the two business partners climbed aboard the wagon. When they had both settled into the repaired seat, Roshan clicked his tongue and gently snapped the repaired reins. He guided the repaired wagon easterly, drove it through a narrow alley to Washington Street, and turned right. A few minutes later, he eased the wagon to the front of the general store where Gustus had told him to buy the supplies. The two friends dismounted the wagon and walked up two wood steps to the boardwalk. When they arrived at the entry door, they read a large hand-painted sign nailed into the siding to the left of the door:

NO CHINA MEN
OR INDIANS
ALLOWED

Roshan read the sign then asked Longwei, "What does this mean?"

Longwei appeared unconcerned. "It means you must buy the supplies alone while I wait outside. I may not enter this store."

Roshan clenched his fists and fumed, "But this is of the stupid, if you care to know if my opinion is true enough."

Longwei attempted to console Roshan. "I do not disagree with your opinion, my faithful business partner. But since we are already two days late—and Gustus De Angeles must certainly believe we have stolen his money, wagon, mules, and fled from Silver City—we should not waste any time arguing with the owner of the store. I will wait outside while you buy the supplies. Think of the 'room of plenty screwing noise' if we have to stay in town tonight."

Roshan relaxed his hands. "I will do of you say, but do not think Roshan will be of the happy when he buys the supplies alone to his friend."

Hesitant to draw attention to the regrettable sign by loitering in front of it, Tseng Longwei strolled south on the boardwalk after Roshan entered the general store. He walked along the jagged shadow line beneath the uneven shade of connected canopies. He passed by a saloon that smelled of stale vomit and strong perfume, a clothing store with a young woman placing green and blue fedoras on two partially-clothed dressmaker's dummies behind a dusty window, two small offices of unknown purpose, an apothecary (or so it claimed), and finally a small store specializing in candy and notions. He stepped off the end of the boardwalk, walked across the pulverized soil of a nameless alley, and stepped up to the continuation of the boardwalk fronting the next block of buildings. Three women in sooty dresses and drab bonnets approached him as he arrived at another general store; they quickly darted into the store and watched him pass by through a large window next to the entry door. The three women waited a minute, then exited the store and scurried north, one glancing back repeatedly and the other two whispering. Longwei took no notice of the women, and continued on along a string of buildings without boardwalks or canopies and several more nameless alleys. When he had reached the front of a building advertising itself as both a hotel and an undertaker, a large bearded man wearing frayed suspenders and knee-high leather boots approached. The man quickened his pace and refused to yield, forcing Longwei to step aside. When Longwei swerved to avoid a disastrous collision, he tripped on the base of a pine casket leaned up against the front of the building and fell to his hands. He sucked in a deep breath, pushed himself up, patted the dust off his knees, turned briskly to continue his walk, and nearly collided with a second man dressed in a black suit with streaks of dust across his right sleeve.

The suited man eyed Tseng Longwei's shiny black hair and black tunic, then held out a ragged shred of paper. "I'd like to invite you to church services this Sunday." Longwei noted the paper but did not say anything. The man continued, "It's in the back room of the saloon on the corner of Washington and Avalanche. You can't miss it." Longwei plucked the paper from the man's hand but still said nothing. The man suggested, "You might want to come in the back door, because I don't think the owner would be too happy if you came in through the front." Longwei held the paper close to his face to examine the penciled text but still did not speak. The man persisted, "I don't suppose you speak English. Why don't I just take that notice back. You never know when I might run out, and I don't have any paper left to make any more."

Tseng Longwei folded the shred of paper twice and slid it into a pocket beneath the hem of his black tunic. "Is it not odd to hold church services in the back of a saloon? What kind of church would do such a thing?"

The man, surprised by Longwei's flawless English, did not answer the question with much thought. "The Lutheran Church, of course."

Longwei frowned. "Can you not use the big white church north of town?"

"No. The church you speak of belongs to the Catholics. I already asked and they declined. I think they're still a little upset by Martin Luther's antics during the Reformation."

Longwei nodded. "So I've heard. And what is the name of the man who holds church services in the back room of a saloon?"

The man bowed his head slightly. "Name's Manfred Herrmann, and at this point I'd hold church services in the very bowels of hell if I had to."

"When you describe it in such a way, the back room of the saloon does not sound at all bad. Is it acceptable to bring a friend?"

"I would be delighted if you would bring a friend. Is he Chinese like you?"

"No, he is from Alaska. But I must warn you: he is a bit loud at times. I hope this is not a problem. And when he begins to talk, he may not stop for a very long time and when he is finished you still do not know what he has said. I hope this also is not a problem."

Manfred pulled a second shred of paper off his stack and wadded it into Longwei's hand. "Take another notice to give to your friend. Talking in a loud voice is not a sin. And talking for a long time without saying anything is also not a sin, even though it is tempting to think so—especially with politicians."

Longwei accepted the second notice. "I will give it to him, but you may have a different idea of the definition of sin after you meet him."

Longwei returned to the general store (the one with the regrettable sign) in time to watch Roshan toss the last sack of flour on the back of the repaired wagon. The surly mule tried to bite Longwei's elbow again when he walked by. Roshan, drenched in sweat after loading the wagon without help, used his hat to wipe his forehead and neck. "I did not think you had the idea of return after the sign of angry words and I did not see of you load on the wagon when I load the wagon in alone with no help from not a one, if you see of my thought."

Tseng Longwei bowed deeply. "I did not mean for you to do all the work, Roshan, but I was delayed by a conversation with a most interesting person who has invited both of us to church on Sunday. It is to be held in the back room of a saloon. I know you will find it acceptable."

Roshan jammed the soggy hat on his head. "In the back of saloon? What kind of church do you find in such of a place?"

"I asked the same of this man, and he said you can find the Lutheran Church in the back of a saloon. But we can talk more of this on our return to Mahogany Gulch. It is now late in the afternoon, and we will just make it back before dark if we hurry."

Roshan climbed up to the wagon seat and grabbed the reins. "Yes, we will just make of it before the dark of night has become…" and then he scowled at the mules, "…if the mule of plenty stupid do not find of the rock in the road in one more of the time."

Longwei pondered the mule that had tried to bite his arm. "I believe these mules are in some ways smarter than you or me. I suggest you tell them to proceed and let them choose the speed and route. In my humble opinion, this is the only way to allow the possibility of arriving at Mahogany Gulch alive."

CHAPTER SEVEN

A few miles north of Silver City
November 6, 1871

Joshua Hotah and his beloved appaloosa—who still did not possess a name because it was still not in Joshua's nature to give a name to a horse—both sniffed the crispness of an autumn breeze and squinted into the hazy rim of sun drifting low along the mountainous horizon to the southwest. Joshua spoke in soothing tones to the faithful animal. "The sky is strange today." The appaloosa sniffed up and down. "I can see you think it is strange too. I fear the cold of winter is very close now." The appaloosa whinnied. Joshua rubbed her neck. "I know I have many times complained about the scorched lands we have passed through, but we may soon yearn for the heat we once cursed. When our journey is finished, we should search for a place where it is not too cold or too hot." The appaloosa softly chortled her agreement with this idea.

The churning wheels of an approaching stagecoach clattered distantly behind Joshua and the appaloosa, interrupting their conversation. Joshua twisted in the saddle and braced his hand against the appaloosa's rump, and a cluster of three vertebrae crackled in his lower back. His eyes traced the winding road back to a modest hill a little less than a mile away, and he waited. Four seething horses and a stagecoach erupted above the smooth crest of the hill moments before Joshua's back popped a second time. Encouraged by the rhythmic snap of the driver's whip, the enraged horses drove the advancing stagecoach down the center of the lumpy road directly at Joshua and the appaloosa. Apparently unconcerned,

Joshua rotated slowly forward and yawned without bothering to cover his mouth. When his lips had closed, he pulled the reins gently to the left and the appaloosa danced aside. When Joshua clicked his tongue the appaloosa settled into a relaxed pose. The four horses and stagecoach rumbled by in a shower of pebbles and a swirl of choking dust.

Joshua and the appaloosa watched the stagecoach diminish to a small dot before it vanished around a mountainous switchback. Joshua spit three times and rubbed the side of his nose with a dirty finger. "You are lucky to not have to pull a stagecoach for a job. I do not think you would like it much." The appaloosa snorted and clicked her hoof on the ground. "I know you do not always like riding with me either, but I think it is better for you than pulling a stagecoach. Did you see those unhappy horses? Not a single one was smiling. Remember those horses next time you feel like complaining." The appaloosa shook her head from side to side and sniggered. Joshua bent down and spoke near the appaloosa's ear. "You think what I just said is funny? Then maybe I should sell you to the man who owns the stagecoach when we get to Silver City and you will find out if it is really funny or not." The appaloosa stomped her foot again, a little harder this time. "I do not much like this road either. Too many wagons and stagecoaches and people who I do not like the look of. We should find a better way to Silver City."

When Joshua straightened up, he glimpsed a slender column of bluish smoke in the westerly limit of his vision. He squinted when he turned to observe the vaporous plume. When he had convinced himself that the smoke belonged to a campfire, he pulled the reins and clicked his tongue. "It is growing late in the day, and I do not want to travel on such a busy road when the sun will begin to set in a few hours. I think we should find a place to camp for the night." The appaloosa snorted and trotted off the road toward the smoke. "No, of course I do not know who owns the campfire, but it is not too far away. I think we will soon find out."

The unfettered appaloosa waited near a ragged stand of mountain mahogany trees while Joshua crawled on his belly a hundred feet away. A small brown squirrel—searching for the last of his provisions before the onset of winter—chattered nearby and darted behind a splintered stump. The setting sun glinted around the gnarled branches of the nearest mahogany. A cool breeze fluttered across the rocky ground and rustled through the trees. The appaloosa sniffed the air then bent down and nibbled at a clump of yellowed grass. When she raised her head to chew, she watched Joshua roll along a fractured boulder and peek around the side. The appaloosa tilted her head in amusement and blinked when Joshua suddenly jumped to his feet and began running back. When Joshua arrived at the appaloosa's side, he appeared excited about something.

"There is a single teepee with a nice fire nearby and a small stream within a short walk. There is a woman tending the fire, and someone is sleeping next to the fire." Joshua raised his foot to the stirrup and swung himself into the saddle. "I do not imagine the woman will mind if we sleep by the fire tonight. We will collect some wood and tend the fire in return for her hospitality." The appaloosa chortled. Joshua nudged the animal with his heels and gently tugged on the reins. Joshua and the appaloosa walked by the fractured boulder then negotiated the loose soil and rocks of the hillside down toward the campsite. When they reached the toe of the slope, the terrain leveled out and the firmness of the ground improved and the regularity of troublesome rocks diminished. The appaloosa circled the teepee and stopped about fifteen feet from the ring of stones around the fire. Joshua could now see that the woman was huddled near a small boy wrapped in a threadbare blanket. The woman had parted her black hair neatly down the middle and braided each side into a ponytail secured at the end with a strip of green cloth. A necklace of colored beads and another of leather and elk teeth hung down across the front of her long buckskin dress. A simple leather belt secured the dress around her slender waist. Knee-high moccasins, decorated with more colored beads, adorned her sturdy legs. Joshua dismounted, led the appaloosa up to the fire, and knelt down without releasing the reins. Now he could hear her sobbing. Joshua petted the appaloosa's nose. "She is Nez Perce. It is odd her husband is not around. It is also odd she does not look at us when we are only standing a few feet away. I am afraid I only learned a few words from the Nez Perce warrior who sold you to me. I will try those words first. If we are lucky she might speak a little Sioux… or maybe some English."

Joshua cleared his throat to announce his presence. "Ta'c halaxp, manaa wees?" (*Good afternoon, how are you*)

The woman quickly rolled to her knees, her tear-glistened hand brandishing a knife. She raised the knife and hissed something back at Joshua, but he did not understand any of it.

Joshua tried again. "Do you speak any English?" The woman did not appear to understand. Joshua asked the woman if she spoke any Sioux, and she frowned. Joshua stood and caressed the appaloosa's nose. "Since you do not understand Sioux or English, and I only speak enough Nez Perce to buy a horse, I will speak to you in English and hope you understand something of what I say. I do not want to hurt you or the boy. We only wish to camp by the fire tonight. We will even gather wood for you."

The woman hissed more incomprehensible Nez Perce words at Joshua and jabbed the knife in his direction.

Joshua spoke to the appaloosa. "I do not think the woman understood much of what I said, and she seems angrier than before. I think it is time to find some wood. When the woman sees me return with the wood, maybe she will believe we mean her and the boy no harm. You wait here while I collect the wood." The appaloosa grunted at Joshua. "No, I do not think she will stab you with the knife. Do not be such a baby. I will not be gone long."

When Joshua returned with an armful of gnarled branches, the woman had lifted the boy to a sitting position and was attempting to give him some water, but he would not drink. Joshua piled the wood by the fire, crept up to the boy, and knelt down. The woman shuddered, and Joshua could see both fear and grief in her sweet eyes. She did not pick up the knife this time. Joshua held up his right hand and slowly moved his left hand to the blanket. He pulled the blanket down until he could see the boy's swollen belly. He touched the belly and the boy squealed and kicked his feet. The woman reached for the knife but Joshua grabber her hand. He quickly repeated his earlier introduction. "Ta'c halaxp, manaa wees?" (*Good afternoon, how are you*)

Joshua's gentle voice and tender grip calmed the woman, and she answered, "Ta'c wees." (*I am good*)—she actually said more than this, but Joshua did not understand any of it.

Joshua pointed at the swollen belly and continued in English. "The boy does not look good to me. I do not know what is wrong with him, but it is very bad and if he does not see a doctor soon I think he might die. I must take him to Silver City tonight." Without thinking, Joshua used the sign language his Sioux mother had taught him to gesture the individual signs for "white man, chief, and medicine," (which together meant "doctor") and then finished with the individual signs for "die and sleep" (which together meant "dead").

The woman's face darkened. She repeated the words, "Silver City," and quickly made the signs back to Joshua for "white man, chief, and medicine." She did not sign the words "die" and "sleep."

Joshua touched the woman's hand. "You do not speak English or Sioux, but you know the sign language for doctor."

The woman formed the signs for "white man, chief, and medicine" again, and said, "Silver City" before jabbering a flurry of Nez Perce words he did not understand.

Joshua stood and regarded the appaloosa. "It is late in the day, but I think we must take this boy to town and find a doctor before the night is finished." The appaloosa nodded. "Thank you my friend. I will try to pick the boy up, and we will see if the woman allows us to leave without trying to stab us with the knife."

The woman stood without the knife in her hand, and said, *"What a strange man you are who talks so much to his horse. But it is even stranger to hear the horse talk back."* Joshua understood the Nez Perce words for "horse" and "man," and assumed the woman had simply given him her blessing to take the boy to town. The appaloosa kept a keen eye on the knife while Joshua lifted the boy up to the saddle.

Nearly five-foot and four-and-one-half inches from heel to crown, once-flowing auburn hair now cut just below the ears and silvered by too much care during the final months of the Civil War, the slender figure of her youth concealed by plumpish waist and hips, her face aged with subtle lines but still pretty in a way—Guinevere Dupree removed the reading glasses she had found necessary after reaching the age of forty-three and set them next to the neatly-penned journal where she recorded the daily events, random thoughts, and unfulfilled aspirations of her life. Someone pounded a second time on the door to the pair of rooms that constituted her little medical clinic,* but this time with more anxiety than the first. She glanced at the pocket watch she used to check a patient's heart rate, stood, and approached the door. The anxious fist pounded a third time just before she swung the door open. Guinevere strained to discern the shape of a man carrying a small boy wrapped in a blanket in the dim light of the hallway. The boy moaned, but the stoic man said nothing.

Guinevere initiated the conversation when the man did not speak. "Can I help you?"

The man allowed three unpleasant seconds to pass before responding. "I am looking for the doctor. A woman in town told me I could find him here."

Guinevere did not take offense. "I am Dr. Dupree." She repeated her earlier question. "How can I help you?"

The man paused again. "You are a woman. I thought all white doctors were men."

Guinevere explained, "What you say is generally true, especially out here in the wilderness. But you have found the exception and the same question remains unanswered: how can I help you?"

The man did still not answer this simple question, and suspicion tempered his voice. "It is strange you are in the same building as the undertaker."

Guinevere answered drolly, "I assure you it is only a coincidence. I did not choose this address because of its convenient location in the same building as the undertaker. Do you care to step into my office? I assume you'd like me to look at the boy."

The man's suspicion abruptly deepened. "How did you come to be called a doctor?"

---

* Amusingly, Dr. Guinevere Dupree's "clinic" is located near the southern end of Washington Street across from the War Eagle Hotel in a two-story building housing both an annex of hotel rooms and the facilities of the local undertaker, but this is another story altogether.

Guinevere answered, a little peevishly, "You mean, do I know what I'm doing? Well, I served more than three years with five different doctors during the war, in which time I witnessed more suffering and death than I believe you can ever imagine. After the war—and upon failing to find a suitable husband—I decided to become a doctor. I was fortunate enough to gain admittance to the New York Women's Medical College in 1868."

This brief résumé appeared to satisfy the man, and he carried the boy into the kerosene light of the office. "He is very sick. I fear he may die if someone does not help him. I brought him here because a woman in town told me you might be willing to see him."

Guinevere rested her hand on the boy's forehead. "He is quite warm, but let's check his temperature to be sure. Bring him into the back room." Guinevere walked past her desk and opened a narrow door. She stepped aside and the man carried the boy into the next room. She followed the man in, lighted a kerosene lamp, and closed the door. "Set him on the table. How long has he been like this?"

The man shrugged. "Like what?"

Guinevere opened a drawer and pulled out a thermometer. She shook the thermometer three times. "In his current condition?"

The man shrugged again. "I do not know for sure, because his mother does not speak any English or Sioux, and I only speak enough Nez Perce to buy a horse. I think seven or eight days. Maybe more."

Guinevere dipped the end of the thermometer in a small bottle and then slid it between the boy's cracked lips and beneath his swollen tongue. "Eight days or more? Goodness." She waited a short while, retrieved the thermometer, and then remembered her reading glasses (which she had left in the front office). She scurried into the next room, donned the detestable lenses, scurried back, and viewed the thermometer in the unsteady light of the kerosene lamp: 102 degrees, plus or minus. "Yes, he does have a fever. Has he been vomiting at all?"

The man scratched his ear. "Vomiting?"

"Yes, vomiting. Throwing up."

"Yes, he did when we left camp. I think he may have done it several times during the ride to town, but nothing came up. He also complained a lot, although I could not tell much of what he was saying because he is Nez Perce like his mother."

Guinevere set the reading glasses on the table next to the kerosene lamp. "Help me hold the boy up. I have to remove his shirt." The man lifted the boy's shoulders and he squealed. When Guinevere pulled the shirt from the boy's arms, he squealed again. "Now lay him back down … gently please. The poor boy is in a great deal of pain." The man lowered the boy's head to the table, and he squealed a third time. Guinevere studied the boy's stomach. "The boy has some abdominal swelling." She pressed her fingers against the boy's lower right abdomen. The boy convulsed in pain and whimpered. "Has the boy passed any gas?"

The man shifted his weight from one foot to the other. "Passed any gas?"

"You know—farted. Has the boy been farting?"

The man answered the question with a growing tone of anger. "I did not spend any of my time on the way to town listening for farts. And the wind was not favorable to allow me to smell any of the farts if the boy had farted. But I can tell you this: I did hear my horse fart at least five times, and I farted at least two times. Why do you ask so many stupid questions? You can see for yourself the problem is not if the boy has farted. If you are worried about farting, you should go outside and check my horse's ass and leave the boy alone."

Guinevere decided that she liked this man. "There is no need to check your horse's ass. I must ask you to leave the room now. The boy has appendicitis, and the only way to save him is to perform an appendectomy."

The man frowned. "Perform a what?"

"An appendectomy. I will have to surgically remove his appendix."

"Surgically remove?"

Guinevere made an unfortunate attempt to simplify. "Yes, I will have to cut the boy open and snip out the appendix and sew him up again."

The man shuddered. "Have you done this cutting and snipping before?"

Guinevere's confidence faltered a bit. "Well, not exactly. But because I have taken a special interest in the subject of surgery, I had the good fortune to observe Dr. William Parker* of New York perform an appendec-

---

*   William Parker began performing appendectomies in New York beginning in 1867. A fellow named Hancock performed the first deliberate appendectomy in 1848.

tomy on three different occasions." She quickly added, "And I paid very close attention to the entire procedure … every single time."

The man squeezed his hands into fists. "This does not fill me with much hope. I have watched men skin and gut a buffalo many times more than three, but this does not mean I know how to do the same."

"Please do not worry. I know I can do it. I promise I will not fail."

"I do not worry about whether or not you can cut the boy open. Even a butcher can cut the boy open. I worry about carrying a dead child back to his mother if you kill him."

"The boy will die anyway if I do not perform the appendectomy."

"So you say, but you are only worried about whether the boy has farted or not. This does not make me think you know what you are doing."

Guinevere's voice settled into a more resolute timbre. "I implore you to trust me on this. If you do not, the boy will surely die. Now please leave us alone. I must get to work immediately. You may wait in the other room or go outside, but please leave."

"Will the boy not die of pain when you cut him open?"

"No. I will put him to sleep with ether, something I learned to use during my last months in the war. He will feel no pain during the procedure. I promise."

The man's expression hardened and he crossed his arms. "You make too many promises. I will not leave the boy alone with you in this room. If you kill him, I must witness the death so I can tell the mother."

Guinevere crossed her arms in rebuttal. "Alright then. Since you insist on staying, I insist that you help me perform the procedure. But first, you must wash your hands with chlorinated lime water and scrub your fingernails clean with a hand brush. I will find a fresh gown for you to wear." Then she smirked, "I assume you will not faint when I make the incision."

"Make the incision?"

"Cut him open."

The man grinned and rolled up his sleeves to begin washing his hands. "I will not faint when you cut him … make the incision. I have seen much worse."

Guinevere relaxed. "Fine. And since you insist on staying, please tell me your name so I can address you directly during the operation. We managed to avoid a proper introduction when you first arrived."

The man nodded. "My name is Joshua Hotah."

Guinevere held out her hand and they shook. "A pleasure to meet you, Joshua Hotah." After releasing his hand, she said, "I neglected to inform you of something important: the boy should not travel for at least two days after the surgery."

"Two days? But where will he stay during these two days?"

Guinevere pulled a clean white gown from a drawer. "He can stay with me. I'll make up a bed for him."

"And what will I do during the time when the boy cannot travel?"

Guinevere unfolded the gown. "I suggest you ride back to his mother and explain what is happening."

Joshua hesitated. "I do not think I should ride back to the mother. She will come after me with a knife if I return without her son. Maybe I should just stay here."

Guinevere appeared unconcerned. "Suit yourself. Now, I have to ask you one more stupid question before we begin."

"What kind of stupid question?"

"Is it really true you do not know how to skin and gut a buffalo?"

The boy moaned.

CHAPTER EIGHT

Saloon on the corner of Washington and Avalanche
November 6, 1871

Excerpt from
A Concise History of the West
by Muireall Anne Ravenscroft
Courtesans and Nymphs du Prairie

During the age of feudalism,* the court typically func-
tioned as both the center of government and the abode
of the ruling monarch. This arrangement encouraged a
complex intermingling of political and social life,
and eventually prompted the advent of the "courtier,"
originally a female attendant who served in a position
of trust at a sovereign's court. Before the emergence
of the Renaissance in Italy during the late Middle
Ages (14th century), monarchs and other ruling officials
often depended on these courtiers to convey messages
to visiting dignitaries when the information was too
important to hand over to a mere servant. During the

---

* Feudalism was a political and economic system of
Europe, from the 9th to about the 15th century, based
on the holding of all land in fief or fee, and the
resulting relation of lord to vassal characterized
by homage, legal and military service of tenants,
and forfeiture.

Renaissance, likely because of the proclivity of ruling couples to marry only to preserve bloodlines or to establish alliances, upper-class married men and women often led essentially separate lives and, consequently, found it necessary to seek companionship and physical gratification outside of these marriages of convenience from a more sophisticated type of courtier, the "courtesan." In Renaissance Italy, the word "cortigiana" (feminine of "cortigiano," the Old Italian word for "courtier") came to mean "the ruler's mistress," and later, a well-educated woman (often trained in the arts of dancing and music) who provided companionship to wealthy and powerful men in exchange for social status and other benefits. The English borrowed the word "courtisane" from the French in the 16th century, and, by dropping the e, transformed it to "courtesan" while at the same time maintaining the associated meanings of "court mistress" and "prostitute." Today, the English word "courtesan" carries the primary meaning of a woman prostitute, particularly one whose clients are members of a royal court or men of high social standing and great wealth.

There are several courtesans worthy of mention who thrived from the time of the Renaissance into the 19th century of the American West. Tullia d'Aragona (c. 1510-1556) was born in Rome and became one of the most celebrated courtesans of the Renaissance. Although not considered particularly attractive by the standards of the time, she achieved success through the clever application of her intellect, and is today considered a noteworthy philosopher and poet. She wrote Dialogue on the Infinity of Love in 1547 while an attendant at the court of Cosimo de Medici, the Duke of Florence. Marion Delorme (1613-1650) was a French courtesan famous for her intimate relationships with several important men of the times including George Villiers (2nd Duke of

Buckingham), Louis II de Bourbon, and Cardinal Riche-
lieu. She was popularized by author Victor Hugo in a
five-act play titled "Marion Delorme" and first presented
in 1831. Jeanne Antoinette Poisson (1721-1764), more
famously known as Madame de Pompadour, was a member
of the French Court and the "official chief mistress"
of Louis XV from 1745 until her death. She was noted
for her intelligence, beauty, and social refinement, as
well as her keen interests in both interior design and
literature. Frances Villiers (1753-1821) was one of
the more infamous mistresses of the Prince of Wales in
the years before he became King George IV. She was a
grandmother and mother of ten children when the affair
began in 1793. And Cora Pearl (1835-1886) -- born Emma
Elizabeth Crouch in Plymouth, England -- courted the
likes of the son of King William III of the Netherlands
and the half-brother of Napoleon III. After living in
London during her early life, she moved to Paris where
she accumulated significant wealth and is said to have
bathed nude before dinner guests in a silver tub of
expensive Champagne on more than one occasion. But she
was also capable of less frivolous behavior, and during
the Franco-Prussian War of 1870 she freely offered her
several homes to provide shelter for wounded soldiers
and also paid for doctors and medicines out of her own
pocket.

The courtesans of the American West lived and worked
in what were called "parlor houses." The best parlor
houses resembled respectable mansions, with this subtle
difference: red lanterns were hung below the roof eaves
or near the main entry to advertise the true purpose of
the building. After stepping through the front door,
guests usually encountered a lavishly-adorned parlor
(thus the name) lined with elegant sofas, chairs, and
tables, and often incorporating a piano. The larger
parlor houses offered game rooms and a dance hall and

provided musicians, singers, dancers, and even jugglers to entertain the guests. First class parlor houses maintained well-supplied cellars with fine cigars, the best bourbon, and expensive liquors and wines. Nearly every parlor house employed a bouncer to protect the girls from excessively-rough customers and to deal with those who refused to pay the bill. Parlor houses typically employed 6 to 12 girls, as well as a madam who managed the house and enjoyed the additional benefit of entertaining only those guests she preferred. In the very best parlor houses, the girls could be seen only by appointment, and often demanded as much as $50 for a single night.* Some courtesans split their earnings with the madam of the parlor house, but many paid a flat fee by the night or week.

Not all women of this profession were fortunate enough to enjoy the special benefits of working in a high-class parlor house and to be called courtesans. During the California Gold Rush of 1849, prostitutes were labeled "ladies of the line" and "sporting women." Cowboys called them "soiled doves." Other common terms included "daughters of sin," "doves of the roost," "scarlet ladies," "painted ladies," and, particularly evocative, "nymphs du prairie." If the parlor house was at the top of the pecking order, the bordellos and brothels could be considered the next level down. These establishments typically eschewed both the finery and subtlety of the parlor house, instead relying on a more direct approach: after five minutes of conversation, sometimes a short dance, and possibly a stiff drink at the bar, it was off to the girl's room. Even lower than the women

---

* By comparison, the going rates in the frontier generally ranged from $5 per night at the nicer establishments down to $1 or less for the majority of nymphs du prairie.

who worked the bordellos and brothels were the saloon prostitutes. And lower still were the women who worked independently out of small houses or cabins called "cribs." The purpose of the cribs was often advertised by the same red lanterns used at the more sophisticated parlor houses, and occasionally a madam would operate a string of cribs for older women who were no longer employable at the main parlor house. Below the women who worked in cribs were the street walkers, but they were typically found only in larger cities. However, at the very bottom of the profession were the women who provided services to the military at the remote forts of the west. The settlements that grew up near the forts were usually too small to justify a parlor house, and the madam of a good parlor house would not admit a poorly-paid soldier in any case. Instead, special districts called "hog towns" thrived near the forts, and were places where soldiers could spend their meager earnings on gambling, drinking, and the services of a few women who were not "qualified" to work in a crib, bordello, or parlor house.

Women entered the profession for various reasons. The 19th century offered limited economic opportunities for women, and if a young bride was abandoned by her husband, or stranded in a remote western town by the death or murder of a husband, the outlook could rapidly turn grim. Most women had no useful skill with which to support themselves, and likely believed they had no other way to survive. Some followed the regrettable path of their mothers because they had known of nothing else. Particularly poignant were those who entered the profession because they had been seduced by an opportunistic villain and then discarded, or much worse, raped: these unfortunate souls were instantly viewed by society as lost, regardless of the circumstances that had forever stolen their virginity. But whatever the reason, the

initial decision was often only the beginning of a tragic descent into darkness because of the considerable
dangers associated with the profession, even for those
"fortunate" enough to work in a well-managed parlor
house. Tuberculosis, known at the time as consumption,
was a persistent concern. There was always the risk of
contracting a sexually-transmitted disease, primarily
syphilis. Some women died after botched abortions. Sui-
cides were common. And violence was a steady threat. In
fact, my research found over 100 documented cases of
violent deaths related to prostitution, but the number
is likely far higher because many communities did not
maintain adequate records of such events. In one particularly shocking case, a young woman who had not even
reached the age of twenty....

John Ravenscroft pushed the page of manuscript aside and stared
dreamily through the window to the rain-shrouded mountains beyond
the valley to the north. "Remarkable. Taking a bath in a silver tub of
champagne...right out in front of the dinner guests. Must have been
quite a party."

Muireall jabbed vigorously at her needlepoint and scoffed, "I bet you
would have liked to have seen it."

John blushed and stammered a little. "I didn't...say...I would have
liked to have seen it. I said it must have been quite a party." He tapped
his fingers on the armrest of his chair. "But it sure would have been
something to see."

Muireall calmed her tone and loosened her grip on the needle. "Is that
all you took away from the manuscript? If true, I may decide to remove
this bit of information if men find it such a distraction from the primary
points of the article."

John straightened up and watched the first drops of an afternoon rain
shower splatter across the window sill. "I wouldn't remove it. I don't think
men will find it distracting at all. Although I must say the thought of it certainly fires the imagination. How do you think they kept the champagne
fresh before she got into the tub? They must have uncorked hundreds of

bottles at the same time and poured them all at once. Otherwise, the stuff would've gone flat."

"Honestly John, I have no idea how they poured the champagne into the tub. Does it really matter?"

"Do you think the bubbles tickled?"

"That does it. I'm crossing out the reference to Cora Pearl's silver tub with a fat ink pen as soon as I get the chance. I can see now how it temporarily renders men incapable of lucid thought."

"Oh come now. My thoughts are perfectly lucid. As a matter of fact, I don't think my thoughts have been this lucid for many weeks. Although it's true I might find the image of a naked Cora Pearl stepping into her silver tub of champagne in front of dinner guests somewhat distracting during my client meeting tomorrow morning. Maybe a nice dinner and a good night's sleep will clear my mind of any thoughts of silver bathtubs full of champagne and...."

The rain intensified against the picture window. A deep rumble of thunder rolled in above the outlying waves of the Pacific Ocean. The cat jumped up to the window sill and swatted at one of the rivulets streaking across the glass. Muireall scoffed again. "I doubt anything will clear your mind at this point. I think you should cancel the meeting."

John hastily changed the subject. "Looks like rain tonight, don't you think? We could use a good dose of rain to settle the dust. I'll close the front door."

"No," said Muireall. "Please leave the door open. I like the smell of the rain and the sound of the thunder." She took a deep breath and listened.

Priscilla Kimball pulled the hem of the gray skirt above her knees and suppressed the urge to retch when she dropped down to the floor and involuntarily gulped a big whiff of stale vomit. She jerked herself up and covered both mouth and nose, but too late: a lingering taste of the sour aroma had already clung to the roof of her mouth. She twisted away from the vomit and inhaled a breath of the room's musty air, and while still looking away fished around in the bucket of soapy water she had carried into the dingy space until her fingers snagged the torn rag sticking to the bottom. After quickly sucking in a second breath and then holding it, she wrung the rag twice to squeeze out excess water and again fell to her hands and knees to clean up the mess left by one of the establishment's more important clients. She inspected the small room while swirling the rag along the margins of the acrid mess. Bright vertical lines illuminating the sides of the window blinds provided the only light. A dented porcelain wash basin and an empty kerosene lamp with a burnt wick rested on a simple wood table under the window sill. Someone had shoved the bed against the peeling paint of the wall, and someone else had torn the stained bottom sheet halfway down the middle. Numerous stains of different sizes, shapes, and colors decorated the wood floor planks. And a small painting of a naked woman standing next to a tree and pouring water from a white vase adorned the wall opposite the bed. Priscilla dipped the rag into the pail and squeezed, then went to work on the vomit again. Her mind drifted away to thoughts of her wedding reception, and she did not hear the door open behind her.

A strapping miner named Jacque—sufficiently drunk to blur his vision, temporarily wealthy due to the modest discovery of a small gold nugget at an otherwise useless claim, and wearing his cleanest long underwear and wool socks—shuffled quietly into the dim room. He blinked twice before he located Priscilla's enticingly-naked legs and youthful derrière. He watched her posterior move seductively back and forth as she cleaned up the vomit. And then he could no longer resist. He took one step forward, dropped to his knees, and yanked the skirt up. Priscilla shot up at the unexpected touch and hurled the rag across the room where it stuck momentarily on the wall before tumbling to the floor. Jacque grabbed the collar of her blouse and shoved her back down with his left hand while flailing at her vulnerable undergarments with his right. Priscilla tried to fend him off by reaching back and poking with her fist, but he released the collar and twisted her arm behind her back. She tried to kick him in the crotch, but he raised his knees and pinned her ankles against the floor. When Jacque had Priscilla under control, he spoke to her in slurred tones. "No need to get upset, little missy. This'll only take a minute ... or maybe two."

Priscilla winced when Jacque pushed her arm up higher and pulled her bloomers down. Tears ran down her flushed cheeks when her ankle scraped against a nail sticking out of a floor board. She gagged again when he forced her face down into the sloppy pool of vomit. She lifted her face up and screamed, "Get off me! Get off! You're hurting my arm!" When his fingers touched her sex, she shrieked.

Jacque smirked, "Well, I found the right spot. Now all I got to do is pull this dang thing out and get proper lined up." He fiddled clumsily with the crotch buttons of his long underwear. When he had finally unloosed the last button—"

The door flung open and slammed against the wall. Nadia stood in the opening clothed in the exotic lingerie of her trade and brandishing a hickory axe handle. After discerning what had caused the scream, she backhanded the axe handle in a smooth arc and smashed it across Jacque's shoulder blades. He did not immediately release Priscilla, so she slapped the side of his head with an accurate forehand stroke.

Jacque rose up and covered his throbbing ear with his free hand, maintaining a tight grip on Priscilla's arm with the other hand. He turned to discover his assailant. "Nadia, what did you do that for? I paid good money for this little whore, and I was just about to get my reward when you barged in here and messed things up."

Nadia raised the axe handle and prepared to strike again. "Get off her, Jacque. You're in the wrong room again, and Priscilla's not for sale. Get off her now before I split your head down the middle like a ripe pumpkin!"

Jacque released Priscilla's arm and staggered up, his chin aligning with the top of Nadia's head. "Dammit, Nadia, why didn't you say so in the first place before whacking me with an axe handle? You could'a broke something."

Unsympathetic, Nadia did not back away from the burly man now towering over her. "Jacque, you're still in the wrong room. And Priscilla's not a whore. Don't ever call her that again. Now get out of here before I lose my temper."

Jacque rubbed his ear and attempted a weak smile, but the ear began to throb. "I sure would hate to see you lose your temper." He pushed by Nadia and shuffled into the dark second-floor hallway without closing the door.

Priscilla Kimball bent down over the narrow table by the open window in Nadia's pleasant little room and washed her face in the cool water of a basin (decorated with colorful flowers) and perfectly centered on a round linen doily. The sweet air refreshed her lungs and the morning sunlight warmed her back. When she had finished, she dried her face on a soft cotton towel and sat on a chair with a seat cushion embroidered with brown mountains, green trees, and a blue river snaking diagonally from corner to corner. She swung her feet back and forth and folded her hands on her legs, looking more like a little girl than a young woman. "Your room smells nice, Miss Nadia. It's not like the other rooms. The other rooms are dark and smelly, but yours is filled with the sun. I like your room."

Nadia restored the hickory axe handle to its home beneath the bed. "Are you all washed up now? That was quite a mess you were dealing with."

Priscilla sniffed. "Yes, Miss Nadia, and I'm not finished cleaning the mess up, either. I'll have to clean it up soon, before Miss Margaret finds out I'm not getting my work done and kicks me out. I can't afford to lose this job."

Nadia sat on the bed and crossed her legs. "Don't worry, Priscilla. You can rest here a few minutes. When you feel better you can go back to the room and finish cleaning up. I'll talk to Margaret if she tries to kick you out."

Priscilla swung her legs a bit faster. "Thank you, Miss Nadia." Her legs slowed down again. "And thank you for rescuing me from that awful man. I don't know what I would have done if you hadn't come by. I tried to whack him, but he was too strong for me." A subterranean explosion boomed on War Eagle Mountain and echoed down the valley.

Nadia offered a different perspective. "Jacque's not such a bad fellow. He was just drunk and got a little confused. He wouldn't have bothered you if he'd known you're the cleaning lady. He just thought you were one of the wh—" Nadia stopped without finishing the last word of her sentence, then decided to finish it with a different word. "…courtesans."

Priscilla lowered her hands to the sides of the chair and squeezed the seat cushion. "What's a courtesan, Miss Nadia? I haven't heard the word before."

Nadia answered directly. "A courtesan, Priscilla, is a woman who provides intelligent conversation and intimate companionship to men of high social standing or great wealth."

Priscilla scrunched her face as she thought about this definition. "Are you a courtesan, Miss Nadia? I thought you were a whore."

Nadia winced at the sound of the word. "No, Priscilla. I like to think of myself as a courtesan, because I have higher aspirations than simply working here the rest of my life."

Priscilla added a rocking motion to the swing of her legs. "Have you always been a courtesan, Miss Nadia?"

"No, Priscilla. I was supposed to be a school teacher, but something terrible happened before I started." She repeated in a trembling whisper, "Something terrible."

Priscilla's legs stopped swinging. "What happened, Miss Nadia?"

Nadia looked away from Priscilla's youthful face. The sound of a wagon pulled by eight mules rumbled in the street below and reverberated off the canyon of storefront buildings. "The same thing that almost happened to you, Priscilla."

"You mean with Jacque?"

"Yes, I mean with Jacque."

Priscilla hopped up from the chair, skipped across the small room, and sat on the bed next to Nadia. "Thank you for whacking Jacque in the head with the axe handle. He was really big, and you whacked him really good. I appreciate it."

"You're welcome, Priscilla. You are truly welcome." Nadia wiped her eye.

Priscilla began bouncing her heels in unison off the bed frame. "Are you saying... you're not planning to be a courtesan the rest of your life?"

Nadia sniffed. "No, Priscilla. Because I can never again work as a school teacher, my dream is to make enough money to move to California and buy a nice home with a view of the ocean. I'd like to have my own garden too. It's either that or marry a fine gentleman of means, which I don't really believe is likely given my current occupation. I hope to raise a family someday too. But right now, this all is just a dream."

Priscilla smiled broadly. "But it's a beautiful dream, Miss Nadia. Do you think it's going to happen any time soon?" She touched Nadia's hand.

Nadia squeezed Priscilla's hand. "I hope so, Priscilla, because I'm not sure how much longer I will last."

CHAPTER NINE

A masked ball before winter
November 7, 1871

S itting in a bentwood rocking chair (recently imported from Chicago) and rocking back and forth next to a barrel of pickles in The Sommercamp Emporium & General Store, Manfred Herrmann sulked. At the same time, he felt guilty for sulking. And then, after wallowing in an extra measure of guilt, he abruptly stopped rocking and lifted the wood lid on top of the barrel and reached inside and pulled out an enormous pickle. He glared at the pickle with a look of disdain before gnawing off a big chunk and munching on it, his expression quickly turning nearly as sour as the pickle.

William Sommercamp watched Manfred bite about two inches off the end of the dilled cucumber while he swept the floor next to a table loaded with boots and shoes and wool socks (and a display of leather shoe strings). When he had finished sweeping a small pile of debris into a metal dust pan, he emptied the dust pan into a small trash can. "Manfred, you're eating one of my pickles. I thought you hated pickles."

Manfred gnawed off another bite and chewed it into small chunks. "I *don't* like pickles, William. And if you want to know the truth, I can hardly stand to even look at one. I'm just punishing myself for sulking. Nothing upsets me more than when someone sulks, and since I can't seem to stop feeling sorry for myself, I just thought I'd eat one of these pickles to balance things out." Manfred rocked a few more times before swallowing the sour chunks.

William Sommercamp rested his broom against the boot and shoe table and gestured with the dust pan. "Maybe you should try to do something to cheer yourself up instead of punishing yourself with one of my dilled pickles. I might have trouble selling them if word gets out about what you're doing."

Manfred lowered the pickle and glared sourly at William. "What a ridiculously logical suggestion. And did you have any specific ideas, or are you just wasting my time with meaningless small talk?"

William Sommercamp set the dust pan on the table and hooked his thumbs behind his suspenders. "As a matter of fact, I do. Why don't you go to the masked ball at the Masonic Hall tonight? If I remember correctly, it should get started in a couple of hours. The town's never done one before, so who knows what might happen."

Manfred bit off another inch of pickle. "Never done what before?"

"A masked ball."

Manfred rocked and glowered at the pickle. "I don't really see how a masked ball would cheer me up, but it doesn't matter anyway because I can't go."

William Sommercamp sat on the boot and shoe table. "Why? You have something else going on tonight?"

"No, I don't. The problem is...I don't have a mask. I certainly can't go to a masked ball without a mask."

"Shoot, Manfred. I'll give you a mask for free so you can go to the ball. Anything to keep you from giving my pickles a bad reputation."

"I appreciate it, William, but there's another problem. I'm not really much of a dancer. Why should I bother to go to a dance if I can't even—"

William snapped his suspenders. "You don't have to dance at all, Manfred, if you don't want to. You can just sit off to the side and watch everyone else dance and listen to the music. You might even find the opportunity to talk to some folks about your new church. Tell you what... I'll even let you take a second pickle with you, just in case it doesn't work out. Then, if the need arises, you can really punish yourself. Just promise me you won't tell anyone you got the pickle from my store."

Manfred sulked a little more. "Don't think I can afford the price of this masked ball."

William grinned. "No problem there, Manfred. It's free. Silver City is picking up the cost."

Manfred squeezed the half-eaten pickle. "It sounds like you're telling me there's no way I'm getting out of this."

William snapped his suspenders even louder to celebrate his triumph. "That's right, Manfred. Grab yourself an extra pickle and I'll go fetch a mask for you. I think a plain black mask is just the ticket for a preacher like you."

Manfred stood, reached into the barrel, and fished out a second pickle. "Are you going to the masked ball?"

"Of course. Wouldn't miss it for anything. As I said, who knows what might happen?"

After William Sommercamp returned with the mask—a plain black one devoid of any decoration—Manfred accepted it without pleasure. Defeated, he nodded weakly and trudged away from the pickle barrel. Before leaving the store, he muttered back to William, "I'll go to the masked ball tonight, but I plan on eating this second pickle before the evening's out. You can count on it."

William snapped his suspenders a final time before shouting, "See you there, Manfred. And don't forget to wear your mask!"

Manfred slouched on a three-legged stool with two wobbly legs and sulked. He leaned back against the rounded wood trim at the top of the wainscot, reached into an inside coat pocket, and fingered the second pickle to make sure he hadn't lost it. The masked ball had failed to improve his disposition, particularly when the band—an ad hoc group consisting of two fiddles, a concertina, a banjo, an upright piano in desperate need of tuning, and a lone percussionist playing tambourine and castanets—burst into an overly-exuberant rendition of *Oh! Susanna*.* Somewhere near bar 27, when the musical balance between the concertina and banjo suddenly collapsed, he thought of devouring the pickle right then and there and heading back to his little cabin to sulk in private. He nearly pulled the pickle out, but after squeezing it a few times decided instead to make one

---

* Stephen Foster (1826-1864). *Oh! Susanna* was first published in Cincinnati, Ohio in 1848.

more attempt to enjoy the dance—and thereby improve his attitude—by observing the numerous attendees. He knew nearly everyone, and a few had actually accepted one of his handwritten notes announcing the new church in the backroom of the saloon on the corner of Washington and Avalanche, although he had yet to see any of these individuals attend one of his services.

He adjusted the position of the mask on his nose, to see through the holes better, and made a closer study of the band. He noticed that Nadia, one of the women who worked upstairs at the saloon, was playing the concertina—although she had dressed more like a school teacher for the dance and he nearly did not recognize her. He briefly considered the idea of asking her to accompany the hymns on Sunday mornings, but then his thoughts were distracted by some sort of commotion at the front entry. Manfred swiveled on the round seat of the three-legged stool to observe the commotion without straining his neck. Two men were arguing and waving their arms at each other, but he could not hear what they were saying above the blended melodies of the banjo and fiddles. A third man, clearly one of the Chinese who lived somewhere on the outskirts of town, stood by the doorway with his hands together. One of the men pushed the other. The second man pushed back, and it looked like a brawl for sure. Manfred stood and prepared to intervene, but just as he took his first step toward the impending clash, a young woman wearing a dress the color of a clear morning sky and a mask the color of fresh clouds stepped through the doorway and walked right up to the two men. She touched each man on the shoulder, said a few words (which Manfred could not hear), and the men immediately separated and removed their hats. One man said something to her, but the other man remained silent. The young woman nodded and slipped between the two men, and after taking three nimble steps paused to survey the room with her hands neatly folded in front and her black leather shoes pressed together beneath the white-trimmed hem of her dress. Her gaze appeared to stop on a dapper young gentleman dressed in a neatly-pressed pinstripe gray suit, brilliant white shirt, black string tie, and debonair gray mask with black trim. She waved at the gentleman, and walked over to him and stood at his side. The gentleman kissed her hand and they began chatting. Manfred squinted to improve his vision and recognized the fancy shirt and string tie. He had given the dapper gentlemen one of the church notices late in the afternoon about a week ago, and the fellow had actually accepted the shred of paper and said he would think about attending. *What was his name? New attorney in town. Some sort of accent, probably British, but not sure. Strange name. Very Strange. Csongor. Csongor. Last name started with a T. Csongor. Yes, that's it. Toth. Toth's the last name. Csongor Toth. Nice fellow. Should stop by his office and speak with him sometime. Maybe early next week.*

Manfred refocused his attention on the woman in the sky-blue dress because she was the only activity at the masked ball he found interesting, and because she reminded him of someone. *What is it about this woman? She looks familiar. The short-cropped black hair? Yes. The way she folds her hands? Yes. But there's more. What is it, exactly? The slenderness of her waist? No, that's not it. It's something else. Something else. Something—I've got it now. It's the way she walks. It's the tilt of her head. But how is it even possible? How could it be? It makes no sense at all to find her in Silver City. No sense at all. Can't imagine why she would....*

He adjusted the mask because it had slipped again and the band launched into a new piece of music he did not recognize. Dancing couples glided across his vision and obscured his view of the young woman and the dapper gentleman. He stood and pushed up on his toes, but could not see them above the crowded dance floor. Afraid he would lose sight of the young woman, he charged forward and weaved his way through the melee. When he broke through the other side, he found himself standing a mere six feet from the young woman in the sky-blue dress. But before he could turn away, Csongor Toth waved to him.

"Mr. Herrmann. Please join us for a moment."

Manfred attempted a look of surprise, but the mask probably concealed it. "Mr. Toth. Nice to see you again." Keeping his eyes on Csongor Toth, Manfred stepped forward and shook his outstretched hand."

"This charming young lady is a dear friend of mine, and she is in desperate need of a reliable escort for the evening. You see, she prefers not to dance with just any man."

Although this statement astonished Manfred, he responded casually without looking at the young woman. "Yes, I can appreciate the dilemma. Some of these fellows are a little rough around the edges." Then he added clumsily, "I wouldn't want to dance with any of them either."

Csongor glanced at the young woman before continuing his conversation with Manfred. "Yes, of course. But the problem is, Mr. Herrmann... she prefers not to be the one to ask for a dance. She is waiting for said gentleman to ask her first."

Manfred finally acknowledged the young woman, but avoided her eyes by staring at the elfish curve of her chin. "Oh, yes, yes. I agree completely. I wouldn't have it any other way."

Csongor Toth persisted. "So what are your thoughts on the matter?"

The question perplexed Manfred, but the mask concealed his confusion. "What are my thoughts on what matter?"

Csongor did not betray his amusement. "What do you think about escorting this charming young lady this evening?"

The mask did not conceal the surprise in Manfred's voice. "Me? Are you asking me to dance with her this evening? But we've never met before."

Csongor deftly countered, "A mere formality, which I shall rectify in a moment. But first, you must agree to accept the task at hand."

Manfred swallowed hard. "I'm not much of a dancer. I can do the waltz a little, but I'm pretty flat-footed with the other dances. I wouldn't want to step on her toes."

Csongor presented his closing argument. "Nonsense, Mr. Herrmann. Dance as much or as little as you wish. She will not mind. But stay by her side as her knight in shining armor this evening, and she will be forever grateful. Do you agree to these terms, Mr. Herrmann, or do you plan to throw her to the wolves?"

Manfred swallowed even harder. "Well, if you put it that way, I suppose I have no choice but to accept."

Csongor smiled beneath his mask. "Thank you, Mr. Herrmann. I know you are about to embark on an onerous task, and I applaud your courage for accepting. Now, before we part, may I introduce you to your companion for the evening?"

Manfred sighed. "Yes, by all means."

Csongor nodded. "Mr. Herrmann, I would like to introduce you to Miss Alexandra Smythe of Liverpool, England. Miss Smythe, I would like to introduce you to Mr. Manfred Herrmann, the new Lutheran Pastor of Silver City." Manfred opened his mouth to say something but then froze, forcing Csongor to continue. "It would be appropriate, Mr. Herrmann, to kiss her hand. Do not be afraid. She has promised me that she will not harm you in any way." Manfred froze with indecision. "I'll tell you what, Mr. Herrmann; I shall speak to the band this very moment and request a waltz for the next dance. This will help the two of you get off on the right foot." Csongor Toth walked over to the fiddle player and whispered in his ear as the band concluded playing the final notes of *Turkey in the Straw*.* The fiddle player nodded, said something to the piano player, and then the two of them began playing an unusual version of the *Blue Danube*.† The other musicians joined in after a few measures. Csongor Toth returned and found that Manfred had still not moved. "Alright, Mr. Herrmann, the time for action has now arrived. Please kiss Miss Smythe's hand and then ask her to dance. No more excuses."

Alexandra Smythe raised her arm, and when Manfred held her hand and lowered his lips to kiss it, he was surprised to see a chipped finger nail and two scraped knuckles. Even so, when his lips touched the top of her hand a shiver fluttered down his back before exploding somewhere near his tail bone.

Near the final measures of the *Blue Danube*, another couple bumped against Alexandra Smythe, and her bosom pressed briefly against Manfred's chest. She had not talked to Manfred during the dance, and he had said nothing to her, but now the dance had ended and couples were dispersing to the perimeter of the dance floor. Alexandra decided that she had no choice but to speak first. "Mr. Herrmann...."

Manfred finally found his voice. "Yes, Miss Smythe?"

"I'm afraid I must ask you a question."

"Yes, Miss Smythe?"

"What is it you have in your coat pocket?"

Manfred glanced down at the pocket. "In my coat pocket?"

---

* *Turkey in the Straw* is based on an American folk song dating from the early 19th century and popularized in the 1820s. The composer is in dispute.
† Austrian Johann Straus II (1825-1899) composed the *Blue Danube* in 1866.

"Yes, in your coat pocket. It is really none of my business, but I thought you may want to remove whatever it is before we dance again."

Manfred reached in his jacket. "Oh, my coat pocket. I had forgotten about it. It's just a pickle, Miss Smythe."

Alexandra could not resist further inquiry. "A pickle? Do you often carry a pickle in your coat pocket?"

"No, this is the first time. But I don't think I'll need it now."

"Then, may I suggest that you remove it before the next dance?"

"Yes, Miss Smythe. I'll get rid of it. Right away."

Alexandra's eyes glimmered behind the mask. "Please call me Alex."

Manfred fingered the pickle as he searched the room for an appropriate place to discard it. "Yes, Miss Smythe."

CHAPTER TEN

Commotion at the masked ball
November 7, 1871

Waiting patiently on the second floor of the Masonic Hall a few inches inside the doorway to the large social room with his hands clasped together and his head bowed deferentially, Tseng Longwei listened to Roshan "negotiate" with the burly doorkeeper who had blocked his entry to the masked ball. Longwei had initially suggested that he should take a walk while Roshan attended the dance by himself. Roshan had listened to this idea respectfully, but then immediately confronted the doorkeeper in a most unpleasant manner. Regrettably, the doorkeeper had not backed down, and was now locked in an escalating conflict with Longwei's well-meaning business partner. Roshan's unique understanding of the English language did not improve the doorkeeper's appreciation of the key issues under discussion.

Roshan puffed his chest, but the burly doorkeeper still did not retreat. "Listen to my lips speak much the truth, my man of big who is too of the idiot, if you ask my opinion to me. If Roshan cannot walk to the dance with Longwei, this is of the largest of the stupid to think of and you should know about it later before the sooner is now."

The burley doorkeeper clenched his hands and loomed menacingly to counter Roshan's puffing chest. "Listen here. This fellow's a Chinaman, and I've got strict orders from the organizers of the masked ball: no Chinamen is allowed. If you want to come to the masked ball, you have to leave the Chinaman outside."

Roshan listened intently, then sputtered his rebuttal. "No, you listen of the here, and I will speak to you of the other way. Longwei and Roshan are of business partner together, and together they must do of all things. It is not the possible for Roshan to dance when Longwei is not in the nearby. It makes the sense of no."

The burly doorkeeper frowned. "I don't know what you just said, but whatever it was, the Chinaman's not getting into this dance."

Roshan waved his arms and retorted with a short but effective outburst. "Is of the much stupid and big idiot!"

The burly doorkeeper waved his arms too and bellowed, "If you ask me, the only big idiot here is you!"

Roshan lost all self control, and, without thinking of the consequences, shoved the burley doorkeeper. When the doorkeeper budged only a quarter of an inch, Roshan privately admired the man's strength. The doorkeeper lost all patience as well, and pushed Roshan back. When Roshan also budged about a quarter of an inch, the doorkeeper appreciated his adversary's brawn. Undeterred by the strength of his adversary, Roshan prepared to push the doorkeeper even harder—or maybe just slug him on the chin—but before he could act a young woman wearing a dress the color of a clear morning sky and a mask the color of fresh clouds stepped briskly through the doorway. To the astonishment of both Roshan and the doorkeeper, she walked into the middle of their conflict, hesitated briefly, then touched each man on the shoulder with a disarming caress. Roshan immediately unpuffed his chest and the doorkeeper stopped looming.

The woman spoke to Roshan and the burly doorkeeper in soothing words. "Good evening my fine gentlemen. Can you tell me if I have arrived safely at the masked ball?" Instantly deflated by the woman's gentle touch and seductive brogue, each man stepped back and removed his hat.

Enchanted by the woman's charm, the doorkeeper did not bother to consider that, with a room full of people wearing masks and other assorted disguises, the question ignored the obvious. "Why, sure, ma'am. This here's the right location for the masked ball. You can go right on in."

Roshan's eyes followed the young woman when she glided by, but he did not attempt to say anything to her. He quietly returned his attention to the burly doorkeeper. Seeing an opportunity to calm the dispute, Tseng

Longwei rushed ahead and set his strong hand on Roshan's forearm. "Roshan, do not start a fight for my sake when no good will come of it. This man will never yield."

Roshan squashed his rumpled hat back on his head and glared at the burly doorkeeper. "Alright, my business partner of many time. I will walk to the ball of mask and you will walk of the outside and we will find the other to the late of clock. I do not like it in this way, but this man will not feel the sound of my hand on his lips because you say of it."

The doorkeeper jammed his hat back on too. "I still don't have any idea what you're talking about, but you need to listen to the Chinaman before you get yourself in a whole heap of trouble."

Longwei bowed to the burly doorkeeper. "I respect you for doing your job." Then he turned to Roshan. "I will see you after the masked ball has ended. Do not worry about me. The sky is clear and full of stars. I shall walk in the fresh air of the evening complacent in my humble thoughts."

Roshan grumbled, "I do not like of it, but I will do it what you say."

Longwei bowed to the doorkeeper one last time before saying to Roshan, "Thank you, my business partner of many time."

Tseng Longwei escaped the bedlam of the Masonic Hall and walked to the middle of the dirt roadway between the buildings fronting Jordan Avenue to the west and the meandering banks of Jordan Creek to the east. He convinced his mind to ignore the foot stomping music pouring though a pair of open second-floor windows, and instead focused on the calming sounds of the waters of Jordan Creek flowing pleasantly beneath the bridge-like building. When the music intensified beyond even his ability to ignore it, he hiked south. He negotiated an irregular pattern of smooth stones across a small tributary of Jordan Creek, then wandered along the rear of a two-story female boarding house with connected storage building. He crossed the eastern end of a narrow alley between the storage building and one of the town's more important liveries, then angled easterly back towards Jordan Creek. He occasionally glimpsed a lantern in a cabin window twinkling through the trees and bushes growing along the shores of the creek. After passing the narrow end of a foot bridge, he weaved amongst a group of shanties clustered behind a wagon shop and stable. The pungent aroma of horses and mules gathered in the attached corral saturated the night air. When he emerged from the cluster of shanties, a burst of fiery embers swirled into the sky near the creek a few hundred feet away. Longwei headed directly toward the sparkling light. When he had taken only twenty steps, the crackle of a bonfire echoed around his ears and a dense column of smoke pulsing with flaming light merged into his sight. He improved his pace and lengthened his stride, and when the last legitimate structure south of town no longer obscured his view, the comforting scene of many people gathered around a blazing bonfire instantly justified his decision to leave Roshan at the masked ball. When he approached within twenty feet of the bonfire, his nimble mind quickly assessed the gathering's demography: three old men, two old women, four young men, six young women, and nine children of various ages and genders—all Chinese.

Tseng Longwei quietly slipped into an open space between a young woman and an old woman and introduced himself in halting Mandarin: "Good evening my friends. My name is Tseng Longwei, and I have travelled far to spend this evening with you in the town of Silver City."

An old man standing nearby responded in fluent Mandarin. "Welcome to our gathering, Tseng Longwei. Your Mandarin is not too bad, but I fear not everyone here will understand it."

Longwei pushed his hands out to feel the heat radiating from the swirling flames. "I was born a peasant in the mountains of Guangxi Province and learned to speak Cantonese as a child. I did not learn Mandarin until much later in life, and therefore do not speak it as well. I apologize if I sound a bit rough from lack of practice."*

The old man nodded. "Not at all. There are many here from the southern lands of China who will understand your Cantonese better.

---

* Although Cantonese and Mandarin share much common vocabulary, the two languages are not mutually intelligible because of significant differences in pronunciation and syntax. Both are tonal languages—different tones impart different meanings to the same sound—but Mandarin uses four tones while Cantonese requires more than six. The two languages also incorporate a number of different vowels and consonants. Written Mandarin and Cantonese use the same characters with a few exceptions.

Amazingly, I live as your opposite: I learned Mandarin as a child and Cantonese as a youth. If you care to speak in your native language, I will translate what you say into Mandarin so we may all—with the exception of one who does not hear well anyway—understand."

Longwei bowed and responded in Cantonese, "As you prefer, but I am not sure I have much more to say, especially to the children."

The old man poked at the fire with a charred stick and a plume of sparks erupted from the glowing embers. "Nonsense. We had just prayed for the arrival of a storyteller to enliven our evening, and behold, you have appeared out of the darkness."

Longwei pressed his hands together inside the joined sleeves of his tunic. "I have never considered myself a storyteller. You must still wait for an answer to your prayer."

The old man chuckled and poked the fire again. "This is where you are wrong, Tseng Longwei. I am convinced that you are the answer to our prayer. Whatever you might think of yourself, you must either tell us a story or go someplace else so we are not required to look upon our disappointment in the flesh."

"Are you saying I cannot stay by the fire unless I tell a story?"

"It is precisely what I am saying. Please gather your thoughts and begin the story when you are ready."

Tseng Longwei cleared his throat. "If you insist, but understand that you have been forewarned of my profound inadequacy as a storyteller."

The old man announced to the gathering that Longwei would tell a story in Cantonese, and that he would repeat it in Mandarin so all would understand. When he had finished his proclamation, he turned to Longwei and said, "All, particularly the children, are ready to hear your story. Remember to pause at intervals to allow time for me to translate as you go. Please begin."

Longwei gestured his consent, but did not immediately begin. His gaze plunged into the depths of the fire, and then raised skyward to the stars. After he had sufficiently studied the constellations* —and picked out the

---

* Chinese constellations are based on star groupings developed by ancient Chinese astronomers, and are therefore quite different from western groupings derived from Greco-Roman astronomy. There is no "Orion" in the Chinese night sky.

ancient star groupings he would use to create the outline of his story— he opened his mouth and spoke.

"Many thousands of years ago, in a mythical land existing only among the stars of the heavenly sky, a munificent blue dragon ruled the people of the eastern kingdom with kindness and wisdom. The blue dragon was not alone in the heavens. A black tortoise ruled the people who lived in the wintry northern kingdom. A white tiger ruled the people of the autumn lands of the western kingdom. A fiery red phoenix ruled the summer people of the southern kingdom. And most importantly, a powerful emperor ruled the lands of the middle kingdom and watched over all the lands with much concern.

"The blue dragon lived in a glorious castle close to the boundary of the middle kingdom, and in the castle the dragon kept his most prized possession: a young princess of the most astonishing beauty, a beauty so wondrous that few dared to look upon her for fear of being struck instantly blind. The princess lived in a high tower protected by stone ramparts and a personal guard of fierce soldiers, for the blue dragon wished to cherish the beautiful princess for many years to come. The leader of the guard was a member of the blue dragon's most decorated regiment: a young man born to modest peasants who, by virtue of personal industry and discipline, had risen to the rank of colonel and had entered the ring of the blue dragon's most trusted servants.

"One morning, when the sun settled low in the sky and dew hung on the flowers of the meadow, the blue dragon approached the colonel and said these words to him: 'As you know, my most trusted colonel who I have known for many years, the princess who you guard is my most valued possession of all my possessions in the eastern kingdom. It is because of her importance to me that I ask you at this time to vow you will never let anything happen to her, even at the cost of your own life.' The colonel bowed obediently to the blue dragon, and answered with deep reverence: 'munificent blue dragon, who rules the eastern kingdom with grace and compassion, I promise to you that I will never allow any harm to come to the princess, who I know you love dearly, even if such obedience should cost me my own life.' To this answer, the blue dragon smiled, and said: 'You are a faithful servant, my trusted colonel. I will rest peacefully during the long nights because I know my cherished princess is safely under your protection.' The colonel bowed a second time, and the blue dragon winged away to attend to the many other pressing matters of the eastern kingdom.

"Some years later, when the princess had become even more beautiful because her growing intellect and wisdom had given her countenance a distinctive glow, a dispute arose between the emperor of the middle kingdom and the blue dragon of the eastern kingdom. In reaction to the dispute, which I will fully describe in a moment, the emperor summoned his five feudal kings and the great general of the heavens to a special gathering of much importance. Because it was a beautiful day of clear skies and warm weather flowing in from the southern kingdom of the red phoenix, the emperor ordered the gathering to take place in his favorite celestial meadows to the east of the palace. Here the emperor had previously ordered his master of construction to erect a magnificent outdoor palace complete with roofs of gold floating effortlessly above intricately-carved columns, fragrant gardens planted with flowers of every imaginable kind, ornately-painted benches with cushions of fine silk, walkways of the smoothest hand-hewn stone, and waterfalls flowing with the purest water of the middle kingdom. When all had gathered, and the emperor had taken his seat with the crown prince to his right and the imperial concubine to his left, the emperor began: 'I have called this gathering to discuss an issue of the gravest importance. To fund the construction of four new palaces—to be positioned at the gateways to the northern, eastern, southern, and western kingdoms—I have requested the black tortoise, white tiger, red phoenix, and blue dragon to each pay a significant tribute to the middle kingdom. After lengthy negotiations, the complexity of which only your emperor can fathom, all have agreed with the exception of the blue dragon. I have therefore decided, although this decision greatly saddens me and has nearly moved me to tears, to take up arms against the eastern kingdom and to extract the tribute by force. This will demonstrate to the other kingdoms that such disobedience will not be tolerated. Because the time for action is already upon us, I directed the great general of the heavens to prepare a battle plan early this morning.' The great general of the heavens and the five feudal kings all bowed their heads in obedience to the emperor's great power, and departed the celestial meadows to begin preparations for battle.

"When word of the emperor's gathering reached the blue dragon, he immediately ordered his army to prepare for war, and he once again approached the colonel and reminded him of his promise to protect the beautiful princess with his very life. Three days passed, and the war began with thunder and lightning and the rush of celestial chariots. The army of the blue dragon, outnumbered by the superior forces of the emperor, fought with great valor and sacrifice, and at first won several victories, casting the outcome of the war into doubt. But over the span of several months, the armies of the five feudal kings slowly and inexorably advanced across the eastern kingdom until the blue dragon and his remaining forces were compelled to take refuge in the castle. Without hesitation, the emperor laid siege to the castle and demanded the unconditional surrender of the blue dragon and immediate payment of the tribute. And also without hesitation, the blue dragon refused both demands. The emperor demanded surrender and payment every day for the next thousand days, and the blue dragon refused a thousand times.

"The emperor eventually grew impatient of the blue dragon's steadfast disobedience, and decided to take the castle by frontal assault of the main gate, even though such an attack could result in the loss of thousands of his soldiers. Because the clever blue dragon had planted many traps around the castle, the emperor directed the celestial cow herders to clear a safe path to the main gate of the castle in front of the advancing infantry. Many cow herders and cows died, but when the path was cleared the armies of the five feudal kings moved ten wagons loaded with barrels of gun powder next to the castle's main gate. The soldiers of the blue dragon rained thousands of arrows down on the attackers and poured great caldrons of boiling oil on their heads, but to no avail. A few minutes later, a monstrous explosion ripped the main gate's massive doors off their hinges and shattered the stone walls. The armies of the five feudal kings poured into the castle and slaughtered all who resisted them.

"The colonel had watched this entire affair from one of the high parapets protecting the tower of the beautiful princess. Although he had twice promised the blue dragon he would protect her, when he heard the explosion and saw the soldiers of the five feudal kings storm through the gate he was overcome by fear and fled from his obligation. When he had reached the base of the tower, the colonel hid in a narrow alley for several hours. He killed one of the soldiers of the five feudal kings and donned his uniform to conceal his identity. Later, when the colonel was making his way out of the castle and looking for a way to escape, he walked through a large central courtyard. When he had reached the middle of the courtyard, he was greeted by the most horrifyingly nightmarish scene. There, on the other side of the courtyard, stood the blue dragon in chains. And to teach the blue dragon an eternal lesson, the emperor had ordered the beautiful princess stripped naked and her neck and hands bound into heavy wood stocks to cause her everlasting humiliation in front of the soldiers of the middle kingdom.

"When the colonel witnessed the plight of the princess—and could not avert his eyes from her sublime nakedness—he felt deep shame for both his unholy desire and his failure to protect her. Concealed by his disguise, he furtively crossed the great courtyard. Along the way he found a discarded skirt and jacket, and when he had reached the princess he pulled the skirt around her legs and tied it at her slender waist and cut the front of the jacket open with his sword and draped it around her shoulders. Their eyes met briefly, and the Princess implored, 'Please save me, favored colonel of the blue dragon.' But the colonel could not find the courage to speak to her, and simply turned away.

"The colonel jogged across the courtyard, weaving between several groups of enemy soldiers along the way. When he arrived at a narrow passageway and prepared to make his escape, he stopped to glean one last view of the beautiful princess, but his eyes met the unforgiving gaze of the blue dragon instead. The colonel averted his gaze in shame, and fled down the passageway and out of the castle. He later convinced a boatman to transport him on a river leading to the north, where he could hide in the winter kingdom of the black tortoise. And there he lives to this very day, wandering a strange land in endless disguises and consumed by shame because of his failure to protect the beautiful princess."

All were silent around the bonfire until the old man who had asked for the story coughed. He finally spoke after throwing a small log on the fire. "Not exactly a story for young children, but very good nonetheless. You may stay, Tseng Longwei."

Tseng Longwei bowed his head to the old man and stared pensively into the fire. "Thank you. I hope to prove worthy of your hospitality."

"You already have," the old man answered.

CHAPTER ELEVEN

A bath at the War Eagle Hotel
November 7, 1871

Gordania Sinclair plunged to the bottom of the bathtub—a hammered-copper single-slipper tub imported from San Francisco at great expense by the owner of the War Eagle Hotel—when heavy footsteps tromped beyond the locked door separating the second floor bathing room from the dimly-lighted hallway. After holding her breath until bubbles seeped from her nose, she gradually emerged from below the surface of the water. She arranged floating mounds of soap foam with her hands to adequately conceal her torso. Resting her neck against the rolled edge of the copper tub, she tilted her head to better see through the double-hung window of the small room, and noted the clarity of the evening and the new stars appearing in the darkening sky. A thin remnant of twilight outlined the mountains to the west before fading to deep purple beneath the lowest stars. She folded her hands across her stomach, closed her eyes, and soaked. When the water had cooled and no longer provided adequate pleasure, she pushed herself up and stepped out of the tub onto a round mat and dried herself with a white cotton towel. She finished the process by rubbing the towel vigorously over her head to dry the short-cropped black hair, which reminded her of her grave predicament whenever she viewed her reflection in a mirror. She folded the towel over the back of a chair, crossed her arms, and allowed herself a few seconds to admire the sky-blue dress she had sewn especially for the masked ball (she had hung the dress on a wood rack more often used by men to hang coats and pantaloons). She had thought of sewing a black dress to maintain the perfection of her disguise, but had finally rationalized that only a white dress might expose her true identity and that she could safely wear any other color.

After she had sufficiently examined the dress, she shifted her gaze to the full-length mirror standing next to the coat rack and critiqued the hideous scar in the flickering light of a kerosene lamp sitting on a small side table. She dropped her arms, raised her left hand, and gently ran an index finger along the length of the scar from her neck down to its jagged termination a few inches below the right clavicle. When she had first worn the blue dress, the scar had peeked mockingly above the rim of the collar. Dismayed, she had hastily removed the dress and added a narrow strip of material to fully conceal the imperfection. She covered the scar with her hand, but could still visualize every detail of the blemish beneath the closed fingers. She might have stood there longer, but the same heavy footsteps that had startled her before tromped down the hallway heading the opposite direction and ended her reverie. She lowered her hand from the scar, gathered a pair of powder-blue stockings from the back of a chair, and began to dress.

After adjusting her undergarments until they did not chafe or bind, she removed the derringer (the one Csongor had given her at the train station in Boston) from a leather valise. She stroked her thumb across the silver-finished-over-and-under barrels and dark walnut grips, then pivoted the barrels open to confirm the presence of two .41 caliber cartridges. She clicked the barrels down and slid the small pistol into a cotton holster she had sewn into her bloomers just above the right knee. She practiced removing the derringer three times, and each time pretended to shoot the scantily-clad woman facing her in the full-length mirror. She attempted an aggressive fast draw on the forth try, and juggled the pistol up in the air and nearly dropped it before catching it by the barrel with her left hand. She apologized for her clumsiness to the image in the mirror, and pushed the miniature pistol into the cotton holster until it rested comfortably against her thigh. She jiggled her leg up-and-down and side-to-side to confirm that the weapon would not accidently dislodge while dancing (or worse, fire off a round and shoot her partner in the foot). Satisfied with the security of the weapon, she reached for the glorious sky-blue dress.

Alexandra Smythe—a dress the color of a clear morning sky flowing across shapely legs and a mask the color of fresh clouds concealing impish eyes—descended the straight run of stairs from the second floor and glided across the hotel lobby. She maneuvered efficiently around a grouping of three fabric-covered chairs and a small table and walked toward the main entry. A young clerk, sitting on a stool behind the high counter in front of the hotel office and reading a dime novel, lowered the book and observed Alexandra with keen interest as she glided by. When her hand touched the doorknob, the clerk called out to her. "Excuse me ma'am. The owner wanted me to ask if you found the bathing accommodations acceptable. Did you?"

Alexandra released the knob. She hesitated before turning and walking fearlessly up to the counter. "Please tell the owner I found the accommodations quite acceptable. I will surely use them again in the future." Her nose crinkled beneath the mask.

The clean aroma of her freshly-washed body and the seductive lilt of her words distracted the young man, but then he remembered his duty as the hotel clerk. "Yes ma'am. I'll be sure to pass what you said on to him. I know he'll be pleased to hear it."

To the great disappointment of the young clerk, who had anticipated a longer conversation, Alexandra simply said, "Thank you," and quickly exited the War Eagle Hotel. She hesitated on the wood boardwalk in front of the hotel to savor the cool night air and observe the emerging constellations of the western skies. She waited for the dust to settle after an empty wagon rumbled by, then lifted the hem of her dress and stepped into the street. She did not know the precise location of the Masonic Hall—the site of the masked ball according to William Sommercamp—but she soon found a couple wearing colorful masks and followed them as they headed north on Washington. The couple walked all the way to Avalanche before turning right and then turned right again on Jordan. After a short distance, Alexandra followed the couple east through an alley between a tin shop and a cigar store before arriving in an open area fronting the Masonic Hall. A narrow footbridge crossed Jordan Creek to the south of the two-story structure, and the waters of the creek flowed smoothly beneath the building. Alexandra listened to the pleasant sound of the flowing creek until a wave of rambunctious music and stomping feet issued from a pair of open second-floor windows. She pushed a finger into each ear and proceeded to the main entry.

When she arrived at the top of the stairs and then the doorway leading to the source of the music and foot-stomping, a commotion between two large bearded men prompted her to wait. She took the opportunity to chat to the man standing next to the doorway. "Good evening, sir. I assume this is the masked ball everyone has been talking about for weeks."

The man bowed his head. "You have assumed correctly."

She felt a pang of nostalgia in her stomach as she admired the man's long black ponytail, although her longing did not include the color of it. "What are these men arguing about? It appears to be creating quite a commotion."

The man bowed his head again. "I am sorry for the disturbance, but my friend and business partner Roshan is attempting to convince the doorkeeper to allow my entrance to the party. The other man has said I am not allowed."

Alexandra squeezed the folds of her dress. "How unfortunate. Would you like me to talk to your friend and the doorkeeper? Maybe I can help."

The man shuddered. "Please do not endanger yourself on my behalf. I am perfectly happy to console myself with a long walk. I have told Roshan this same thing three times, but he has refused to listen."

Alexandra watched while the intensity of the commotion increased and the men began shoving each other. "Please excuse me, but I think it is time to make my entrance." She walked up to the men and touched each of them on the shoulder, and asked, "Good evening my fine gentlemen. Can you tell me if I have arrived safely at the masked ball?" To her surprise, the men instantly separated and, to her amusement, politely removed their hats.

The doorkeeper, a burly man of obvious strength, responded to the peculiar question (while the other man appeared dumbfounded). "Why, sure, ma'am. This here's the right location for the masked ball. You can go right on in."

Alexandra nodded respectfully before walking directly between the surprised men. She marched forward three quick steps and abruptly halted with her feet pressed together and her hands folded neatly in front. She squinted through the eyeholes of her white mask and scanned the occupants of the crowded room. When her eyes fell upon a striking young gentleman dressed in neatly-pressed pinstripe gray suit, brilliant white shirt, black string tie, and debonair gray mask with black trim, she waved. The young gentleman waved back, and she walked over to him. When she arrived at his side, the young gentleman bowed and kissed her freshly-washed hand.

When he had completed the kiss, the young man did not immediately release her hand. "If you will allow me the gentle touch of your hand a few moments longer, my lovely Alexandra, then my attendance at this dreary social event will be justified beyond what I thought possible."

Alexandra pulled her hand away. "Oh stop it, Csongor. I'm not in the mood to be teased, even by you."

Csongor smirked with subtle refinement. "I apologize, my bonnie maiden, if you think my intention is to tease. Please rest assured that you are safe to accept my words at face value."

Alexandra scrunched her eyes behind the white mask. "If I didn't know you better, I'd think you were teasing me again. But let's talk no more of it. Were you successful in luring Mr. Herrmann to the masked ball? I didn't see him when I arrived."

"Quite successful. My little ruse with William Sommercamp did the trick, and he has arrived as planned. The man you seek is sitting forlornly over there on a ridiculous three-legged stool." Csongor pointed vaguely in the direction of Manfred Herrmann. "But I trust his hopelessness will soon be assuaged by the arrival of the charming Alexandra Smythe, recently of Liverpool."

"Then I should go to his side quickly, before this endless teasing causes me to swoon."

Csongor bowed slightly. "As you wish, but I am pierced to the core of my soul if you believe the deepest musings of my heart are not authentic."

Alexandra touched Csongor near the elbow and curled her lip in a pixie smile. "Goodbye, Csongor. Enjoy the dance. Maybe you will find other young women to tease. And if you are lucky, one of them may actually enjoy it."

Alexandra began to take a step, but Csongor unexpectedly held her arm with a firm but affectionate grip. "Do not depart my side yet, my elusive lass, for the man you seek appears to be heading this way. I suggest that you look deeply into my eyes and pretend not to notice him. When he arrives, I will pretend to introduce you as if nothing is amiss."

Alexandra clicked her heels together and looked into Csongor's eyes. "Are you sure he is heading this direction? Maybe he's decided to leave and I should cut him off?"

"Quite certain, my dear. In fact, he has emerged triumphantly from the horde of dancers that once blocked his path and now stands a mere two strides away. Keep your eyes on me, and follow my lead." Csongor turned casually and feigned surprise at the sight of Manfred Herrmann, then encouraged him to approach with a cavalier wave of his hand. "Mr. Herrmann. Please join us for a moment."

Manfred acknowledged Csongor's invitation with apparent surprise. "Mr. Toth. Nice to see you again." He stepped forward and shook Csongor's hand. Alexandra waited for Manfred to notice her, but he did not look her way. She decided to say nothing, and to simply follow Csongor's lead as he had advised.

Csongor gestured with an upturned palm toward Alexandra, and spoke in a professional but relaxed tone. "This charming young lady is a dear friend of mine, and she is in desperate need of a reliable escort for the evening. You see, she prefers not to dance with just any man." Very clever, thought Alexandra, but also very peculiar because she had suggested nothing of the sort. She decided to say nothing—for the moment.

Manfred nodded toward Csongor. "Yes, I can appreciate the dilemma. Some of these fellows are a little rough around the edges." An accurate observation, thought Alexandra. But then he continued with, "I wouldn't want to dance with any of them either." Alexandra raised her hand to her lips and pressed back a giggle.

Csongor turned his head sharply and glared sternly into Alexandra's eyes in an obvious attempt to encourage Manfred to do the same. When Manfred still refused to look at her, Csongor continued, "Yes, of course. But the problem is, Mr. Herrmann . . . she prefers not to be the one to ask for a dance. She is waiting for said gentleman to ask her first."

Alexandra turned her head to receive Manfred's eyes, but when he turned his head he focused lower—on the lips or possibly the chin. Manfred held this odd position as he replied, "Oh, yes, yes. I agree completely. I wouldn't have it any other way."

Alexandra sensed both frustration and amusement in Csongor's voice, but to his credit he did not give up, and asked, "So what are your thoughts on the matter?"

Manfred countered indifferently, "What are my thoughts on what matter?"

Now Alexandra felt both frustration and amusement, and she began tapping her foot on the floor, but not in rhythm with the music. Csongor persevered by asking, "What do you think about escorting this charming young lady this evening?"

To Alexandra's surprise, Csongor had artfully maneuvered Manfred Herrmann into a corner. "Me? Are you asking me to dance with her this evening? But we've never met before."

This declaration astounded Alexandra. Until this moment she had imagined that Manfred crossed the dance floor because he recognized her. Now that she realized he had not, she regretted bringing the small pistol because it might prove a reminder of the unfortunate incident on the train. But more importantly, how would Csongor respond to this aggressive rebuff? Alexandra had to wait only a second for Csongor's clever retort: "A mere formality, which I shall rectify in a moment. But first, you must agree to accept the task at hand."

Manfred swallowed with difficulty. "I'm not much of a dancer. I can do the waltz a little, but I'm pretty flat-footed with the other dances. I wouldn't want to step on her toes."

Alexandra's eyes closed behind the mask. Clearly this man had no desire to spend even the briefest moment in her company. But as she prepared for disappointment, Csongor Toth presented his closing argument and won the day. "Nonsense, Mr. Herrmann. Dance as much or as little as you wish. She will not mind. But stay by her side as her knight in shining armor this evening, and she will be forever grateful. Do you agree to these terms, Mr. Herrmann, or do you plan to throw her to the wolves?"

Alexandra thought this a bit melodramatic, but marveled at Csongor's obvious gift of debate. Manfred swallowed hard a second time, and finally succumbed. "Well, if you put it that way, I suppose I have no choice but to accept."

Alexandra could hear the triumph in Csongor's voice when he replied, "Thank you, Mr. Herrmann. I know you are about to embark on an onerous task, and I applaud your courage for accepting. Now, before we part, may I introduce you to your companion for the evening?"

To Alexandra's surprise, Manfred Herrmann appeared crestfallen when he answered: "Yes, by all means." She determined at that moment to release him from his obligation to escort her after the first dance. An onerous task indeed!

Csongor nodded. "Mr. Herrmann, I would like to introduce you to Miss Alexandra Smythe of Liverpool, England. Miss Smythe, I would like to introduce you to Mr. Manfred Herrmann, the new Lutheran Pastor in Silver City." Alexandra watched Manfred open his mouth to say something, but before he could speak a word, Csongor interrupted, "It would be appropriate, Mr. Herrmann, to kiss her hand. Do not be afraid. She has promised me that she will not harm you in any way." Alexandra had made no such promise, but maintained silence as she waited for Manfred to take her hand. Unfortunately, he remained as still as a marble statue and did not immediately take her hand. Csongor resolved the awkward moment by suggesting, "I'll tell you what, Mr. Herrmann; I shall speak to the band this very moment and request a waltz for the next dance. This will help the two of you get off on the right foot." Amidst the final rousing chords of *Turkey in the Straw*, Csongor Toth strode confidently over to the fiddle player and whispered in his ear. The band then commenced an odd arrangement of the *Blue Danube*. When Csongor returned, Alexandra noted that Manfred had somehow maintained the same statuesque pose, and had even taken on the pallor of a marble statue. Csongor took aggressive steps to force Manfred Herrmann to action. "Alright, Mr. Herrmann, the time for action has now arrived. Please kiss Miss Smythe's hand and then ask her to dance. No more excuses."

Alexandra Smythe raised her hand, and when Manfred's kiss arrived she felt his lips tremble.

By the time the imposing grandfather clock standing in an adjacent corner of the room chimed twelve times to proclaim the beginning of a new morning, Alexandra Smythe and Manfred Herrmann had danced together well over a dozen times. In contradiction to Csongor's instructions, Manfred had allowed one fellow the chance to dance with Alexandra, but thereafter had refused the entreaties of nine consecutive men whom he considered excessively rough around the edges. The last individual complained that Manfred was not following the rules; Manfred had told him bluntly to file a complaint with the organizers of the dance if he didn't like it.

After a brief absence, Manfred returned to Alexandra's side with two glasses of lemonade. "The lady told me this might be a little sour, because she got distracted when she was adding the sugar. I guess we'll find out soon enough."

Alexandra accepted her glass contentedly. "Tell me Manfred, have you found it such an onerous task to spend your entire evening with me? Surely there are other women here who might interest you. And now the time for you to meet them has passed."

Manfred sipped the lemonade and smacked his lips twice. "This lemonade is pretty sour. I'm not sure she put much sugar in it at all." Then, without thinking, he took another sip. "No, not at all, Alex. I can't even remember spending a more delightful evening with anyone. And I must confess to you: it was my intention to do so the moment I saw you walk into the room."

Alexandra lowered the glass to her right knee. "Really? But Csongor had to use all of his charms to convince you to dance with me. I listened to the entire discussion."

Manfred attempted a smile, but the lemonade prevented it. "I must make a confession to you, Alex. I thought I recognized you when you entered the room, but it seemed too improbable to find you here in Silver City. When I walked over to where you were standing with Csongor, I couldn't summon up the courage to take a good look at you. I kept on waiting for you to say something so I might recognize your Liverpool accent, but you never did. I remembered the hair, but I couldn't be sure with the blue dress. And the mask...."

"When you told Csongor we had never met...."

"This was partially true because I couldn't be sure it was you. And it was partially untrue, because the way you walked into the room and tilted your head... well, I shouldn't really say anything more or I'll embarrass myself and you'll think I'm a fool. You probably already think I'm a liar, but I'm not too worried about it because I know the good Lord has promised to forgive my transgressions."

Alexandra finally tasted her lemonade. "Yes, I'm sure God has a long list of transgressors to forgive every day." She frowned when the lemonade flooded across her tongue. "Goodness! This lemonade *is* sour. I fear it may take me the rest of the night to finish it. I hope you don't mind waiting."

Manfred pulled a chair around and sat directly in front of Alexandra, his knees separated from hers by an electrified gap of only two inches. He slurped from his glass of lemonade and leaned forward. "Take your time. And if you do manage to finish it, there's plenty more where that came from."

In an apparent display of modesty, Alexandra slid her hand over her right knee and rested it on top of the derringer.

CHAPTER TWELVE

An English lesson… of sorts
November 8, 1871

Two hours after the grandfather clock had chimed twelve times, give or take a minute, Roshan gave the burly doorkeeper one final stern look as he prepared to stagger from the second floor of the Masonic Hall. He had no intention of speaking to the oafish brute, but when he arrived at the door he found it impossible to control his tongue. Holding fast to the doorframe with his left hand, Roshan jabbed angrily at the doorkeeper with his right. "I hope you are of the happy to lose my friend and man of business on the outside where I may not to find any of him again in the nearest time of the morning to early see." Roshan burped lustily without covering his mouth. "It is on the head of you when Roshan can find the friend in not the good. Do not be the sorry of me if you know what I hear."

The burly doorkeeper, worn out from a long night of thankless guard duty and incessant foot-stomping music, could not rouse the energy to continue the fight with Roshan. "Good luck to you," he said. And noting that his former advisory appeared a little tipsy, he warned, "Watch your step going down those stairs. Looks to me like you had a little too much to drink. I don't want to have to clean up any extra messes before I leave."

Roshan swung around and charged through the doorway. Before miscalculating the distance to the stairs and missing the top step, he yelled back, "Do you not worry much of Roshan. He is never too much to drink, of this you can be—" His voice trailed away in a rhythmic series of comical "harrumphs" as his buttocks bounced neatly against each tread all the way to the bottom.

When Roshan disappeared, the burly doorkeeper rushed to the top of the stairs. When he looked down, he found Roshan sitting cross-legged with his elbows leaned back against the second tread. When he lowered his view more, he found Roshan's hat. Unsympathetic, the burly doorkeeper picked up the rumpled hat, pretended to brush it off, wadded it up into a tight little ball, and threw it down the stairs with every ounce of strength he could muster. The burly doorkeeper marveled at his good fortune when the hat bounced off the back of Roshan's head. Still unsympathetic, he yelled, "You forgot your hat."

Embarrassed but undeterred, Roshan pushed himself up on wobbly legs, shook his head to clear the blurry images smeared across his retinas, reached down and picked the hat up from the floor, unfolded it, and crushed it on his head. In a fleeting moment of grace, he yelled up the stairs, "Thank you my man of the good for finding of my forgetful hat to be sure." He punctuated the end of his sentence with another lusty belch.

Momentarily unsettled by Roshan's good manners, the burly doorkeeper answered, "You're welcome. See you at the next dance." He almost added, "*and next time don't bring any Chinamen with you unless you want a heap of trouble,*" but decided to let it go.

Without waving or saying anything more, Roshan stumbled through the front door into the cool night air of the empty street in front of the Masonic Hall. The band had already gone home and the dancing had stopped and someone had closed the two second floor windows: the building now reclined silently in the night. He sucked in a breath to clear his head, but it didn't help much. He thought about looking for Tseng Longwei, but decided it made more sense to head back to the wagon and wait for him there. Maybe Longwei was already asleep in the back of the wagon. Maybe he should go to sleep in the back of the wagon himself because it would likely be foolish to drive back to Mahogany Gulch alone in the dark, especially in his present condition. On the other hand, the mules could probably find the way home in the dark by themselves while he slept in the back of the wagon, but this would diminish his purpose as the driver. And what if they hit another rock? Better to find the wagon and wait for Longwei there. Roshan stretched his shoulders back, sucked in another breath, and shuffled off to the north. A long building of freight stables and jumbled roofs blocked any view of Jordan Creek or the cabins beyond to the right, but to his left kerosene lights still flickered through a few second story windows and the ground floor dining room of the Idaho Hotel. A pretty young woman carrying a lantern and a round tray entered the dining room; when Roshan took his eyes from his path and followed her across the room his foot glanced off a tree root and he nearly fell to the ground. Regaining his balance, he averted his gaze from the young woman and plunged ahead into the darkness.

When Roshan reached the northeast corner of the Idaho Hotel, he angled left along the first floor kitchen and walked a meandering path down a narrow alley before arriving on Jordan Avenue. He turned left, walked about fifteen paces, stopped directly in front of the hotel, walked three more paces, and stopped again. He began talking to himself in Russian. *"I cannot believe it. I have forgotten where the wagon is parked again. Tseng Longwei always remembers where it is parked, but I am never so lucky and he is not here to point me in the right direction."* He looked south down Jordan and then shambled around and looked north. *"Maybe the wagon isn't even parked on Jordan. Maybe the wagon is parked on Washington."* Given this possibility, Roshan forged across the street toward Avalanche. When he reached the corner of Avalanche and Washington, the lights and piano music and laughter coming from the corner saloon distracted him from his search for the wagon. A man blundered through the front door of the saloon, wobbled to the front of the boardwalk, took three clumsy strides into the street, and collapsed face-down with a revolting thud. Roshan spoke to himself, again in Russian. *"Since the wagon and Longwei are nowhere to be found, it makes sense to wait in the saloon until daylight... especially since the departure of this satisfied customer has provided the space."* Roshan moseyed over to the man, and observed that the poor bastard had lost one of his boots. The man groaned and smacked his lips, and then hiccupped. Roshan spoke to the man in Russian. *"You cannot sleep here in the middle of the street, my drunken acquaintance. Please allow me to move you to a safer place."* The man coughed and began drooling. Roshan knelt down, rolled the man to his back, hooked his hands beneath the man's armpits, dragged him across the street and over the splintered boards of the boardwalk, and positioned him sitting upright against the front of the saloon. A little more sober after the hard work of moving the man, Roshan switched back to English. "You will be of the safest never in the street when the mule or wagon—who can say of which at the time of night we have with us?—will run on the top of you when you do not know it and cut the legs to a different place. I would not want to see of such a thing in my time of life, if you want to hear of my many truth." When the man offered another greasy hiccup, Roshan decided that he could do no more and proceeded to the front door of the saloon.

Inside the saloon, the blotchy light provided by three dust-caked lanterns hanging from the high ceiling (and a few more glowing on tables) appeared surprisingly bright to Roshan's fully-dilated eyes. Two glowering men and one brightly-dressed woman stood by the long bar to the right. To the left three men played cards at a table next to a window overlooking Avalanche. At the back of the saloon a wood-trimmed opening led to a gloomy room and narrow stairs ascended through the ceiling. Just beyond the end of the bar, tucked in under the stairs, a man wearing a white shirt and colorful vest played a sorrowful melody on an upright piano in desperate need of maintenance. A woman dressed completely in black from her chubby neck down to the soles of her feet sat alone at the nearest table to the left. Attracted by her wholesome physique, Roshan walked to the table and sat in a chair next to her. The woman did not immediately speak, forcing him to begin the conversation. "Tell me, my woman of goodness who wears of the blackness you cannot imagine unless you hear yourself or one surely tells of it... can you tell of the one who is of the owner in the saloon we sit, to be sure?"

After a long day of dealing with too many idiots, Margaret's reserve of patience had diminished to a precarious level. "I knew I should have gone to bed. Another useless foreigner in my saloon who can't speak a word of American."

Roshan chuckled. "Yes, is maybe of the truth of it if you say, but if you hear my lips you can tell me of the owner to see my question of the look for the something of the strangest you can't believe it when your lips hear of it."

Margaret sighed and tapped her fingers on the table. "Not only a foreigner, but a sex pervert too." Then she mumbled, "Lord, can't you send me a normal customer once in a while? I'd even be thankful if you'd

bless me with one a week. Shoot, I'd even be happy with one a month."
She glared straight at Roshan. "Let's go with one a week. Yes, I'd be happy
with a week. Is it really too much to ask?"

Roshan slapped his knee and cackled robustly. "It is of the good one,
but can you tell me who the owner of the strange?"

"You're looking at the owner. Now what is this strange request? I can
hardly wait to hear all about it."

"You are of the owner? This is of my day of the much luck. Now hear my
lips when I tell you this. I have of hope to find the whore of the strangest
on this night."

"This must be my lucky day too. Please go on."

"Now listen of the close or you misunderstand: the whore who looks
for me can speak of the English and both the Russian. Is this of the not
strangest you have heard in time of it?"

Margaret looked at one of the ceiling lanterns. "Thank you Lord." She
dropped her eyes to Roshan. "Why, you are one lucky fellow. I've got just
the gal for you." Margaret yelled across the saloon to the woman standing
at the bar. "Beverly, go upstairs and get Nadia. I've got a really special
customer just for her."

Beverly yelled back without budging, "She just got back from the
masked ball. I think she was heading to bed."

Margaret scowled. "Do as I say and go find her right now. If she's in
bed, get her out of bed. If you don't, you get to deal with the special customer—all by yourself."

Beverly sniffed, strolled to the back of the saloon, and plodded up the
narrow stairs. She came back with Nadia a few minutes later. Nadia had
just finished storing the concertina in its case and had not yet changed
from the high-collared white blouse and ankle-length gray skirt that gave
her the appearance of a school teacher. She bowed slightly when she
spoke to Margaret, and then glanced at the wall clock behind the bar—
just past 2:30 in the morning. "You wanted to see me?"

Margaret sneered and dipped her head toward Roshan. "Sure did. I've
got a fresh customer for you, a man who's looking for someone who
speaks Russian."

Moving only her eyes to glimpse Roshan, Nadia noted the uncombed
beard, dirty shirt with sleeves rolled up different lengths, and silly grin.

She decided to decline the offer. "It's late, and I'm about to head to bed. Beverly's up working. Why don't you send him off with her?"

Margaret answered the question with palpable scorn. "Now there's a fine idea, Nadia. I forgot that Beverly speaks Russian too." She instantly transferred her wrath to Beverly. "Beverly, why don't you speak a few words of Russian to this fellow?"

Beverly complained, "I don't speak no Russian, Margaret. You should know better."

Margaret fell back in her chair and laughed, then rolled forward until her ample bosom smooshed against the table. "How could I forget something so obvious? Now I remember: Nadia's the one who speaks Russian. How silly of me." She spoke derisively to Nadia. "Looks like this man is your responsibility for the night. Now take him over to the bar for a couple of drinks and then get your ass upstairs and earn your keep before I lose my temper and say something I shouldn't."

Less than pleased with her predicament, Nadia chastised Roshan in fluent Russian. *"What were you thinking, coming in here in the middle of the night asking for someone who spoke Russian? Are you out of your mind, or are you just a simple fool who likes to ask stupid questions?"*

When Roshan heard the beauty of his mother tongue, his heart swelled with sudden affection for the woman who had spoken it. *"Your Russian is superb, but I do not think you were born in mother Russia. Nonetheless, your beautiful words fill my heart with the warm glow of nostalgia for my homeland!"*

Roshan's words calmed Nadia, and she answered, *"No, I was not born in Russia. I was born in San Francisco only a month after my parents arrived in this country, but my mother died in childbirth so I never knew her."*

This unexpected information saddened Roshan. *"I am sorry to hear this. No one deserves to be without a mother, especially a young girl in a strange land."*

After listening to this gibberish, Margaret shot up and slammed both hands on the table. A beer glass rattled and nearly fell over. "Nadia! Enough of this pointless drivel. Now get this fine gentleman over to the bar for a drink like I asked."

Nadia smiled contemptuously at Margaret, and invited Roshan to the bar in the sweetest Russian she could muster. *"As you can see, Margaret is quite the witch. She even dresses in black like a witch. The only thing missing is her broom, which I believe she keeps hidden under her dress in case she needs to suddenly fly away. Shall we adjourn to the bar where we can enjoy our conversation free of her witchy interruptions?"* Nadia smiled at Margaret more politely and fluttered her eyes.

Roshan stood and held out his arm for Nadia to take. *"It would gladden my heart to accompany such a lovely woman—especially one who speaks Russian like a beautiful cherub—to yonder bar."*

Nadia set her hand on Roshan's arm, and they strolled to the bar. When the bartender looked over, Nadia asked Roshan, *"What would you like to drink? Whisky?"*

Roshan had originally intended to improve the quality of his intoxication when he entered the saloon, but now he changed his plans. *"No, I think not. Now that I have found you, I would prefer a large cup of hot coffee, if you have it."*

Nadia removed her hand from Roshan's arm. *"Suit yourself, but the bartender will charge you more for coffee than a glass of whisky because he'll have to brew a fresh pot."* She waved at the bartender; he walked slowly along the back of the bar until he stood directly across from Nadia. "My special guest would like a large cup of fresh coffee."

The bartender picked up a dirty shot glass and began cleaning it with a stained rag tucked into his belt. It's past two in the morning. Tell your guest to move along to one of the hotels if he wants a cup of coffee after midnight."

Nadia cooed, "Now John, it won't take you long to make it. And you don't appear very busy at the moment. Should I fetch Margaret and ask her opinion?"

The bartender stored the glass beneath the bar with a sharp click. "Don't you dare get Margaret involved in this. She'll just tell me to make the coffee, and probably dock my pay at the same time. I'll go make it right now, but I'm not going to like it and I'm going to charge your special guest extra for all the trouble he's causing me."

Nadia quipped, "Thank you John for understanding. I already warned him you'd charge extra." She turned to Roshan and asked in Russian, *"Is this alright with you?"*

Roshan touched Nadia's hand, and she did not pull it away. *"I just got paid this week by Mr. Gustus. It should not be a problem, although the price of things in Silver City always surprises me. I am used to paying less in places like Seattle and San Francisco."*

Nadia's voice lifted. *"You have been to San Francisco?"*

Emboldened by Nadia's interest in San Francisco, Roshan slid his fingers a nearly imperceptible distance across the top of Nadia's hand to stroke it without appearing to do so intentionally. *"Yes, a little over three years ago. I escorted a shipment of lumber from Seattle to a construction project in San Francisco. But I only stayed a few weeks. After I bought a good horse and some supplies, I rode east straightaway."*

When the bartender returned with the coffee, he scoffed, "Here's your coffee. I hope you don't' want any sugar or milk, because if you do you're plumb out of luck."

Roshan opened his mouth to protest, but Nadia raised her hand and touched his lips. "Fine, John. I'm sure my guest prefers his coffee black." She turned to Roshan and continued in Russian, *"Isn't that right, mister… why, I don't even know your name. How thoughtless of me to have forgotten to ask."*

Roshan pulled Nadia's hand away from his mouth and gently squeezed it. *"Do not worry of it. My name is Roshan Kuznetsov, but please call me Roshan—like everyone else does."* He reached across the bar, shoved his fingers through the handle of the ceramic cup, drank some of the coffee, set the cup down, and wiped his hand across his lips. When Roshan addressed the bartender directly, Nadia heard his first words of English: "I must say this of you, my man of good goodness—if you have time to hear of my lips say to it—but this coffee is of the much hot I do not know of before the today. To make of this is hardly to believe one can see, if you know what is it I tell you when you listen in the time of now."

Nadia shivered, and scolded in English, "Goodness gracious. That was the most impressive display of needless words I've ever heard, and I've heard quite a few."

Roshan interpreted this as a compliment, and felt new inspiration to speak more English. "Thank you of the very much, to see my lips say to the coffee of this man in the saloon who knows of nothing to see of—"

Nadia touched Roshan's lips again. "Shush, Roshan. I don't think a second flurry of needless words is necessary to make your point, although I'm not sure what the point is." Roshan tried to speak again, but Nadia pressed a little harder. "No, don't say a word." She switched back to Russian. *"Roshan, I do not want to hurt your feelings, but if you were a student in my class I would never tolerate such pointless ramblings."*

Roshan pulled Nadia's hand away from his lips. *"You were a teacher?"*

A little embarrassed by her present livelihood, Nadia clarified, *"Sort of. I was hired once to teach children in a real school house, but something happened before the first day of school and I had to leave town."*

Roshan swigged another gulp of the really hot coffee. *"Something happened? What could possibly have happened to make you leave before the first day of school?"* He nearly said: *"...and become a whore,"* but held his tongue.

Nadia's expression hardened. *"It is not something I care to talk about."*

Roshan instantly noticed the change in Nadia's face and smoothly diverted the conversation. *"It does not matter. And as far as I am concerned, if you were hired to teach children, then you are a teacher. It does not matter whether or not you actually taught the children. It is the same."*

Nadia relaxed. *"Thank you, Roshan. I appreciate your kind words."*

An idea exploded in Roshan's head. *"Nadia, I have an idea. My English is pretty good, as you may have noticed; but nonetheless, would you be willing to teach me to speak English even better? I would be thankful if you would."*

Nadia balked at the idea. *"Well, I don't know..."*

Margaret, who had grown impatient watching the lack of progress, unexpectedly appeared. "Nadia, isn't it time for the two of you to get upstairs?"

Nadia explained, "I was just discussing the possibility of giving Mr. Kuznetsov English lessons." She thought of saying something snippier, but resisted the temptation.

Margaret snorted, "English lessons? Are you serious? Tell you what, Nadia. I don't care if you want to teach him English or anything else between the sheets. The rate's still the same and my cut's still the same."

Nadia hissed, "Fine, Margaret." She spoke to Roshan in Russian. *"Shall we retire upstairs to my room and begin the lesson? As you just heard from the resident witch, the rate's the same."*

Roshan nodded and tugged Nadia away from the bar with both hands. *"Yes. I want to begin my English lessons as soon as possible. What do you think we should study tonight? I am very excited to speak English even better than I do now."*

When Roshan pulled her away, Nadia announced loudly in English so Margaret could hear: "I suggest we begin with a study of basic sentence structure, Mr. Kuznetsov, particularly the organization of the subject and predicate. I think I still have a small chalkboard and some chalk we can use for the lesson."

Margaret smacked the top of the bar and snorted even louder as Nadia and Roshan rushed toward the narrow staircase, "Go ahead, Nadia. You show him how to stick his subject into your predicate. The rate's still the same and my cut's still the same."

Without looking back, Nadia replied caustically, "Thank you for reminding me, Margaret. I almost forgot."

CHAPTER THIRTEEN

A business meeting after the masked ball
November 8, 1871

T he hour of two in the morning had arrived, and Csongor Toth waited for the door to his office to open. His business associates, Seth, Jackson, and Miguel—and a new man who claimed the moniker of Jeb Wheezer—sat impatiently in hard wooden chairs scattered to his left. At exactly 2:02 am, the door opened with a long metallic squeal and the man named Elijah Brown entered the room. The door squealed again when he closed it.

Csongor stood behind his desk and noted the time on his pocket watch. "I must assign someone to oil those hinges. The high pitched sound is quite annoying." He dropped the watch into a coat pocket and, without betraying any particular sentiment, measured the man now standing in his office. "You are late, Mr. Brown. The time of our meeting was set at exactly two o'clock. According to my watch—which I take great pains to maintain in an accurate condition—it is now two minutes after the appointed hour. This is not an auspicious beginning to our future business partnership."

Elijah Brown rested his hand on the curved handle of the Smith & Wesson Model 3 revolver* carried in a simple black-leather holster hanging from a stiff black-leather belt. The color of his pantaloons

---

* Smith & Wesson introduced this single-action, cartridge-firing, top-break revolver in 1869. Elijah Brown's pistol is chambered for the .44 S&W American centerfire cartridge.

roughly matched the color of the holster, and the color of his shirt achieved a shade only slightly lighter than the pants. His black-leather boots matched the hue of the holster, and the flat-brimmed hat, set at a slightly forward angle on his head to express unrivaled self-confidence, matched the tone of the shirt to complete the utter blackness of his attire. Elijah Brown did not appear to care that the moment of his arrival did not coincide with Csongor's pocket watch, nor did he believe in the purported accuracy of the timepiece. He explained dryly, "I had a little business to clean up in Dodge City, otherwise I would have arrived on time."

Csongor nodded. "Just so. As you may have already discerned from the odd expressions of my business associates, we were not expecting an Ethiopian shootist."

Elijah Brown blinked. "Beg pardon?"

Csongor waved his left hand in the air. "An African, Mr. Brown. We were not expecting an African. With a name like Elijah, I assumed you would have at least some knowledge of the Bible."

"Didn't come from Africa. I was born in Texas."

"Your place of birth makes little difference to me, Mr. Brown. But now we have a different issue on the table. Stated quite frankly, Mr. Brown, I had assumed all gunmen were white. I had no idea you were not when I made the decision to send for you."

Elijah Brown tapped his thumb on the hammer of the revolver. "I'm glad to leave if you don't think I'm right for the job. But I'd expect to be paid for my trouble."

Csongor noticed a feathery curl of paint peeling off the wall in the distance a few inches above the peak of Elijah's black hat. "That won't be necessary, Mr. Brown. Your credentials are impeccable, and I see no reason why we shouldn't come to a mutually-beneficial agreement. Please sit and we shall discuss the business at hand."

Jackson scowled when Elijah Brown stepped toward the chair, and blurted, "I can't believe you're going to hire a n—"

Csongor held up his hand to cut Jackson off. "Hold the thought, Jackson. Might I remind you that your job is to listen, and to speak only when asked? I will conduct the negotiations with Mr. Brown. The color of his complexion is not your concern."

Jackson's hands squeezed into fists and his boot vibrated ominously against a loose floor board. "But it is my business if you're going to hire a good for nothing n—"

Csongor snapped his fingers so loudly that Miguel jumped in his chair. "I'm warning you, Jackson. If you cannot hold your tongue as I have instructed, I will have no choice but to ask Miguel and Seth to escort you outside. If more encouragement is required, I can certainly invite Mr. Wheezer to participate in the task as well. Do I make myself perfectly clear?"

Jackson slumped in his chair and his foot stopped vibrating, but he did not unclench his fists. "I'll shut up, but I don't much like it." Then he muttered, "Don't much like it at all."

Csongor gestured and Elijah Brown sat in the last unoccupied chair in the room—without releasing his hand from the Smith & Wesson Model 3. "Excellent. Then since we are in agreement about the format for the meeting, let us begin." Csongor settled into his chair, opened a dark wood box on his desk, and selected a cigar. He skillfully bit off the end and spit it into a waste basket by the side of the desk. He pulled open a narrow pencil drawer above his knees, found a wood match, struck it on the front of the drawer, drew the flame into the cigar to light it, and exhaled a haze of bluish smoke above the desk. He asked Elijah, "Would you care for a cigar, Mr. Brown?"

Elijah removed his hand from the pistol, but kept it close. "No thanks, Mr. Toth. Never found much use for the habit."

Csongor sucked on the cigar and exhaled more smoke as he spoke. "Whisky? I can offer a very expensive brand imported from Scotland. I'm sure you would find it quite satisfactory."

Elijah quipped, "Don't have much need to drink neither. Don't like the way it throws off my aim and clouds my thinking."

Csongor spit a bit of tobacco leaf onto the floor and rubbed his bottom lip with the tip of his little finger. "A pity, but I'm sure my business associates will not mind because there will be more for them ... although I am still not convinced they appreciate the superb quality of this imported product of Scotland."

Elijah straightened up in the chair. "Not here to talk about whisky or cigars. The telegram said you had an important business proposition.

Also said you thought I was the right man for the job and I'd get paid a lot of money if I got the job done. That's why people hire me in the first place: because I always get the job done."

Csongor relaxed against the back of his chair and puffed lightly at the cigar between sentences. "Yes, of course. I did send the telegram, and I'm sure you are curious to hear of my proposition. Let me begin by saying that the business I have in mind involves some killing. I assume this will not pose a problem for you, Mr. Brown."

Elijah Brown appeared deep in thought before announcing, "I don't mind killing, but it depends on what kind of killing you got in mind."

Csongor flicked an ash into a ceramic ash tray, balanced the cigar on the rim of the tray, and pressed the tips of his fingers together just below his cleanly-shaved chin. "An excellent observation, Mr. Brown. I can see that you are a practical man who does not kill only for the love of it… as some do. Then let me present the full details of my idea, and you can decide for yourself."

Elijah Brown folded his arms across his chest and stretched out his legs. "I'd appreciate it. Like you said, I generally want to know what I'm getting into before I agree to anything."

Csongor stood to allow the opportunity to roam the office freely while talking. He did not pick up the cigar, and the smoke rose in a slender plume before dispersing near the ceiling. "Let me begin, Mr. Brown, by offering some background. The typical Silver City resident maintains an unwholesome fear of Indian attack at all times. In my opinion, this fear is generally unfounded, because the most recent incident of which I am aware occurred a long time ago, in 1864 to be precise. In this particular year a group of twenty-one intrepid men pursued and then cornered three-hundred Indians in a rocky canyon with, as you might imagine, less than satisfactory results. I will not go into details, but you can probably picture how this turned out on your own. However, because of this truly gruesome affair a deep-seated fear of Indians still persists to this day, and I have an idea to turn this fear into a lucrative business enterprise."

Jackson could not keep his mouth shut. "How you going to do that?"

Csongor glared briefly at Jackson before looking away. "I will let this interruption go, Jackson, as your question is germane to my presentation."

Jackson whispered in Miguel's ear, "What does 'germane' mean?"

Miguel shrugged and whispered back, "I don't know. Maybe he'll explain later."

Csongor strolled to the double-hung window near the front door and peered into the darkened street. "As with all good ideas, my plan is simple. I will offer protection from the Indians to the locals, particularly those with outlying mining claims. But to guarantee financial success, I must first create a new incident: one which will adequately intensify fear in every heart."

Elijah Brown demanded, "What kind of incident? I'm not sure what you're getting at."

"I'm glad you asked, Mr. Brown. I will arrange for a group of Indians from one of the regional tribes to dispatch an innocent family and burn their wagon to the ground... after said family has travelled some distance from Silver City, of course." Csongor used his thumb to rub a smudge off the glass.

Elijah Brown snapped, "What do you mean by dispatch? You gonna send them a letter?"

"I have no intention of sending anyone a letter, Mr. Brown. By 'dispatch,' I mean terminate, exterminate, eliminate, eradicate, extirpate, liquidate, immolate, annihilate, assassinate, depopulate, obliterate, purge, destroy, execute, slay, massacre, slaughter, butcher... or something along those lines. Please feel free, Mr. Brown, to insert your favorite action verb into the discussion."

Elijah Brown smirked, "Don't know a thing about no action verb, but I do know there's no way you can talk an Indian into killing for you. Your plan is not as simple as you say."

Csongor pivoted away from the window, faced Elijah Brown directly, took one step forward, and slid his hands into the pockets of his pantaloons. "Therein rests the inherent beauty of my plan. I don't have to communicate with any Indians. This is because you, Mr. Brown, will complete the task for me. You may have to hire a few unscrupulous locals to assist, but when you have finished the job no one in Silver City will suspect my connection to the crime in any way."

"Your plan don't make a lick of sense. Why is anyone in Silver City going to believe Indians did it when it was actually me?"

"Must I state the obvious? Because you, Mr. Brown, will dispatch the family and mutilate the bodies using Indian weapons and techniques. And, of course, you will take scalps. There must be scalps."

Elijah Brown abruptly stood and squeezed the grips of his Smith and Wesson Model 3. "You must be crazy. No way I'm going to kill women and children." His hand twitched on the revolver. "I'll go a step further, Mr. Toth: no way I'm killing an innocent father neither. If you want to do this kind of killing, you'll have to find somebody else or do it yourself."

Csongor walked casually back to the desk, sat in his chair, picked up the cigar, flicked off an inch of ash, and enjoyed a deep breath of fragrant smoke. He slouched in the chair and gazed dreamily at the ceiling as he exhaled. "I must inform you, Mr. Brown, that I am profoundly disappointed in your response to my proposal. I had no idea your willingness to kill would be constrained by such an extreme sense of morality. I would not have sent for you if I had known this important bit of information beforehand. I strongly recommend that you add this exception to your resume to properly inform future clients of your limitations."

Elijah Brown shook his head. "You're just plumb crazy." Speaking forcefully, he declared, "I expect to get paid for my trouble before I leave town. I turned down another job in Tombstone to come here."

Csongor puffed the cigar, "Of course, Mr. Brown." He opened a side drawer and procured a small leather pouch. "Jackson, please escort Mr. Brown back to the Idaho Hotel. When you have arrived safely at said destination, present him with this pouch of gold dust as compensation for his professional expenses." Csongor tossed the pouch across the room.

Jackson snatched the pouch out of the air, then stood and grabbed Miguel and Seth by their shoulders and pulled them to their feet. "Sure thing, boss. You still want me to handle this like you said before?"

Csongor sniffed. "Like I said before? Oh yes, yes, of course. Please handle it like I said before. And when you have finished your work, return here with your associates. Unfortunately, we are now compelled to discuss an alternate plan." After crushing the cigar into the ash tray, he intoned, "Although it pains me to suggest it, we may have to participate in a more direct manner than I had originally planned. This will certainly increase the risk of discovery, but I'm confident something can be worked out to guarantee a satisfactory result. Oh well. Such is life in the wilderness. One must be flexible to survive. Goodbye, Mr. Brown. Safe travels to your next assignment, wherever that might be."

Elijah Brown touched the brim of his hat. "Thank you, Mr. Toth. I hope you will have no hard feelings if I say you should try some other line of work."

"Of course, Mr. Brown. No hard feelings whatsoever. And I hope you will keep our little conversation to yourself. I'm sure you understand what I mean." Csongor arranged some meaningless papers on top of his desk.

Elijah Brown nodded. "Of course, Mr. Toth. I'm a professional. I promise not to tell a sole about this meeting, even though it might be pretty tempting."

"Thank you, Mr. Brown. I would expect nothing less from, as you say, a professional such as yourself."

With the meeting apparently adjourned, Elijah Brown strode through the front door into the dark street. Jackson, Miguel, Seth, and the new man Jeb Wheezer, followed closely behind.

The mongrel of a dog had emerged from behind a ramshackle cabin shortly after Tseng Longwei had said his goodbyes at the bonfire, and now he could not convince the beast to leave. He swung around and pretended to throw a rock at the pathetic creature, then quickly trotted away. The display momentarily deterred the animal, but when Longwei glanced over his shoulder, the dog reappeared in his peripheral vision. Longwei stopped and turned again, and attempted to convince the dog to find someone else to bother with logic. "Listen to me, dog. You must go someplace else. I have to find my friend Roshan and return to Mahogany Gulch in the wagon. It does not make good sense for you to follow me. You are just wasting your time." The dog panted softly and thumped its tail against the ground. Longwei folded his hands together and tried a different argument. "If you follow me, I will not give you any food. You are better off returning to where you came from." The dog stood and panted loudly and whimpered. Longwei continued, "Do you not understand what I am telling you? You cannot come with me. Please go." Longwei trotted away, and the mongrel of a dog followed.

When Longwei approached the wagon, with the dog now very close to his side, he could see Roshan taking a nap in the back. He walked up to the wagon and prepared to wake Roshan so they could begin the journey back to Mahogany Gulch, but when he looked more closely he realized the man taking a nap in the back of the wagon was not Roshan. Longwei said to the dog, "This is very strange, dog. I thought this was Roshan in the wagon, but now I see it is not. It is a man with no boots dressed only in long underwear." The man groaned, and when Longwei pushed the man on the shoulder to wake him up, he felt something sticky. Longwei rubbed the sticky substance between his thumb and fingers. He pulled a wood match from his pocket and struck it on the wagon wheel. When the flame erupted, Longwei could see that the curly black hair of the man's head, and the arms and back of his long underwear, where drenched in blood. Longwei stared at the blood until the match singed his finger. He tossed the match to the ground and said to the dog, "This man is in very poor health. Fortunately, a Good Samaritan has placed him in my wagon, allowing me to find him and offer my help." The dog tilted his head and his tail thumped the ground. "I agree we should take him to a doctor. I have been told about a new doctor who has opened a place in the building across the street from the War Eagle Hotel. I think we should take this poor man there now. I fear he may die if we stand here and do nothing." The dog jumped and barked. "Be quiet, dog. You will wake up the dead if you bark in the middle of the night." Tseng Longwei walked to the back of the wagon, pulled the man closer, and then lifted him onto his shoulders. As he prepared to take a step, Longwei grunted to the dog, "He is a very big man, but I think I can carry him to the new doctor if I do not think only of myself. It is not too far from here." Longwei trudged away from the wagon with the broken and bloodied stranger slung over his back. The mongrel of a dog trotted along by Longwei's side.

Excerpt from

A Concise History of the West

by Muireall Anne Ravenscroft

Of Dime Novels and Shootists

Regrettably, too many Americans (and likely many Euro-peans as well) have learned much of what they know of the old west from dime novels. Because I believe this phenomenon is especially pervasive when considering the common perceptions of the shootist, or, more prosaically, the gunman, this presumption can be illustrated through a review of several of the more lurid examples specific to the genre.* However, before beginning this exposition, it would be useful to review a brief history of the dime novel itself.

Irwin P. Beadle & Co. (later Beadle & Adams) published what is considered the very first dime novel in 1860. Titled "Malaeska: The Indian Wife of the White Hunter," it was the initial book in a series called "Beadle's Dime Novels." Produced as an inexpensive paperback, it established a style and format that would continue for many years. Although originally considered an experiment, the company ultimately sold millions of copies of its various dime novels, prompting many others to produce similar books and thereby igniting a successful publishing market that has extended into the 1900s. The earliest dime novels were roughly four by six inches and typically 100 pages in length, but publishers soon began trying out other formats. As an example, "nickel weeklies" were produced to cost less than dime novels by using larger pages with multiple columns to squeeze more text into fewer sheets of paper. Examples of this variation include Beadle's "Half-Dime Library" and Street & Smith's "Tip Top Weekly." Intended to appeal to a diverse audience of readers, the earliest dime novels presented stories of adventure and romance on the American frontier. Other popular

---

* Although the number of published dime novels was vast and encompassed nearly every genre, my research focused on the dozen examples I selected and purchased at a university bookstore specializing in used, rare, and out-of-print books. Because dime novels were manufactured with the cheapest possible materials, it is unlikely that many will survive the passage of time unless they are archived by private collectors.

settings included historical events, such as the Civil War, and the sea. In later years tales of the west -- particularly cowboys, Indians, and outlaws -- became increasingly popular. Usually published in a numbered series and often updated with a new title every week, most dime novels incorporated illustrated covers (some in color) foretelling the daring exploits to be found within the fragile pages.

And now let us examine a few examples from my modest collection of dime novels (and nickel weeklies). "The Masked Avenger or Death on the Trail," an 1873 book from Beadle's Dime Novels, No. 286, written by Colonel Prentiss Ingraham, has a cover illustrated with said avenger shooting a man at some distance while kneeling precariously on a rocky outcrop. The avenger sports a large ring in his left ear and a bandana trails rakishly from beneath the back of his sombrero. The first few paragraphs of the novel set the tone for the remainder of the story:

A bivouac of bandits! A wild, picturesque scene, never beheld except on the far frontier, where civilization's footprints have left few traces, or in the wildest recesses of Mexican scenery, where the robber and the renegade, the Comanche and the wild beast have their haunts.

An encampment of robbers! men (sic) outlawed from the marts of the world where honesty is enthroned; men who have dyed their hands in human blood, and bartered their souls to Satan.

A more evocative description follows, but near the end of the first chapter, the author finally provides indisputable proof of the Masked Avenger's shooting prowess:

Ere an answer could be returned there came the distant report of a rifle; a small puff of smoke broke from the foliage on the hillside, and with a cry of agony, Red La Roche sunk to the ground, while a stream of blood trickled from a small bullet-wound in his temple.

We can only assume that the Masked Avenger was indeed aiming for Mr. La Roche's temple, a remarkable shot by any standard, and that he employed a small caliber round that did not explode from the other side of the man's face as would have been the result with the minie ball commonly employed during the Civil War. At the beginning of chapter two, we learn that the Masked Avenger was not kneeling on a rocky outcrop as shown on the cover, but instead took the astonishing shot while mounted on a horse. The author also appears confused about the extent of foliage on the hillside:

Devoid of foliage, the little spur of the hillside was a rocky pedestal upon which stood the horseman, for both steed and rider, being photographed against the blue sky, appeared more like statuary than objects of life, as, having reloaded his weapon, the man sat motionless in the saddle, one hand firmly holding the bridle-reins, the other grasping the deadly rifle, as if to bring it into immediate use again, should occasion require.

Now the reader is even more astonished, as it is discovered that the Masked Avenger was not only sitting on a horse, but took the shot with one hand because his other hand was "firmly holding the bridle-reins." The author describes the Masked Avenger's colorful attire a few paragraphs later:

Attired in a Mexican suit of black velvet, embroidered with gold braid, and ornamented adown (sic) the sides of the pants pants (sic) with gilt bell-buttons, the erect and graceful form was displayed to remarkable advantage, fully exhibiting the power and agility of the man, whose face was completely hidden by a closely-fitting mask of steel, such a covering for the face as the knights of old were wont to wear when clad in full armor.

I am not a shootist myself -- I have only fired a rifle and a revolver once each as part of my research -- but I imagine the shot was made even more difficult with a "closely-fitting mask of steel" in the way. But now on to the second example, a nickel weekly published in 1901 as part of Frank Tousey's "Pluck and Luck Complete Stories of Adventure" series titled "Jack Hawthorne of No Mans (sic) Land; or, An Uncrowned King." The author is listed as NONAME: one can only assume that the book's content was too controversial for the times and that the writer preferred anonymity to public scorn. The full-color cover displays a saloon scene in which a young cowboy with flowing golden locks and wearing buckskin and sombrero is brandishing a six-shooter aimed at a bearded man crawling on the floor while the bartender and five other men casually witness the fracas in the background. The dialogue beneath the illustration reads: "I said you were going to crawl, and now I'll prove it," he continued. "Get down on your hands and knees, and crawl for that door, or as surely as I'm Jack Hawthorne, I'll have you carried out, feet first; crawl, I tell you!" I don't agree with much of the punctuation, but Mr. NONAME evidently believed that a generous sprinkling of commas and semicolons improved clarity. Chapter 1, subtitled "Wasp's Nest," begins with these harrowing words:

"I think I have the drop on you, Black Harry, but if you are not entirely convinced of the fact, just lower your hands a little and I'll prove it by laying you out cold!"

Skipping ahead more than a few paragraphs but still on the first page of the opening chapter, which is impressively dense with text....

At the middle of one of the card tables, and therefore the most conspicuous, stood Jack Hawthorne of No Man's Land, with a self-cocking six-shooter held firmly in his extended right hand, the muzzle pointed directly at Black Harry's heart.

And skipping ahead again to the middle of page two where we are regaled of Jack Hawthorn's proficiency as a shootist....

The moment he was strong enough to hold weapons in his hands, he began to study their uses, and his wonderful proficiency amounted almost to magic.

Indeed, many who knew him, and who had the shoots of superstition still sprouting in their ignorant hearts, said openly that he practiced black art, and was a veritable imp of the devil.

Of every known weapon he was a complete and perfect master.

With the revolver, even the quickest were slow when compared to him, and he would send a ball as unerringly from one position as another.

Jack was the only man in the region who never allowed a weapon to show upon his person.

To meet him upon the road one would suppose him to be unarmed, and yet, if the occasion required, he would stretch out his arms, while a six-shooter, small of size, but of large caliber, would seem to materialize in his grasp.

The report would follow instantaneously, and the missile, without any apparent effort on Jack's part, would strike exactly upon the object he had intended, no matter how small.

He had been known upon one occasion to actually shoot a revolver out of the hands of a man who had "got the drop on him," effectually disarming his adversary with no injury being inflicted beyond a natural numbness of the hand and wrist, resulting from the sudden shock.

After reading this stirring little description, I can see that the Masked Avenger was a rank amateur when compared to Jack Hawthorne of No Man's Land. And now to my third and final example, a juicy nickel weekly published by Street & Smith in 1902 (only five years ago) titled "Nick Carter and the Kidnapped Heiress or The Recovery of a Great Ransom." The writer's attribution is "By the author of NICHOLAUS CARTER" at the beginning of chapter one, but no other name is given. The full-color cover illustration shows four outlaws, two with guns slung from their belts, overpowering a young man dressed in dark brown suit and black felt bowler and holding a revolver in his left hand. The young man has been forced against a large boulder, and the third man looms above him with a rope in his hands, ostensibly to tie the young man up. Three other men can be seen in the distance, apparently panning for gold. The caption beneath reads: "Patsy was seized violently from behind." The book begins innocuously enough with these lines:

"Mr. Carter, can I trust you?"
It was in the great detective's own house that this question was asked.
"Well," was Nick's quiet answer, "if you had any doubt on the matter, why did you come to me?"
His caller looked nervously at the floor.
"There's no use in talking to me," Nick went on, "unless you do trust me." A detective can do nothing for a client who does not give him his confidence absolutely."

"Of course," the other assented; "I did not mean to offend you."

"You haven't offended me."

"I am so disturbed by it, you see. So much depends on secrecy. It is so terribly important that I found it difficult to make up my mind to consult anybody on the matter; and yet I know by your reputation that you are a perfectly trustworthy man. There is nobody in the States more so."

With this pompous endorsement completed, we must now look to Canada or Mexico to find a more trustworthy individual. Later in the book, a different detective, an associate of Nick Carter with the unlikely moniker of "Patsy," demonstrates his credentials as a shootist:

Quick as a flash, therefore, without moving from his place, and before Bloody Sam could cock his revolver again, Patsy drew one of his own barkers and fired.

Nobody in the room knew what he was about till they heard the bang! and saw the puff of smoke that rolled away from in front of the detective.

"I don't dance for anybody in Helena, see?" said Patsy, quietly.

"Wow, ouch! dang!" (sic) howled Bloody Sam, as his revolver flew from his hand.

Patsy's bullet had struck it on the butt.

It not only caused Bloody Sam to drop the weapon, but it numbed his fingers.

And the bullet did another thing.

Glancing from the place where it stuck Sam's revolver, it flew across the room and hit another man on the cartridge belt, doing no harm, but startling that man fearfully.

Shooting a revolver out of a man's hand and causing numbness appears to be a pattern in these books. But,

as far as I know because I have only read a dozen dime
novels, not even Jack Hawthorne perfected the art of
the ricochet. It also appears that publishers of dime
novels must have paid their writers by the paragraph,
which is the only reasonable explanation for....

John Ravenscroft scythed off another swath of shaving cream and whis-kers beneath his chin then rinsed the straight razor in the basin. He raised the blade to commence another run, but then lowered it and observed the reflection of Muireall's knees and head in the mirror. "Do you still have those, those, what did you call them … dime novels?"

Luxuriating in the hot water and bubbles of the porcelain tub, Muireall answered lazily, "Yes, I still have them. I might need them for more research. Why do you ask?"

John tapped the straight razor on the edge of the basin. "Oh, I don't know." He turned and spoke to Muireall directly. "I was thinking I would try to give them a good read. That's all."

Muireall scooted up a little and the sudsy water swirled around her shoulders. "Why would you want to read them? You should've gotten the idea from my manuscript that I don't think much of them. I actually think they are rather poorly written, and some of them are really quite trashy. I don't think you should bother. I'm sure it would be a waste of your time."

John gestured with the straight razor. "But I *want* to read them. Your limited excerpts only served to whet my appetite for more. I have to find out what happens to the Masked Avenger. And that Jack Hawthorne fellow, what a shootist he is! Although, I must admit, Patsy the detective is an amazing shootist in his own right."

Muireall sat up completely; the sudsy water swirled around her breasts and her knees disappeared beneath the surface. "Jack Hawthorne and the others are ridiculous fictional characters. I doubt anyone can shoot in the manner portrayed by the alleged writers. If you paid any attention at all, you would understand my deep objection to this sort of drivel and its negative effect on our understanding of American history."

"Is it true that you purchased only twelve books? Is the bookstore where you bought them nearby? Do they still cost only ten cents?"

Muireall stood and water streamed down her legs. "Please hand me my towel. The bath is no longer pleasurable for me. I need to get ready for our dinner party anyway."

John grinned through the shaving cream. "I'll hand you the towel when you answer my questions."

Muireall covered her bosom with her arms. "That's absurd. Hand me my towel."

John seized the towel from the rack and held it just out of Muireall's reach. "It's not absurd. Answer the questions. Then you shall have your towel."

"You would make me stand in the bath unclothed until I answer your silly questions?"

John moved the towel a bit closer, but when she reached for it, he yanked it away. "It appears that I shall win whether you answer the questions or not."

Muireall sighed. "Oh, for goodness' sake. Yes I purchased only twelve books and no the bookstore is not nearby and yes I paid only ten cents each. Satisfied?"

John dropped the razor into the basin, opened the towel, and affectionately wrapped it around his wife. "That wasn't so hard, was it?"

Muireall stepped from the tub and began vigorously drying. "It was excruciatingly hard, if you must know."

John picked up the straight razor and prepared to finish shaving. "Oh, I forgot to ask. Where did you hide the twelve copies and where exactly is this bookstore located?"

Muireall dried her hair and secured the towel around her torso. "Now that I have my towel, you shall never know."

CHAPTER FOURTEEN

The strange dream of Joshua Hotah
November 8, 1871

S mudgy penumbras flitted beyond the diaphanous veil of mist but Joshua Hotah could not make them out even though the shadows appeared at times to drift closer when he glimpsed them from the corner of his eye but they also appeared to move away at the same time when he saw them from the corner of his other eye and he really could not say which direction they went. He reached out his hand and pulled a swirl of the warm sticky mist to his mouth and pressed the warm sticky mist against his lips and licked it with his tongue and it tasted like the acrid smoke of burning cottonwoods when he played by the river as a child and lightning struck the dry ground and ignited the prairie grasses until they roared with great leaping flames and surged with billowing clouds of black smoke all around him and made him run. He slowly chewed the mist and swallowed it and the taste of foul decay gushed against the back of his tongue and he tried to gag but then did not feel the need and he fell to his knees and prepared to press his finger against the back of his tongue to gag again but when his hands touched the ground it also felt warm and sticky like the mist. Still on his knees he straightened up and raised a hand to his face and finger-rubbed his face and the inside of both nostrils and the inside of both ears and the smell of blood flowed down into his lungs and the sound of blood poured through both eardrums and throbbed deep inside his head. He raised up and stood because he imagined something creeping up from behind because he thought he heard the sound of creeping between the pounding throbs of the blood pouring through his ears and he tried to turn around to look but his feet refused to move and his head would not turn and he soon realized he could only look straight ahead and could not look behind to see if some fearful creature with sharp fangs and claws and glowing eyes now loomed behind where he could not see and that his feet truly would not move even when he tried to move them with all his strength.

A white raven the color of the moon on a cloudless winter night appeared not from the sky but hopped comically out of the mist jumping on both legs at the same time until it stood directly in front of Joshua and the white raven cocked its head to look up at Joshua and spoke after a long time of looking but maybe it was only a few seconds because it was hard to tell in the mist when Joshua Hotah still worried about the fearful creature standing behind him. "I have waited for you Joshua Hotah many years and now you have finally arrived and I have something to tell you but you must still wait longer to hear what I have to say because I am not ready to say it quite yet but promise I will say it in my own good time if you will promise to wait for me."

Joshua allowed his thoughts to plunge into the mystical blue eyes of the white raven and he tried to take a step closer to the white raven so he could see it even better but his feet remained trapped in the warm sticky ground that smelled like blood and after trying many more times he decided to just stand there and to never again try to walk or turn around. "Why can't you tell me now because I don't know how much time I have before I must leave and I didn't know a raven could talk anyway and why didn't you fly from the sky because it is strange to see you walk on the ground when you can fly?"

The white raven hopped closer to Joshua and then cocked its head the other way and studied Joshua's face to be sure it was really Joshua Hotah and not someone else who the white raven had no desire to talk to because his message was meant only for Joshua Hotah and not for some other interloper the white raven had no desire to talk to. "It surprises me you did not know ravens could talk because I do not know one who cannot talk and surely you must have talked to a raven before now but it does not matter because I have changed my mind and have decided to tell you now because I am no longer not quite ready because I am now quite ready to tell you and there is no reason to wait any longer."

Joshua Hotah dropped to his knees again because he could not move his feet to step closer to the white raven but he could drop to his knees and move closer and he even found that he could bend forward a little if he rested his hands on the front of his legs so he did this and his knees sunk a little deeper into the warm sticky ground but he did not care. "I do not know if I should trust you raven because my mother has told me stories about you and I am concerned you are a trickster and only misery and death follows in your dark wake."

The white raven's large white beak smiled and this surprised Joshua because he did not know a beak could smile but he also did not know a raven could talk in the first place and one could say that if a raven could speak words one could understand then it made sense the raven could also smile. "Do you believe everything your mother has told you Joshua Hotah because if you do or even if you do not I will take you to see her now and you can ask her this question for yourself and you can believe what you want to believe."

Joshua stood and tried to move his feet again and amazingly the warm sticky ground released his feet and he could move them but when he tried to swing around to look behind to see the fearful creature he knew waited behind he still could not do it. "I have been searching for my mother a very long time and I would very much like to talk to her and ask her many questions if you will take me to her and we will find out if you are a trickster or not if you still have the courage to take me to her."

The white raven hopped away on two feet in the direction of the shadows flitting beyond the obscuring mist and then yelled back at Joshua Hotah to follow. "Follow me into the warm sticky mist to find your mother if you have the courage to do it Joshua Hotah because I am not afraid of what she will say like you are because I have already talked to her many times before today."

Joshua followed without hesitation because the white raven hopped away with haste and when Joshua tried to increase the pace of his strides the warm sticky ground sucked at his toes and the bottoms of his feet which felt naked even though he could see his moccasins but somehow he managed to keep up with the white raven even when it changed directions and he followed the white raven through the mist until at one point he could not see anything but the warm sticky mist because it covered his eyes and filled his nostrils and filled his ears and he was aware that he could not see or breath or hear but somehow he managed to follow the white raven until the two of them reached a small opening in the mist and an old woman sat cross-legged next to a fire with no flames but the warm sticky mist poured out of it and she wore a beaded leather dress secured at the waist and moccasins and leggings the color the mist and her long hair was the color of the mist and her skin was the color of the mist and everything about her was the color of the mist and the white raven abruptly faced Joshua Hotah and pointed a slender white wing directly at Joshua Hotah and then at the old woman the color of the mist. "This is your mother the one you are looking for so ask her any questions you care to ask for I am not afraid of what she will say to you when you ask the questions you have in mind because I already know the questions you will ask before you have even thought to ask them and I also know the answers before you hear them."

Joshua fell to his knees in front of the old woman the raven claimed was his mother and the warm sticky ground sucked at his knees and he rested his hands on his knees and the woman raised her head and looked at him through vacuous eyes the color of the warm sticky mist and Joshua could not remember if this old woman presented the visage of the woman he remembered as a child. "Are you my mother like the raven says or has the raven tricked me with false words because I remember when you told me many years ago to beware of the raven because it is a trickster and I am not sure you are the mother I remember as a child?"

The old woman who the white raven claimed was the mother of Joshua Hotah opened her mouth and spoke words without moving her lips which struck Joshua Hotah as strange but he listened anyway because he wanted to find out if the raven had tricked him or not and this was the only way to do it. "I am your mother the raven speaks the truth and you should listen to the raven because I was wrong when I told you when you were a child to not trust the raven because it is a trickster but the raven has already told me you have come to my campfire to ask me questions and I am ready to answer the questions after you have asked them."

This pleased Joshua Hotah because now he believed this old woman was truly his mother as the white raven had promised and he was wrong not to trust the raven because now his mother had finally admitted the raven was not a trickster and he could trust it. "Where do you live because I would like to visit you when I get the chance because I have been searching for you a very long time and still have not found you?"

The old women who had closed her mouth after speaking opened her lips again and again spoke without moving her lips but it did not matter because Joshua Hotah could understand every word even though the sight of it was quite strange. "I live next to this fire without flames and you may come to visit me anytime you wish because I yearn to talk to you again and hold you in my arms again as I did when you were a child before you were lost and I will wait here for you so I can talk to you and hold you."

Joshua Hotah felt warmth in his heart when the old woman spoke these words without moving her lips and believed the old woman was truly his mother who he had searched for many years and now had found with the help of the noble white raven who led him through the mist to this place next to the fire without flames. "I too would like you to speak to me and hold me in your arms and this is why I have asked you where you live so I can find you but now I must ask you if you know where my father lives because I have also searched for him many years and have not found him either but maybe you know where he lives because you know where you live?"

Again the old woman opened her mouth because she had again closed it after speaking and her lips still did not move when she spoke but by now it did not bother Joshua Hotah anymore when his mother spoke without moving her lips because he had grown accustomed to it. "I do not know where your father lives because I have not seen him in many years but if you ask the raven it will take you to your father and you can speak with him but before you go I must tell you one more thing you should know before you go to see your father."

Joshua forced himself up from the sticky ground and prepared to walk away from the old woman who was his mother sitting by the fire without flames and follow the white raven into the warm sticky mist to find his father but before leaving he sank down until his ear nearly touched lips that did not move when his mother spoke and listened for an answer to his question. "What is it you wish to tell me mother?"

The lips did not move. "Do not trust the white raven my son or you will surely die."

This disturbed Joshua Hotah and he floated up to ask his mother another question but when he tried to see her one last time his mother had vanished and he found himself following the white raven through the mist again which didn't make any sense but he didn't have much time to think about it because he had to fight against the warm sticky ground which sucked at his feet again when he tried to walk faster to keep up with the scampering white raven who hopped even faster than before. "Where are you taking me raven because I would like to know where I am going and I didn't have time to ask my mother another question but at least I know where she lives and I can find her again and ask the question I did not ask before?"

The white raven elevated its white beak and spoke to Joshua Hotah with warbling tones not sounding much like a raven but the white raven liked to hop along on the wet sticky ground instead of flying so maybe it did make sense that the white raven could sound like another bird that could not talk. "I am taking you to see your father because you said you wanted to talk to him and we are nearly out of time and must travel with speed before he vanishes like the old woman who is your mother and you cannot ask the questions you desire to ask."

Joshua Hotah felt the warm sticky ground sucking at his toes when he tried to walk faster but could not walk faster and the white raven hopped faster and faster and he didn't have any trouble keeping up with the white raven even though he felt like the warm sticky ground was slowing him down to the pace of a tortoise sunning itself on a rock by a lake and not moving at all. "How far must we walk to find my father because I do not think I have the strength to fight the ground much more although I am not tired which is strange because I should feel very tired because the ground is pulling at my feet but I do not feel tired at all?"

The white raven plunged through a particularly moist and sticky wall of mist and Joshua Hotah followed like he had been told and the white raven and Joshua Hotah nearly fell headlong into a vast opening in the mist littered with many dead carcasses of buffalo stretching away as far as Joshua Hotah could see and the carcasses were covered with countless white ravens who looked like maggots they were so thick and the white raven spoke to Joshua Hotah and pointed with a slender white wing when he had finished speaking. "I hope you will not mind if I have invited some of my friends to feed on the dead buffalo while you talk to your father and ask him questions but we do not have much time so you must ask him the questions very soon before he vanishes like the old woman who is your mother and you can find him over there gutting a freshly killed buffalo and when he finishes I will feed on the carcass if you do not mind."

Joshua Hotah squinted through the warm sticky mist in the direction of the white raven's pointing wing and saw a man the color of the mist stooping over a buffalo also the color of the mist and cutting it open with a long knife and inside the buffalo guts squirmed and poured out of the gaping wound and spilled out over the ground and squirmed around on the ground still alive and Joshua walked up to the man who the white raven said was his father and tapped the man on his shoulder which was the color of the mist and the man sat on the haunch of the gutted animal with the guts snaking around his feet but the man did not appear to care and Joshua Hotah bowed respectfully and asked his question. "Are you the man the raven has told me is my father because if you are the man then I have some questions to ask you and I must ask the questions very soon because the raven says I do not have much time left to ask them?"

The man wore a shaggy beard the color of the mist and an uncombed moustache the color of the mist and his hair was also the color of the mist and his clothing and hat and boots too and he spoke in the same manner as the old woman who the white raven said was Joshua Hotah's mother by opening his lips to speak but the lips did not move when the words emptied out onto the ground and mixed with the buffalo guts squirming around like many snakes. "Yes the raven knows of what he speaks because I am your father and I have waited a long time for your arrival because the raven told me you would arrive someday but I never imagined it would take this much time and now there is little time left to talk as the raven has told you so please ask your questions very soon before the buffalo move because I have to follow them when they do."

Joshua Hotah nodded to the man the white raven said was his father and lowered to the ground close to the squirming buffalo guts and the guts noticed Joshua Hotah's knees and began slithering around Joshua Hotah's legs and over his feet and began to climb up his legs until they reached his belt but then stopped for some reason Joshua Hotah did not understand. "Where do you live now because I would like to come and visit you when I get the chance because I have been searching for you a very long time and still have not found you?"

The man who the white raven said was Joshua Hotah's father looked away from Joshua Hotah and his lips that did not move could not be seen and again stabbed his long knife into the body of the buffalo carcass and more guts squirmed from the fresh wound and spilled out over the carcass and onto the warm sticky ground and slithered around like many snakes. "I do not live anywhere because I follow the buffalo wherever they travel through this land and I never know where to find myself when I move with the buffalo but if you follow the raven he knows where I live even though I do not live in the same place much longer than you might think but because there is not much time left and before you must leave I must tell you something very soon because it is important for you to know of it."

Joshua Hotah touched the arm of the man the white raven said was his father just as the man drove his long knife into the buffalo carcass again and more guts erupted from the wound and spilled out over the warm sticky ground. "What is it my father?"

The man did not look up from his work. "Do not trust the white raven or you will surely—"

Always the light sleeper, Joshua Hotah promptly sat up when the agitated pounding of a man's hand on the door across the hallway resounded inside his ears. He rolled to his knees and stood before checking the Nez Perce boy, still asleep on the only bed in the small room. He opened the door and peered into the dusky gloom of the hallway. A lantern sitting on a small table several rooms down the hall had run out of fuel during the night, but Joshua's eyes usually worked well in the dark and he easily discerned the extraordinary image of a very small man carrying a very large man on his shoulders and pounding on the door to Guinevere Dupree's clinic. He waited until the door opened before stepping into the hallway and gently closing the door behind because he did not want to interrupt the Nez Perce boy's sleep.

The very small man spoke to Guinevere Dupree in a calm voice. "Are you the new doctor in town? I was told you would see a man such as this."

Guinevere pulled the robe she had hastily donned more tightly around her neck. "Yes, I'm the new doctor." She studied the very large man slung over the small man's back. "Should I assume you have brought me a new patient?"

The very small man grunted. "You have assumed well. Do I have your permission to set this man down? He is very heavy, and my knees are beginning to hurt from the weight of him."

Guinevere backed away from the doorway and waved toward the side room where she had snipped the Nez Perce boy's inflamed appendix two days earlier. "By all means. You may set him down on the table in the next room."

Joshua Hotah watched the very small man disappear into the clinic. He listened to the very small man speak with Guinevere Dupree but the words of both were not clear enough to understand. After several minutes, the very small man came out of the clinic and closed the door. The man bowed to Joshua before declaring, "Good morning to you. I apologize if I woke you from a sound sleep. It was not my desire to do so."

Joshua lowered his chin but kept his eyes on the very small man. "You do not need to apologize to me. I was having a very unpleasant dream. I am happy it is over, even if I did not hear the final words of my father."

The very small man pushed his hands into his sleeves. "My name is Tseng Longwei, and it would interest me to hear of your dream. In China, before my travels to Silver City, I often listened to the dreams of others and told them the meaning of the dreams. Some have said I possess a gift."

Joshua rested back against the wall of the hallway and folded his arms. "My name is Joshua Hotah. It is only a few hours before the sun rises and I am tired of sleeping in a small room where you cannot see the sky. If you walk outside I will tell the dream to you, because the memory of it has not left me. But I must warn you: the dream was very strange and it may be impossible to find any meaning in it."

Tseng Longwei bowed and motioned toward the main entry door with a gracefully-upturned palm. "Tell me the story of your dream and we shall see if there is meaning or not. After you, Joshua Hotah."

The two men reconvened outside in the chill of the early morning and sat on the covered boardwalk fronting the two-story building across the street from the War Eagle Hotel. They did not immediately discuss the strange dream. After sharing a few trivial stories of recent experiences, the men talked about the years before Silver City. Tseng Longwei told

Joshua of the great battle that led to the fall of Nanjing, of the naked woman in the courtyard who likely died the next morning, of his regrettable escape to Shanghai, of the horrific passage through the frightful storm on the East China Sea, of his work on the great railroad in the mountains of California, of his first meeting with Roshan Kuznetsov, and of his great fortune in finding work at Mahogany Gulch. Joshua Hotah told Longwei of his time as a scout with the white soldiers, of meeting his half-brother at the gully where all of the soldiers died except one, of his search for his mother and father, of finding the Nez Perce woman who lives a few miles from Silver City, and of taking her son to the woman doctor who made the child sleep before cutting him open like a dead buffalo. When Joshua had finished, he waited several minutes in silence before telling Tseng Longwei every detail of his strange dream.

After hearing the story of Joshua's dream, Longwei also rested silently for a time before interpreting its meaning. He began by asking, "Have you seen this white raven before?"

Joshua scratched an itch just behind his right ear. "What does it matter if I have seen the white raven or not?"

CHAPTER FIFTEEN

Saloon on the corner of Washington and Avalanche
November 10, 1871

T he unwashed man—who reeked so robustly of stale sweat he would have attracted a flotilla of horse flies on a hot summer day—flung his head back and noisily gulped the whisky until the last drop splashed against his tongue. Convinced he had completely drained the finger-smudged tumbler, he wiped his shirt sleeve across his lips and bounced the glass on the table when he lowered it. He wiped his mouth a second time, coughed up a gob of dirt-streaked phlegm and swallowed it, and picked his nose and deposited the fresh booger under the table. He attempted to improve Margaret's brooding visage by offering a dubious promise. "I'd pay good money for the privilege, Margaret. You know I'm good for it. Have I ever let you down before?"

Margaret, dressed in black from the top of her neck to the bottom of her boot heels (as was her custom), smiled a sly little smile and drummed a pudgy little finger on the table. A wagon rumbled down Avalanche and distracted her while she talked. "I just don't know, Andrew. Somehow it doesn't seem right when I really think about it. It just doesn't."

Andrew frowned and lifted the empty glass and used it as a theatrical prop to gesture more emphatically. A cold swirl of wind gusted across the roof and rattled a loose strip of metal flashing near the base of the stove pipe. The gust sucked a breath of air from the cast-iron potbelly stove squatting near the middle of the saloon and a half-burned log crackled a shower of glowing embers against the double-swing feed doors. "What don't seem right about it? It's my idea in the first place, not yours, and I promise you're gonna make a lot of money 'cause me and some other fellows I knows about would be willing to pay top dollar for the privilege. What's there to think about? Sounds pretty simple to me. All you gotta do is say yes and then start making a lot of money."

Margaret's sly smile waned. "Everything you say makes good business sense, but there's plenty of people in town who might not take kindly to the idea." The same wagon turned south onto Washington and rumbled across the front of the saloon.

Andrew set the glass down, gently this time. "Might not take kindly to the idea? Like who?"

Margaret groaned to express her disgust of Andrew's abject ignorance of local politics. "Like Father Nero, for starters. He's a first-class pain in the ass, if you ask me. And the new preacher, Manfred Herrmann. I don't know much about him…yet, but I do know he talked me into letting him hold church services right here in the back room without having to pay a dime. He's sure to find out sooner or later. He hasn't caused me much trouble yet, but who knows what he might try if I did what you say."

Andrew smirked. "You worry too much, Margaret. How's he gonna find out if you don't tell him about it? Just keep your mouth shut like usual and he'll never know the difference."

Margaret cackled, but not because she thought Andrew had said anything funny. "Oh, you'd be surprised how clever these religious fellows are at finding things out, especially when it comes to stuff they think is sin. It's what they do for a living." A chubby cat with orange fur, white stripes, and a long puffy tail hopped up on the table and cuddled next to Margaret's hand. The cat trilled loudly when Margaret began stroking the cat behind its ears.

Andrew suddenly appeared concerned about the hygienic practices of Margaret's saloon. "How come you let this cat get up on the tables and bar? It you ask me, that's what's not right. Who knows where it's been or what it's gotten into or what it's been eating. Makes me sick just to think about it walking all over everything whenever it pleases."

Margaret cooed sarcastically, "Poor Andrew…worried about an innocent animal who never meant you any harm, but willing to pay good money for something that even makes *me* wonder. And I've seen and heard just about everything you can imagine."

Andrew picked the glass up again and used it to point at Margaret's smirking face. "That ain't funny, Margaret. You know darn well the cat makes me sneeze and my peepers itch. Why don't you tell it to go sleep over by the stove like the lazy animal usually does?"

"That's the stupidest thing I ever heard, Andrew. Cats do whatever they want. This cat is going to sit on this table as long as it wants, and it's not going to sleep by the stove until it darn well feels like it."

"Then maybe I should just give it a good swat in the behind with the back of my hand to convince it to leave." Andrew set the glass down and raised his hand.

Margaret held her hand protectively over the cat's butt. "Don't you dare touch my kitty. If you even try, it'll be you who gets a good swat in the butt, and not with my hand."

Andrew scoffed, "I don't know why you're so protective of the little beast. If anyone but you tries to pet the dang thing they more likely than not will get clawed. It mostly sleeps by the stove during the day, and wanders around the saloon standing on tables looking out the windows and yowling at night. Can't possibly be good for business, if you ask me. I don't even know if it's a girl or a boy. Have you even given the dang thing a name?"

Margaret pulled the cat a little closer and it purred even louder. "He's a boy cat, and I haven't given him a name. I'm still thinking about it."

Andrew guffawed and slapped his thighs. "Well then, why don't you give it a name that fits, like *Mister Completely Useless.*"

Margaret slid the cat off the table and held it in her lap. "You're really cruel, Andrew. I'm surprised you had the guts to say that to my face. And he's not completely useless because he keeps the place free of mice and other varmints."

"You have mice in this saloon?"

"Not anymore."

"And what kind of other varmints are you talking about?"

"Mostly rats, I suppose."

"You have rats in this saloon too?"

"I already told you. Not anymore."

Andrew glared at the purring cat. "You're gonna get orange cat hairs all over your pretty black dress, not to mention the cat spit."

Margaret patted the cat a little harder. "Not worried about any orange hairs or cat spit. I'm more worried about what you want to do after paying me a lot of money. I'm trying to decide if all the trouble it's going to cause is worth it."

Andrew picked up the glass once more. "Oh, now we're back to where we started? I thought you forgot all about it because you was too preoccupied with the cat. I'm glad to see you still know what's important around here. Then have you decided? Makes me hard just thinking about it."

The cat jumped down and sauntered over to the potbelly stove. Margaret brushed a few orange cat hairs from the front of her dress. "No, I haven't decided yet. I'm thinking about either George or Frederick, but I'm liking Frederick because it sounds more dignified to me. George is such a common name." Another gust of wind vibrated the stove pipe.

Andrew snarled, "Oh for goodness sakes Margaret! I wasn't talking about the silly cat's name. I was talking about my offer to pay top dollar for it. Like I said, I'll even get some of my friends to chip in. Of course, if they did they'd expect to get something special for it. They're not going to pay good money for the same old stuff, you know."

Margaret rested her elbows on the table. "Stop pushing me, Andrew. I'm still thinking about it because she's only fourteen. If she was a little older it wouldn't bother me at all, but fourteen just sounds a mite young."

Andrew acted surprised. "She's fourteen? Dang, I thought she was only thirteen."

"No. She's fourteen. She'll be fifteen in a month or two."

Andrew slouched in his chair and pouted. "That's too bad, Margaret. I already told a bunch of my friends you were working a thirteen-year-old whore here at the saloon. They're going to be mighty disappointed to find out she's already growed to almost fifteen."

Margaret scrunched her face into a frightful grimace. "Why would you go and say such a darn fool thing when I haven't even decided if I'm going to do it or not? You trying to get me into trouble before I even deserve it?"

Andrew grew more cantankerous. "If you're not going to make her available then you ought to just get rid of her right now because she drives me crazy when she bends down to clean something off the floor with her cute little ass waving around like that. Drives me plumb crazy, and I'm not the only one. You should ask around and you'll find out she's driving a lot of your customers crazy. I swear to you, Margaret, you're going to make a lot of money. If I was you, I'd fib about her age and tell everyone she's thirteen anyway. Just think about the extra business you'll bring in."

Margaret appeared deep in thought. After ten seconds she looked around until she spotted Priscilla Kimball cleaning something off the floor near the piano. She snapped her fingers twice. "Priscilla. Get over her. I want to talk to you about something."

Priscilla balanced a hand broom and dust pan against the end of the piano and capered diagonally across the saloon until she stood at Margaret's side. She folded her hands in front. "Yes, Miss Margaret?"

Margaret waved at one of the empty chairs next to the table. "Sit down, my little darling. This might take a few minutes to explain."

Priscilla dutifully pulled the chair out and sat up straight as her mother had always told her and pressed her knees together and folded her hands on her lap as her mother had also always told her. "What is it you wanted to explain to me, Miss Margaret?"

Margaret began her presentation deceptively. "Tell me how you've been getting along here at the saloon, Priscilla. Had any problems since your unfortunate misunderstanding with Jacque? I heard it was a humdinger of a day."

Priscilla looked down at her folded hands and her cheeks flushed pink. "No, Miss Margaret. No other misunderstandings. I think everyone's afraid Miss Nadia will whack them on the head with her axe handle if someone tries something like that again. She keeps it under her bed, but I think I'm the only one who knows about it."

Margaret slapped the top of the table and chuckled. "That's a good one, Priscilla. You don't need to worry none. If I had to guess, I'd say half the residents of Silver City know Nadia keeps a hickory axe handle under her bed. And more than a few of them have felt the sting of it."

Priscilla's youthful face expressed honest surprise. "Really?"

Margaret stopped laughing and her jaw tightened. "Really. Now, let's stop talking about Nadia's axe handle and get down to business." She scooted her plump bottom forward on the seat of the chair. "I've been thinking it's about time for me to give you a promotion around here. I think you've got a lot more to offer the saloon than just cleaning up and making beds and the like. What do you think about a promotion, Priscilla?"

Priscilla swung her feet back and forth beneath the chair. "I don't know, Miss Margaret. What would I have to do if you give me a promotion?"

Margaret sniffed. "Such a clever girl. Someday you'll be a business-woman like me."

"You really think so?"

"I know so, my dear. Now, all you'd have to do is to entertain a few special customers from time to time. You could get started tonight … if you wanted do. We could work out the financial details later."

"Would I get paid to entertain the special customers? I don't get anything but room and board now. And I still don't know what I'm supposed to do to get the extra money." Priscilla swung her feet a little more exuberantly.

Margaret raised her hands and pushed the tips of her fingers together. "Like I said, such a clever girl. Of course you'd get paid, my darling. What's the point of a promotion if you don't get paid extra?" She grinned cunningly.

"How much would I get paid?" Priscilla let her feet dangle to a stop.

"I haven't felt this generous in years, but I'd pay you ninety cents for each customer, and not a penny more." Margaret folded her arms together and squeezed.

Priscilla began swinging her feet again and completed five repetitions before saying, "I want two dollars per customer, and not a penny less."

Margaret unfolded her arms and sputtered, "Two dollars! Too clever for her own good, if you ask me!" She relaxed a bit. "It pains me to the bone to say this, because I'm barely making a profit as it is, but I'd be willing to increase my offer to a dollar-twenty-five … but only if you work on Sundays whenever any of the special customers wants."

"I'd be willing to go down to a dollar-seventy-five … but only if I get Sunday mornings off, 'cause that's only fair."

"Why, you little witch! I'd go broke in less than a month if I had to pay that much. A dollar-fifty for each satisfied customer, and you only get every other Sunday morning off. That's my final offer. Take it or leave it."

Priscilla jumped to her feet and stretched out her hand. "Deal!"

Margaret stood too, but when she tried to shake Priscilla's hand, Nadia blocked her way. Margaret fumed, "Nadia, what do you think you're doing? I was about to give Priscilla a promotion. Get out of my way so I can shake her hand and finish the deal."

Nadia's voice trembled. "I'm not going anywhere, Margaret, because there's no way I'm letting you turn Priscilla into a whore."

Priscilla clarified the agreement. "She's not trying to turn me into a whore, Nadia. I've just got to entertain some special customers from time to time, except every other Sunday when I get the morning off."

Nadia kept her eyes on Margaret. "Sit down and be quiet, Priscilla. We'll talk about this later." Then she said to Margaret in a menacing whisper, "No way at all."

Andrew snarled, "This ain't none of your business, Nadia. You'd best stay out of it, if you knows what's good for you."

She snapped her gaze to Andrew. "I'll tell you what's good for me, Andrew. I'm thinking of getting that hickory axe handle right now and using it to beat you around the head until you're on your knees blubbering like that little thirteen-year-old girl you seem to be so fond of. Is that good for you?"

Andrew pushed his hands under his armpits and mumbled, "When you put it that way...."

Margaret dropped her hand. "Thanks, Nadia. You just cost me a lot of money. A lot of money. But I understand how you feel about it. Perfectly natural you'd want to protect the little darling. Tell you what: I'll just take another three dollars out of your salary every day and we'll call it even. It'll make up for my lost profits, and your precious little Priscilla can keep cleaning up vomit and changing dirty beds for room and board. Is that good for you?"

Nadia's lips tightened. She wedged her fists against her hips and advanced until her nose hovered about an inch from Margaret's. "Fine, Margaret. But the only witch in this saloon is the one I'm looking at right now." When Nadia had finished these words, she understood implicitly that her beautiful dream to make enough money to move to California and buy a cozy home with a view of the ocean had vanished. Forever.

Chapter Sixteen

He that is without sin among you
November 28, 1871

G athered in front of the Idaho Hotel, the agitated mob—made up of eleven who objected to the idea on legitimate moral grounds and fourteen who wanted to see for themselves if it was really true for more prurient reasons and nine who fell somewhere in-between these two possibilities—listened with great interest to the eloquent oration of one Samuel B. Peters, an upstanding and highly-regarded deacon of a noteworthy congregation in Boise City. Mr. Peters, accompanied by his wife and two close friends, hooked his thumbs behind the lapels of his black frock coat and puffed out his chest. "...and I promise you this day, citizens of Silver City, that God will surely rain fire and brimstone down upon the heads of those sinners who have instigated this outrage against humanity." The low voices and whispers of the mob blended together into an incoherent murmur. Samuel B. Peters jabbed an index finger to the sky and continued, "Why, the very idea of offering up a thirteen-year-old girl as a prostitute...to be abused by older men in the most unspeakable ways...sends shivers up my spine and fills me with deep shame for my fellow man."

A woman held a hand over her mouth and gasped. The incoherent murmur amplified and then quickly diminished. A man standing near the back of the crowd yelled, "Burn the place down, that's what I say. Burn it to the ground!"

The suggestion energized the mob and many nodded, but Samuel B. Peters repeatedly pushed his hands down toward the ground before advising restraint. "Please calm yourselves, my brothers and sisters. Please calm yourselves." The mob calmed itself. "If these evildoers were hiding in a single building far from town, I would agree with you. But such an act could set the entire town afire and harm those who are truly innocent. Is this what you want, my friends, to slaughter everyone for the sake of a mere handful of sinners?"

Jackson, Seth, and Miguel sauntered up to the rear of the crowd just in time to hear the man yell, "Burn the place down...." Jackson asked the fellow standing next to him, a miner wearing long underwear and pants held up with suspenders but no shirt and his left cheek bulged out with a wad of chewing tobacco, "What's going on here?"

The man spat and some black goo stuck to his lip. "Nothing much. Just some fellow from Boise City saying we should burn the saloon down. But he's afraid we might set the whole town on fire and slaughter the handful of truly innocent people who live here. Looks like he's maybe changing his mind about it."

Miguel's gloomy disposition improved when he heard this. "I can blow it up for him if he wants. Just tell me which saloon it is and I'll get started right away."

The man spat again, and a rivulet of tobacco juice drooled down his chin. "The saloon on the corner of Washington and Avalanche. Seems they got a whole stable of thirteen-year-old whores who just arrived in town. The preacher man from Boise says we're all gonna burn in hell 'less we do something about it."

Jackson grumbled. "How come I didn't hear about them thirteen-year-old whores before now? I would of done something about it all by myself if I'd a known."

Seth sneered, "I bet you would, but not what I'm a thinking."

Jackson clenched his stained teeth and snarled, "Shut up, Seth. You don't know a darn thing about nothing, especially thirteen-year-old whores."

The man with chewing tobacco drooling down his chin held up his hand. "Quiet. The preacher man from Boise is saying something again."

Samuel B. Peters squeezed the fingers of his right hand into a fist and shook it at the mob. "No, we won't burn them out. We are civilized people, after all. We will march down to the saloon and publicly demand an end to this monstrous practice, and we will not leave until our demand is met. Who here has the courage to follow me to the saloon and confront the brood of vipers dwelling within its walls?"

Miguel asked the man with chewing tobacco drooling down his chin, "What's a brood of vipers? They have a bunch of snakes in there?"

The man wiped the sleeve of his long underwear across his mouth and spat again. "Never seen any snakes in there either. He must be talking about some other place."

Jackson barked impatiently, "Doesn't matter what he's talking about. Let's go over there and see those whores he's talking about. Might have some fun at the same time."

Samuel B. Peters swung his arm overhead in a wide arc and pointed in the direction of the saloon on the corner of Washington and Avalanche. "The time has come to take action my brothers and sisters. Onward to confront this brood of vipers. Onward to cleanse this town of despicable sin. Onward to put right an unspeakable wrong. Onward! Onward! Onward!" Samuel B. Peters began marching toward Avalanche and the mob lurched forward.

The man with chewing tobacco drooling down his chin followed a pair of Cousin Jennies, and Jackson, Seth, and Miguel followed right behind him. Still thinking about the snakes, Miguel said, "There's those brood of vipers again. I still don't know what's going on. Don't much like snakes. Not going to stick around if there's snakes about."

Jackson snarled, "Stop worrying about them snakes. The only thing that matters is we might have some fun."

Seth agreed. "Yeah, stop worrying about them snakes. Just worry you might not get the chance to blow something up."

Samuel B. Peters exhorted the mob onward as it rounded the corner onto Washington. "Onward to smite the evildoers, my friends. Do not flee from your moral obligation. Take heart. Have courage. Onward, I say! Onward!"

Priscilla, who had just cleaned up a dried-up headless mouse from beneath the potbelly stove, heard a cacophony of odd noises on Washington and skipped to the front door and looked out the window next to the door. She watched a group of about three dozen people gather in front of the saloon and a man in a black frock coat shake his fist at the people and then point at the saloon. Alarmed, she yelled for Nadia. "Miss Nadia. There's something funny going on out front. You better come and take a look."

Standing at the bar with a guest, Nadia caressed his arm. "Would you excuse me a moment? I should go see what's bothering Priscilla. I won't be long." The man consented and Nadia walked to the front door and stood next to Priscilla and squinted through the window. "Where's Margaret? Have you seen her this morning?"

Priscilla clapped her hands. "Yes, Miss Nadia. She left right after breakfast. Said she had to go on some sort of errand and didn't know when she'd get back. I haven't seen her since."

Nadia swore. "Darn. She's always on some errand when something bad is about to happen. I don't know how she does it."

"Does what?"

"Manages to be gone whenever there's trouble. It must be a gift."

"A gift?"

"No matter. You stay away from the window. I'd better find out what's going on. It doesn't look like we can wait for Margaret." Nadia opened the front door and stepped outside. The late morning sun drifted low in the southern sky and the heavy wood columns supporting the canopy roof cast long shadows over the wood boardwalk. A cold gust from the north pushed a swirl of dust around Nadia's feet and lifted the hem of her frilly dress. A dog barked across the street. The man in the frock coat stopped talking and the crowd turned silent when Nadia appeared. She recognized many of the faces in the crowd. When no one spoke, she asked innocently, "Is there something I can help you folks with?"

Samuel B. Peters raised one foot to the boardwalk, rested his arms on his elevated knee, and asked calmly, "Are you the proprietor of this saloon?"

Nadia answered sweetly, "No, I'm not the owner. She's not here right now. Is there something I can help you with?"

Jackson slithered behind the man with the tobacco drooling down his chin and yelled, "We want to see them thirteen-year-old whores. Bring 'em out so we can see what they look like." The incoherent murmur swelled.

Nadia adjusted the shoulder strap of her frilly dress and clasped her hands in front to hold the hem down against the wind. "I don't know what you're talking about. I've never heard of such a thing. You can come inside and look for yourself if—"

Samuel B. Peters held up his hand and cut her off. "No. No. No. We will not enter this den of iniquity. Nor will we cast our eyes upon the despicable things that dwell within. We are here to ...."

Manfred Herrmann placed the half-empty coffee cup down on its saucer but did not immediately release his finger and thumb from the white porcelain handle. He kept his eyes on the cup as he spoke to the priest sitting across the table. "I suppose it's time to be moving along. Almost noon, and I still have a few errands I'd like to get done before I head back to the cabin."

Father Nero Aguilar rubbed his forehead. "I suppose we have sat here talking and drinking coffee long enough for one day. And I also have an errand or two I'd like to accomplish before the end of the day. Same time next week?"

Manfred released the cup. "Yes, same time next week. I'm already looking forward to it." The two men stood and shook hands. Manfred walked from the dining room into the hotel lobby. He waved when he passed by the young clerk sitting on a stool behind the high counter in front of the hotel office. The young clerk lowered a dog-eared dime novel he had read four times before and waved back. Manfred walked through the front door of the War Eagle Hotel and across the wood boardwalk to the eave of the canopy at the front of the building. He shaded his eyes with his left hand and glanced at the sky a little below the sun. He shoved his hands into his jacket pockets and walked north. After maneuvering around a line of four children following a woman carrying a baby in one arm and a basket in the other, he noticed an unusual commotion down the street near Avalanche Avenue. He squinted, and discerned a large crowd of people gathered in front of the saloon where he held church services every Sunday morning. He hastened his pace and dashed over to the boardwalk to avoid an approaching freight wagon. After crossing an alley, he rushed by a general store, a tailor's shop, and Csongor Toth's law office. He nearly ran into a freshly-shaved man exiting the barber shop. He apologized before proceeding with increased speed past a store selling drugs and jewelry, a saloon, a cobbler's shop, another saloon, another saloon, and yet another saloon, and finally another barber shop until he arrived at the front of the saloon on the corner of Washington and Avalanche.

Manfred Herrmann walked up to Nadia and stood by her side. He looked the crowd over, then asked Nadia, "What's going on here, Nadia? Some sort of meeting?"

Nadia appeared rattled. "This…man is accusing the saloon of employing thirteen-year-old prostitutes, but I've told him it's not—"

Samuel B. Peters interrupted, "And who are you, might I ask? Are you the owner of this saloon? Because if you are, we have profoundly serious business to discuss with you."

Manfred looked down on the stranger in the black frock coat because the man had still not stepped completely onto the boardwalk. "No, I'm not the owner. Name's Manfred Herrmann. And who, might I ask, are you?"

"Samuel B. Peters of Boise. And what is your business in this affair, if you are not the owner of this manifestation of Sodom and Gomorrah which condemns us all by offering a thirteen-year-old prostitute to satisfy the most unspeakable desires of men?"

Manfred shrugged. "I'm a local pastor, and Nadia happens to be a friend. What's all this about a thirteen-year-old prostitute?"

Samuel B. Peters wheezed, "You are a friend of this woman of sin?" The crowd murmured.

"Yes I am. She plays the concertina for my church services…every Sunday morning."

"What kind of pastor would befriend someone who works in a brothel?"

Without shame, Manfred answered, "I guess a Lutheran pastor."

Samuel B. Peters pointed an accusatory finger directly at Manfred's face. "A Lutheran? Now I've heard all. Have you considered that you may have condemned your very soul by association with this lady of the night?" The crowd murmured.

Jackson, sensing a keen opportunity to incite the crowd to violence and have some fun, cupped his hands around his mouth and screamed, "Drag the whore into the street and strip her. Burn the place to the ground! Strip her naked and burn the place down!" He nudged Seth when he had finished.

Taking his cue, Seth yelled, "Strip her! Teach the whore a lesson she will never forget. Burn the saloon. Burn it!"

Miguel suggested an alternative solution to the problem. "Don't burn it down. Blow it up!"

Others in the crowd echoed the call to action, and three scruffy men standing next to Samuel B. Peters aggressively mounted the boardwalk and prepared to carry out the various recommendations of the crowd.

Manfred moved in front of Nadia and protectively pushed his arms back around her sides. "Anyone who wants to take Nadia will have to get by me first."

When the three men hesitated, Jackson shouted, "She's a whore and a sinner. Drag her into the street and strip her of sin!"

Manfred nudged Nadia closer to the front door. "Get inside, Nadia." He held up his hand to discourage the three men, and, believing this would calm the crowd's overheated emotions, declared in a booming voice, "He that is without sin among you, let him first cast a stone at her."

This was Jackson's chance. He picked up a smooth stone and rolled it around in his hand. "Whatever you say, preacher man." Not having paid much attention to the Bible verse Manfred had quoted, he flung it at Manfred instead of Nadia. But his aim was off, and the stone glanced off Nadia's head just above her left eye. Nadia stumbled and pressed her hand against the wound. Blood flowed between her fingers. Manfred seized her arm to prevent her from falling.

Jackson casually picked up a second stone and rolled it around in his hand again. "Ready for another one, preacher man?" Jackson reared back and prepared to throw again, but before he could begin a good forward motion a shotgun blast shattered the air behind him. Jackson jumped and spun around, and his derisive glare found the reclusive countenance of Conrad Airingsail. Jackson did not drop the stone. "Why, it's the little four-eyed pipsqueak of a cowpoke who don't know how to talk. Who invited you, you good-for-nothing pipsqueak?" Conrad motioned with the shotgun for Jackson to drop the stone. Jackson cocked his arm back. "How 'bout I just throw this here stone down your throat? A little pipsqueak like you ain't going to do anything about it anyway." Conrad lowered the shotgun and fired the second barrel into the ground in front of Jackson's feet. A few of the pellets bounced up and struck him in the shins. Jackson flinched his legs apart and dropped the stone. "Why you stupid fool. You could'a shot my foot off." Conrad refused to back down. "But now we'll see who's the real fool, 'cause you just used up your last shot." Jackson reached for the Smith & Wesson he had stolen from Elijah Brown, but before the barrel had cleared the top of his belt Conrad Airingsail dropped the shotgun to his side and drew the small-caliber five-cylinder revolver from his shoulder holster and aimed it directly at Jackson's nose. Jackson slowed for a moment, but then continued to pull the gun out. He froze when Conrad Airingsail cocked the hammer.

Manfred stepped between Conrad and Jackson. "Stop, Conrad. There's no need for bloodshed. I think we can resolve this issue peacefully if you will give me the chance." Conrad slowly lowered the revolver and stepped back. Manfred turned and faced Jackson. "Give me the gun, Jackson, before Conrad does something regrettable."

Jackson scoffed, "I don't give up my gun to nobody, especially a preacher man."

Manfred warned sternly, "If you do not give me the gun of your own accord, I will be forced to take it from you."

Jackson chortled, "You think I'm going to let a preacher take my gu—"

Manfred struck Jackson in the center of his face with a splendid left jab. As Jackson began falling backwards, Manfred reached out and plucked the Smith & Wesson from his hand. Jackson crumpled to the ground holding his nose. Blood gushed from both nostrils. Manfred calmly handed the gun to Conrad Airingsail. "Do you mind taking care of this, Mr. Airingsail? I have no need for such tools of violence."

Jackson kicked his feet and cried incoherently, "You broke my nose. You broke my nose, you stupid good for nothing...."

Manfred ignored Jackson and spoke directly to the crowd while holding his hands up as if giving them a blessing. "Please return to your homes, my sisters and brothers. There's nothing more for you to do here. Please return to your homes." Startled (and impressed) by what they had just witnessed, the unruly mob slowly dispersed. Samuel B. Peters and his wife and his two friends departed for Boise City on the afternoon stage.

CHAPTER SEVENTEEN

War Eagle Mountain near Mahogany Gulch
December 1, 1871

D riven onward by a cold front advancing relentlessly over the Owyhee Mountains, the first bona fide snowstorm of winter shrieked across jagged peaks and swirled deeply into river valleys and blasted rocky cliffs and whirred through plunging mountain saddles and pummeled ancient trees clinging to precipitous slopes. A week earlier, the temperature had quickly dropped before a light dusting of snow settled pleasantly on the streets and rooftops of Silver City, but only a day later the air warmed and melted away any trace. The power and breadth of this new storm did not present the look of an ephemeral event, and as the rising sun attempted to brighten the gray-veiled skies and icy morning segued into icy afternoon the intensity of the wind and the depth of the surging waves of snow amplified until the blizzard had rendered the winding mountain road between town and Mahogany Gulch impassable.

Trudging through knee-deep snow near Mahogany Gulch, Tseng Longwei made his way back to the cabin. Secured across his shoulders in a canvas sling, an impressive load of hand-split firewood gave him the appearance of a medieval hunchback and provided an excellent sail for the wind, which tried to knock him down every few steps. He squinted to protect his eyes from the razor-sharp snowflakes because his hands were both occupied with the sling, and he closed his eyes completely when the intensity of the wind increased beyond his willingness to resist it. Obscured by the blizzard during his last dozen steps, the cabin blurred back into his view when the wind momentarily abated. Cheered by the knowledge of his imminent arrival, Longwei quickened his pace. When he had taken only three steps, a frightful gust knocked his advancing leg inward and he tripped and plunged headfirst into the snow. The load of firewood rolled out of the canvas sling over the back of his head and scattered across the drifting snow. Longwei crawled forward and fished around in the snow with his hands, blindly searching for the errant firewood. His fingers touched one piece of firewood, and another, and a third, but then his fingers began aching from the cold. When he had located all but one and reloaded the sling, he struggled to his feet and staggered the last few steps to the front door of the cabin. He kicked at the door with his foot, and within seconds Gustus De Angeles opened the door and invited him in. "Where you been? I began to think you'd maybe decided to walk to town and give the firewood to someone else."

Tseng Longwei stumbled into the cabin, lowered the sling to the dirt floor, and brushed snow from his arms. "It is still confusing to me, Mr. Gustus, why the wood pile is stored such a great distance from the cabin. Why do we not store the firewood next to the cabin where it will not be such a long walk to carry it?"

Gustus gathered up two pieces of wood and walked over to the potbelly stove, a distance of only two steps. He opened the single-feed door and rammed the chunks in one after the other. "That's better. Now maybe we won't all freeze to death. Nothing worse than freezing to death. Done it a few times before and I can tell you there's nothing worse." He warmed his hands over the stove. "Except maybe dying of thirst. Done that a few times too."

Longwei brushed the snow off the front of his legs. "If you would give your permission, it would please me to build a small roof on the side of the cabin to store firewood. I could build it after the winter, if you would provide the materials."

"Suit yourself, but you can build it on your own time, and I ain't paying for no materials neither. I need you helping with the new shaft, not wasting time building some cockamamie roof on the side of the cabin so you don't have to walk as far." Gustus clapped his hands and then rubbed them together vigorously.

Roshan and a black man—the one Tseng Longwei had carried to the doctor—sat on rough-hewn chairs at a rough-hewn table playing cards with a grimy deck missing the Seven of Clubs, the Ten of Spades, and the Queen of Hearts. Roshan shuffled the deck and dealt out two hands in the manner he had learned from the trombonist on the USS Ossipee. He spoke to the black man sitting across the table after the last card spun away from his hand. "It is of the odd one to me, if you ask of who is my opinion, you do not remember a word of who is you and from where you arrived. Is of my opinion, if you ask it to me, not the you."

The black man arranged his cards with great skill, even though he could not recollect where he had learned to play the game. "I can't explain it, but I just don't remember a dang thing. Can't remember my name or where I came from or even why I ended up here."

Roshan assessed the strength of his hand: a three, a five, two sevens, and a queen. He regretted the loss of the cards from the deck. "Then we should tell of you the new name, who we may call of you the something to know of it when we speak. This is of the most to me."

Longwei hopped over to the potbelly stove to avoid tripping on the firewood scattered on the floor and held his aching hands in the rising heat. "Yes, this is a good idea. We should give you a new name if you cannot remember the old one."

Gustus pulled a pipe from his vest pocket, stuffed the bowl with tobacco, and lighted it with a flaming stick retrieved from the potbelly stove. "Only reason to give him a name is if he's sticking around, and only way he's sticking around is if he does his fair share of the work. I'm running a mining operation here, not a charity hospital. This cabin was already too crowded when I was living here all by myself. Now there's no room to speak of at all with a Chinaman, a fellow who can't speak a word of American anyone can understand, and a beat up Negro who can't remember his name filling the place up. I can't even change my coat and my mind at the same time."

Longwei turned away from the potbelly stove and shoved his hands into the opposite sleeves of his black tunic. "You have spoken of many important things, Mr. Gustus. But I would like to speak to all of you of my sincere appreciation of our friendship." The storm outside the cabin intensified. The walls of the cabin creaked and the wind whistled through the trees. A branch jittered noisily against the roof.

Roshan threw his cards on the table in disgust. "How can I think of me to win without the cards who are lost? It is always of the cards who are lost I must need to win the poker."

The black man sniggered. "You just need to stop asking for them lost cards. You ain't never gonna get four queens, and there's the simple truth of it."

Gustus began rummaging through the food supply looking for a few potatoes and a tin of bacon. "If we have to listen to one of them long speeches you're so fond of, then I'm going to start making some dinner. I can at least get something useful done at the same time."

The black man mixed the cards using a uniquely-personal overhand shuffle technique. "I don't mind listening to your speeches. They're kind of relaxing, if you want my opinion." He dealt another hand.

Gustus banged a grease-and-smoke-blackened cast-iron frying pan on the cooking surface of the potbelly stove, cut off four slabs of bacon into the pan, sliced up two gnarled potatoes on top of the bacon, and sprinkled pinches of salt and pepper over the whole mess. "Nothing relaxing about his speeches, if you ask me. They're just long and complicated and hard to listen to." He set the coffee pot next to the frying pan to heat up the coffee he had made an hour earlier.

Tseng Longwei bowed, meditated a few seconds, and then commenced—just as the bacon began sputtering in the fry pan. "Thank you all for listening to the lowly words I am about to say. It now seems many years since I was an officer of high rank in the great army of the Taiping Heavenly Kingdom under the worthy leadership of the holy Hong Xiuquan. But when I allow time to contemplate the truth, I soon realize that only a few months more than seven years have actually passed since the unfolding of those important events."

A series of scratching sounds on the door interrupted Longwei's oration. Gustus poked at the slabs of sputtering bacon with a two-pronged fork and then spoke to no one in particular. "Will someone get off their lazy ass and see who's at the front door? Anyone who pays attention can see I'm busy cooking up this bacon."

Roshan threw his cards on the table again. "This hand is of the most crappy you can be sure. Roshan will see of the who is in the door."

Longwei motioned to Roshan to remain seated. "Please stay as you are, Roshan. I am already standing, and the door is within my reach."

Roshan stood. "I do not care of opening the door. It is the good time to take off my legs and I do it with glad on my heart."

Gustus shook the two-pronged fork at Longwei. "Will someone please just answer the darn door?"

Longwei unlatched the door and pulled it open. An icy gust of snow-laden wind swirled into the small cabin and blew several playing cards off the rough-hewn table. Everyone looked, and there stood the mongrel of a dog Longwei had befriended the night he found the black man sleeping in the wagon. The dog offered an expression both sad and expectant at the same time, but did not enter the cabin. Longwei exclaimed, "It is the dog who followed me from Silver City. It appears he desires to come into the cabin because of the storm."

Gustus drove the fork into one of the slabs of bacon and flipped it over. "That mangy animal is not coming inside this cabin. It's already too darn crowded in here."

Longwei took sympathy on the dog. "But it is very cold outside. If you will look at the dog you will see that it is shivering." Another gust blew snow into the cabin. "I am sure the dog will not cause trouble if it comes inside."

Gustus stood silently while cutting off another slab of bacon and slamming it into the frying pan. "I give up. Invite the mangy thing in. And close the door before we all freeze to death." He muttered something no one except the dog could hear.

Longwei waved the dog in and closed the door. The dog skittered straight over to the potbelly stove and curled up on the floor next to Gustus's foot. Gustus glanced down at the mangy beast and muttered something unintelligible then resumed flipping the slabs of bacon and poking at the slices of potato.

Longwei continued, "As I was saying to you earlier, my friends, the time that has passed from the events I spoke of has seemed much longer than the truth. But even so, the final battle which led to the fall of Nanjing and the terrible slaughter of many great warriors and innocent cow herders still burns vividly within my thoughts each and every day. At the end of the great battle, when all hope was lost and there was no longer any purpose in my own death—even though I had caused the death of many of the Emperor's greatest soldiers with my magnificent sword—I made my way to Shanghai like a shameful rat where I again experienced much tragedy and disappointment. My lofty rank in the army of the Taiping Heavenly Kingdom, and the false arrogance that had grown within my soul for having achieved such rank, no longer held any meaning for me. I was reduced to the poverty of my peasant roots and forced to pull wealthy Americans and Germans around the city in my humble rickshaw. When I had saved enough money to escape the city, I again experienced much tragedy during a frightful storm on the great sea, a storm which terrified me beyond the words necessary to describe it to you. The only thing that sustained me during this terrible storm was the kindness of one sailor who spoke mostly in foul words but who understood the sea and did not fear it as I did. I arrived safely in the city of San Francisco after many unpleasant weeks, and although I was thankful to leave the boat, I again experienced many hardships and tragedies on the great railroad in the endless mountains of California. The false arrogance of lofty rank began to fade from my understanding during this time, and the first true appreciation of my humble life began to unfold in my heart. But the transformation of my arrogance had not yet completed itself. I met my good friend and business partner Roshan at the finish of my work on the railroad, and together we experienced many more humbling adventures on the great trail until the day we arrived in Silver City. Still my arrogance was not completely washed away, even though this is often impossible for me to believe when I consider the many unfortunate events since the fall of Nanjing. But now I gladly confess to all of you on this day: the glorious poverty and splendid deprivation I have finally achieved in this small cabin with the three of you has finally crushed my pride into worthless dust and convinced me to appreciate the life I have been given." Longwei bowed deeply at the waist. "Thank you, my dearest of friends, for this heavenly gift of understanding. I shall cherish this gift always, even to the day of my death."

Continuing his bad luck, Roshan slapped his cards on the table and folded. "You are full of the much to be sure horse manure again, my business partner and friend."

The black man gathered up the cards. "I liked his sermon. If you ask my opinion, I thought it made a lot of sense."

Roshan picked up the Jack of Spades from the floor and handed it to the black man. "If you believe to it, you are full of the much horse manure in the too."

The bacon sizzled and Gustus pulled the fry pan off the potbelly stove. "Enough talk. Time to eat some bacon."

The mangy mongrel of a dog raised its head, sniffed at the greasy-blue smoke permeating the tiny cabin, and whimpered expectantly.

Longwei bowed. "Before we eat, tell me what you think of the name of John Smith? I have heard the name before, in one of the many general stores we have visited. I think it is suitable for our new friend."

The black man shuffled the cards and dealt a new hand. "Sounds good to me, but I'd like to change back to my real name when I remember what it is, if it's alright with you."

Roshan closed his cards then fanned them open again. "John Smith is of the good name for you, because it looks much of you. And Roshan will not stop in your way when you remember of the real name."

Gustus smacked a slab of bacon on a metal plate. "Call him whatever you want, but I don't give a darn because I'm getting hungrier by the minute. Who wants bacon?"

The dog tilted his head and thumped the floor with his tail.

CHAPTER EIGHTEEN

Sunday morning at the back room of the saloon
December 3, 1871

In Nadia's skilled hands the concertina* wheezed out a reedy but convincing accompaniment to *A Mighty Fortress is Our God*. Manfred Herrmann waved his arms in a useless attempt to teach his "congregation" the words to the hymn since he could not yet afford hymnals—not that a ready supply of hymnals would have made the slightest difference. A winter breeze rushed along the ridgeline of the second-story roof and whistled an annoying pitch about twenty-cents flat of C-sharp. The bed in the room directly above Manfred's head creaked metrically about eleven beats per minute off the pace Manfred had chosen for the hymn, at one point accelerating to a perfectly bothersome three-against-two rhythm. When Manfred and Nadia and the congregation reached half-way through the third verse, the upright piano in the next room burst into a rousing performance of *Camptown Races*[†] in a different key and meter altogether and within seconds the entire musical extravaganza disintegrated. Defeated by the boisterous melodies and chords of the upright piano, Nadia lowered her arms and slowly pressed the concertina into a little ball on her lap; the mournful drone of the reeds faded away into a poignantly fitting death. She removed her hands from the instrument and touched the large

---

[*] Nadia is playing a hexagonal-ended, twenty-button, German-made concertina.

[†] *Camptown Races* is a minstrel song composed by Stephen Foster (1826-1864) in 1849 and published by F. D. Benteen of Baltimore in 1850.

dressing above her left eye where the stone had struck, then lounged in her chair and repositioned the concertina.

Manfred lowered his arms and reviewed his ragtag congregation sitting in armless-stiff-backed wooden chairs borrowed from the saloon. To his left, four men from one of the hard rock mines on War Eagle Mountain sat clustered together near a window: a Chinaman with long black hair, a muscular black man with an impressive shiner and a cauliflower ear, a grizzled old geezer who swore a lot, and a fellow who spoke a muddled and nearly indecipherable version of the English language. More to the right and separated from the four men by a good three feet sat the enigmatic Conrad Airingsail, his soiled wide-brimmed hat jammed down to the top of his spectacles and his soiled multicolored bandana pulled tightly beneath the nose. Conrad had entered the room unnoticed after the beginning of the hymn, but a vague scent of fresh manure, likely emanating from his spur-festooned boots and stained chaps, had announced his tardy arrival to everyone. To Conrad's left sat a young lady named Priscilla who Manfred had met only a few minutes before the beginning of the service. And close by Priscilla's side sat Nadia with her concertina. Yearning to see Alexandra Smythe again, Manfred glanced back at the opening to the back room of the saloon several times during the hymn, but she never appeared—even though he had invited her at least three times before her sudden disappearance from the masked ball nearly a month ago.

Manfred folded his arms across his chest as nonchalantly as he could manage and addressed the congregation in a calm tone. "Not bad for our first try. I thought the second verse was particularly splendid. But I think it's best to set this hymn aside for now and practice it again next Sunday. Why don't we proceed to a few readings from the Bible before I begin the sermon?" When he picked up the well-worn *King James Bible* from a round table by his side, he glanced back again to see if, perchance, Alexandra had yet wandered into the saloon. He faced the congregation with a clear look of disappointment and clumsily flipped through the pages of the Bible until he found the lesson he had chosen. "I shall read from the Psalms, number 23." He cleared his throat. "The Lord is my shepherd. I shall not want. He maketh me to lie down in green pastures: he leadeth me beside the still waters. He restoreth my soul: he leadeth me in the paths of righteousness for his name's sake. Yea, though I walk through the valley of the shadow of death, I will fear no evil: for thou art with me; thy rod and thy staff they comfort me. Thou preparest a table before me in the presence of mine enemies: thou anointest my head with oil; my cup runneth over. Surely goodness and mercy shall follow me all the days of my life: and I will dwell in the house of the Lord forever." Manfred began thumbing through the pages again. "And now I shall read from the New Testament, the book of Romans, Chapter Eight, Verse—"

Roshan Kuznetsov waved his hand. "Excuse of me to have the question, if you do not have the mind of it to ask."

This surprised Manfred. In his limited experience, no one had ever asked a question in the middle of the readings. "A question? A question about what?"

Roshan looked at Nadia before framing his question. "A question of this salami you have just of course spoke to we of it to be sure." He looked at her again when he had finished, seeking a nod of approval for his improved English.

Nadia held up her finger. "Mr. Kuznetsov, may I offer a suggestion?"

"Yes, you might always offer to Roshan the suggestion of what you speak. It is of my most pleasure to hear of it any of the times you may say of it in the now."

Manfred's eyes flitted back and forth between Roshan and Nadia. "A question about a salami? What salami are you referring to?"

Nadia suggested, "Say this to the pastor: I have a question about the Psalm you just read."

Roshan stood, scrunched his face in deep concentration, and addressed Manfred directly. "I have of this question about this salami to read."

Nadia stood. "I have *a* question, not *of this* question."

Roshan scrunched even harder and squeezed his hands into writhing lumps. "I have a question about this salami."

Nadia corrected again, "I have a question about the Psalm."

A little frustrated, Roshan asked Nadia, "Is my question not of the salami? What is this Psalm you speak of to Roshan?" He writhed his hands some more.

Manfred noticed that Conrad Airingsail's eyes appeared to smile at the amusing exchange between Nadia and Roshan, but he could not tell for sure because the man's mouth remained hidden beneath the bandana. "Mr. Kuznetsov, I was reading a *Psalm*, not a salami. I'm afraid you have confused the two words."

Roshan plopped down hard on his chair. "There is of the different between the two of these when you speak of the words to me?"

Nadia corrected again. "Too many words, Mr. Kuznetsov. Too many words. Say this: There is a difference between the two?"

Roshan attempted to repeat Nadia's words. "There is a many different between of two?"

Manfred intervened. "There is a great difference, Mr. Kuznetsov, between a Psalm and a salami. A Psalm is food for the soul; a salami is food for the stomach."

Gustus De Angeles perked up at this comment. "I know you're the preacher and I don't know a thing about anything but prospecting and mining, but, if you ask my opinion, that don't make a lick of sense."

The black man offered an observation. "Why, it makes perfect sense to me. Here's how I see it: you can lick a salami, but you can't lick a Psalm."

Gustus harrumphed, "That don't make a lick of sense neither. Why can't you lick a Psalm? Don't see any reason why you couldn't…if you put your mind to it."

Manfred inhaled and exhaled deeply and flipped through the pages of his Bible. "Why don't we set this discussion aside for another time, and move on to the next reading? Maybe we'll have better luck with a reading from the New Testament." Manfred sucked in another deep breath. "The book of Romans, chapter eight, beginning with verse thirty-five: Who shall separate us from the love of Christ? Shall tribulation, or distress, or persecution, or famine, or nakedness, or peril, or sword? As it is written, for thy sake we are killed all the day long; we are accounted as sheep for the slaughter. Nay, in all these things we are more than conquerors through him that loved us. For I am persuaded, that neither death, nor life, nor angels, nor principalities, nor powers, nor things present, nor things to come…."

Roshan waved his hand again. "Excuse of me once in the again, if you can hear of my lips to speak the words to know of what it is said. But how is this to be of the killed the day all along? Is it not the possible?"

Gustus De Angeles complained, "I was thinking the same thing. That don't make a lick of sense."

Nadia held up her finger again. "Mr. Kuznetsov, if I might offer another suggestion, I would recast your question in this way...."

Manfred looked back at the door, hoping to see the lovely Alexandra Smythe glide into the room and calm his lost soul.

In full compliance of his agreement with Margaret, Manfred picked up any loose objects and swept the floor clean and returned the chairs and tables to their original positions. When he had finished, he sat for a good twenty-five minutes before deciding to head back to his cabin. When he stood to leave, Alexandra Smythe unexpectedly entered the room. She stepped into the wintry light glowing through a nearby window, pressed the toes of her black shoes together beneath the hem of the black dress she had worn on the train from Chicago, and folded her hands. "Oh dear. Have I arrived too late for the church service?"

The ache in Manfred's chest, which he had forgotten during the pandemonium of the church service, reemerged. "Why no...I mean yes... in other words, yes, you have arrived too late. But I think it is better to have not arrived on time. It wasn't much of a service, at least in the traditional sense. It turned out to be more of a Shakespearean comedy. Or maybe it was more of a tragedy. To be honest, I'm not really sure what to call it."

"I see...but I'm still sorry to have missed it. I had a few chores to finish up and I didn't watch the clock like I should have."

Manfred refreshed his memory of Alexandra's pretty eyes, the pixie turn of her lips, and the crispness of her short-cropped hair. "Chores are important." Her hair was longer than he remembered. "Would you like to sit by the potbelly stove in the other room for a few minutes? I can probably talk the bartender into making a fresh pot of coffee." Her eyes were prettier too.

"It is not my habit to sit with men next to a potbelly stove in a saloon, particularly one with a brothel upstairs."

Manfred's pulse increased about ten beats a minute. "We...we...could walk to the War Eagle Hotel and sit in the dining room. I don't think there's a brothel within fifty feet of that establishment."

Now Alexandra's pulse increased, and she demurred. "It is both cold and windy outside. I don't think I'm interested in walking across town for a cup of coffee."

Although he had visited the Idaho Hotel only once, it offered his last hope to extend his liaison with Alexandra. "We could walk over to the Idaho Hotel and get a cup of coffee and something to eat there. They have a nice dining room next to the billiard parlor, and it's only a short walk from here."

"I am also not accustomed to sitting with men in a billiard parlor."

"We don't have to go into the billiard parlor... unless you want to play a game of billiards. The dining room's separate."

"Well, I suppose...."

Manfred charged forward. "Good! Then it's decided. Grab your coat and let's head over. I'm finished cleaning up here."

After a short walk on Avalanche then across Jordan then through the lobby of the Idaho Hotel then into the dining room at the back, Manfred and Alexandra sat at a small rectangular table covered with a white table cloth and a glass vase full of flowers and a half-full kerosene lantern. Manfred sipped his cup of coffee and watched the activity in front of the freight stables across the street. The dull gray skies suggested the possibility of snow.

Manfred set his cup down and judged Alexandra's temperament to be receptive. "You know, I don't even know where you live." She lifted the cup to her pixie mouth, sipped some coffee, set the cup down, and folded her hands without saying where she lived. He had possibly miscalculated her mood. "Well, no matter. I didn't invite you here to pry into your personal affairs. I just thought you should know a few things about me before we go any further."

Alexandra unfolded her hands. "But Manfred, we shared a great deal at the masked ball."

"True enough, but there are some important things I didn't share with you, and it's been bothering me that I didn't, especially when I thought I might never see you again."

Alexandra offered an elfish smile. "Don't be silly, Manfred. Of course you were going to see me again. It's just... I'm very busy and don't get into town much."

Manfred shifted and rested his elbow on the curved back of the chair. "I'm glad to hear you had full intention to see me again, but the dance was nearly a month ago." He quickly corrected his untoward accusation. "It doesn't really matter. I'm just glad to see you right now." Impetuously, Manfred reached across the table and grasped Alexandra's hand. "I must tell you something very important."

Alexandra squeezed Manfred's hand and whispered impishly, "What is so important that you can hardly wait to tell me?"

A darkness flowed across Manfred's face. "During the war, I killed many men, probably hundreds before I was done. When I entered the seminary after the war, I made a sacred vow to never kill again. Even so, I still see the faces of some of the men I killed—in my nightmares. One young boy in particular haunts me, sometimes even when I am awake."

Alexandra squeezed Manfred's hand again. "You were a soldier in the war. You had to kill to survive. Many men killed in the war. Why is it important to tell me this? I would never hold it against you."

"Because…you see…the problem is…the problem is this…I enjoyed the killing."

Alexandra shivered, but swiftly came to Manfred's defense. "Surely it was a fleeting emotion brought on by the daily horrors of battle?"

"I don't think so. The other day a crowd of people tried to hurt a friend of mine in front of the saloon. One man threw a stone and hit her in the head, and then tried to draw his pistol. Instead of turning the other cheek, I punched him in the nose and took the gun from him."

"Turning the other cheek is an admirable goal, but it sounds to me like you did the sensible thing…under the circumstances."

Now Manfred squeezed Alexandra's hand. "What you say makes good sense, but there's more to it."

Alexandra blinked. "More?"

"Yes, there is. I wanted to kill him. Only my sacred vow prevented it."

Alexandra released Manfred's hand and lifted her cup to sip some luke-warm coffee. While still cradling the cup in both hands, she said, "Thank you for sharing your secret with me. I admire you even more because of it, and I promise that I shall never tell anyone." She lowered the cup to the table and wiped her lips with a napkin. "But you are not alone. I can assure you that we all have secrets." After she said this, she did not speak more of herself.

CHAPTER NINETEEN

A visit to the doctor
December 4, 1871

Monday shimmered clear and bright. The slanting warmth of morning sun dazzled over the snowy mountains of Jordan Valley and warmed the snowcapped roofs of Silver City until the surface of the snow evaporated in rising waves of lucent vapor. The percussive melody of a blacksmith's hammer pounding hot-glowing rods of iron flat against the face of an iron anvil reverberated down the streets and alleys and echoed pleasantly off the distant trees and mountainsides. The iron-rimmed wheels of a freight wagon loaded with freshly-cut slabs of ice and pulled by six mules churned up the fresh snow and underlying dust into a muddy trail of freezing ruts running south down Washington Street. A floppy-eared dog of uncertain breed sauntered up to the front of the War Eagle Hotel and lifted its hind leg and peed on the boardwalk. The dog sniffed eagerly at the yellow stain before trotting away. A woman and her young daughter—both wearing clean white bonnets, dark wool jackets, brown leather shoes, and carrying large and small but otherwise identical baskets—scurried along the boardwalk across the street from the War Eagle Hotel before swerving into a general store that had opened for business only a few minutes earlier. A Chinese cook—his wrinkled apron stained with grease—staggered five steps from the back door of the Idaho Hotel kitchen with a large basin of dish water before flinging the soapy-brown liquid across the fresh snow in a steamy cascade. Three men—each one with beard, felt derby, wool vest and jacket, and wool pants tucked into knee-high leather boots—strolled from the saloon on the corner of Washington and Avalanche and headed for the Idaho Hotel for a breakfast of biscuits and gravy and hot coffee. About a mile north of town, the New York and Owyhee Mill vibrated the frigid air with the constant din of whirring shafts and spinning cams and the persistent beat of twenty iron stamp heads pounding a smoothly-flowing river of ore. A subterranean blast rumbled in one of the deep shafts on the far side of War Eagle Mountain a few miles to the south: an explosion more likely felt than heard by the residents of Silver City.

Roshan Kuznetsov twisted his rump in the hard chair and cupped a calloused hand behind his ear. "Did you hear of the noise which is of the now?"

Nadia, sitting in an equally uncomfortable chair, turned her head to look at Roshan's cupped hand. "Did I hear what? I didn't hear a thing. But I did feel the floor shake a little."

Roshan lifted his feet a few inches above the floor. "Yes, there was of it. The floor is of the shaking too and the noise in the ear is of the same, if you hear my eyes to speak of it."

Nadia parted her rouge-painted lips to suggest a more succinct and graceful sentence, but before she could say a word Dr. Guinevere Dupree swung open the door to the back room of her two-room clinic. "Sorry to make the two of you wait, but this is going to take at least half an hour."

Nadia asked, "Is it something serious?"

Guinevere sighed. "I suppose one might call it serious, especially the fellow in the back room. He shot off his big toe trying to demonstrate his quick draw technique to a bunch of drunken friends. He brought the toe with him in a cigar box and wants me to sew it back on, but I already told him the only thing I planned to do with it was plunk it into a bottle of formaldehyde so he can show it to his grandchildren and tell them a good story." The man groaned. A bit out of character, Guinevere simpered and winked before withdrawing into the back room and closing the door.

Roshan grinned and slapped his legs; two puffs of dust ejected into the air. "Because of these big toe who is shooted in the off the two of we have many of the chance to practice of the English in the time of the toe in the bottle of the farm-of-hides."

Nadia touched the dressing above her eye and sighed, "I suppose it would be a good way to pass the time. What would you like to talk about?"

Roshan deliberated before saying, "We should talk about you and the plans you have of the life you think of living before the now in the California of the garden and who can see the ocean if it looks at it."

Nadia corrected, "We should talk about you and your plans for the future."

Roshan frowned. "But I do not want to talk of the Roshan. I want to talk of the you."

Nadia decided not to argue. "Fine. Then let's talk about my plans for the future."

Roshan crossed his arms and nodded aggressively. "Good. You begin the first of it to give a start to the good. I will hear of the good with my lips and speak the best of English you should be proud to see of it when you speak the again."

Nadia held three fingers to her lips and cleared her throat with a delicate cough. "There's not much to tell, really. My plan is to save enough money to purchase a train ticket to California and buy a nice house with a small garden and a good view of the Pacific Ocean. I heard someone say the sunsets are breathtaking and the crashing waves inspiring. I also hope to have a family with at least four children. I've actually had pleasant dreams of long walks on the beach with my family. But at this point, as you can plainly see, my house on the ocean and family of four children is only a dream." Nadia folded her hands and closed her eyes.

Roshan cleared his throat too, but not delicately and without covering his mouth. "It is of the goodly plan, if you think of asking to me. Do you think it is of the possibly to make the money enough for it ... this ... this house of beach and breathing sun?"

The corners of Nadia's mouth dipped. "Probably not. I'm afraid recent financial events may require me to remain in Silver City much longer than I had anticipated." But then she joked, "But I have another plan, if the first one doesn't work."

"And of this plan is the what?"

"It's quite simple, actually. A wealthy gentleman will someday arrive in Silver City and ask me to marry him. This gentleman will provide the financial means to fulfill my dreams, and we shall move to California and buy a beautiful home with a view of the ocean and sit in rocking chairs outside on warm summer evenings next to the garden and watch the sunsets and crashing waves and raise a family of at least two boys and two girls and go for long walks on the beach and live happily ever after, just like in a fairytale."

A shadow of melancholy fell across Roshan's face. "Do you not think of it the love of one who has for you would be of the enough when there is not the wealthy?"

"What do you mean?"

"I mean of this to say: if the one who loves you with the most is asking of the marry then is this of enough? What is the money if the love is not inside with it?"

Nadia touched Roshan's hand. "Very sweet, Roshan, but I'm afraid the reality of life has crushed any desire I might have had to marry only for love. I decided a long time ago to marry someone who is rich so I can escape the cesspool of a life that is slowly drowning me." Nadia noticed the sadness in Roshan's eyes and quickly added, "But if I'm very lucky, maybe I can learn to love the wealthy gentleman later. I suppose anything's possible, given enough time. But I'm confident I will love my children, whether or not I love their father."

This statement did not soften Roshan's growing despair, and a dull pain emerged in his gut and wriggled around inside his stomach before ascending to the center of his heart. "It is of the much sad to hear of it love is lost to you in the day, but I think to understand."

The narrow door to the back room swung open and a man about thirty years in age with his right foot bandaged up to the ankle and a small glass jar wedged under his left arm and his right hand brandishing a cane stumbled into the office. Dr. Guinevere Dupree trailed behind. "Now you come back to see me in a few days. I want to make sure there's no blood poisoning. If there is, I'll have to take the whole foot off. And make sure you keep the dressing clean and dry. If it gets dirty or wet, come back right away."

The man held up the jar and examined his big toe. "Too bad you couldn't sew it back on. I sort'a liked my big toe. Sorry to see it sitting in this here jar instead of my foot."

Guinevere slapped the man on the back. "You're lucky you only shot the toe off. Be glad half your foot isn't floating around in a jar."

The man nodded. "I suppose you're right. Thanks for seeing me. I'll come back in two days, like you said." He grunted as he hobbled out of the office into the hallway.

Guinevere motioned Nadia and Roshan into the back room. She asked Nadia to sit on the table, then she peeled off the dressing above Nadia's eye and examined the wound. "The wound's healing quite nicely. I'll go ahead and remove the stitches."

Nadia asked, "Do you think it will it leave a mark?"

Guinevere pulled her reading glasses down to the tip of her nose. "Maybe a little one, but I don't think anyone will notice unless they look really close … or you point it out to them."

Nadia shuddered. "I have no intention of telling anyone about this terrible incident. If anyone ever asks, I will tell them I hurt myself falling out of a tree as a young girl."

Guinevere touched the wound. "Suit yourself, my dear. Now let's get those stitches out so you can be on your way. This should only take a few minutes."

With the stitches gone and the bill paid, Nadia and Roshan departed the two-story building housing both an annex of hotel rooms and the facilities of the local undertaker. When the fresh morning sunlight flashed across their faces, Nadia began speaking to Roshan in Russian. *"Thank you, Mr. Kuznetsov, for accompanying me to the doctor's office. I appreciate your concern. But I'm sure you have more important things to occupy your time, and I must return to the saloon. There is no need for you to tag along."*

Roshan answered in Russian, *"It was my pleasure to accompany you to the doctor's office, but I have no intention of letting you walk back to the saloon alone. I shall stay by your side until you arrive safely."*

Nadia objected, *"There really is no need for you—"*

Roshan raised his hand. *"I cannot think of anything more important than escorting you back to the saloon. I must insist that you allow me to do so. Please do not force me to argue with you."* Roshan bowed and offered his arm to Nadia.

Reluctantly, Nadia slid her hand around Roshan's arm and the two stepped off together. *"If you insist on escorting me, then I must insist on giving you a free English lesson when we have arrived safely at the saloon. It is the least I can do to reward such chivalry."*

Roshan remembered Nadia's plan to make enough money to buy a house in California. *"I will not be held responsible for any further delays to your plan to move to California by accepting free services. I will pay a fair price for my English lesson as usual. The pleasure of escorting you back to the saloon is reward enough."*

Nadia seized Roshan's wrist. *"Then I will not argue with you. But I must therefore insist that we speak only English from this point."* Nadia began speaking in English. "Tell me, what new words have you learned this week?"

Roshan stammered, "New words of the English in the week of now? You have much the surprise to Roshan and he must think to tell you, if you have the listen."

Nadia slowed her pace. "Take your time. There is still some distance to the saloon. Can you think of even one word?"

Roshan scrunched his face and announced, "Yes, I can think of the one word. Ridiculous. This is of the new word to this week for Roshan to know of."

"Very good. And can you tell me the definition?"

"Yes. It is the word of Mr. Gustus to say after many Roshan tells of anything to do in the cabin of very small in the Mahogany Gulch."

Nadia slowed her pace a bit more. "I see. But I think a better definition is something that is absurd or preposterous."

Roshan turned his head. "And what is of the absurd?"

Now Nadia stammered, "Why, I suppose you would say that something is absurd if it is ridiculously nonsensical."

Roshan squinted. "Nonsensical? And what is of the nonsensical?"

Nadia tried again. "Let's see. I would say something is nonsensical if it is foolishly absurd."

When they arrived at the boardwalk in front of the saloon at the corner of Washington and Avalanche, Roshan reverted to Russian. *"English has to be the most ridiculous language ever conceived. It appears to go in circles until it ends up at the same place you started."*

Nadia tried to comfort Roshan. *"I know it seems impossible at times, but you just have to stick with it. It will come to you eventually."*

Roshan heroically reverted to English. "I'm of glad you think of it too. Right of the now I think Roshan is the ridiculously nonsensical foolishly absurd one of us."

"Why Mr. Kuznetsov, I *am* impressed. You used all four of the new words in a single sentence, and it actually made sense ... " Nadia brushed a fleck of lint from Roshan's shoulder before saying, " ... more or less."

Roshan jiggled his head and a slab of snow fell off his hat and spattered on Nadia's shoes. He smiled when he realized she had tricked him into a free English lesson after all. At this moment, when he thought of Nadia's dream to buy a home in California with a view of the ocean and small garden and have a family with four children and go for walks on the beach with the crashing waves and sunsets, he decided to pay her double for his next lesson.

CHAPTER TWENTY

The time for action has arrived
May 5, 1872

T he cruel storms of winter now receding from remembrance, and
the promise of favorable weather now fully upon the cusp of a lumi-
nous spring morning, Ferd Tucker struggled to adjust the leather harnesses and iron fittings of the four oxen lollygagging in front of the prairie
schooner while Joniah rearranged the family's meager possessions in the
back. About sixty feet away, just beyond the easterly terminus of the wood-
sided-gable-roofed livery, Seth and Clarinda played a spontaneous game
of slap tag in the narrow alley snaking between a general store and a candy
and notions shop before connecting unevenly to Washington Street.

Seth punched Clarinda on the arm with his closed fist as she tried to
dart away. Clarinda bawled at her older brother, "You did it way too hard.
I'm gonna tell pa you hit me on purpose, then you'll get a whipping before
we leave today. You'll get a whipping for sure."

Seth objected to the accusation. "Didn't hit you on purpose. It was an
accident. And if you tell pa and I get a whipping I'll just hit you again later
when he's not looking except a lot harder 'cause that's what a little tattletale like you deserves."

Miguel Cervantes relaxed casually against the wall of the candy and
notions shop and listened with keen interest to the arguing children. He
chewed a splintered toothpick as he walked over to the children. "Hey,
you two: no more fighting. It's not right to fight."

Clarinda, still rubbing her arm, objected to the stranger's assertion.
"We weren't fighting. Just playing a little game of tag."

The strange man alarmed Seth. "Don't go talking to strangers, Clarinda. You know what ma and pa says."

Miguel spat a small chunk of the toothpick to the ground. "He's right, little girl. You listen to what your brother says." He offered a sly warning. "You wouldn't want to get into trouble on the day you're leaving town, would you? Is that your wagon in front of the livery?"

Clarinda exclaimed proudly to the friendly stranger, "Yes it is. Father and mother are getting ready to head out today. They said we'll be in Boise City before we knows it."

Miguel spat another chunk and lowered his hands to his knees. "And when might that be, little Clarinda? I suppose you'd want to head out soon to take advantage of the daylight."

Clarinda puckered her lips and scrunched her nose. "Pretty quick, I reckon, but I don't really know for sure 'cause ma and pa are still working on the wagon." She relaxed her face and smiled. "But I think they're almost done."

Seth grabbed his sister's arm and pulled her away from the stranger. "C'mon Clarinda. We have to get back to the wagon."

Miguel Cervantes gallantly flicked the brim of his hat. "You have a safe trip now." When the children were gone, he spat the mutilated toothpick to the ground and hustled away.

Joniah clambered down from the back of the wagon holding an old bucket. "Ferd, you seen the children? It's getting to be about time to leave and they're nowhere to be found."

Ferd pulled a leather harness taught. "Last time I saw them, they was chasing each other down that there alley. Haven't seen 'em since, but I heard 'em screaming a few times, so I know they're alright."

Joniah spread her feet and pressed both hands against her hips. "Heard them screaming a few times so you know they're alright? Well I never! I suppose you expect me to go find them all by myself."

Ferd dropped both knees to the ground and bent down to inspect the wood tongue running between each pair of oxen. "I don't mind looking for 'em, but if you want it done right this minute you'll have to go find them yourself. If you haven't noticed, I'm sort'a busy right now harnessing up these oxen, and if you ask me they ain't helping much."

Annoyed, Joniah pushed back her bonnet. "Fine, but I want to leave right away when I get back. I don't want to spend one more second in this unforgiving town, which, I would like to point out, was your idea to come to in the first place. We should've gone to Oregon like I wanted to in the first place. That's what we should'a done."

Ferd straightened up. "If I remember correctly, you didn't complain much when we decided to go to Silver City instead of Oregon. Matter of fact, I remember you were kind'a excited about the idea when that fellow at the mercantile suggested it in the first place."

Joniah crossed her arms defiantly and grunted, "That's not exactly how *I* remember it, but if *you* want to remember it that way, I'm not going to argue with you."

Ferd stood and brushed the dirt from his knees. "I'll go find the children now since you talked long enough for me to finish with the harnesses. A lot better than standing here arguing with you anyhow."

Before Ferd could take a step, Clarinda ran up to him with mock tears streaming down her pink cheeks. "Seth punched me on the arm, and he did it on purpose. Do you want to look at the mark it made?"

Seth suddenly appeared right next to his distraught sister. "Did not punch her on purpose. It was an accident, and she's a tattletale. We was just playing a game of slap tag, and she's a sore loser, if you ask me."

Clarinda implored, "You gonna give him a whipping before we leave town?" She pushed her lip out and sobbed.

Ferd had already used up his limited reserves of patience arguing with Joniah. "I'm gonna give the both of you a whipping if you don't get in the wagon right now. Your mother is ready to leave and I'm tired of hearing about how much she don't like Silver City and we should've gone to Oregon instead."

Joniah helped the children climb into the back of the prairie schooner. "I made some room for the two of you to lie down, if you want." She walked to the front of the wagon, climbed up to the seat, snuggled next to Ferd, and proclaimed, "I'm ready to leave."

Ferd snapped the leather reins and the four oxen lurched forward with a shuddering tug. "Suit yourself, but I didn't think Silver City was all that bad." Without saying a word, Joniah folded her arms across her bosom and glared straight ahead.

Csongor Toth listened to Miguel's words with perceptible ennui. Seth and Jackson slouched in their usual chairs in front of Csongor's polished desk. Seth tapped the scuffed heel of his grubby boot against the chair leg. Jackson fidgeted with a new pistol, then pulled out a handkerchief and polished the barrel and front sight. When Miguel had finished his report about the wagon family, Csongor masked a small yawn before flipping his hand in the air with a jocular snap and announcing to his three associates, "Gentlemen, at long last … at very long last … the time for action has arrived." Csongor folded his hands behind his back and began wandering around the office. "Jackson, round up the horses and prepare them for the upcoming adventure. Seth, collect the Indian clothing, bows and arrows, and related accouterments procured from those hopeless savages at Fort Hall.* Make sure nobody sees you. Miguel, prepare to follow that wagon with haste; report back to me without delay when the family has traveled exactly one mile from town. At that time, we will each leave separately before reconvening at a time and place to be announced. There we shall don our Indian attire and prepare for battle." Csongor ceased pacing and pointed grandly to the ceiling. "When we have finished our work today, the good citizens of Silver City will beg for our protection from the bloodthirsty savages who are about to press in from all sides of the town. Then, gentlemen, through the proper application of our unholy canard, we shall become wealthy beyond our wildest dreams." Csongor rubbed his hands together in an aberrant display of delight.

Jackson didn't even bother to ask what the word "canard" meant, because he really didn't care anyway. After sitting up in the chair, he simply replied, "Whatever you say, Mr. Toth. Whatever you say." He stood, jabbed the handkerchief into his pocket and the pistol into his belt, and declared, "Time to go, boys. Time to go."

Clarinda held tight to the jittering tailgate of the prairie schooner and watched the receding buildings of Silver City. When the wagon neared the top of a lumpy hillock, she noticed a man on horseback following

---

*   The U.S. Government had relocated the Bannock Tribe to a reservation at Fort Hall by 1869.

some distance behind. She squinted and thought she recognized the man. She yelled to her older brother, "Seth, I think there's a man following us."

Seth sat up and looked though the arched canvas opening at the rear of the prairie schooner. "What man are you talking about? I don't see nobody."

Clarinda yelled a little louder, "The man who talked to us in the alley when we was playing slap tag. The one who was interested in where we were going. I think he's riding behind us right now. Come and see for yourself."

Seth crawled to the back of the wagon to take a good look for himself. "I don't see the man who talked to us in the alley. I don't see nobody at all. You must be going crazy again."

Clarinda quickly turned to confirm what she knew she had seen, but the man had vanished. "He was there, and I'm pretty sure it was the man who talked to us in the alley."

Seth rolled his eyes and scoffed, "You are going crazy again, and we've hardly started our trip to Boise City."

The dappled light of morning filtered through vertical gaps in the rough-hewn siding of the barn and sparkled on floating dust. The earthy fragrance of freshly-cut hay permeated the damp air. A gentle breeze creaked the rusted hinges on a loose door. The pioneers of Silver City had constructed the barn on Jordan Creek at the northern end of Washington Street about seven years earlier. The intent of the barn was to provide feed for horses and mules and oxen before they began the long climb north over the Owyhee Mountains toward Boise City, but this morning the barn provided a splendid shroud of concealment for the birth of the unholy canard of Csongor Toth.

Jackson barked at Miguel, "You got the mule loaded yet? We need to get riding before the wagon family gets out of range. At this rate we won't leave before noon."

Miguel snapped back without looking up from his work. "I'm going as fast as I can. It ain't easy packing up these bows and arrows so nobody can see them. If you think you can do it faster, then come over here and give it a try yourself."

Dressed in riding boots and pants, tweed jacket, spotless bowler, and sporting a new riding crop imported from Boston, Csongor Toth crooned, "Patience, gentlemen. Patience. We are in no particular hurry at the moment. The wagon we seek is pulled by four oxen whose pace is no faster than a slow walk. I could probably catch the family on foot in less than two hours."

Seth mounted his horse and watched Miguel tie off the last burlap sack of Bannock Indian accouterments. "You can walk if you like, but I'm riding."

Without a wisp of passion, Csongor Toth simply replied, "Just so, my comrade. Just so."

Ferd and Joniah watched the four horsemen—and one heavily-laden mule—gallop by the prairie schooner and vanish around a switchback about a half-mile down the road after kicking up a choking wall of dust. Joniah took particular interest in the dapper gentleman dressed in riding boots and tweed jacket, because when he pulled up even with the front of the wagon he slowed enough to tip his bowler. She did not recognize the man, but he acted like he recognized her.

Ferd watched the man doff his hat to Joniah before kicking his horse into a fierce gallop to catch up with the other men. Ferd snapped the reins to the plodding oxen. "What was that all about? You know this fellow?"

Joniah blushed. "I swear I've never seen him before. I have no idea why he did that."

Ferd's voice trembled with suspicion. "Well it sure seemed like he knowed you. Not every day a man tips his hat like that to a woman."

Joniah crossed her arms. "I don't know what you're thinking about, Ferd Tucker. I never seen him before in my whole life, and that's the truth of it."

Ferd snapped the reins again, a little harder, and the four oxen continued at the same pace. "Not thinking about anything. Just seemed like he knowed you, that's all."

Joniah said no more, and the oxen plodded.

Jackson swore. "This shirt don't fit worth a darn. Who'd you buy it off of? Some sort of midget Indian?"

Miguel snarled back while he hopped around on one foot trying to pull on a pair of leather breeches (with a colorful bead motif) that didn't fit all that well either. "Don't know who it came from, but you only have to wear it for an hour, so stop your fussing."

Jackson held his arms out and the sleeves reached three-inches short of his wrists. "And another thing, this shirt stinks to high heaven. You should've washed it before packing it up and bringing it out here."

Csongor Toth intervened. "Gentlemen, please calm yourselves. The wagon will arrive within minutes. We do not have time to argue about the bouquet of the clothing."

Seth sat on the ground and pulled on a pair of oversized moccasins. "What's 'bouquet'?"

Now Jackson snarled at Seth. "You heard the man. You don't need to know what the boss's fancy words mean to know he wants you to finish getting dressed before the wagon gets here."

Seth stood and squirmed his toes inside the moccasins. "Just wondering. How do you 'spect me to improve my 'cabulary if I don't ask questions?"

Csongor Toth positioned a red headband across his forehead and tied a figure eight knot in back, then slung a quiver of arrows over his shoulder. "The wagon will arrive any moment. Gentlemen, or should I say Indians, collect your weapon of choice and take your positions in the manner we discussed."

Pulled by the four plodding oxen, the prairie schooner ascended a long, upward grade, and after rolling over the top of the hill began a relatively-steep descent down toward a tree-lined bend in a narrow creek. Joniah held her hand above her brows and squinted at the creek. "Is this the same creek that runs through town?"

Dozing a bit, Ferd had not noticed the creek until Joniah pointed it out. "Don't know for sure. Might be, but don't know for sure." Then he noticed four men standing in a line across the road. "What's going on here?"

Joniah, still looking at the creek, asked, "What's going on where?"

Ferd rubbed his neck. "There's four men standing in the road, and if I didn't know better I'd say they were the ones who—" The sharp crack of a rifle shot resounded off the mountains. Ferd slumped to his left without releasing the reins. The oxen continued plodding toward the bend in the creek and the four men standing in the road.

The startling rifle shot yanked Joniah's attention to the four men. She shifted around to ask Ferd what he was talking about and noticed he was slumped over. She closed her mouth and looked a little closer and saw a stream of blood drooling from a ragged hole in his back. She touched the gurgling hole and held the blood-smudged fingers close to her face. The oxen plodded toward the four men. Joniah tried to grab the reins from Ferd's hands, but they slipped away and fell to the side. The oxen plodded toward the four men. Joniah screamed into the back of the wagon, "Seth and Clarinda, run back to town and get help. Run now! Run! Run!" The oxen plodded toward the four men. Joniah reached behind the seat and pulled out an ax. She kissed her fingertips and touched Ferd's lifeless cheek before stepping off the wagon, marching toward the four men, and brandishing the ax as threateningly as she could manage.

Csongor Toth chastised Jackson. "Was that truly necessary, my dear Jackson? I thought we had all agreed to dispatch the family with arrows and knives? I had no idea you intended to shoot anyone when you brought that thing along."

Jackson shoved the lever down on his Winchester Model 1866 and clacked it up to load another round. "I had a clear shot. I was afraid they might get away if we just stood here and waited for them to get down here."

Csongor leaned on his bow and mused sarcastically, "Oh yes, I can see your point now. Those oxen might have suddenly reared up on their hind legs and spun around in the middle of the road before executing a hasty retreat back to Silver City. Such an event would have required us to walk somewhat briskly to catch up."

Seth noticed movement beyond the wagon. "The two of you might think this is funny, but there's someone running away from the wagon.

And there's a woman coming this way with an axe. And she don't look too happy, if you ask me."

Csongor sighed, "Now see what you have done, Jackson? We will now be forced to improvise because of your thoughtlessness."

Seth asked, "What does 'improvise' mean?"

Jackson snarled, "Shut up, Seth."

Csongor Toth intoned, "Alright, gentlemen, here is the new plan. Jackson, you take the axe away from yonder approaching woman and tie her to the wagon exactly as I have instructed. Seth and Miguel, apprehend those children and bring back their scalps." Csongor adjusted his red headband. "And please try to act like real Indians when you accomplish your assigned tasks. We are, after all, professionals."

Clarinda and Seth, alarmed by the shot and the way their mother had screamed, did not ask any questions. They scurried to the back of the prairie schooner, leaped to the ground, and ran. Holding his younger sister's hand to keep her from falling, Seth repeatedly glanced back as they stumbled to the top of the hill. When he stopped to catch his breath, two Indians darted by the wagon and headed up the hill. Seth pulled Clarinda over the hill and then to the side of the road. "There's no way you're gonna outrun these fellows. You've got to hide in the bushes by that tree." He pointed. "I'll try to lead them down the road. When it's dark and nobody's around, you walk back to town and get help. Understand?"

Clarinda sniffed and tears streamed down her cheeks. "But what if they catch you?"

Seth waved his finger in her face like his mother would have done. "Don't you worry none about me. Just get yourself behind that bush, and don't move or make a sound or go nowhere until after dark." Seth grabbed Clarinda's shoulders, spun her around, and pushed her. "Now get before I sock you a good one."

Clarinda hopped off the uneven shoulder of the road, tripped on a rock, ran to the bush her brother had pointed at, and hid with her face pressed into the ground. She heard the Indians run by, and then she heard whooping and hollering somewhere down the road. She waited for what seemed to her a very long time. She pushed up on her little hands and scuffed knees and peeked through the top branches of the scrubby bush. One of the Indians had returned, and with the sun at his back he leaped off the road and charged straight at her. She dropped to her stomach and hid her face and sobbed.

Joniah struggled against the ropes that pulled her right arm backwards over the top of the wagon wheel and stretched her left arm to the side. She pushed up on her toes to relieve some of the pain in her shoulders before scowling at the man standing a few paces in front of her. She spat her words at the man. "You ain't gonna get away with this."

Csongor Toth pulled an arrow from his quiver. "My dear Jackson, kindly remove the lady's clothing to allow me to observe the position of her legs."

Jackson pulled out a large knife and sneered, "All of it?"

Finding the arrow a bit warped, Csongor dropped it to the ground and acquired another. "Of course not, Jackson. I should have expressed myself more clearly. Please leave her undergarments in place. We are not, after all, uncivilized heathens."

Jackson licked the tip of the knife. "With pleasure." When he had finished removing her bonnet and cutting off the dress and a few other items he didn't think were necessary, he stepped back and admired his work.

Joniah glared at Csongor. "What're you a fixing to do now?"

Csongor raised the bow and nocked the first arrow. "Not that it is any concern of yours, my dear, but I'm 'a fixing' to recreate the martyrdom of Saint Sebastian as portrayed in the painting by Dutch artist Gerrit van Honthorst—a painting I have had the opportunity to view at great length on several occasions. I can therefore assure you that I have taken the time necessary to memorize every important detail. This should only require a few minutes of your time, and then we shall be on our way and will trouble you no more."

Joniah finally remembered. "I know you. You're the man who tipped his hat back there on the road." She gritted her teeth and sputtered, "I hope you... burn in hell for this."

"How sweet of you to remember our brief but tender rendezvous. And thank you for the charming personal sentiment. Now, my unfortunate darling, it is time to begin." Csongor pulled the bowstring back and took aim.

CHAPTER TWENTY-ONE

An unexpected act of kindness
May 5, 1872

The Nez Perce woman impaled four thick cuts of fresh elk backstrap on a sharpened juniper stick. After adjusting the spacing of each chunk of meat, she positioned the stick on top of a pair of flattish rocks about six inches above the fire. Blood dripped into the glowing coals and vaporized into hissing steam geysers. She allowed the meat to cook until it sizzled, then grabbed the stick at both ends and gave it a smooth one-quarter turn. She repeated this process six more times, then lifted the stick from the rocks and coaxed the backstraps onto a tattered square of leather with the sharp blade of her bone-handled knife. She kneeled down and sniffed the savory cuts and sprinkled a few pinches of salt over the meat. She had traded her necklace of elk teeth to a Silver City man for a small bag of salt, and very little of the precious seasoning remained. She thought to herself that she should make another necklace of elk teeth and find the same man to trade for another bag of salt, but this would require the killing of another large elk.

Riding on the appaloosa together, Joshua Hotah and the Nez Perce boy trotted from a ragged stand of mountain mahogany trees. The appaloosa pranced across the small stream that flowed within a few hundred feet of the Nez Perce woman's teepee, then cantered up close to the cooking fire. Joshua Hotah swung the boy down to the ground and dismounted.

The Nez Perce boy spoke to his mother in English. "We no shoot elk today. We see elk, but we no shoot elk. Elk far away."

Joshua Hotah dropped to his knees and warmed the dirty palms of his hands over the fire. "It is cold today. I hope the sun is warmer tomorrow, because I have grown tired of the cold." He sniffed the aroma of the cooked and salted elk backstraps. "You have been busy today. The elk meat you have cooked smells good. I think I will enjoy eating what you have made."

The Nez Perce woman wiped the blade of the bone-handled knife on her buckskin dress. "Thank you, Joshua Hotah. Good morning," but unlike her son, this was nearly the extent of her willingness to speak English.

Joshua Hotah stabbed one of the backstraps with the tip of his knife, raised the meat to his mouth, and bit off a morsel. He spoke to the Nez Perce woman as he chewed. "You have cooked this meat with much skill, but you should try to say more English. Your son has learned many English words, far more than I thought he could in six months. I think he almost sounds like a white man when he speaks."

The Nez Perce woman looked down and smiled broadly. "Thank you, Joshua Hotah. Good morning."

Joshua swallowed the chewed backstrap. "Say this: Thank you, Joshua Hotah. I will try to speak more English."

The woman stammered, "Thank you … Joshua Hotah. I will try … speak more … good morning."

Joshua gnawed off another bite. "Better, but you should try to speak like your son."

The woman scrunched up her face with the appearance of great effort and said, "Thank you, Joshua Hotah. I will … try speak more." She handed a cut of elk backstrap to her son.

Joshua comforted the woman. "It is enough English for now. We will practice more after we have finished the elk meat."

The boy tugged Joshua Hotah's sleeve. "Is there horse to ride today?"

Joshua winked at the appaloosa. "Yes, you can ride the appaloosa today, but only if you stay near the camp. I do not want to see you getting into trouble. The appaloosa is one who looks for trouble and often finds it. You do not need more trouble in your life."

The boy opened his mouth to speak more English words, but the sharp crack of a rifle shot rang out in the distance. Joshua Hotah quickly looked in the direction of the shot and listened for another. When the echo faded away and the mountains remained silent, he stood and finished the last of the elk meat and licked the knife clean, taking care not to cut his tongue on the sharpened blade. He spoke to the woman without facing her. "If you will forgive me, I must ride to the sound of the shot and take a look for myself. When I return, your son can ride the appaloosa, as I have promised. Try to practice some English with your son while I am gone."

The Nez Perce scrunched her face again. "Thank you, Joshua Hotah. I will try speak more. Good morning."

The appaloosa did not understand the necessity of searching for the source of a stray rifle shot, but nonetheless agreed to race along the uneven dirt road at a steady gallop when urged onward by Joshua Hotah. It would have sorely disappointed the animal to have known that Joshua did not himself know why he was riding toward the shot, especially when he could have stayed in the pleasant camp with the friendly Nez Perce woman and her funny son who had learned to speak many English words. But the familiar resonance of the rifle shot, and the direction from which it had originated, compelled Joshua to investigate, and as he approached the source of the shot he unknowingly provoked a sequence of events that would forever alter the path of his life.

After riding by a tree-lined bend in a narrow creek, the appaloosa ascended a steep hill and slowed to an easy walk. Joshua soon spotted a wagon pulled by four oxen, except the oxen where not pulling and the wagon was not moving. The appaloosa stopped fifty feet downhill from the wagon. Joshua pulled his Henry repeating rifle from its sheath, dismounted smoothly, and lifted the rear sight to his eye. His keen vision found a man with open eyes and drooping mouth sitting in the seat but bent over awkwardly to the side. He walked up to the man without speaking, and noticed an oozing bullet hole to the left of the man's heart. Joshua lowered the rifle barrel but kept the butt pressed against his shoulder as he slinked along the side of the wagon and swung around the back. He stopped briefly to look into the rear of the wagon, but found only a few chairs, a small desk, a leather-strapped chest, a few wooden casks, some tools, several boxes, food supplies, and a metal bucket filled with rocks. He lifted the rear sight to his eye again and peeked around to the other side of the wagon. And there, tied with hemp ropes to the iron-rimmed wheel in a strange manner, he found a dead woman pierced with arrows in her stomach, left breast, right thigh, and left arm. He lowered the rifle and studied the odd expression on the woman's face. He stepped closer to the woman and inspected each of the four arrows, beginning with the one piercing her leg. He considered whether or not he should poke her in the shoulder, but instead leaned forward until his nose stopped only a few inches from hers. He thought of holding his hand over her heart to confirm that she was as dead as her pallid color indicated, but before he could decide she opened her eyes. Joshua Hotah did not frighten easily, but when the dead woman's eyes opened he swore in Sioux and jerked back. When the dead woman did not talk and Joshua had calmed himself, he asked, "Who has done this terrible thing to you?"

The dead woman swallowed twice before speaking words that rasped her swollen tongue. "It weren't Indians who did this."

Joshua repeated his question. "Who did this to you?"

The dead woman answered, "It was white men who was dressed like Indians." Then she begged, "Please help my children. I don't know what happened to them."

Joshua dropped the Henry rifle to his side and rested the butt on the toe of his moccasin. "Where are your children? I will help them if you can tell me where to find them."

The dead woman coughed. "Please help them. Their names are Seth and Clarinda. They are very young." She inhaled a wheezy breath.

Not knowing what to do, Joshua feigned confidence. "I will find your children. Do you know where I should look for them?"

The dead woman arched her back away from the iron rim of the wheel and groaned softly. "Up the road. Look for them there."

Joshua nodded, and jogged up the road to search for the dead woman's children. He loped back to the wagon after twenty-minutes. This time the dead woman did not frighten him when she opened her eyes.

The dead woman asked Joshua, "Did you find my children?"

Joshua fidgeted with his rifle and looked down at the dead woman's swollen feet. "I found your children and they are both safe." He nearly recoiled at the wound from the arrow piercing the dead woman's breast. "I hope you will forgive me for not bringing them here to talk to you.

I don't think it is right for them to see their mother in this terrible way." Joshua hesitated, then explained, "I asked them to wait by a big tree a long walk from here. I will take them to Silver City when I finish turning the wagon around. I gave them a canteen so they could both have a drink." He finished his report with, "Your little girl is very pretty."

The dead woman attempted a weak smile, and asked, "What is your name? I wish to thank you properly for saving my children."

"My name is Joshua Hotah."

"Thank you, Joshua Hotah, for saving my children. I appreciate it."

Joshua remembered the man sitting bent over in the front of the prairie schooner. "Is your husband sitting in the wagon?"

"Yes, he is my husband. He is dead."

"Yes, I have noticed he is dead. I will bury him for you."

"Thank you, Joshua Hotah." The dead woman dropped her chin against her chest and shuddered. She used the last of her strength to rise up again and gaze into Joshua's eyes. "Can you do one more thing for me, Joshua Hotah?"

"I will do anything you ask."

The dead woman lifted her arrow-pierced leg, then let it fall lifeless until her toes rested on a patch of blood-soaked mud. "Will you please kill me, Joshua Hotah? I don't care to suffer no more. I don't mind going to Heaven now because I know Seth and Clarinda are safe."

Joshua cradled the Henry rifle above his elbow. "I will do as you ask, but first you must also tell me your name."

The dead woman rasped, "My name ... is Joniah Tucker, and I want you to know ... I already ... forgive you for this ... unexpected act of kindness." Joniah gazed contentedly upon Joshua Hotah's face one last time.

Joshua Hotah raised the rifle and aimed at the center of Joniah's faintly-beating heart. "Good-bye, Joniah Tucker. I hope you have a good trip to Heaven." He pulled the trigger. Already weak and near death from pain and loss of blood, Joniah's eyes fluttered briefly before she died. Joshua Hotah cut the ropes binding Joniah's arms, laid her on the ground near the wagon, and methodically broke off the four arrow shafts close to the wounds. He found a remnant of Joniah's dress beneath the wagon and used it to cover her torso and part of her legs. He called the appaloosa with a shrill whistle, then rode up the road to fetch Joniah's dead children.

When he returned, he arranged the children next to Joniah—Seth to the right and Clarinda to the left—and positioned Joniah's lifeless arms around them. He found a rusty shovel and a dull pick with a splintered handle in the back of the wagon, hiked down the road to a pleasant stretch of ground overlooking the tree-lined bend in the narrow creek, and began digging. The appaloosa followed Joshua down to the creek and kept him company as he toiled in the rocky soil, but did not say anything.

A Preview of
Book 3: Nor Things to Come

By Muireall Anne Ravenscroft,
award-winning author of *A Concise History of the West*
and other acclaimed works of nonfiction.

As I explained at the conclusion of *Book 1: The Perilous Journey Begins*, I originally vacillated when Rich Ritter inquired if I had any interest in editing the manuscript of *Nor Things to Come: A Trilogy of the American West*. My indecision derived from my limited experience with fiction writing: to date I have only written in the nonfiction genre. However, with encouragement from my husband, because John knows that I have decided to begin work on a fictional novel—that is, when I have sorted out the storyline to my satisfaction—I agreed to the opportunity. After a year of editing and intense collaboration, I continued my association with Mr. Ritter by writing the synopsis of *The Perilous Journey Begins*, which I trust you read thoroughly before plunging into this second volume of the trilogy. I am therefore pleased that Mr. Ritter has asked me to write a preview of *Book 3: Nor Things to Come*, because it confirms his appreciation of my previous efforts.

In the preview of *Gathering of the Clans*, I wrote, "As with all great stories, *Book 1* has ended with many unanswered questions." Although you may find it difficult to believe, this statement is even more pertinent to this second book of the trilogy. Of particular concern are the precarious circumstances of Joshua Hotah. After discovering Joniah Tucker tied to a wagon wheel and pierced with arrows, he shoots her through the heart to end her misery. I fear that Joshua's unexpected act of kindness will invite only more misery. And what of Csongor Toth? He has proven that he cares for Gordania by saving her twice, but with the horrific massacre of the wagon family he has also proven that he is unpredictable and dangerous. Manfred Herrmann has shared his darkest secret with Alexandra. Is their relationship doomed because of this disturbing revelation? Priscilla Kimball appears to have chosen an occupation that rewards backbreaking work with endless peril. Nadia has protected her to this point, but what if she is distracted when Priscilla needs her most? Longwei and Roshan have taken John Smith (actually the shootist Elijah Brown) to Mahogany Gulch to help work Gustus De Angeles's worthless claim. Will this dubious relationship lead to comedy or tragedy (or possibly both)? And what of our enchanting heroine Gordania Sinclair, who was given the moniker Alexandra Smythe by Csongor to conceal her true identity? Once delightfully innocent but now irreparably flawed, will the tragic death of Meredith Brewster haunt her to the very end? Because I have no intention of diminishing your enjoyment of this story, you will find no predictions here. But, as this is a preview, I do feel obligated to present a few hints of the delicious events you can anticipate in the final book of this magnificent trilogy.

In the first seven chapters of *Book 3*, you will learn more of Csongor Toth's infamous past—including his psychologically lurid infatuation with a flirtatious peasant girl at the age of 14. None of this new information will calm any misgivings you may have of Csongor's potential for unspeakable evil. Joshua Hotah will encounter all manner of calamity after making the decision to transport Joniah and her children to Silver City on a travois. I do not want to give away any particulars, but I can promise that the townspeople will not herald him as a hero. Already swimming in a cesspool of depravity at the saloon on the corner of Washington and Avalanche, Priscilla Kimball will not improve her status when she attempts to befriend Joshua Hotah. Alexandra Smythe will meet Csongor at the Idaho Hotel, supposedly for a game of billiards and dinner, but instead of playing billiards she announces that she is concerned for Manfred's safety because he is walking around town asking people to donate money for the Indian's legal defense. In what should have been an innocent request, she asks Csongor to intervene. Will his apparent indifference portend more wickedness to come? Csongor's plan to sell protection from Indians will lead his three henchmen—Jackson, Seth, and Miguel—to Mahogany Gulch, where they will engage Gustus De Angeles in an unfortunate confrontation that will change everything.

The unsettling events of the next seven chapters will almost certainly cause profound apprehension. You will meet Reginald Simpson, the prosecuting attorney who slicks his hair down with oil (consistent with his personality) and is looking for an opportunity to improve his stature in the community. Judge Roy Parker will make his appearance in the story. His colorful language, heavy-handed use of the gavel, and desire to always move things along because it's time for the next meal will not give you much confidence in the legal system. After earlier asking Csongor to stop Manfred from raising money for the Indian's legal defense because she was concerned for his safety, a change of heart prompts Alexandra to ride to Manfred's cabin and implore him to do something to save Joshua. The meeting does not go well when Manfred attempts to explain to Alexandra that he is powerless to influence the outcome. He changes his mind the next day and embarks on a desperate play that may endanger his friends. An unusual incident at Mahogany Gulch nearly kills Roshan and Longwei (as well as John Smith). The incident will alter the trajectory of their business partnership. Csongor will arrange a nocturnal meeting with Manfred at a livery—with potentially devastating consequences. Roshan will ask for Manfred's counsel on a questions that is, "…of the simple and not of the simple of the same time." And, finally, Csongor will meet at his office with Jackson, Seth, and Miguel to offer a provocative business proposition. Monsieur Hector Faure, who first appears in chapter 6, will mysteriously reappear after the meeting to offer his deviously learned advice to Csongor.

I cannot say much of the final seven chapters because to do so would give away too much of the story and spoil the many surprises awaiting you. I will not even tell you if the surprises are pleasant or tragic. But I can provide a taste of the final chapters. A day of reckoning will arrive, followed by a day of confusion. Manfred will further risk jeopardizing his relationship with Alexandra by sharing his plans with her during a picnic on the sun-dappled hills above Silver City. Tseng Longwei and John Smith will achieve enlightenment at Mahogany Gulch while building a new cabin. Roshan and Nadia will engage in a spirited discussion in Russian at The Sommercamp Emporium and General Store. Manfred will write his last words in a diary. Later that same night, he will discover the truth after a confrontation with Csongor Toth.

The closing scene will take place outside Guinevere Dupree's medical clinic in 1872, but the surprises do not end here. The epilogue, which spans only a few pleasant hours on a crisp spring day in Mendota, Illinois in the year 1882, will offer one final revelation that I know you will find most astonishing—that is, if you have not already figured it out. And now I must conclude this preview, as John and I have to pack for a trip to San Francisco to discuss my new book with the publisher. Adieu, dear reader, until me meet again at the beginning of *Book 3*.

CHAPTER NOTES

CHAPTER ONE

1. Due to a ten-day trip to New Orleans to attend an AIA convention, several summer visitors, a bit of surgery, a Juneau Symphony concert, and a few other excuses which I do not care to share with you, I permitted myself a six-week hiatus before commencing the first draft of Book 2. But I did not let the time pass aimlessly. During the final weeks of this sabbatical I read the following before starting the first chapter:

> Adams, Mildretta. *Historic Silver City: The Story of the Owyhees.* Tenth Printing. Homedale: Owyhee Publishing Company, 2001.
> Welch, Julia Conway. *Gold Town to Ghost Town: The Story of Silver City, Idaho.* Moscow: University of Idaho Press, 1982.
> Nettleton, Helen. *Interesting Buildings in Silver City, Idaho.* Fifth Printing. Homedale: Owyhee Publishing Company, 1998.

I found each of these personal accounts of the history of Silver City fascinating and useful, and recommend them to anyone interested in further study. I used information from the first two books, in part, to write Muireall's excerpt titled "Silver City: The Jewel of the Owyhees," although each book's account of the "Blue Bucket Legend" is quite different. I should also explain that I purchased my copy of *Gold Town to Ghost Town* at Pat's What-Not Shop on the corner of Jordan Street and Avalanche Avenue mere seconds before Julia Conway Welch entered the store: I managed to talk her into signing it for me.

2. I've just returned from my third trip to Silver City, Idaho. Kris and I flew into Bozeman, Montana on Sunday, July 24, 2011, where we rented a car and stayed the night. We drove to Sheridan, Wyoming the next morning to resolve some personal business. The daytime

temperature hung just a degree or two below 100 during our two days in Sheridan—a bit higher than the middle fifties we had left behind in Juneau—and only cooled to the high eighties during the evenings. On Wednesday the 27th we drove north to the junction to Highway 14 then west through Ranchester, across the Bighorn Mountains to Burgess Junction and Shell, then on to Graybull and Cody, through Yellowstone National Park (had to pay $25 for a day pass to enter the park), across the state line into Idaho, then down Highway 20 to Rexburg (we could see the Teton Range to the east on the way), Rigby, Idaho Falls, Blackfoot, and finally Pocatello (home of Idaho State University) where we stopped for the night. The next morning we continued on Highway 86 to American Falls, took the junction west on Highway 84 to Twin Falls, Mountain Home, Boise, Nampa, and arrived at Caldwell (where the daily temperature had cooled to 97 degrees F) around three in the afternoon. We stayed in Caldwell at the home (with central air conditioning—thank goodness!) of our close friend Yvonne until Sunday morning, then packed her car with provisions and two dogs before heading south to the Owyhee Mountains and Silver City. We arrived around two in the afternoon at Von's "cabin" on the hillside east of the main town, released the dogs, carried our luggage into one of the bedrooms, and then enjoyed an afternoon rest before cocktails at six (a Silver City tradition, I'm told). That night we ate taco salad on the porch overlooking Silver City and enjoyed a thunderstorm with horizontal bolts of lightning flashing amongst dark clouds some miles west of Florida Mountain. An hour later heavy rains pelted the cabin's metal roof for nearly two hours before abating, but I rather enjoyed the sound of it. Illuminated by an antique lamp powered by the cabin's new solar panel electrical system, we played cards at the kitchen table until around midnight. Kris and I slept well that night and enjoyed a cool breeze flowing in through an open window next to the double bed. The next morning (Monday), Von cooked pancakes and bacon for breakfast, and the three of us enjoyed a long walk beyond the south end of town in the hot morning sun. Although the temperature was probably 10 degrees cooler than Caldwell, I managed to burn the backs of my legs—likely because I was 3,500 feet closer to the sun. Upon our return to town we strolled into Pat's What-Not Shop and visited with Pat for twenty minutes. Pat said she would keep an eye out for a good map of Silver

City (circa 1870), and I purchased the following additional resources to support my research:

Chadwick, Alta Grete. *Tales of Silver City.* Third Edition, revised 1994.

Owyhee County Historical Society. *War Eagle Mountain Field Guide: Historical and Mining Road Log.* Prepared by Wilma Lewis Statham with H.R. 'Rusty' Statham and William P. Statham. Revised Edition, July 2003.

The field guide includes a superbly-detailed map of the historic mines and sites on War Eagle Mountain and around Silver City. After lunch and an afternoon nap, I walked back down the hill and photographed 360-degree panoramas at each of the primary street intersections. I also checked bearings from several key points with my Cammenga Military Lensatic Compass (I had cleverly preset the magnetic declination for Silver City before leaving Juneau). That evening we ate dinner on the porch again (marinated flank steak and noodles, corn on the cob, salad, and red wine), enjoyed homemade pie for desert, and bathed pleasurably in a cool breeze flowing in over the mountains from the northwest. The next morning I dragged myself out of bed around eight, dressed in shorts and sandals, and hiked up the hill to snap a few additional panoramic photos from above the town. When I returned to the "cabin" we ate omelets and drank coffee for breakfast and Kris and I helped Von clean up. We departed for Caldwell around noon. After successfully negotiating the winding 23-mile road out of Silver City, we stopped at the Owyhee County Historical Society Museum in Murphy and I made contact with the new director—a graduate of Boise State University. I told him about my work on *Nor Things to Come: A Novel of the West,* and he recommended that I include a Basque sheep herder in the novel. We stayed in Caldwell at Von's home that night, and flew out of Boise for our return to Alaska the next afternoon.

CHAPTER TWO

1. Originally a small log structure built in Ruby City to house miners and prospectors, the War Eagle Hotel was moved to Silver City around 1864. According to Alta Grete Chadwick in *Tales of Silver City,* two men named Way and Mayes expanded the log structure after the relocation, although she does not describe the functional purpose

or extent of the addition. John Grete Sr. purchased the building in 1878 and constructed another addition and a separate boarding house across the street, bringing the total number of rooms to 35. Other hotel spaces included an office (with high counter to check in guests), parlor, barroom, and dining room. Alta Grete Chadwick notes that the hotel always employed two Chinese cooks (supervised by her grandmother), and that the hotel was noted for the quality of its food. Unfortunately, I have not yet located a photograph or detailed description of the dining room, and have therefore resorted to my writer's imagination.

2. Today in Silver City, services are conducted once a month during the summer at *Our Lady of Tears* Catholic Church. The steep-roofed-white-painted building—complete with stained glass windows and a bell tower above the main entrance—is located on a rocky hillside near the northern end of Morning Star Street.

3. In the pamphlet titled *Interesting Buildings in Silver City, Idaho*, Helen Nettleton writes: "In 1868 the Community Church in Ruby City had been bought, remodeled and dedicated as St. Andrew's Catholic Church. In 1879, after Silver City had eclipsed Ruby City, it was sold and there was no church again until 1882 when the Graham building, opposite the Idaho Hotel, was remodeled and dedicated to Our Lady of Tears." She also notes that the Episcopal Church constructed the existing church in Silver City between the years 1896 and 1898, held services whenever convenient, and then gave the building to the Catholic Diocese of Boise in 1928. I have therefore fictionalized the presence of *Our Lady of Tears* Catholic Church in Silver City during the early 1870s to support the storyline, and, more importantly, to create an obvious disparity between the religious facilities of the Catholic Church and the Lutherans. I have also fictionalized an official presence of the Lutheran Church in Silver City, but I'm convinced they would have sent someone like Manfred Herrmann if they had known about the place at the time.

4. Although I made my best effort, I could not locate a floor plan of the War Eagle Hotel and, unfortunately, the building no longer exists. I therefore combined a street-level photograph of the front of the building with a birds-eye view taken from the hillside to the southwest to extrapolate a likely arrangement of the lobby, office, saloon, and dining room. I suppose I could have placed the meeting between

Father Nero and Manfred Herrmann at the Idaho Hotel, which is still standing and which I recently visited, but I heard that the War Eagle Hotel had the best food in town (see note #1 above).

Update: When I worked through the first draft of chapter 12, I discovered that the 1903 Sanborn Map Company map of Silver City (noted below in chapter 3 note #1) does illustrate the basic ground floor plan layout of all buildings, including the War Eagle Hotel. The hotel office (lobby) and saloon front Washington Street, while the kitchen and dining room are located at the rear of the hotel looking easterly onto Jordan Avenue across a wide opening between two buildings. I have revised the chapter to match these conditions. See chapter 12 note #1 for comments about the number of floors and other issues at the saloon on the corner of Washington and Avalanche.

CHAPTER THREE

1. The only general store remaining in Silver City today is the "Hawes Bazaar" on the eastern side of Washington Street between Second Street and Dead Man's Alley—just down the way from the site of the War Eagle Hotel. Helen Nettleton records in *Interesting Buildings in Silver City, Idaho* that a Mr. William F. Sommercamp arrived in Silver City in 1864 and operated a general store for many years, but she does not indicate the date of construction or the original name of the store. A fellow named Richard S. Hawes purchased the building in 1885 and converted it into a restaurant, which he operated until 1894. In that same year, he relocated to DeLamar where he opened another general store. Although I never confirmed the original date of construction, I did find another photo of the building on page 106 of *Gold Town to Ghost Town: The Story of Silver City* (Julia Conway Welch) with the following caption: "The Hawes store, formerly Sommercamp's store." However, because the word "store" is not capitalized, I can only assume that the word "Sommercamp's" indicates the possessive case and not the name of the store. In the Idaho State Historical Society Digital Collections, I found a map of Silver City prepared by the Sanborn Map Company in 1903 that shows four general stores on Washington Street alone (as well as more saloons than I bothered to count). The map does not provide any of the names of the stores. I have therefore chosen to create a fictional name and

to make a reasonable assumption for the date of construction: *The Sommercamp Emporium & General Store - Est. 1867.* I have spent a great deal of time searching for an interior photograph of one of the general stores in Silver City, but have failed to find anything. I will let you know when, or if, I do.

CHAPTER FOUR

1. New York Summit was named after the New York and Owyhee Stamp Mill. According to the Owyhee County Historical Society *War Eagle Mountain Field Guide*, this 20-stamp mill was built and running by autumn of 1865. It was used primarily to process ore from the various hard rock mines operating on War Eagle Mountain.

2. In Muireall Anne Ravenscroft's excerpt titled *From Las Medulas to Silver City: The Techniques and Implements of Mining*, the paragraphs on Roman mining techniques and definitions of terms were derived primarily from *Wikipedia* and *The American Heritage College Dictionary* (Fourth Edition), respectively. The paragraph on the construction and operation of the gold rocker was derived primarily from the following article and website: *Do it Yourself, Old Time Gold Rocker Box*, (nevada-outback-gems.com/design_plans/DIY_rocker/Rocker_box.htm).

3. My selection of Anaheim as John and Muireall's destination is not capricious. My parents moved from Des Moines, Iowa to El Monte, California in 1958, and then to Anaheim a year later. I completed first grade in El Monte, but the Anaheim City School District provided my education from the second grade through high school. I attended Loara Elementary School, Trident Junior High School (now a community center), and Loara High School. My sister, Robin, attended the same schools two years behind me. We both participated in band: Robin played the flute and bassoon and I played percussion and tuba. My mother taught first grade for many years at Clara Barton Elementary School. My father worked as a comptroller (I believe this is correct, but my memory is fuzzy on this point) at Aerojet General in Downey, and later as a cost analyst at Aerojet General in Fullerton. I remember him talking about the engine and fuel tanks on the Apollo Lunar Module. When the family moved to Anaheim, Disneyland was only a few years old and orange groves bordered our small two-street neighborhood on three sides. I have many fond memories of playing with friends in those groves—although the play could turn scary at night, especially when a rotten orange zinged by your head in the

dark. Anaheim, now the tenth largest city in California, was founded in 1857 by German farmers and vintners. This original colony, which consisted of 200 acres, is now the "downtown" area inside the boundaries of North, East, South, and West Streets. The name "Anaheim" is a composite of "Ana," from the nearby Santa Ana River, and "heim," the German word for home. Anaheim therefore meant "home by the river" to the original German colonists. At first they planted grapes for wine, but a plague wiped out the vineyards in the 1870s. The community responded to this tragedy by planting groves of citrus trees, as well as walnuts and chili peppers. These early farmers and vintners did not, however, limit themselves to farms and vineyards. They were also writers, artists, and musicians. When the time came to construct the community's first public buildings, they did not build administrative facilities: they built a school and an opera house. (www.anaheim. net/article.asp?id=216)

CHAPTER FIVE

1. The General Mining Act of 1872—the current federal law that governs mineral rights and the right to explore for and mine minerals on federal lands—is deeply rooted in the traditions of the Greek and Roman Empires and the precepts of English and Spanish law. From ancient times to the present, three basic principals have remained consistent: 1) Governments have generally held mineral rights; 2) Miners have generally maintained the right to enter land to explore for and mine minerals; 3) Miners have been required to pay a fee for this privilege to land owners or the government. The Greeks operated mines on Mount Laurion from 700 to 200 B.C. and produced the first extensive body of mining literature—and the first recorded mining lawsuit. Under Greek law, minerals were the property of the state. The Romans searched relentlessly for precious metals: a map of the Roman Empire coincides remarkably well with the distribution of mineral wealth in Europe, Asia, and North Africa. Under Roman law, the State operated existing mines in conquered territory (sometimes leasing to public companies and individuals), but mines discovered through exploration were operated by individuals who had to pay a fee to Rome. During the Dark Ages* that followed the collapse of

---

* The Dark Ages encompass the early part of the Middle Ages from 476 to around 1000.

the Roman Empire and into the Middle Ages,* Europe was chaotically governed by hundreds of potentates who consistently agreed that minerals were their property. Over time the chaos evolved into a practical set of mining laws, first formalized in 1185 in the charter of the Bishop of Trent. Under these laws, the State held the mineral rights, miners were given the right to freely enter the land to explore and mine, and miners were expected to share any discovered wealth with the State. In 1201 a charter of King John granted free right of entry to miners, but usurped the rights of the landlords. The landlords later compelled King John to moderate this claim. Spain first developed codes in the middle of the 16th century to deal with mining in the colonies of the New World. These laws incorporated the right of free entry to public and private lands, the requirement to register a claim, and the right to exploit the claim without further specific authorization. Unfortunately, the Spanish Crown imposed increasingly higher royalties as new gold mines were discovered to the point that production decreased, many new discoveries were not reported at all, and smuggling and official corruption became the norm. These problems were partially corrected by the promulgation of the Spanish Royal Codes in 1783. In 1602, Richard Carew's *Survey of Cornwall* extensively recorded and clarified known customs and rights of mining that were later maintained in broad principle well into the 19th Century. The principles embodied in the *Survey of Cornwall* included the following: 1) Miners were allowed to freely enter public lands and stake claims; 2) Mineral rights were limited to the vertical boundaries of the claim; 3) The miner had to pay a fee to the landowner; 4) Miners could not legally enter lands where the landowner also held the mineral rights, but were allowed to negotiate a private arrangement with the landowner. In the early years of mining in the United States, miners generally followed the Spanish Royal Codes of 1783 and English law. A few early U.S. laws were passed, such as the 1807 law addressing lead mines and salt springs, but not until the California gold rush of 1848 and the discovery of silver in Nevada in 1854 did the U.S. Government feel compelled to explore a more comprehensive mining law. Disagreement imme-

---

* The Middle Ages are the period in European history between antiquity and the Renaissance, often dated from 476 to 1453.

diately ignited between the Federal Government and the State of California, and many proposals were offered by both sides including taxing the mines, leasing of mineral lands with permits sold to mines, and administration of mineral rights solely by the State of California. After much discourse, Congress passed the Lode Law in 1866, which was amended to include placer claims in 1870. It is important to understand that the Lode Law (as amended) substantially conformed to the rules and regulations commonly used by the miners of the time. In 1872, Congress further amended the Lode Law to include protection of agricultural rights and to establish a consistent set of Federal rules. This act became known as the General Mining Law of 1872, and, with the exception of additional minor amendments, the law remains substantially intact today. (*A Short History of Mining Law* by Jonathan DuHamel, December 19, 2011, TucsonCitizen.com)

2. The Pulteney Distillery was founded in 1826 in the town of Wick in northeast Scotland by James Henderson during the height of a legendary herring boom. Because there were no road links with Wick during the early years, the distillery depended on shipping by sea for both supply of barley and export of malt whisky. Wick soon became renowned for two specific products: herring and whisky, both of which the city exported to the world in vast quantities. Today the distillery is the most northerly on the British mainland. I have attempted to purchase a bottle of Old Pulteney in Juneau—as background research for this novel, or course—but have come up short. I may be forced to order a bottle or two to further my studies. (www.oldpulteney.com/history-distillery-history.php)

> Update: Somehow aware of this predicament, my oldest son gave me a bottle of Old Pulteney 12-Year for Christmas. We saved it until New Year's Eve before conducting suitable research. I have recorded my review within the context of Csongor Toth's fictional description. Forgive me for not including the words "nose," "notes," "finish," or "maritime" in the dialogue.

CHAPTER SIX

1. Julia Conway Welch devotes an entire chapter to the Chinese experience in *Gold Town to Ghost Town: The Story of Silver City, Idaho.* She begins Chapter 9 with this introductory statement: "The treatment of the Chinese in Idaho followed the pattern already set by its

neighboring states. Mining laws and union organizations discrim-
inated against them, vigilantes took it upon themselves to punish
them, and they were fair game for all kinds of pranks and humil-
iations." Although the Chinese immigrated to America in large
numbers throughout the 19th Century during the so-called "first
wave" (over 300,000 by 1880), the estimated Chinese population
in the Owyhee region of southern Idaho during the 1870s was only
700. The Chinese of Silver City lived in wall-to-wall rows of unin-
teresting buildings fronting the southern end of Jordan Street—
near the present-day picnic grounds. In the 1880s and 1890s this
Jordan Street "Chinatown" offered a variety of facilities including
dwellings, an assortment of stores, lottery rooms, and gambling
houses. Opium was sold in a few of the gambling houses. A document titled *A Historical, Descriptive, and Commercial Directory of
Owyhee County, Idaho*, published in 1898 and known by the residents of Silver City as the "Blue Book," had one listing for a Chinese
business: "Song Lee, Chinese Merchandise and Wood Contractor."
By the 1920s only three Chinese residents remained in Silver City:
King Tan, a handyman and occasional merchant; Ah Moon, who
lived in a house decorated with splayed kerosene cans; and Little
Dick, the cook at the hotel.

CHAPTER SEVEN

1. The original inhabitants of the area that is now the State of Idaho
   included the Kootenai, Coeur d'Alene, Palouse, Kalispel, and Salish
   in the northern panhandle; the Nez Perce in the central region; and
   the Paiute, Shoshone, and Bannock in the south. The Nez Perce
   were first discovered by Lewis and Clark in 1805. At the time the
   tribe occupied an area that is now western Idaho, northeast Oregon,
   and southeast Washington. According to Lewis and Clark, the Nez
   Perce roamed between the Blue Mountains in Oregon and the Bitter
   Root Mountains in Idaho, and occasionally crossed over the mountains and travelled as far east as the headwaters of the Missouri River.
   Through the Treaty of 1855, the Nez Perce relinquished title to
   all of their lands to the United States except for a large reservation
   encompassing the Wallowa Valley, an area west of the Snake River in
   what is today the northeastern corner of Oregon. However, in 1863
   Calvin H. Hale (Superintendent of Indian Affairs of the Washington
   Territory) and Indian Agents Samuel D. Howe and Charles Hutchins

consummated a supplementary treaty with several bands of the Nez Perce nation that excluded the Wallowa Valley from the reservation. The Wallowa Valley and vicinity were subsequently surveyed as public lands and declared open to settlement in 1867. Following the counsel of his father—Old Chief Joseph, who died in 1871—Chief Joseph (also known as Young Joseph) repudiated the Treaty of 1863 and claimed the Wallowa Valley as the sacred home of his band. This decision ultimately led to the Nez Perce Indian War of 1877, which ended in October of the same year 40 miles south of the Canadian border in the foothills of the Bear Paw Mountains after a 1,400 mile fighting retreat from pursuing U.S. Cavalry. (www.native-languages.org/idaho.htm, www.accessgenealogy.com/native/tribes/nezperce)

2.   Although I spent several hours on three separate days searching the Internet, I found only a few useful Nez Perce words and phrases, and I found nothing at all during my hunt for an authentic Nez Perce girl's name. Fortunately, I did find the following phrases: "Ta'c halaxp, manaa wees?" (*Good afternoon, how are you?*), and "Ta'c wees." (*I am good.*). I also found the following words: "m'a min" (*horse, appaloosa*), "qoq'a lx" (*buffalo*), "sa'qant' yx s'a qan" (*eagle, bald*), and "x'axa c" (*bear, grizzly*). Your guess is as good as mine on the correct pronunciation. (www.nezperce.com/npedu13-2a.html)

3.   My research of American Indian sign languages focused primarily on whether or not the Sioux and Nez Perce both used sign language, and if so, could they have communicated with each other using sign language in 1871. After significant effort and numerous dead ends, I finally discovered an article on sign history by William Tomkins[*] that included the following notation: "Chief Joseph of the Nez Perces [sic] said that his tribe learned the language from the Blackfeet, some 80 years earlier, and yet it is a well-known fact that these Indians used gesture speech long before that time." In a separate article titled *American Indian Universal Sign Language,* William Tomkins discusses his investigations with: "... Blackfoot, Cheyenne, Sioux, Arapahoe, and other Indians of recognized sign-talking ability." Between the two articles then, it is clear that the Sioux and Nez Perce are connected

---

[*]   The article includes this elaborate subtitle: *Some Research With Reference to the Origin and Wide Dissemination of Indian Sign Language in North America.*

by mutual association with the Blackfoot, and evidently used a sign language universal to the Plains Indians of North America. The latter article also includes an elaborate "dictionary" of signs and numerous graphic charts illustrating key signs, some of which I used to determine that the word "doctor" would have been constructed using the individual signs for "white man, chief, and medicine," and that the word "dead" would have been constructed using the individual signs for "die and sleep." I did not try to describe the signs used in the story because of the needless complexity this would have introduced. For example, this is how the sign for "medicine" is described: "Hold right hand close to forehead, palm outwards; index and second fingers separated and pointing upwards, others and thumb closed; move hand, upwards while turning from right to left in a spiral." The punctuation is quoted verbatim. (http://inquiry.net/outdoor/native/sign/history.htm, www.manataka.org/page310.html#Introductory Notes)

4. The first genuine medical school for women, the Women's Medical College of Pennsylvania, was established in 1850. Elizabeth Blackwell, who entered the Geneva Medical College (Geneva, New York) in 1847, later founded the New York Women's Medical College in 1868. Modeled after the medical school in Edinburgh, Scotland, the very first American medical school began in 1765 at the University of Pennsylvania (Philadelphia). Other notable medical schools of the period included Dartmouth (1798), Harvard (1803), Maryland (1807), Ohio Medical College (1819), and Worthington Medical College (1832). By the late 1860s, university medical students studied "...anatomy, physiology, chemistry, and therapeutics, followed by *materia medica*,* pharmacy, obstetrics, and elementary surgery. But few schools, even in 1870, offered any laboratory or clinical work." However, to gain a fundamental understanding of the state of medicine in the American West, it might prove useful to review a chronological outline of selected events relevant to the storyline of the novel:

   a. During the time of the American Revolution, it is estimated that less than 400 of the 3,500 practicing doctors held university degrees.

---

* *Materia medica* is a Latin medical term for the body of collected knowledge about the therapeutic properties of any substance used for healing.

b. Doctor Benjamin Rush (1745-1813) trained more than 3,000 doctors in the dubious practices of bloodletting, sweating, diuretics, vomiting, and blisters to treat a wide range of ailments.

c. Digitalis was used to treat cardiac patients as early as 1815, although doses were sometimes too large and resulted in death.

d. Dr. John L. Richmond performed the first caesarean section in 1827 in rural Ohio using only a pocket case of instruments. The child died, but the mother survived.

e. The stethoscope was in general use by 1826 and the clinical thermometer by the 1830s. Doctors also commonly used the otoscope (the familiar medical device used to look into the ear) by the 1860s.

f. Dr. Crawford Long first used ether to produce surgical anesthesia in 1842. Dr. W. T. G. Morton operated on an etherized patient for the first time in 1846 at Massachusetts General Hospital. In 1847 in Edinburgh, ether was first used to achieve a painless childbirth; however, the practice was not widely accepted in Great Britain until Queen Victoria gave birth to Prince Leopold using ether.

g. In 1847 Dr. I. T. Semmelweis managed to reduce the death rate in the maternity ward of the Vienna General Hospital from 12.4% to 1.27% in only two months by requiring his students to wash their hands in chlorinated lime water and to scrub their fingernails with a hand brush. Nonetheless, the hospital administrators were not convinced and did not adopt these procedures.

h. Elizabeth Blackwell (noted above), the first traditionally-trained woman doctor in the United States, received her diploma in 1849 after overcoming considerable opposition.

i. In 1855, during the Crimean War, Florence Nightingale introduced hygienic standards into military hospitals.

j. Henry Gray published *Anatomy of the Human Body* in 1858. The book remained a standard text on the subject for more than a century.

k. In 1865 Joseph Lister began using a continuous spray of carbolic acid (now known as phenol) during operations and developed a lint bandage soaked in carbolic acid, thus initiating the age of antisepsis.*

---

* Antisepsis is the prevention of infection by inhibiting or arresting the growth and multiplication of germs. Antisepsis implies the idea of scrupulously clean

l. At Harvard from the years 1866 to 1879, medical students attended only two lecture courses, which required a little less than four months to complete. If the medical student could also provide evidence of three years of study at another medical school or under the mentorship of another doctor and pass a nominal examination, they were awarded a degree in medicine.

m. By 1870, there were over 62,000 physicians in the United States serving a population of nearly 40,000,000 (according to the census), and the existing medical schools were turning out an additional 2,000 doctors each year.

n. I felt compelled to conclude with the following direct quotation from the Christine Jeffords essay (cited below) as I am not quite sure how to recast this fascinating information in my own words. "Typical charges [of a country doctor in the American West] included the following: sterilization and bandaging of a cut (not requiring stitches), 20-50c.; lancing of a carbuncle, 50c.; use of syringe, $1; bleeding, $1-$2; treatment of a wound made by a bullet that went clean through, the same; removal of a bullet, $1-$5; cleaning, stitching, and bandaging of a wound, $2; cupping, $2-$5; correction of a broken nose, $4; surgical operations, $5-$25 (presumably depending upon difficulty); delivery of a baby, $25-$50 (though most demanded only $10), plus a 50% surcharge by night."

(*Doctors, Healers, and Health: The State of Medicine in the Old West*, an essay by Christine Jeffords).

5. A fellow named Hancock performed the first deliberate appendectomy in 1848. The medical community generally perceived this as an extreme procedure and did not readily accept Hancock's advice. Not until 1867 did William Parker of New York again practice the techniques advocated by Hancock, but because he understood the principals of antisepsis previously introduced by Sir Joseph Lister (see above), he succeeded where Hancock had failed. Hancock recommended the operation from the fifth to the seventh or the eleventh to the fourteenth days. According to the Mayo Clinic the symptoms of appendicitis *may* include the following:

---

and free of all living microorganisms.

a. Aching pain that begins around your navel and often shifts to your lower right abdomen
b. Pain that becomes sharper over several hours
c. Tenderness that occurs when you apply pressure to your lower right abdomen
d. Pain that worsens if you cough, walk, or make other jarring movements
e. Nausea
f. Vomiting
g. Low-grade fever
h. Constipation
i. Inability to pass gas (this symptom is a critical part of the story)
j. Diarrhea (see item h. above)
k. Abdominal swelling

Although I did not find specific evidence, I have assumed that the above symptoms were generally understood in 1871 and have therefore used them freely in the story. (*History of Appendicitis Vermiformis: Its Diseases and Treatment*, an essay by Arthur C. McCarty, M.D., University of Louisville 1927; MayoClinic.com)

CHAPTER EIGHT

1. Now that it is finished, I must reveal to you that Chapter 7 nearly did me in. I don't know why it caused so much suffering and required so much time, but it did and I'm happy to move on to Chapter 8 and let Muireall Anne Ravenscroft take over the next few pages. She is the better writer anyway.

2. I used the following primary Internet and other resources to write Muireall Anne Ravenscroft's excerpt in Chapter 8 titled *Courtesans and Nymphs du Prairie*:

> *The American Heritage College Dictionary* (Fourth Edition), Wikipedia (which noted that the sources for the article titled "Courtesan" are unclear),
> http://home.infionline.net/~ddisse/aragona.html (*Other Women's Voices: Translations of Women's Writing Before 1700*),
> http://scandalouswoman.blogspot.com/2008/11/cora-pearl-english-beauty-of-second.html,
> www.legendsofamerica.com/we-paintedlady.html (*Painted Ladies of the Old West*, an article by Kathy Weiser)

CHAPTER NINE

1. In the pamphlet *Interesting Buildings in Silver City, Idaho*, Helen Nettleton explains that the Masonic Hall was originally built as a planing mill to produce finished boards for construction purposes, and that the Masons began using a second floor room for social purposes around 1868. The Masons purchased the building in the middle 1870s and remodeled it in 1892. In the book *Historic Silver City*, Mildretta Adams confirms that the building was built as a planing mill in the 1860s, and adds that both the Masonic and Odd Fellows lodges were established in Silver City in 1865. She notes that the building has been used by residents for social gatherings and dances, but does not record the year when such uses began. In *Gold Town to Ghost Town*, Julia Conway Welch writes that in the later years of Silver City (1930s) dances held in the Masonic and Odd Fellows Halls attracted outsiders from Murphy and other towns including Jordan Valley, Oregon, but she does not mention any dances at the Masonic Hall in the late 1860s or early 1870s. The website

    http://ednapurviance.org/silvercity/silvercityidaho.html

    displays numerous photographs of present-day Silver City, and states that the locals began using the second floor of the Masonic Hall for entertainment purposes in the late 1860s, including masked balls. The website does not indicate the year of the first masked ball. Given this information, I have quite possibly fictionalized the occurrence of a masked ball on the second floor of the Masonic Hall in 1871.

CHAPTER TEN

1. The following selected information is summarized from an essay titled *The Chinese Language(s): An Overview for Beginners* by David K. Jordan, Professor Emeritus of Anthropology, UCSD.
    a. The phrase "Chinese language" describes a number of mutually unintelligible but historically-related languages, or groups of dialects, spoken by the Han people of China.
    b. Mandarin, the most common language, is spoken in north, central, and west China. The Mandarin of Beijing has been the language of government for centuries.
    c. Important non-Mandarin languages, or dialect groups, include the following:

    i.   Cantonese, which derives from the city of Canton, is spoken in the Guangdong province and was once the most common dialect in the Chinatowns of North America.

    ii. Hakka is spoken in parts of Guangdong and Fujian provinces.

    iii. Hokkien, also called Southern Min, is spoken in southern Fujian and Taiwan provinces.

    iv. Foochow, or Northern Min, is the dialect of the northern Fujian province.

    v. Shanghainese is the language of the lower Yangzi Valley and Shanghai.

    vi. Xiang is the language of Hunan province.

d. Taken together, the groups of dialects that compose verbal Chinese are spoken by approximately 94% of the population of China. The remaining 6% speak Tibetan, Mongol, Yao-Miao, Thai, Uigur, and other non-Han languages.

e. Although not directly relevant to the storyline, it is useful to know that the dialect of Beijing was chosen as the official national language of China in the twentieth century. This is the "Chinese" usually taught in schools outside of China.

f. Written Chinese uses hieroglyphics, which are called "characters" in English. The largest Chinese dictionary lists nearly 50,000 characters, although there is a theoretical possibility of 190,032 compound characters. The writing system is largely independent of the sounds used in spoken Chinese, and therefore can be understood by the speakers of all dialect groups of China.

2. I used two primary resources to write Tseng Longwei's bonfire story of the blue dragon and beautiful princess. First, a single-page document titled *Simplified Chinese Seasonal Star Map (Latitude: 22.5 degrees N)*. I found it on the following website:

www.lcsd.gov.hk/CE/Museum/Space/StarShine/HKSkyMap

This particular star map shows the night sky at the noted latitude at 10 pm on November 1, 9 pm in the middle of November, and 8 pm at the end of November. Because the latitude of Silver City, Idaho is 43.01 N, the star map is not a perfect match, but I deemed it close enough for the purposes of a fictional story. Second, an article titled *The Chinese Sky* from the following website:

http://idp.bl.uk/education/astronomy/sky.html

Although not particularly relevant to the story, this article offered the following selected tidbits of fascinating information:

a. The ancient Chinese believed events in the sky directly correlated with events on earth. They also believed the emperor was the Son of Heaven, and that he had been given a mandate to rule by Heaven itself. Because of this mandate, the emperor expected his astronomers to watch the sky very closely and to predict important events—such as eclipses of the sun and moon and Halley's Comet—accurately. Because of this expectation, Chinese astronomers began recording the timing and physical appearance of Halley's Comet* over 3,000 years ago. If the astronomers failed to correctly predict an important astronomical event, the emperor's power would appear diminished and his political adversaries might feel sufficiently emboldened to rebel.

b. The Chinese sky is divided into five regions called *gong*, which are aligned with the north, south, east, west, and a middle region. The middle region is considered the most important because it houses the celestial image of the emperor and his family, as well as important civil and military officials. Each of the other four houses is associated with a specific animal, color, and season of the year. The Black Tortoise (*Xuan wu*), a symbol of longevity and often paired with a snake, is associated with the north and winter. The Blue Dragon (*Qing long*), generally considered by the Chinese as both benevolent and auspicious, is associated with the east and spring. The Red Bird (*Zhu que*), sometimes seen as a phoenix and representing good fortune, is associated with the south and summer. And the White Tiger (*Bai hu*), thought by the Chinese to guard the spirits of the dead, is associated with the west and autumn.

c. The Chinese sky is further divided into 28 segments called mansions or lunar lodges (*xiu*). The Chinese calendar system was based on the phases of the moon, measured by observing the position of the stars in the 28 mansions, as well as the time of the solar year.

---

* Halley's Comet appears in the sky every 70 to 75 years.

CHAPTER ELEVEN

1. Although I could not establish an exact date, the War Eagle Hotel did not enjoy the luxury of indoor plumbing until some years after 1871.* Gordania's (or Alexandra's—whichever you prefer) bath would therefore have required hotel staff to heat the water separately and fill the tub by hand using buckets. According to an article titled *History of Plumbing in America* in the July 1987 issue of Plumbing and Mechanical Magazine, The Tremont Hotel, built in Boston in 1829 and designed by a twenty-six-year-old architect named Isaiah Rogers, was the first American hotel with indoor plumbing. The four-story building incorporated eight water closets on the ground floor and bathrooms in the basement. The bathrooms were supplied with cold water piped from a roof-mounted storage tank and furnished with bathtubs of copper or tin fitted with a small furnace at one end. Although I am not certain how this worked, the water supposedly circulated until heated to the desired temperature. Five years later, the Astor House of New York City—also designed by Isaiah Rogers—surpassed the Tremont Hotel by offering 17 individual bathrooms on the upper floors, each with a water closet and bathtub, to serve the 300 guestrooms of the six-story building. The Tremont Hotel and Astor House were the first American buildings constructed with significant indoor plumbing, but these were relative anomalies. Consider the Statler Hotel of Buffalo, which created a sensation in 1908 by offering "A room with a bath for a dollar and a half." I present the following supplementary points of interest from the same magazine article for my civil and mechanical engineering friends:

   a. The use of cast iron pipe for municipal water mains first occurred in Philadelphia in 1804. The city sold its discarded wooden pipes to Burlington, New Jersey.

   b. Primarily in response to a growing need for improved fire protection, New York City constructed the Croton Aqueduct in 1842. The system transported water from a huge reservoir in Croton 40 miles north of the city to secondary reservoirs on 42nd Street and in Central Park. These secondary reservoirs fed

---

* In *Historic Silver City: The Story of the Owyhees*, Mildretta Adams writes that John Grete, Sr. purchased the War Eagle Hotel in 1878, and that he later built a waterworks to supply clear spring water to the building.

a system of underground mains, which then supplied buildings with running water.

c. By 1871, the year of this chapter, the population of Tucson, Arizona had grown to 3,000 people and the town boasted a brewery, two doctors, several saloons, and one bathtub.

d. The city of Chicago is credited with construction of the first comprehensive sewage system in the country. The system was designed by E. S. Chesbrough in 1885 and modeled after systems developed earlier in New York City.

e. An outbreak of amoebic dysentery during the 1933 World's Fair in Chicago was ultimately traced to faulty plumbing in two hotels, and resulted in 98 deaths and 1,409 documented cases of illness.

CHAPTER TWELVE

1. While perusing the Sanborn Map Company 1903 map of Silver City* so that I could accurately describe Roshan's path from the Masonic Hall to the saloon on the corner of Washington and Avalanche, I discovered an unfortunate fact: this particular building is listed as a one-story structure—not two-stories as I had originally assumed. I considered moving the action of this and earlier chapters to a two-story saloon a few buildings down the street (the only one I could find on the map), but because "the corner of Washington and Avalanche" is such a pithy little description I have decided to maintain the fiction of a two-story saloon at this location. It is unclear from the map whether or not the saloon is directly connected to a back room, which is designated as a contiguous dwelling on the map, but it is certainly possible that the connection may have existed over 30 years earlier in 1871.

CHAPTER THIRTEEN

1. Horace Smith and Daniel B. Wesson formed their first partnership in 1852 in Norwich, Connecticut to market a lever-action repeating pistol using a fully self-contained cartridge. This initial venture did not prove successful, and Smith and Wesson were forced to sell their fledgling company to a shirt maker named Oliver Winchester. Years later, in 1866, Winchester's company used the original lever-action

---

* This map was first referenced in the Chapter 3 notes and later in an update to the Chapter 2 notes.

design created by Smith and Wesson to launch the now famous Winchester Repeating Arms Co. In 1856 Smith and Wesson formed a second partnership to produce a revolver designed to fire the rim-fire cartridge they had patented in 1854. Smith and Wesson had previously secured patents for the pistol—the first successful self-contained cartridge revolver in the world—and subsequently enjoyed considerable financial success. Prompted by the approaching expiration of these patents, Smith and Wesson completed a new design in 1869—the Model 3 American—and began marketing the pistol in 1870. The introduction of this large caliber cartridge revolver quickly established the Smith & Wesson Company as a world leader in the manufacture of handguns. The first major clients for the new handgun were the United States Cavalry (which purchased 1,000 units for use on the western frontier) and the Russian Imperial Government. (www.smith-wesson.com)

2. I found a limited number of references when I searched the Internet for information on black gunfighters. When I finally typed in "black cowboys" the number of hits improved dramatically, and several of these sites included a few references to black gunfighters. An article titled *Black Cowboys* on the Texas State Historical Society website (www.tshaonline.org) briefly mentioned that "...a few [black cowboys] who followed the lure of the Wild West became gunfighters and outlaws." Furthermore, many of the first black cowboys were born into slavery, and after the Civil War found a better life and encountered less racism on the open range of the West. The article also stated that many African Americans participated in the great cattle drives of the late 1800s, and a few eventually owned their own ranches. Several black cowboys followed careers as rodeo performers.* Others were hired as federal peace officers in Indian Territory. An article titled *Likable Old West Swindler Ben Hodges* on the website http://jy3502.hubpages.com describes the exploits of Benjamin F. Hodges. His mother was Hispanic and his father was a buffalo soldier with the Ninth Cavalry in San Antonio, Texas. He arrived

---

* A black cowboy named William Pickett (1870-1932), born in Texas to former slaves Thomas Jefferson and Mary Virginia Elizabeth (Gilbert) Pickett, became one of the best rodeo performers in the country. He is credited with having invented the sport of bulldogging (called "steer wrestling" today), and was inducted into the National Cowboy Hall of Fame in 1971.

in Dodge City, Kansas in 1872 and found that the wildness of the town suited his particular skill sets of card cheat, swindler, and master forger. Although not exactly described as a gunfighter, his photograph in the article shows him wearing a western-style holster and six-shooter and carrying a rifle. A third article titled *African American Cowboys* by Brad A. Bays (Encyclopedia of the Great Plains, http://plainshumanities.unl.edu/encyclopedia/) notes the following: "Folk memory and white writers have preserved many infamous black gunfighters and murderers, such as Ben Hodges of Dodge City and Cherokee Bill, who terrorized Indian Territory." This article makes no other mention of black gunfighters, instead focusing on African Americans as drovers, horsemen, blacksmiths, cattle drive cooks, and rodeo performers. Interestingly, the article also notes that with the surplus of unemployed whites after the Civil War, "...the African American cowhand became more of an anomaly in the Great Plains by the mid-1870s."

CHAPTER FOURTEEN

1. Somehow I've managed to maneuver myself into the proverbial corner. I wrote a detailed story outline before I began working on the first draft of this novel—a document of 16,875 words and 24 single-spaced pages completed in April 2010 after two months of work—and, in general, have followed it closely. But inspired by my research of medicine in the American West, I deviated significantly from the outline in Chapter 7. Here is my original plan for this chapter:

Chapter 7

November 5, 1871

Joshua Hotah arrives a few miles away from Silver City, and finds a Nez Perce squaw and her 12-year-old son. The squaw speaks some English, so they are able to communicate to a point. They also use sign language. (research required) The squaw and her son are beginning to starve, and Joshua can see that they will likely not make it through the winter without his help. Begrudgingly, he agrees to stay though the winter, but insists that he will leave in the spring to renew his search for his parents. A few days later, Joshua goes hunting. The son wants to go with him, and Joshua, who clearly does not like children, objects. The squaw insists so they leave the camp together. They run into a bear, and the bear mauls the son before Joshua can kill it with his rifle. Joshua packs the injured child on his horse and rides back to the squaw's camp. Joshua will make the decision in a few days to take the son to the doctor in Silver City.

In the actual story, Joshua Hotah has already travelled to Silver City with the Nez Perce child by the end of Chapter 7, and not because the child was mauled by a bear. And it gets worse. Here is my original summary for Chapter 14:

Chapter 14

Just before noon, November 8, 1871

Joshua Hotah decides that the squaw's son will not survive unless he takes him to the doctor in Silver City. The squaw is frightened about what might happen to her son in town but Joshua makes a travois* for the son and rides to Silver City anyway. When he rides down the main street he is generally shunned by the townspeople. He asks several people where he can find the doctor and they flee from him. He finally runs into Manfred who has pity for him and leads him to the doctor's office. When they enter the office, the doctor, an Irishman named Sean Gallagher who drinks too much but does not give a crap about the color of one's skin, is already caring for Ezekiel Smith in the back room with Longwei's help. The doctor comes out to look at the son and says, "My, but it's been quite a day already...and not even noon yet." He takes the Nez Perce child in and cares for his wounds. Longwei and Joshua strike up a conversation. Joshua talks about his search for his parents and his temporary sojourn with the squaw and her son on the outskirts of town. Longwei talks about his travels from China. They conclude the conversation as friends.

And now it gets much worse, because I changed the character of the doctor from Sean Gallagher, who now exists only in the original story outline and these chapter notes—a death by literature, I suppose—to Guinevere Dupree, a character I have already grown quite fond of. I also altered the black gunfighter's name from "Ezekiel" to "Elijah" as well, but this is a minor problem. I finished the first draft of Chapter 13 nearly two weeks ago, and because of these substantial

---

* A travois is a conveyance formally used by Plains Indians consisting of a frame slung between poles and pulled by a dog or horse.

breaks from my original story outline I have struggled to begin work on Chapter 14—which now must be completely recast. With each passing day of inactivity I have grown more apprehensive. Will this lapse of creativity signal the end of *Nor Things to Come: A Novel of the West*? Will my failure to follow the story outline with my typically Teutonic precision condemn me to an eternal oblivion of writer's block? Will my shortsighted fondness of Guinevere Dupree force me to end my work and change the title to *Nor Things to Come: An Unfinished Novel*? I think not, because a glimmer of optimism presented itself after I finished lunch last Sunday at one of Juneau's Asian restaurants. Although run by a delightful Japanese family and offering an elaborate Sushi bar, I ordered off the Chinese menu and therefore received a fortune cookie at the end of my meal. When I opened the cookie and read the little strip of paper concealed inside, my salvation presented itself in the following message: "You will find your solution where you least expect it." And then, during a Bible study last night on the story of Joseph in the Book of Genesis, the solution did indeed present itself.*

2. The Common Raven (Corvus corax)—a large sooty bird with thick neck, shaggy throat feathers, knife-like beak and, in flight, a long wedge-shaped tail—has followed the migrations of humans across the Northern Hemisphere for hundreds of years. Historically, the raven lived on the Great Plains in collaboration with the American bison (buffalo) and wolves. Today, the raven continues to live in wilderness areas throughout much of the North American continent, but is also reestablishing its former range in the forests of the east and moving into urban areas. Geographically and ecologically, the Common Raven is one of the most widespread naturally-occurring birds in the world. The year-round range in North America extends from Mexico across the western states to Alaska and eastward over most of Canada. The raven is also found in Europe, Asia, and North

---

* I thought it prudent to bury information about yet another change to the original story outline in a footnote, and assume that only the most dedicated readers will find it. The original outline did not include Csongor Toth's artful transformation of the guileless Gordania Sinclair to the enigmatic Alexandra Smythe (Part 1, Chapter 16). This specific flash of creativity, an event for which I have no explanation, has added a tantalizing aura of mystery to the character of Gordania Sinclair that I never anticipated.

Africa. Although related to crows, the Common Raven is less social and more likely to be seen alone or in pairs except at food sources. Ravens are confident, inquisitive, and graceful in flight. The Common Raven has held a special place in the folklore of many cultures. Native Americans of the Northwest have venerated the raven as the creator of the earth, moon, sun, and stars, but also regarded the bird as a trickster. In the literature of Western cultures, the raven has often symbolized death, danger, and even wisdom.* (www.allaboutbirds. org/guide/Common_Raven, http://bna.birds.cornell.edu/bna/ species/476)

CHAPTER FIFTEEN

1. By definition, a "potbelly" is a protruding belly. A "potbelly stove" is therefore a stove with a protruding belly. My Internet search yielded very little history of the potbelly stove, although I did find some useful information in a blog by the Good Time Stove Company. Here are a few of the more interesting tidbits: 1) Potbelly stoves were fabricated entirely from cast iron; 2) Potbelly stoves could burn either wood or coal; 3) Generally available in small, medium, and large sizes, the burn time ranged from a low of 6 hours for a small potbelly stove to a high of 14 hours for a large stove; 4) Many potbelly stoves incorporated a flat top for cooking or warming a pot of coffee; 5) The ring sticking out around the middle of the potbelly stove was designed to prevent people from bumping into the stove and burning themselves; 6) Other common features of the potbelly stove included single- or double-swing feed doors, large ash pits, cast iron feet, and draft controls; 7) Potbelly stoves were commonly found throughout the American West in general stores, one-room school houses, railroad stations, and many other frontier establishments; 8) The ACME Stove Company, one of the premier manufacturers of potbelly stoves in America, sold several products in Sears Roebuck Company mail order catalogs including the "ACME Giant," which the company claimed could burn anything; 9) Other manufacturers of potbelly

---

* "Then this ebony bird beguiling my sad fancy into smiling, By the grave and stern decorum of the countenance it wore, 'Though thy crest be shorn and shaven, thou,' I said, 'art sure no craven. Ghastly grim and ancient raven wandering from the nightly shore— Tell me what thy lordly name is on the Night's Plutonian shore!' Quoth the raven, 'Nevermore.'"

stoves included Glenwood, Crawford, Jewel, Kalamazoo, Red Cross, Winter, and Sears; 10) The Boston and Maine Railroad Company fabricated its own potbelly stoves and placed them in railroad stations and train depots, box cars, and cabooses. (http://goodtimestove. blogspot.com/2008/07/learn-all-about-antique-pot-belly.html)

CHAPTER SIXTEEN

1. Manfred quoted from the *King James Bible*: John Chapter 8, Verse 7. During the Hampton Court Conference (on the future of the church) in 1604, a group of moderate puritans persuaded King James I of England of the need for a new translation of the Bible; he ordered work to begin that same year. Six different companies of translators were ultimately established, and translations of the various books of the Bible were completed in 1608 and finalized in London in 1610. After numerous printing difficulties, the *King James Bible* was first published in 1611. The Pilgrims carried this Bible to America in 1620. (www.kingjamesbibletrust.org/the-king-james-bible)

CHAPTER SEVENTEEN

1. Reserved.

CHAPTER EIGHTEEN

1. Nadia's instrument is a hexagonal-ended, twenty-button, Anglo-German concertina manufactured in Germany in 1864. She originally purchased the instrument (for the price of $2.50) to accompany the instruction of music and singing in her one-room school house. Sadly, she never played the concertina in the classroom because of the tragic events that forever altered the anticipated path of her life.

2. After an exhaustive search of the Internet, including a long and painfully-unsuccessful quest for photos of antique accordions manufactured in the 1860s, I discovered the following article on the history of the concertina in America: *A Brief History of the Anglo Concertina in the United States* by Dan Worrall. Following are several noteworthy facts:

   a. The Anglo concertina first arrived in the United States in the 1840s and was played extensively with both popular and sacred music throughout the middle and late 19th century. By the early 1900s the concertina had all but vanished from American popular culture. After this time, Irish and English immigrants were the primary concertina musicians in America.

b. The exact date of arrival of the Anglo concertina in the United States is not known, but the first American instruction book, *The Concertina Without a Master* by Elias Howe, was published in 1846.

c. Because of the complex history of the instrument's development, a variety of names have applied to the Anglo concertina including the German concertina, the Anglo-German concertina, and the Anglo-Chromatic concertina. Carl Friedrich Uhlig invented the German concertina in 1834 in Chemnitz, Germany. A few years earlier, Sir Charles Wheatstone had independently invented an English system concertina. In the 1850s the English produced an improved German concertina with better reeds and action and two rows of buttons and called the instrument the Anglo-German concertina. Around the same time, Englishman George Jones added a third row of buttons and named his new instrument the Anglo-Chromatic concertina. German builders copied the hexagonal ends and other improvements of the English-made concertinas then manufactured and exported their own Anglo-German and Anglo-Chromatic concertinas. The description "Anglo concertina" is therefore useful as a generic term to represent the entire class of single-action, two- or three-row diatonic concertinas.

d. It is important to distinguish the more expensive and finely-built "English concertina" from the mass-produced and relatively inexpensive "Anglo concertina." The English concertina often appeared in the parlors, concert halls, and social settings of the upper classes. The Anglo concertina was the instrument of choice for the common music of the working classes and was played in dance halls and streets throughout America.

e. The concertina often appears in the paintings, photographs, and drawings of 19th century America. An 1897 painting by George Martin Ottinger titled *The Immigrant Train: Away, Away to the Mountain Dell* displays a group of pioneer singers and musicians walking alongside a wagon train: one of the men is playing an Anglo concertina with obvious exuberance. An early stereoscopic photograph taken in the 1850s shows a musician proudly displaying his violin and Anglo-German concertina. A black youth wearing a quasi-military uniform in a tintype photograph taken circa 1864 cradles a square-ended German concertina in his hands. A photograph of a blackface minstrel troop, circa 1870-1880, shows two singers and four musicians performing with tambourine, Anglo-German concertina, bones, and banjo. And a 1900 photograph of three street musicians playing banjo, Anglo concertina, and guitar presages the approaching decline of the concertina in American social life. Refer to the website below for other examples.

(www.concertina.com/worrall/anglo-in-united-states/index.htm)

CHAPTER NINETEEN

1. If you are following the dates closely (as you should), you will remember that Nadia received her injury from the stone cast by Jackson (Bill Jackson, but everyone calls him Jackson) on November 28th, a Tuesday. December 4th, a Monday, falls six days later. According to the website emedicinehealth.com, the recommended elapsed time before removal of stitches varies by body location as follows: Face - 3 to 5 days; Scalp - 7 to 10 days; Trunk - 7 to 10 days; Arms and legs - 10 to 14 days; and Joints - 14 days. Stitches can be removed all at once in a single visit or over a period of days, depending on the nature of the wound. (www.emedicinehealth.com/removing_stitches/page2_em.htm)

CHAPTER TWENTY

1. The Lewis and Clark expedition first described the Bannock Indians in its written journals in 1805. At the time, the seminomadic Bannock ranged over the lands of present-day western Wyoming and south-eastern Idaho, although they often traveled beyond these regions in the pursuit of buffalo. Lewis and Clark learned of the Bannock Indians during discussions with the Shoshone about the best route across the continental divide. The Shoshone warned the Americans that the Bannock Indians were hostile, prompting the expedition to avoid them altogether by following the northern route through the Lemhi Pass. By 1869 the U.S. Government had forced the Bannock off their traditional lands to a reservation located at Fort Hall, Idaho. Due to starvation and other deprivations, the Bannock Indians began

leaving the reservation in 1878, and in June of the same year joined the Shoshone in an open revolt. The uprising was quickly suppressed, and the tribes were returned to the reservation. Today, the Bannock and Shoshone share the reservation at Fort Hall, Idaho. (www.nationalgeographic.com/lewisandclark/record_tribes_001_11_7.html)

2. In Chapter 8 of *Gold Town to Ghost Town*, Julia Conway Welch describes historical attitudes toward Indians and several incidents arising from these attitudes. In response to an article published in the *Sacramento Union* that praised General Sherman's sympathy for the Indians and appreciation of their sad condition, W. J. Hill wrote in the May 1868 *Owyhee Avalanche* that the general would improve his understanding of the Indian if he took a trip into the interior and, " ... had a fellow passenger killed, himself shot full of arrows and scalped, and the bloody work commenced while having a friendly shake of the hand .... " In 1860, near Sinker Creek, Indians and an immigrant party of eight wagons commenced a running ordeal that ended six weeks later on the banks of the Owyhee River when soldiers from Fort Walla Walla finally arrived to rescue the pioneers. The troopers discovered that the few emaciated survivors of the disaster had eaten the flesh of two dead children to sustain themselves. In 1868, Indians attacked a stagecoach on the road from Silver City to the Owyhee River ferry crossing at a point between stations known as Rocky Canyon. The driver, Nathan Dixon, was killed by the first shot. A fellow named J. P. Merrill took over the reins, but while trying to execute a desperate escape he overturned the coach and scattered the passengers over the roadway. Astonishingly, the passengers managed to regain their composure and drove the Indians off with rifle and pistol fire. One of the passengers, an unnamed woman, even collected Indian souvenirs after the debacle. These and other incidents likely kept the residents of Silver City in an unsettled state during the 1860s and into the 1870s.

3. The Winchester Repeating Arms Company produced lever-action rifles of model designations 1866, 1873 (this was the famous "Gun that Won the West"), 1886, 1892, 1894, and 1895. Manufacturing of the Model 1866 started in Bridgeport, Connecticut in 1867. Each new model incorporated one or more technical improvements, but the most radical enhancement occurred in 1886 when genius gun designer John M. Browning figured out a way to strengthen the

action so that the rifle could fire high-powered rifle cartridges: previous models fired pistol cartridges. The Winchester plant in New Haven, Connecticut closed in 2006, and manufacture of the classic lever-action rifle of the American West was discontinued. (Hunter, Stephen. "Out With A Bang: The Loss of the Classic Winchester Is Loaded With Symbolism." *Washington Post*, January 20, 2006.)

4. Sebastian, a Roman Centurion discovered to be a Christian, was consequently sentenced to death by Emperor Diocletian. Roman soldiers bound him to a stake and shot him with arrows. They left Sebastian for dead, but the arrows did not kill him. The Romans later completed the job by stoning him to death. Dutch painter Gerrit van Honthorst was one of the first artists to portray Saint Sebastian as a half-length figure, slumped forward in a seated position. He probably completed the painting in the city of Utrecht in 1623. (www.nationalgallery.org.uk/paintings/gerrit-van-honthorst-saint-sebastian)

CHAPTER TWENTY-ONE

1. Reserved.